A GROWN-UP KISS

Chase Holloway was no man to tangle with. Talk about notches on a bedpost, he probably had to *replace* the bedposts every six months. No, Chase was too much like a brother to her for a relationship. But he had given her some pretty good pointers about boys when she'd been twelve.

"You know, Maddie, you don't have to forget men completely. I'm sure there's a nice guy out there who wants to settle down."

Gracious, he was just as barbaric in his old Southern values as her brothers.

"You know, you're right, Chase. Forgetting men was a little extremist. Maybe I'll just forget marriage."

His dark eyes widened.

"I can play the field, date lots of guys."

"But—"

"Sure, it's the same as shopping; I try on several different styles of shoes before I buy a pair."

"Shoes? Maddie, you need to watch out—"

Maddie hissed out a breath at his big brotherly tone. "I realize you're more experienced than I, Chase, but I'm not a kid anymore."

He raised a brow, his patronizing expression irritating her even more.

Maddie pursed her lips. "As a matter of fact, I'm a pretty good kisser if I do say so myself." She angled her head sideways to study him. When he simply stared at her in disbelief, she snatched the edge of his shirt. "All right, see for yourself. If my kissing isn't up to par, you can give me pointers."

Marry Me, Maddie

Rita Herron

LOVE SPELL NEW YORK CITY

A LOVE SPELL BOOK®

August 2001

Published by

Dorchester Publishing Co., Inc.
276 Fifth Avenue
New York, NY 10001

ISBN 0-505-52433-3

Printed in the United States of America.

To Lee, the southern-bred father; and
Adam, the macho overprotective brother,
who provided inspiration for the Summers men; and to
Elizabeth & Emily, the feisty, smart southern girls who
keep them on their toes.

I love you all.

Marry Me, Maddie

Chapter One

Maddie Summers's legs wobbled like overused rubber bands as her gaze zeroed in on the neon-green words MARRY ME OR MOVE ON. The special Valentine's Day set of *Sophie Knows,* the leading daytime talk show in Savannah, was a bit more flamboyant than she'd imagined, especially the glitzy red heart announcing the day's topic. Those very words, which had enticed her to appear on the show now flashed like a beacon from a lighthouse tower warning of danger.

"Ladies and gentlemen, we have a special show planned today, which will conclude our weeklong celebration of romance in the steamy South," Sophie announced. Sophie continued with her introduction, looking elegant and savvy in a slinky black satin gown, which accentuated her petite curvy figure. "Recently we've diverted from our usual issue-oriented topics to have some fun. This week's highlights included romance tips from a leading sex therapist, erotic recipes shared by a French chef, a lingerie fashion show designed to spice up your lovelife, and yesterday, we interviewed several popular Georgia romance novelists who keep romance alive year-round with their sensual tales of love and commitment. For our grand finale, we're giving a few special couples an opportunity to tie the knot right here onstage."

Cheers erupted, mingled with whispers and laughter. Maddie grabbed the light pole to steady herself but almost knocked it over. Light flickered and jumped across the stage, earning her a glare from one of the producers. She focused on the crowd. Beneath the applause lay the elemental question that drove people to watch more outlandish talk shows and the question her oldest brother Lance would hit her with as soon as he saw her—what prompted people to air their personal business on camera?

Stupidity. Only a stupid woman would force a man's hand in such a public way.

No, desperation. Only a desperate woman would give a man an ultimatum in front of thousands of strangers.

No, brilliance. Only a brilliant woman would issue such a choice in a public place, laying odds that the man who'd been stringing her along for years would be forced to show some guts and make a commitment.

Good heavens. She was bound to be humiliated.

When Sophie, the talk-show host and one of her best friends, had first mentioned the idea for the show, Maddie had laughed. Then Sophie had described in detail the romantic ceremony that would highlight the final segment of her Valentine series, and Maddie had not been able to resist. The decision to appear on *Sophie Knows* had suddenly seemed like a great idea. Maddie would appear, give her long-standing boyfriend of four years a gentle nudge down the aisle and revive the spontaneity of their too-comfortable relationship.

Although, now, faced with the realization that Savannah's elite society, namely her boyfriend's entire extended family whose descendants had actually founded Savannah, would disapprove of the public whoop-de-do, the ultimatum seemed ludicrous.

Could she go through with it?

Yes, Maddie thought, drawing courage from the energy the vibrant spitfire host emanated. Today, Maddie would find out if Jeff Oglethorpe meant to follow through on the vague promises he'd whispered to her for the past few months or if he'd been blowing smoke up her a—dress.

Excuses be damned.

The strong scent of carnations assaulted her, and she swayed dizzily, squinting through the haze of bright stage lights as she stepped beneath the trellis of white ribbons, roses and baby's breath, which created a canopied sanctuary for the couples who chose to take the plunge today. A piano version of "Love is a Many Splendored Thing" drifted through the speakers, soothing her nerves as Maddie settled into her assigned chair and situated her clothing. She should have worn something a little sexier to tip the scales should Jeff straddle the line on his decision. She'd conned him into appearing by telling him he'd be speaking on Savannah's economic development. Jeff would suck raw eggs through a straw blindfolded if he thought it would bolster his banking business.

Sophie introduced each of the three female guests, then gestured toward a tall, thin, exotic-looking black woman named Vanessa. "Now, we'll let our first guest tell us about herself."

"My man and I have been living together for two years." A row of diamonds glittered along Vanessa's ear. "I don't want to wind up in that never-ending dating game. Other men have expressed interest in me, and if Martin's not the one, I need to know."

"You go, girl!" several spectators shouted.

"Tell it like it is, sister!"

The audience cheered as Sophie welcomed Vanessa's boyfriend, a well-built man dressed in a charcoal-gray suit who vaguely resembled Denzel Washington. A seed of envy sprouted in Maddie at the unbridled moment of lust that rippled between the couple. Had Jeff ever looked at her with that deep hunger in his eyes?

"Do you know why you're here, Mr. Wells?" Sophie asked.

He grinned broadly and squeezed Vanessa's hand. "Is this some kind of contest? Have I won a vacation or a new car?"

The audience chuckled, a smattering of applause rumbling through the crowd.

Vanessa lifted Martin's hand in hers. "Martin, I know you love me."

He nodded and inched to the edge of his seat as if preparing to claim his prize.

"And I love you." She paused for effect. "But I want more than this shacking-up arrangement. I want us to be married."

Martin's stunned expression darted to Sophie, zigzagged to the audience, then flew to the flowered mini-gazebo as if dawning finally penetrated his testosterone-driven brain. No Corvette. No money. No door number three. Finally, he swallowed audibly.

"Marry me, Martin, or . . . or it's time to move on."

A second of hesitation snatched the air from Maddie's lungs as she waited along with Vanessa and the audience for his reply. Finally Martin leaped to his feet, grabbed Vanessa's hand and swung her into his embrace, his voice booming. "Oh, hell, why not, baby. Let's do it."

Vanessa squealed loud enough to damage the microphones and pulled Martin into a passionate kiss. Sophie sprinted out among the crowd and allowed several spectators to voice their thoughts.

"Give them a free honeymoon!" an elderly lady wearing a pink knit suit suggested.

"We have two more guests today," Sophie said. "Vanessa, you and Martin hang around. There's a minister on hand to perform the ceremonies at the end of the show." Sophie winked at the audience. "And we'll discuss that honeymoon, too, when we come back."

The crowd laughed and the couple smooched while Faith Hill's voice purred "The Way You Love Me." Maddie squirmed in her seat, the butterflies now performing cartwheels in her stomach. There would be at least one wedding today. Would Jeff be as enthusiastic?

She twisted her fingers anxiously around the diamond pendant lying between her breasts, memories of her mother surfacing. The pendant had been an heirloom, the only piece of valuable jewelry her mother owned other than her wedding ring. Her mother's wishes were part of the reason she'd clung to Jeff so long. She'd always thought Jeff was the type of man her mother would have liked her to marry. Plus her brothers constantly coaxed her to marry into a good family, claiming their mother would have wanted Maddie to fit into the upper echelon of Savannah society. The Oglethorpes had definitely paved the way for her entry.

Only Maddie had no desire to sip tea from miniature china cups with the elite. She was independent and wanted her own business. In college, Jeff had understood her dreams and encouraged her—unlike her brothers who'd wanted her to settle down, marry and raise babies. The very reason she still hadn't sprung her business plan on them. With Jeff's support, though, they'd have to give her a thumbs-up.

She wished her mother was here now to see her get married. Only what if Jeff said no?

Maybe it was a good thing her mother wasn't here.

Faith Hill's voice faded, and Sophie moved centerstage and introduced the next guest, Deidre. Maddie's shoulders tensed as Deidre's boyfriend entered. His eyes registered surprise when he noticed the Valentine decorations.

Deidre lay one hand over her belly. "I'm pregnant, Stan. And I want you to marry me or move on."

Tears streamed down his ruddy cheeks. "You're really gonna have my baby, Cupcake?"

Deidre whispered a choked reply in confirmation.

"Deidre says you don't want to get married," Sophie said.

He dabbed at his nose, his voice husky when he spoke, "That isn't true, ma'am. I just don't have much to offer a good woman like Deidre. Haven't had a steady job in two years."

Deidre's mouth fell open. The audience chorused a sympathetic sound. Maddie's heartstrings tugged painfully.

Compassion softened Sophie's voice. "If you'd accept our assistance, sir, we'll help you find employment."

He swiped at his cheeks with a handkerchief. "I'd be much obliged. I want my baby to be proud of me." He held out his arms to Deidre, then dropped onto one knee. "Will you marry me, darling?"

Deidre's chin quivered. "Of course I will, you fool." She threw her arms around him and began to sob. "Be My Baby" jangled over the speakers in an upbeat tune, prompting the crowd to clap and sing along.

"Well, folks," Sophie said as the crowd's singing died down, "we're batting two for two here. Let's see if we can go for a grand slam. Maddie, tell us about your situation."

Jeff's excuses for postponing marriage traipsed through her mind like a parade of screeching TransAm race cars. "Well, we've been dating for four years, but Jeff keeps giving excuses for not making a commitment. First, we were too young. Then we both had to attend college." She dug her fingernails into her palms when she realized the crowd leaned forward, hanging on her every word. "Then Jeff needed to establish himself in the business world. But now he's president of the Savannah Savings and Loan, and I've finished school."

Sophie's green eyes glinted with understanding. "Do you think your boyfriend's failure to commit may be an indication of a more serious problem?"

"Exactly." Like he didn't love her. Didn't want to marry her. Had another woman on the side. "I want to know if he's serious or not, because if he isn't, I want to move on."

There she'd done it. Let the floor show begin.

Jeff suddenly appeared, looking confident in a conservative pinstriped custom-made suit. His smile radiated authority, but as his gaze roamed the stage, his expression faltered at the sight of the wedding arch and trellis of roses. Thank goodness the shiny red heart hung behind him so he couldn't see its message.

"Welcome to our show, Mr. Oglethorpe." Sophie coaxed him into a tan chair beside Maddie. "Do you have any idea why you're here?"

Jeff shook his head, straightening the lapels of his jacket so they were perfectly aligned. "Madison said I was invited to speak on Savannah's growing economy."

Maddie winced. The use of her full name clearly indicated he realized he'd been conned. And he wasn't happy about it.

Sophie's eyes glittered mischievously. "I believe Maddie has a surprise for you."

The heat of the cameras radiated around Maddie, almost suffocating her, and the hushed whisper that rang through the crowd sounded painful to her ears. Soon, people would be laughing. . . .

Jeff pivoted in his chair, folding his hands across his bent knee. "Yes, Madison?"

Sink or swim.

Maddie dove into the uncharted waters. With no life jacket. She had a feeling she was going to drown.

"Jeff, I'm sorry for tricking you into coming, but I feel as if we've reached a point in our relationship where we need to make some decisions."

Jeff's patrician nostrils flared slightly as he dipped his chin to give her a private what-the-hell-do-you-think-you're-doing look. Maddie ignored him, her gaze zeroing in on her shoe where a scrap of toilet paper clung to the heel. *Good gracious alive.*

Jeff saw the tissue at the same time and had the nerve to roll his eyes. Maddie's determination was renewed. If their relationship was over, it was over. Better to find out now.

"Can't we discuss this in a more . . ." He cleared his throat, his low voice quivering with unleashed anger, "dignified, private setting?"

Heads angled and craned to hear him. Maddie's lunch surged to the top of her throat.

"Maddie?" Sophie prompted.

Maddie gulped, wishing desperately she'd forgone the spicy Creole at lunch. "We've talked about marriage before but you always have an excuse. I think it's time we either make a commitment or start seeing other people."

"You want to see other men?"

The incredulity in his voice spiked her temper, but she fought to keep her knee-jerk reaction to herself. Because her knee-jerk reaction was to stick her knee in his groin.

She forced a watery smile. "Yes, I want to either get married or move on."

Sophie angled her head toward Jeff. "Now, Mr. Oglethorpe, I believe the ball is in your court."

Chase Holloway stared at the TV screen, unable to believe his eyes—Maddie Summers was on *Sophie Knows,* participating in a episode called "Marry Me or Move On." Maddie's brothers continued to curse and pace the floor just as they had from the moment they'd tuned into the show. When Lance had spotted Maddie, he'd yelled for them to come watch.

Standing up for him in a schoolyard fight, Lance and Reid Summers had befriended Chase when he was just a gangly mean-ass kid. No one had ever defended him before. Not only had they earned his respect that day, but they'd won his loyalty. Odd, since Chase Holloway was a bad boy at heart and until then, had been loyal to no one but himself. His own mama had abandoned him at the Bethesda orphanage when he was only five, claiming he was so mean he would tear up a rock. Her exact words were imprinted in his brain, "You'll probably share a jail cell with your sorry excuse for a father before you're old enough to drive. I don't aim to stick around for pictures."

She'd been right on one part. He was a bad boy. But he'd skimmed through school and avoided serious jail time—mostly because of Reid and Lance.

A diaper commercial ended, and a tampon commercial flashed onto the screen. He turned his head away, feeling his face flush at the feminine products. Why did they advertise that stuff on TV?

He studied Lance and Reid's reactions, wondering when Maddie Summers had grown up and started looking so damned sexy. Hell, he'd known her all his life. She'd been a pest when she was five, a tomboy in her teens and . . . and unavailable as a woman.

She was his best friends' hell, his *blood brothers'* kid sister. Which meant she was practically family to him, practically his *own* little sister.

Which had automatically labeled her off-limits to his lusting libido.

Now, she was going to marry that weasel Oglethorpe. Today. On TV. In front of God and her brothers and the whole city of Savannah.

Unless Oglethorpe bowed out and told her to move on.

The air collected in his lungs in a hot, painful surge.

"What the blazes does she think she's doing?" Lance stopped pacing long enough to slam his fist into the wall. "And look at her, she's got toilet paper stuck on her shoe."

"We don't care how much water a maxi-pad absorbs!" Reid bellowed. "Get back to Maddie!"

"If Oglethorpe hurts her, I'll kill him with my bare hands," Lance mouthed in a more controlled but lethal tone.

"How could he turn her down? She's been blinking and winking and turning men's heads since she was three," Chase said.

"Hell, don't I know it," Lance muttered. "I thought about sending her to live with nuns when she was a teenager."

Chase laughed at the image of feisty Maddie driving the nuns nuts. Oglethorpe would be damn lucky to have a woman like her, Chase thought, suddenly feeling surly. Hot, fiery eyes, sass and spunk and just about as much passion as a sane body could handle. Not that he'd ever experienced her passion—

Lance cursed again, cutting off Chase's thoughts. "They've sure been dating long enough to get married though."

"I told you we should've had a talk with him," Reid growled.

"Yeah, should have hog-tied him and made him do right before she was forced to push the issue," Lance grumbled.

"I'm sure Maddie would have appreciated that," Chase added wryly. The temperamental Maddie he knew would slam her boots in both her brothers' backsides if they'd pulled such a stunt.

"You think she'd have told us about this . . . this ridiculous proposal." Reid passed a beer to Lance, forgoing their usual rule of no drinking before five o'clock. "We should at least be there to give her away."

"Better yet, we could have convinced her to have a church ceremony like Mama would have wanted."

The mention of their mother brought a round of silence from all of them. Chase wasn't sure if Maddie's mother had liked him or just tolerated him, but he'd sure as heck admired her for the way she'd stuck by her boys. Next to him, Lance and Reid had been the biggest troublemakers at Savannah High. They'd been dubbed The Terrible Three in ninth grade and been proud of it.

"Look, guys, you've done the best you could raising Maddie since your mama died. But she's been battling for independence since she tossed her training wheels on the sidewalk at the age of four and barreled headfirst into a tree."

"Ain't that the truth," Lance mumbled.

A Depends commercial flitted on next, and Chase swore. They certainly had all the leakage problems covered with the advertisements. When would they get back to the show?

The commercial finally faded, and Reid waved his hands as the cameras zoomed in on Maddie's face. The cold beer burned in Chase's stomach while he waited on Oglethorpe's reply. Maddie was like a sister to him; he should be happy for her.

Well, maybe she wasn't exactly like a sister, he thought, aware his body thrummed with sexual tension at the sight of her lush legs and silky auburn hair and those rosy pink lips that could form a pout in a second. And those curves? When had Maddie developed full breasts and those luscious hips?

The answer slammed into him. While she'd been gallivanting around with Jeffrey Oglethorpe.

The man she was going to marry in the next five minutes.

Chapter Two

During the break, Sophie had roamed the audience seeking romantic tips, graciously giving Jeff time to ponder his choices. Finally, she returned center-stage. "Okay, Mr. Oglethorpe, I think everyone here, especially Maddie, is anxious for your reply."

Jeff indicated the red heart he'd finally noticed during the break. "Now, Maddie, you know I want us to be married, but there are other things to consider besides our feelings. This TV show definitely isn't appropriate for an Oglethorpe wedding."

Maddie pursed her lips, an onslaught of emotions churning through her. The top being anger at the hint of snobbery she heard in Jeff's voice. Why had she never noticed it before?

"Besides, you've only recently completed your degree. We have to discuss whether or not you'll continue this decorating career."

"What do you mean *whether* I'll pursue it? We talked about my plans in college."

"Yes, but things have changed, Maddie."

"I haven't changed," Maddie said, her temper rising.

Jeff covered her hand with his. "But circumstances have changed, sweetheart. I'm head of the bank now and can handle things financially."

"I want to handle my own finances, Jeff."

"But I'll take care of you, sweetheart. And you can help me by being by my side for social functions," Jeff protested. "We can work together as a team."

Which would be fine if they'd been living in the dark ages! What he really meant was that he wanted her to forgo her own dreams and serve cocktails to his business associates to elevate him on the social pedestal. Where was the support he'd shown her in college?

His selfishness suddenly struck a nerve in Maddie that zinged like a broken violin string. "You don't care about my career?"

"It's not that I don't care, but you won't need a job or have time for one if we marry. Helping me will keep you busy."

"Keep me busy?"

"Well, yes. There'll be lots of social functions for the bank and such."

He would suck every last ounce of independence from her just as her father had done from her mother.

She wanted a man who believed in her, one who would be proud of her accomplishments, not ask her to stifle her dreams for his own goals. A virile, hungry, aggressive hunk who would whisper wild, erotic nothings in her ear and drive her crazy with his tongue and body and make her cry out his name in the dark. An insatiable man who would take her anywhere, anytime, and who wouldn't have to check his pocket calendar to schedule in sex, or even a simple movie.

She wasn't sure whether to laugh or cry, but the truth hit her so vividly she almost shouted. Jeff didn't love her. But even more clear in her mind, she didn't love *him* anymore. Not the man he'd become anyway.

"Um, Maddie?" He reached for her hand and patted it with his slender fingers as if she were a distressed child. "I say we table this issue for a few more months."

Maddie brushed at the wrinkle in her beautiful white sheath. She'd always tried to make her brothers proud. She'd even planned to marry someone she didn't love so they would approve. But she'd wasted four years of her life. Now she'd damn well do as she pleased.

"I'm sorry, Jeff, but I'm not going to table the issue. You're not the man for me." She dropped his hand and stood, then jerked the toilet tissue from her shoe and tossed it at his feet. "It's time to move on."

Jeff shook his foot to dislodge the tissue and clamped his mouth shut in shock. With a strong tilt to her chin, Maddie stalked off stage.

A burst of applause erupted. Maddie slipped out of the side door, kicked off her high heels and headed to her car, ready to move on with her life.

Minus one Jeffrey Oglethorpe.

Chase pumped his fist in a victory sweep. Good for Maddie; she'd finally gotten rid of that ass-wipe Oglethorpe. About damn time.

He opened his mouth to voice his opinion, then firmly closed it when he saw Lance and Reid wearing scowls the size of Texas. They obviously wanted Maddie to marry someone important, someone successful, someone above themselves. Someone like Oglethorpe.

But that wuss wasn't good enough for Maddie.

Chase fisted his hands by his side. Not that he was either. Chase was nothing more than a jailbird's son. A misfit himself with enough scars and bad blood to taint him for life.

Reid slung a pillow across the room and almost knocked over the lamp. "I'll kill him."

"No, killing's too good." Lance crushed a beer can in his fist. "Torture would be better."

Reid nodded, voicing a few painful alternatives.

Chase chuckled to himself, remembering all the childhood brawls they'd gotten into. But they weren't kids anymore, and he was desperately trying to overcome his hard-assed bad-boy reputation.

"I think you should be damn proud of your sister," he finally said. "She's got spunk standing up to that ball-less jerk. He couldn't even give her a straight answer."

Lance and Reid exchanged worried looks. "Yeah, she's gutsy, but you know sweet Maddie."

Sweet Maddie?

"What else could she do? She was only trying to save face."

"Probably crying her eyes out now." Lance's dark eyes filled with worry.

"Poor kid. Her heart must be broken. We gotta do something." Reid drove his hand through his light blond hair, spiking the ends in disarray.

"Yeah, I guess we'll have to pick up the pieces. Just like we always have." Lance grabbed his keys. "I say we get over to her place, quick."

Chase levered himself on the heels of his boots and stood. "You don't think Maddie will want to be alone?"

"No way. She needs us." Reid pounded his fist in his hand. "But first we're going to pay Oglethorpe a visit."

Chase suddenly envisioned bloody bodies and cops and Maddie topping off her day by having to bail her brothers out of jail. He yanked his baseball hat on his head. "I'll follow you over."

"Glad you're in, man," Reid said. "We may need another arm to dig his grave."

Chase shook his head. He hoped he wouldn't have to use his strong-arm tactics to keep his best buds from letting things get out of control. An image of Maddie's wild curls tumbling around her head flitted through his mind, and his body hardened. No, he was not going to think about little Maddie Summers in a sexual way. He was simply going along to keep his friends out of trouble, the same way he'd done a hundred times before.

His presence had nothing to do with the fact that he wanted to see how Maddie was doing for himself. Or to sneak a peek at Maddie's endless legs beneath that stunning slinky white dress.

The evening breeze tossed Maddie's unruly hair into disarray around her face as she rolled her brand-new spit-shiny red VW convertible to a stop in front of her downtown apartment. The ride home had been heaven. The wind, the night sounds, the faint scent of salt air and . . . freedom.

But as she slid into her allotted parking spot on the corner, irritation crawled through her. Chase Holloway, her brothers' best buddy, sat on her front porch in the dark, obviously there to check up on her. Her faithful three-legged cat, T. C., short for Too Cute, lay at his feet in a snoring ball of black-and-white fur. A smile warmed her mouth as she thought of the stray, mangy animal she'd taken in a few months ago. With her love, the cat had flourished and now kept her warm at night. She'd need him even more now that she had no husband prospect in mind. But Chase's sullen frown brought her back to the present.

Where were Lance and Reid? She'd half-expected The Terrible Three to all be there, to have begun her pity party without her, as if they fully expected some great big hullabaloo of a dramatic scene when she arrived home. Men!

They had no idea she'd treated herself to a new car and a shopping trip and didn't need or particularly *want* company. The final coo—comfort food; a chocolate eclair cake sat beside her waiting to be devoured. She'd had a major powwow with herself over the sense of loss she'd experienced over the breakup and had come to some pretty shocking conclusions. She would miss Jeff, much as she would miss a well-worn pair of sneakers that had grown too old to be exciting but comfortable enough to wear on a bad-hair, PMS day. Except come to think of it, she'd hadn't been *that* comfortable with Jeff since he'd graduated; she'd always been keenly aware of his family name and the fact that she had to maintain the proper image to be seen on his arm. Hair could never be messy, clothes untidy or cheap, and heaven forbid she shop at a discount store. She shook her curls around her head and laughed, wondering what Jeff would think if he'd seen her hair flying wild in the wind as she'd driven home. And if he could see her purchases . . .

She'd happened on the day's mind-boggling revelations right in the middle of Victoria's Secret so she'd splurged on a whole array of sexy lingerie, including a black leather thong that was creeping into her nether regions. Then she'd dumped her dependable Volvo at the VW dealership, and bought her new wheels.

She cut off the engine and opened the door, grabbed the cake and juggled her packages in her arms as she maneuvered around the giant azaleas and teetered over the cobblestone steps to her front door. The Victorian house had been divided into a duplex that screamed with character, the ten-foot ceilings and latticework reminiscent of days gone by. Climbing vines of roses wound around the trellis to her bedroom window, reminding her of the set to Sophie's show. And the scene she'd caused with her ultimatum.

Chase sat in the metal glider amid the pots of pink geraniums and hanging baskets of ferns, sliding his big feet just enough to keep the porch swing in motion. Out of the corner of her eye, she noticed his sexy mouth tilt in a tiny smile. Almost sympathetic.

Damn. She did *not* want sympathy, especially from a hottie like Chase.

Maddie dropped the packages on the wrought-iron table. Shadows hovered from the nearby trees, almost completely shielding Chase's face. He'd been watching patiently, she realized, the silent brooding outsider who never seemed to say much, but who always seemed to be around, filling the space with his bad-boy good looks and haunted expression. Keeping his distance as if he knew he wasn't really family, but hovering on the periphery of their lives as if he had no other place to go, as if no one else wanted him. But her family had opened its door and he'd been leaning in the middle of the doorjamb ever since.

Just like T. C. had for a while. A stray mangy cat she could handle. What she didn't need was another overprotective big brother trying to tell her what to do. "I assume Reid and Lance sent you. I'm surprised they aren't here themselves."

"They waited awhile. When you didn't show, they went looking for you."

Maddie rolled her eyes and sank down beside him.

His sharp gaze cut straight to her. "You all right, shortstop?"

She smiled at his use of her childhood nickname and reached for a beer on the circular table beside him. With a flick of her thumb, she popped the top and lifted the cold can to her neck, pressing it against her overheated skin. A shiver rippled up her spine at the sound of Chase's gruff breathing, or maybe it was the ice-cold can. A cacophony of crickets and frogs sang in the background. The faint scent of jasmine and honeysuckle and whatever kind of aftershave Chase was wearing sweetened the balmy air. Odd sensations stirred within her. "I've never been better, Chase."

His dark eyes narrowed perceptibly. "Maybe you should have some coffee or tea instead of drinking, Maddie, you—"

"I'm not twelve anymore, Chase."

His sullen expression said he disagreed. He probably still saw her as a gangly teenager. But she'd save her arguments for her brothers. "I'll let the boys make me some tea when they get here, it'll give them something to do," she said with a wry grin.

Chase's accepting nod eased the tension in her knotted muscles. She relaxed against the swing and watched him fold his big hands together and pop his knuckles, one by one.

Moonlight spilled through the cracks in the awning and streaked the jet-black strands of his hair. Finally he laid his hands on top of his muscular thighs.

Well-worn denim hugged his hips, distracting her from the sounds of a biker sailing by. "You threw Oglethorpe a real curveball tonight."

She grinned, remembering the time Chase had taught her to pitch. He'd spent all afternoon coaxing her to throw balls into a trash can, and she'd hit him as many times as she'd hit the can. One time she'd smacked him in the crotch. He'd walked bowed over for hours. "Yeah, I guess I did."

"He struck out. His loss."

"No, Chase, the man didn't even have the balls to swing." She stretched out her legs, kicked off her shoes and sighed as the warmth of Chase's laughter melted the last of the tension from her body. Then she began to push the glider with her bare feet, setting her rhythm to match Chase's. T. C. crawled up in Chase's lap, plopped into a contented ball and began to purr. Maddie bit her lip, surprised to see the cat take to Chase. He was usually wary of everyone but her.

Shaking off the oddity, she stroked his thick fur. "But I'm all right, you know. I'm sorry if I embarrassed Lance and Reid though."

His tanned knuckle bulged as he patted her hand. "They'll survive."

"I just hope Jeff's parents do. His mother's probably removing my name from every social list in Savannah as we speak."

"She is into all that stuff, isn't she?"

Maddie swallowed a sip of beer. "She lives for all those society functions."

Chase nodded, not quite meeting her eyes. Suspicions inched into Maddie's conscious. He'd said the boys had gone looking for her, but the show had aired at three, and she'd been gone for hours. Her heart fluttered at the disastrous possibility flitting through her head. "Chase, the boys didn't go to Jeff's, did they?"

The corner of his mouth twisted slightly. "Earlier."

Maddie dropped her face into her hands and groaned. "You went with them?"

He nodded again.

She peeked between her fingers. "Please tell me they didn't hurt him."

His feet pushed the glider with a little more force. "Scared him shitless, but Oglethorpe'll survive."

Maddie dropped her hands completely and chuckled. T. C. suddenly raised his head, stared at her, then leaped down and scampered behind the bushes.

"What are you going to do now?" he asked softly.

Maddie shrugged. "Focus on my career. Forget men."

"Ahh, Maddie." His hand brushed hers slightly, a tiny spark of static electricity jolting through her. Maddie frowned, momentarily stunned. As if he'd felt it, too, Chase pulled his hand away and stared at her bare feet, then his boots. A silence fell between them that seemed both comfortable and awkward at the same time.

The creaking sound of the swing lulled her as she studied the outline of his chiseled face. Dark stubble grazed Chase's square jaw, his nose was crooked where it had been broken at least twice in high school, and several stray locks of his too-long black hair tumbled down over his heavy bedroom eyes. A tiny jagged scar splintered his bronze complexion, roving from the edge of his hairline to within an inch of his left eye. She remembered the day he'd gotten the injury, wondered how many more scars he'd added over the years. Each one would tell a story . . .

What was wrong with her? She'd never wondered

about Chase Holloway's scars before. Must be the aftermath of breaking up with one man. You suddenly noticed all the others.

As if he sensed her watching him, Chase raised his head and met her gaze. His jaw tightened, the fine lines at the corner of his mouth crinkling into that killer smile. But his charcoal-black eyes turned a smoky hue that Maddie didn't recognize. She swallowed, astounded by the intensity of emotion hidden in their depths.

Emotions like pain and hunger and need.

Emotions she'd never seen before because she hadn't been looking. Because he was her brothers' buddy. Off-limits to her. Unavailable. Just as she had been to him.

But no more.

She was a free woman. A *fully grown* free woman. And Chase was a free man. The sexiest free man she'd ever known. Good grief, what was happening to her?

She was supposed to be forgetting men.

And Chase Holloway was no man to tangle with. Talk about notches on a bedpost, he probably had to *replace* his bedposts every six months. No, Chase was too much like a brother to her for a relationship. But he had given her some pretty good pointers about boys when she'd been twelve.

"You know, Maddie, you don't have to forget men completely, I'm sure there's a nice guy out there who wants to settle down."

Gracious, he was just as barbaric in his old Southern values as her brothers.

"You know, you're right, Chase. Forgetting men was a little extremist. Maybe I'll just forget marriage."

His dark eyes widened.

"I can play the field, date lots of guys."

"I didn't mean—"

"After all, I want to get my business off the ground before I even consider another serious relationship."

"But—"

"I need to try a lot of men so I'll know when I've found the perfect one."

"I don't know—"

"Sure, it's the same as shopping; I try on several different styles of shoes before I buy a pair."

"Shoes?"

"And it took me at least a dozen different fittings to find a bra that suits me." She could have sworn his dark cheeks flushed before his gaze fell to her breasts. "I may not be model beauty, but I'm not bad either. At least I've developed a few curves."

"Uh, I can't argue with you there."

Maddie yanked her skirt up to mid-thigh. "And I do have nice legs, at least several men have told me that."

"What men?" The glider squeaked as he shifted and tugged at his collar.

"Lots of men, you know guys at school, night-clubs, construction workers."

"Maddie, you need to watch out—"

Maddie cut him off with a hiss. "I realize you're more experienced than me, Chase, but I'm not a kid anymore."

He raised a brow, his patronizing expression irritating her even more.

Maddie pursed her lips. "As a matter of fact, I'm a pretty good kisser if I do say so myself. Maybe I'm a little rusty from only kissing Jeff though." She angled her head sideways to study him. When he simply stared at her in disbelief, she snatched the edge of his shirt. "All right, see for yourself. If my kissing isn't up to par, maybe you can give me some pointers."

Then she jerked his mouth to hers and kissed him like the earth was about to come to an end.

Chapter Three

Chase's hands moved automatically to hover at Maddie's waist as she plunged her tongue into his mouth. Reminding himself that this was Maddie kissing him, he tried to set her away from him, but she seemed intent on driving him wild with her innocent seduction. Or test.

Whatever it was, his body was on fire. About to spontaneously burst into flames from the heat building in his loins. She traced a fingernail down the side of his face and scraped his beard stubble. The simple erotic sound made his body harden. Finally, she broke for air, sipped at his upper lip for a delicious moment, then pulled back and gazed at him. The heady scent of her exotic perfume suffused him, muddling his brain even further.

"Well?"

Well, hell. He narrowed his eyes, faintly aware his pulse had kicked in overtime, and his breathing sounded rough in the stillness of the night, almost as loud as the purring sound close by. The cat? No, a car motor.

A car motor!

"Well, Chase, what do you think?"

He glanced over the giant azaleas and saw Reid and Lance stalking up the sidewalk. *Double hell.* How could he possibly explain why he'd been kissing Maddie? And try as he might to deny it, he had kissed her back. Excuses tumbled through his head—*listen, guys, your baby sister here wanted some pointers.*

Yeah, they'd love that.

"Chase, do you have some suggestions on how I could improve my kissing technique?"

Improve? "Uh, no. I . . . your . . . B-brothers."

He stood, knowing if Lance and Reid had seen him, he was a dead man.

Maddie spotted her brothers, instantly sizing up their moods—their downcast heads, the frowns, the camaraderie of male hormones dominating her porch—not a good sign. To top it off, Chase had had to be so damn patronizing. The boys' gazes swung to her new car, and she sighed.

Not only did she have to deal with her meddling, macho, overprotective brothers and convince them that she had survived the breakup, but she'd also have to convince them a convertible was safe enough for a single female to drive alone at night in the city, and if they'd seen her kissing Chase . . . Boy, she had her work cut out.

Reid and Lance practically tripped over themselves trying to hug her.

"Hey, sis, you okay?" Lance asked in a gruff voice.

"Where the hell have you been?" Reid jammed his

hands on his hips and glared at her. "The show was over hours ago. We've been out of our minds with worry."

"Where did you get that car? Is it a loaner?" Lance asked.

"Whoa, slow down." Obviously, they hadn't seen the kiss. Thank goodness. Maddie pointed to the shopping bags. "I stopped by the mall and the bakery. Then the car dealership." When they started to protest, she held up a warning hand. "The VW is mine, guys. I bought it on the way home."

Lance's shaggy eyebrow shot up. "You bought it?"

"You can't be serious," Reid said. "What if you have a wreck—"

Maddie rolled her eyes in disbelief. "This from the guys who drove motorcycles with bumper stickers that read BAD-ASS BOYS DRIVE BAD-ASS TOYS."

"But that's different, sis, you're a girl," Lance bellowed.

"Newsflash, boys—this isn't the dark ages anymore. Women can actually vote, we've even flown in outer space."

Reid harrumphed. "Don't start with all that feminist stuff."

"You should be happy I didn't get the Miata, that was my first choice."

Reid patted her shoulder. "Okay, sis, calm down, we'll talk about the car later—"

"No, we won't. The convertible is mine," Maddie stated firmly. "I'm keeping it, end of discussion." Reminding herself that her brothers, in their infinitely old-fashioned Southern-bred mentality, meant well, and that they would never accept the fact that she was a grown woman perfectly capable of taking care of herself, she lowered her voice.

"Listen guys, I know you saw the show, but I'm

glad I broke it off with Jeff. Now let's have cake and coffee. I'm dying for some chocolate."

Reid's eyes filled with sympathy. "Uh-oh, she's resorted to chocolate."

"I love chocolate all the time," Maddie said emphatically.

"Look, Maddie, you don't have to pretend with us," Lance murmured. "We know you had to save face on camera, but you're talking to your big brothers now—"

Maddie silenced him with a quick shush. "Read my lips, brother dear. I'm glad my relationship with Jeff is over. I'm ready to move on. Now come on, I'm craving sugar." She forced a smile to placate them, but she knew her efforts were futile. They were certain she was devastated. They expected tears and drama.

She refused to give them either.

Reid pulled her into a bear hug. "We'll kill him for you," he whispered in a dark tone.

Lance widened his stance, his fighting face in place. "Just give us the word, sis, we'll go back and finish the job. He won't even know what hit him."

"What do you mean, you'll go back and finish the job?" Maddie folded her arms across her chest. "I thought you said they didn't hurt him, Chase."

Chase shrugged. "He was fine when I left."

So her brothers had gone back to see Jeff. "Tell me what happened, guys."

"Nothing really," Reid said, resorting to that stammering little-boy act she knew all too well.

"We simply had a little talk," Lance said. "Man to man."

Chase chuckled. "You mean man to wuss."

Maddie groaned. "You did hurt him."

"He'll heal," Reid said with a toothy grin.

"Besides," Lance added, "he can afford a plastic surgeon if the bone doesn't grow back straight."

A mosquito buzzed near Maddie's ear. She swatted at it, wishing she could swat her brothers away. "Please tell me you didn't break his nose. His mother will die—"

"We didn't break his nose," Lance said.

Reid wiggled his fingers. "But he jammed his little pinkie when he hit the pavement."

"Oh, my God, you're bullies!"

"We didn't touch him." Lance tried to look offended but failed miserably. "He was running so damn hard he tripped over his own feet."

The men broke into laughter and once again Maddie hissed. Except for the wuss comment, Chase remained suspiciously silent, a situation that struck her as odd and one she'd deal with sometime later. When she finished killing her brothers.

She squared her shoulders and walked toward them with her most menacing look. "I don't need your help or interference—"

Lance tweaked a strand of her hair in the same tender way he'd done when she was five. "Ahh, Maddie, come on, we're just trying to take care of you."

"Yeah, we promised Mama," Reid added in a rough whisper.

Did they have to go and mention her mother? Moisture immediately welled in Maddie's eyes as she contemplated how her mom would have reacted to today's events. Would she be disappointed in Maddie?

They both instantly noticed the tears and misunderstood the reason. Lance drew her into a hug again. "Shh, now, everything's going to be all right, sweetheart."

Maddie briefly allowed him to console her, but finally drew away, swiping at her eyes. "Reid, why don't you fix me some hot tea. I could use a cup. Would you mind?"

His rugged jaw relaxed slightly. "Sure. I'll be right back."

He hurried into her apartment, looking relieved to be assigned a task he could actually handle. She turned to Lance. He was the oldest of the three, the calmest, the wisest, the one who'd taken care of her and Reid when her parents had died. The one she worried about. The one she knew would be crushed if he learned about the argument her parents had had the night before they'd died.

Concern showed in the set of his jaw. "And you—maybe you could cut us all a slice of cake and make some coffee." She gestured toward the box on the table. "It's chocolate eclair."

He brushed his hand along her chin in that protective I'll-always-take-care-of-you way he had. "Whatever you want, Mad. You know I'm here for you."

Maddie nodded, blinking at the unwanted sting of tears that moistened her eyes. She didn't know whether to hit them both or hug them.

She should have killed them both and put them out of *her* misery, Maddie thought an hour later. Murder would have been easier than enduring their hovering. The boys polished off the eclair cake, gave her a pep talk that she did not need, and over a pot of coffee hinted that Jeff might change his mind and warm to the idea of marriage.

Yeah, with a little more of your intimidation tactics, Maddie thought sourly. She didn't want warm, she wanted *hot*. Someone hot for her and hot over the idea of loving her for the rest of his life. Someone who wouldn't ask her to trade her independence for his own goals. Someone who'd like it when she took control, even in bed.

"Breaking up with Jeff is the best thing I've ever done. Now my life can be my own show; I'll star in it and I won't have Jeff telling me what to do." Maddie lay down her fork, determined to put a positive spin on the humiliating day. "I'm going to date around, explore the single life in Savannah. Maybe I'll get some friends together and we'll make a single women's pact like you guys made that dumb bachelor pact when you were twelve."

"That pact was a good thing," Lance said.

"Yeah, I like my life." Reid mumbled. "I don't have to worry about putting the toilet seat down, have the remote to myself, and a different woman every night."

Maddie laughed. "I'm going to call Sophie and see if she wants to go to Barebones tonight, and there's that drag bar where the Lady Chablis performs, I can't wait to see—"

"You are not going to Barebones," Lance said in a no-nonsense tone.

"Or to see the Lady Chablis," Reid said curtly.

Maddie bristled in spite of the fact that she'd intentionally named the most outrageous bars she could think of to taunt her brothers. "Why not? I'm of legal age, and almost everyone in Savannah has seen—"

"You're a woman, and you're not going," Lance said as if that explained everything.

Reid stood, wincing when his head hit the bottom of a hanging fern pot. "Women like you are meant for places like the Tea House. In a bar, you're prime targets for . . . for—"

"Sexist bachelors like yourselves?" Maddie asked sweetly.

Chase halted the movement of the swing, threw his head back and laughed, cutting off Lance's reply. "Guys, I think Maddie's pulling your leg here."

Maddie shot him a wicked look. "Who says? I missed out on a lot of things dawdling around with Jeff. I'm going to have some fun now."

Lance and Reid groaned. Chase's dark eyes turned blacker than the night. "Then call one of us, and we'll take you, shortstop."

Maddie pointed her fork at them. "Right. Every guy in the place would be all over me, asking me to dance with the three of you hovering around like mother hens."

"We are not mother hens," Reid mumbled. "We're just more experienced."

"And you don't need guys all over you," Lance growled.

"Oh, pull . . . eeease," Maddie moaned. "The only difference between men and women is that you have a—"

"Don't say it, Mad," Lance warned.

"A Y chromosome." Maddie smiled smugly. "Now, let's change the subject."

Lance and Reid quickly shouted, "Here-here."

Chase didn't voice an opinion. In fact, he remained suspiciously silent again, merely giving Maddie another one of those dark, unreadable looks that made her wonder if her black thong underwear was visible beneath the sheer white dress. She crossed her legs and watched Chase's eyes momentarily rivet to her calf where the slitted skirt parted, then fall back to his scuffed-up boots. So, he didn't think she was twelve anymore.

Pleased with herself, Maddie flicked a strand of

hair over her shoulder, aware the bare back of the dress caught Chase's attention as she leaned forward.

Pretending she didn't notice his disapproving look, she continued, "So, how's the new development going?"

Her brothers instantly straightened, both talking at once to fill her in on the houses they'd contracted for restoration and their plans for Skidaway Island.

"Man oh man, the island venture is a great opportunity," Reid said. "Two hundred houses, golf course community, a swimming pool and tennis courts; if things go like we've planned, our company will take off."

"We're going to be included in the Tour of Homes Savannah's hosting for the Reinhardt Foundation," Lance added.

Reid grinned. "With Chase coming on board to design some of the custom projects, The Terrible Three can't possibly fail."

"Think we should advertise that nickname on our business cards?" Lance joked.

Maddie rocked back in the porch swing, a plan taking shape in her mind. "Hey, you guys are going to let me decorate the model homes for the tour, aren't you?"

Lance and Reid both hesitated, reaching for more coffee at the same time. Lance poured his first, dousing it with sugar. "I don't know, sis. You have a habit of jumping from one thing to another."

"Not this time, this time I'm serious."

"That's what you said about art school," Lance said. "Remember when you took that class to draw nudes."

"But you were too embarrassed to draw the men," Reid added. "So, you used your imagination—"

"And the body parts weren't proportioned quite right."

"I was only sixteen," Maddie said, her face flushing. "And I was drawing from memory. I can't help it that you guys were five when I last saw you naked."

"Yeah, but you didn't have to tell everyone we were your models. For God's sakes, we'd just been kids, streaking across the yard."

Maddie laughed. "Your male pride seems to have survived."

"Yeah, but still . . ." Reid began.

"What about that time you decided to join the peace corps," Lance said.

"I really wanted to help people," Maddie said through clenched teeth.

"But you couldn't get past those spiders," Reid pointed out.

"Arachnophobia isn't that uncommon."

"Then you wanted to be a soap-opera star," Lance said.

"Just so you could play kissy-kissy to some punk who didn't even have chest hair."

Maddie groaned. "I know I made mistakes, guys, but I'm grown up now and I finished my degree this time. Please let me work on the project."

Her brothers traded skeptical looks.

"But you haven't gotten established yet," Reid argued, shaking creamer into his cup.

"Don't you need some set-up time before you take on a big project like ours?" Lance asked. "Maybe you should work as an apprentice for someone."

"You could get a job at the hardware store in town," Lance suggested.

"The mall has a furniture store," Reid said.

Chase rose, fumbled with the coffeepot, then

poured himself a fresh cup of coffee, black. "You don't have your business license yet, do you, Maddie?"

Maddie's hand tightened around her tea cup. If she didn't know better, she'd think the men didn't want her to work with them. "I've already applied for my license, and I'm meeting with the bank next week to finalize the loan." She went on to describe her concept of the decorating van on wheels and how much overhead she'd save by using the mobile unit. In fact, getting the loan was almost a done deal, so she'd already ordered the van with her logo on it. It would be ready Monday. She didn't have to tell the boys that part though. "I know there are a couple of high-class design firms in town, guys, but they're going to be pricey, and they don't need your business, I do. I'll cut you a deal. Besides, this tour could be a great way for me to jump-start my business." Maddie took a quick breath, then continued, her excitement gaining momentum. "I already have themes in mind I could incorporate to give each home an individual look and to demonstrate my style."

Lance wiped a drop of perspiration from his cheek. "Most of the people shopping for houses out this way are pretty conservative, Maddie. You can't do anything flamboyant or too contemporary."

"Yeah, the historical society has to approve the restoration projects so none of that weird sponge painting like you have in your bathroom," Reid said.

"And no voodoo paraphernalia or feather headdresses like you hung on the walls in your bedroom," Lance said.

"The voodoo spell is copy of a famous legend," Maddie said. "And that headdress is a Mardi Gras mask I brought back from New Orleans."

"Still, we have to stick to code," Reid added forcefully.

"And you can't quit mid-job like you did on a couple of your other little projects," Lance said.

Maddie's jaw tightened. "I am a professional, guys. You don't have to worry. I know what I'm doing, and I'll finish the job, on time, too."

The boys exchanged uncertain looks, hem-hawed around in a hushed discussion, then finally, very reluctantly, agreed. Maddie jumped up and hugged both of them. "Thanks, you guys. Working with you will be wonderful. I won't let you down, I promise."

"Yeah, okay," Reid mumbled.

Lance scrubbed his hand along his neck. "You'll have to talk to Chase about some of the house designs, the unique features he's including."

Maddie hooked her arm through Chase's, trying to ignore the fact that he hadn't commented on their kiss before her brothers arrived. She must be rustier than she'd thought. "No, problem there. Chase and I will work well together, won't we, Chase?"

Chase's jaw tightened as his gaze roamed over her mouth, then trailed downward over the clinging dress, pausing briefly at the swell of her breasts, her hips, and finally down to her bare toes again where she noticed his eyes linger on her toe ring. Her sparkling red nail polish glittered beneath the light of the moon.

Another disapproving frown flitted onto his brooding face. Still, Maddie could have sworn she felt a current of some primal urge dance between them. Then the minute was gone, and Chase started cracking jokes about her poor sense of direction and how he couldn't imagine her driving a van all over town when she still got lost in the Savannah square. He finished by reminding them that she'd decorated her room with fluorescent painted toilet paper tubes tied together when she was eight.

Once again Maddie had been relegated to kid sister.

She stood, ready to tell him off, when he yanked her back down. Chase brushed his cheek against her ear and whispered, "Here's a brotherly tip: Next time, you might want to go with the white underwear, shortstop."

Maddie's temper exploded. She leaned on her toes and whispered the first comeback that popped into her head. "Heck, Chase, next time, I'll show a little cleavage. And I won't wear any underwear at all."

Chase grimaced inwardly at his inability to hold his traitorous tongue in check. He'd never meant to make that comment to Maddie about her panties, but damn, he'd seen a whiff of that black scrap and her bare butt beneath the dress in the moonlight and nearly choked on his coffee. The fact that Maddie was acting rather strangely herself, talking about barhopping and picking up men hadn't helped either. And that . . . that kiss.

He wasn't sure whether to be worried about her or to warn every single man in Savannah to watch out for the sex siren that had suddenly been unleashed into the city. His poor buddies. They had their hands full.

Recognizing trouble brewing, Chase decided to hit the road and fast. "I gotta get out of here. Maddie looks tired."

Maddie raised one beautiful auburn eyebrow.

He shrugged. "Okay, I'm tired. I have a few years on you, shortstop." *And a few mental calluses and a bad name to boot.*

"We'll head out, too," Lance said.

Reid and Lance hugged Maddie, and Chase waited patiently at the porch edge while they once again offered their condolences. Chase forced himself not to look back as he headed to his truck, afraid moonlight would halo Maddie's curves beneath that white dress and ruin his don't-give-a-shit exit.

He flicked a wave over his shoulder. "See you, kid."

One of Maddie's heels hit Chase's backside, then clunked to the concrete behind him, punctuating her statement. "I am not a kid, Chase Holloway."

Reid and Lance broke into laughter as they walked him to his truck. He'd barely started the engine before Lance began. "Man, I didn't know how to turn down Maddie about the decorating thing, not after what she's been through today."

Reid crooked his arm on the window ledge. "What are we going to do? We can't work with our baby sister underfoot all the time."

"I don't think Maddie's ready for the business world. She's just a kid," Lance complained.

Chase frowned. His buddies obviously had vision problems. Better yet, they needed eye surgery.

"What if she screws up this deal for us? We've been working our butts off to get this business off the ground."

"Why couldn't she have been satisfied marrying Oglethorpe? She could have babies, stay home, throw dinner parties."

Sounded like a miserable life to Chase, especially the dinner party part. He cleared his throat. "Uh, do I have to remind you guys that Oglethorpe turned her down?"

"You heard what he said about her job. He wanted a businessman's wife."

"Mama wanted that for Maddie, too," Reid added.

"But Maddie's excited about her job," Chase said, wondering why he was defending her. Heck, for all he knew Maddie might hang tiki torches in every room or paint the studies pansy pink, or some other weird female color like fuchsia.

"Yeah, I thought this decorating thing was a hobby, figured Maddie would use her degree to make conversation when she was entertaining at dinner parties," Reid said.

A vision of Maddie at one of the droll society affairs, bowing down to some of the ritzy set darted through Chase's mind. He just couldn't picture it.

"What are we going to do?" Lance asked, sounding desperate.

"Why don't you give her a chance?" Chase suggested. "Maybe she'll surprise you and be an asset to the company."

"Yeah, right," Reid mouthed.

"I guess we're stuck." Lance drummed his fingers on the side of the truck. "But she won't listen to the two of us, so you have to be in charge of her, Chase."

Chase nearly knocked the truck into gear. "I . . . I don't think that's a good idea. You two know how to deal with Maddie, you're her brothers, she'll listen to you—"

"Not anymore," Lance argued.

"Man, she followed you around like a puppy dog when she was little, Chase. You were the only one she'd let teach her to pitch," Reid argued.

"And you're the one that talked her out of going out for the football team in high school," Lance said.

"She only wanted to prove a point," Chase said, remembering he'd admired her for her courage. But in the end, Maddie had decided to run for school office and had tried to change things on the political level instead of getting beaten up by a bunch of hulking jocks.

"Yeah, you can deal with her better than us right now," Lance said.

"And someone has to handle her. You know how impulsive she is."

She was impulsive all right. She'd stolen all the football players' jock straps and ran them up the flagpole. Then she'd taken off her own underwear and let them fly beside the boys'. Every male in school had speculated on whether she'd been pantyless at school that day.

"So, you'll do it?" Lance asked.

Chase gripped the steering wheel with white knuckles. An X-rated image of handling Maddie flashed into his mind, nearly knocking the wind out of him.

Lance slapped him on the back before he could argue further. "Thanks, man. You're like a brother to her. Besides, you're the *only* guy we trust with our little sister. Every other man in town would be chomping at the bit to get in her pants."

And see that black thong up close.

"We have to protect the business," Reid added.

Oh, yeah, the business. Chase remembered the bachelors forever pact the three of them had made when they were twelve. They'd renewed their pact when they'd forged their business venture. Marriage and families would only rob time from the company. And right now, the company was the most important thing in the world to Chase. Next to his friendship with Reid and Lance, of course.

He'd grown up an orphan nobody, had been teased his entire life about his jailbird dad, his tainted name. Chase tried to form a mental picture of his father, but the only image that surfaced was prison bars and a number on a pair of orange work overalls. After that, there had been the endless barbs from the other kids about being the son of a murderer. The fights and scrapes he'd gotten into when he couldn't stand the ridicule. Being rejected by a stream of adoptive families. Holidays spent alone. Always feeling like an outcast. Anger had simmered and festered inside him, almost destroying him. He'd promised himself that one day he'd show this town that Chase Holloway was someone worthy of their respect.

Making a success out of this company and building a decent reputation and name for himself in Savannah had to take precedence over a personal life. And definitely over his untamed libido. If he had to handle Maddie for her brothers to ensure success, then hell, he'd accept the job as baby-sitter. He'd just be sure to buy a pair of kid gloves before he saw her next. He'd have to forget that black thong and those delicious-looking cherry-red toenails, too. And that toe ring. And that . . . that insatiable kiss.

Reid poked his side. "Chase, you listening?"

"Yeah, no problem," Chase said. After all, Maddie was almost *his* kid sister.

"But remember," Lance added, "Whatever you do, don't ever tell Maddie we asked you to do this."

Chase nodded. "Don't worry. Maddie will never know."

The last three days had been hell. Friday morning, Maddie dragged herself out of the Lend and Loan, battling depression. First the Small Business Association had turned her down, then every bank in town had dittoed the response. She'd reached the end of her list. Darn it; how could she start her business if everyone in Savannah refused to give her a chance?

The excuses varied, but the results had all been the same. She didn't own her house, so she couldn't use it as collateral. Her brothers had borrowed to the hilt for their own business so she had no one to co-sign a loan for her. Worse, there were the whispered looks behind her back, the raised eyebrows; obviously her TV appearance had been noted, and she'd been blackballed by all the businessmen in town.

She sighed as she thought about splurging on the new car. A dumb impulsive decision. At the time, she'd never dreamed there would be a problem with her business loan. Although she hadn't officially applied for funding, Jeff had hinted there wouldn't be a problem, that he'd put in a good word for her.

And now she had the van payment as well.

But Jeff's support had come before Sophie's show. She should have waited until *after* she'd secured the loan to issue her ultimatum to Jeff. What had she been thinking? Not only was Jeff prominent blue-blood Savannah, but he was on the board of the Savannah Economic Development committee, friends with all the entrepreneurs in town, and he was related to the mayor. He'd probably called everyone he knew and advised them she was a nutcase, not to loan her a dime.

She'd obviously bitten her own self in the ass!

The expression on Jeff's face when he'd seen that flaming red heart instantly materialized in her mind, and Maddie shuddered. She'd purposely avoided his bank this week hoping to secure the money she needed elsewhere. She didn't relish the idea of begging him for money now, not after the way they'd parted, but she had no other choice. She checked her appearance in the mirror, painted her lips a soft plum color to contrast with the dark green suit she'd chosen, climbed from her car, and walked inside the double glass doors.

On the other side of the room, she spotted Jeff leaning against a chrome counter decked with coffee and other condiments. A tall blonde rested her hand on his arm, chatting flirtatiously. Obviously, Jeff had weathered the break-up pretty well.

His gaze lifted, and he looked straight at her, his blue eyes piercing. Frissons of heat danced along her nerve endings at the anger she saw radiating from his expression. She should have worn knee pads for protection when she dropped to the floor to beg for money, she decided. Jeff Oglethorpe didn't intend to make this encounter easy.

In fact, he spent ten minutes talking to the blonde, ten more to his secretary detailing his schedule, then made Maddie wait in his outer office a good twenty minutes after his secretary had disappeared for lunch before he finally allowed her to enter.

She approached his office cautiously. "Um, hi, Jeff."

The mole at the corner of his mouth jumped as his jaw tightened. "If this is about the other day, I don't want to discuss it, Madison."

Maddie bit down on her lip. "Actually, it's not about the other day. Not exactly."

His brown eyebrow raised.

"I would like to apologize for embarrassing you though, Jeff, I never meant to—"

"If you came hoping for a reconciliation, I don't think that's possible now. My mother has barely recovered from that debacle on TV."

His *mother*. What about him?

"I didn't come here to beg for a reconciliation."

He clutched the lapels of his suit jacket stiffly. "Well then, why are you here?"

Maddie momentarily lost her nerve. The strained hum of silence that lingered between them only elevated the tension in the room. Finally, unable to bear the awkwardness any longer, she cleared her throat. "I came here about a loan."

"You want to borrow money from me?" He pulled out a couple of hundred-dollar bills and tossed them toward her. "I'm a little surprised but here, I'm a generous guy, and I don't want any hard feelings. Will two, three hundred be enough to tide you over?"

"I didn't mean I wanted money from you personally. I need a *business* loan, Jeff. From the bank." Heat climbed her neck. "Remember we discussed it before."

"Before you ditched me on TV." He settled into his brown leather desk chair, then leaned back and studied her, a faint look of hurt in his eyes. "You seriously want me to back your business now?"

"Yes. I hate to come to you, Jeff, but I've been everywhere else in town, and no one will help me." She indicated the folder in her perspiring hands. Darnit, she was sweating like a pig in heat, and her panty hose were climbing up her behind, sticking in every nook and cranny. "I've itemized the costs for start-up and included a business plan and a report on the parent company and the franchise I want to buy."

When he simply stared at her, she rushed on, "You know I've wanted to be an interior designer for a long time."

His thin lips quirked sideways. "This venture is risky, Maddie. I think the two elite design firms already established in Savannah would have the market cornered."

"You didn't seem skeptical before."

"Well, as you pointed out, that was before. Now

that I've seen how impulsive you can be, I have a few reservations."

She pressed her lips into a fine line at his insinuation, remembering her brothers' comments. At least her previous meetings had prepared her to argue her case. "There are a lot of new developments popping up, and let's face it, Jeff, not everyone can afford Franchesca's or Dante's. They're pretty upscale and don't cater to middle-income families. I want to cater to them. Plus, I have the advantage of low overhead on my side, and I'll travel to people's homes with samples."

"Franchesca's and Dante's both offer in-home consultations."

"Yes, but at an escalated price. I'll do the first consultation free, get an idea of what my clients are looking for, then give them an estimate on the spot. No fee unless they actually use my services."

Jeff twisted his mouth in thought. "You're talking about one of those low-rent mobile-home decorating vans?"

Maddie fought to squelch her temper. "They're not low-rent. They're called door-to-door decorating vans. Most working people don't have time to drive around to a dozen different stores for estimates and samples, so the whole concept of my business was designed to make decorating more convenient for them. The vans house most of the fabric and wall-covering samples as well as furniture catalogs so the customer doesn't even have to leave her house."

He remained silent for a moment, obviously considering her logic. "How much start-up capital are you talking?"

Maddie handed him the detailed file and business plan she'd written, clenching her hands in her lap as he opened the folder and studied the figures.

"I've met several managers from other franchises and studied profit-and-loss statements as well as reports of their operating expenses. The franchises are profitable. I've also taken a course on merchandising and sales techniques."

"You sound as if you've done your homework but—"

"But what?"

For a brief moment, he let his defenses slip, and Maddie recognized the young man she'd first been attracted to, the eager businessman, the dreamer. She saw the memories flit across his face—the night they'd driven up to the mountains for a romantic picnic, the surprise trip he'd taken her on to Bermuda, the little romantic gifts he used to send her weekly.

Along with those memories, now she saw the regret, the desire, the boyish charm that had once captivated her.

Had she been too hasty in her decision to leave him? When had all the romance stopped—when he'd started working for his family?

"Maddie—" His intercom buzzed and his secretary announced the mayor had arrived early for his luncheon date and a mask slid over his face, hiding his emotions. He was once again transformed into the focused businessman his family wanted. She'd lost the Jeff she once loved.

She was going to lose the loan, too, if she didn't do some fast talking.

"Jeff, you know Lance and Reid won the bid on the new development on Skidaway Island, and they have several restoration projects lined up. They've agreed to let me decorate the models for the Savannah Tour of Homes. It'll be the perfect way to jump-start my business. You've heard of RiverRidge?"

A smug expression flitted into his eyes. "Yes, of course, it's a golf-course community. Mother has friends interested in buying out there, very upscale."

She nodded, tapping her toe on the carpet as if she needed to channel her nervous energy. "I know I can win clients through the tour. Maybe you should study the information I've enclosed about the franchise. You could visit the subdivision before you decide."

"I have to be honest with you, Maddie." He raised his gaze to meet hers, a hint of tenderness in his eyes that reminded Maddie of the good times they'd shared—the young man who'd first awakened her sexual urges, even though they had never consummated their relationship. "Middlemyer, the CEO here, prefers to fund large corporations. He seldom dabbles in small-business loans."

Her stomach knotted. "So you're saying you won't approve my loan?"

He hesitated, fisting his own hands around the file. Maddie could see the indecision within his eyes. "Have you tried the SBA?"

"Yes," she said in a low voice. "They turned me down. No collateral."

"How about the other major banks in town?"

She studied her fingernails. "Ditto."

"Ferguson's Finance Company?"

"No one to co-sign, I even wondered if you'd . . ."

"You want me to co-sign your loan?"

"No, oh, no I didn't mean that . . ."

He drummed his fingers on his desk, anger suddenly flaring in his eyes. "You aren't suggesting I'd sabotage your loan, are you, Maddie?"

"Well, Jeff, I know Lance and Reid paid you a visit and—"

His jaw tightened. "I don't want to talk about your brothers."

"I'm sorry, Jeff."

He hesitated, once again. "After all we shared, Maddie, you don't really think I'd do something so low as to sabotage a loan for you?" His fingers brushed over her palm gently. "I really thought we'd get married someday, you know."

Before his family pressured all the spontaneity and life out of him. Maddie took a deep breath, regrets for all they'd shared and lost clogging her throat. "I'm sorry, Jeff, for even implying such a thing. Please forgive me."

"We could still talk, Maddie." His voice sounded almost desperate. "If you'd just give up this decorating-van idea of yours and help me—"

Her spine stiffened. "I'm not giving up my dreams, Jeff."

His eyes gentle, and for a moment she thought he was going to come across the desk, take her in his arms and tell her everything was all right the way he had when she'd gotten frustrated in college. But in her heart of hearts, she knew things between them had changed. Then the buzzer sounded again, and his secretary reminded him that the mayor was waiting, and the moment was lost. The emotions she'd seen earlier disappeared.

When he met her gaze again, he had his serious work face firmly back in place. "Look, I'll see what I can do, Maddie. Do you have anything you can offer for collateral?"

She fingered the diamond-and-ruby pendant at her breasts, lifted the delicate chain from around her neck and clutched it in her hand. "The only really valuable thing I have is this necklace I inherited from Mom." Surely he wouldn't ask her to sign against the necklace. He knew how much it meant to her.

His blue eyes darkened as he took the delicate jewel and studied the setting. "All right, have it appraised, and I'll see what I can do."

Maddie slid out of her chair and stood, gratitude warring with a sudden attack of nerves and a sliver of anger. "You really want me to borrow against Mom's keepsake?"

His hand closed around the edge of his credenza, his voice gruff. "Middlemyer will expect something as a show of good faith. You're the one who established the new rules now, Maddie. You came to me for a business loan, not a personal favor, that's exactly what you're getting."

"Right." Maddie's chest tightened. She wanted to prove her independence. Here was her chance.

Still, the pendant was the only thing she had left of her mother's. Her father had ordered the ruby and diamonds to be fit in an antique setting for her parents' tenth wedding anniversary. Could she put the treasured jewelry up for collateral?

His eyes narrowed, and she remembered Jeff's comment about marriage; he wanted a businessman's wife, not a businesswoman. She'd issued the ultimatum on TV, but he'd taken control. He'd forced her to choose between him and her dreams. Just as her father had forced her mother to choose.

Lord, how she hated being at the mercy of a man. She wanted her independence, and she'd do anything to achieve it.

Yes, she'd put the necklace up for collateral. In a way the situation was fitting. Her mother had sacrificed her own dreams to care for her father, to try and help him pursue his goals, but she'd lost her own in the process. Maddie would not repeat those mistakes.

She'd take money from Jeff but strictly as a business deal. She'd show her brothers and that infuriating Chase Holloway that she wasn't a kid anymore, that she could be a successful businesswoman. But she'd never give up her independence or her dreams for Jeff.

Or any other man.

Chapter Four

Chase grinned at Daphne, thanking his lucky stars Lance had sent the buxom blonde his way during their Friday afternoon happy hour at the Shrimp Store. The men had met to discuss the problems at the development, mainly the importance of meeting standards and finishing the project on time. One of their backers had warned that if they couldn't make the deadlines or if materials weren't up to code, he'd immediately turn the project over to their competitor. The pressure ball had been dropped hard, landing on his foot when the subject of the tour had arisen. If Maddie didn't do a good job, it would affect sales, which would start a domino effect, trickling back to them. Everything they had was riding on this project. And Lance and Reid were counting on him to make sure Maddie came through.

One pitcher of beer after another had led Chase down the drunken road to thinking about Maddie in other ways though.

Unbidden thoughts, like the fiery look in Maddie's coffee-colored eyes. The seductive curve of her hips, the sexy swagger to her walk, the silkiness of those wild curls that floated over her shoulders like some untamed beast. His body reacted instantly, hot blood rushing through his veins and pooling in his loins. Damn his libido.

Thank God for women like Daphne. Women who liked sex, fast and quick. Women who didn't expect anything but a good time. Women who weren't little sisters to his best friends.

Women who weren't meant to get married any more than he was, or women who weren't tangled up in the business that meant so much to him.

Maddie suddenly appeared. "Hey, you guys, your secretary told me you were here. I had to find you so we could celebrate."

Lance and Reid exchanged confused looks. "What are we celebrating?"

"I got the loan!" Maddie threw her arms around her brothers and hugged them with the same exuberance she had when she'd hit her first homerun. She'd hugged him, too, back then, Chase thought, but now things were too awkward between them. Ever since that kiss . . . He bit his cheek, wishing he could take it back so things could be normal between them again. Especially with the sex goddess Daphne sitting beside him, rubbing her hand up and down his knee.

Lance and Reid asked for details, but Maddie shrugged them off, and waved at the waitress. Sinking into a chair, she looked flushed and beautiful, with her long legs sliding out from that short green skirt. Chase's body automatically stirred.

He glanced at Daphne, deciding to exit and expend his sexual energy where he could—without trouble.

But Maddie cut him off before he could speak. "Aren't you going to congratulate me, Chase?"

He raised his beer, sensing a challenge in her voice. "Way to go, Mad."

She smiled, ordered a margarita, dug a tortilla chip from the bowl, dipped it in salsa and popped it in her mouth. "So we'll all be working together now."

Lance and Reid's panicked expressions darted to him.

Thankfully, Maddie was oblivious. "When can you guys show me the property? I'm dying to get started."

"Uh, sis, we're going to let Chase handle that side of the operation with you," Lance said.

"Yeah, we've got our hands full with contractors and electricians and all that crap. Chase is the man to talk to about that last-minute pretty-it-up kind of stuff."

Maddie's gaze flitted to Daphne, then to Chase. "Later tonight?"

Much later, after I've spent some time with Daphne. "Whenever's good for you."

"How about six?"

"Sure," Chase agreed. Six was fine. That would give him plenty of time to take care of his overactive sex drive.

"Well, you ready to hit that hot tub?" Daphne purred into his ear.

Chase nodded and stood, avoiding Maddie's curious look. Yep, Daphne would make him feel better. Just as soon as he joined her in that sinful sea of iniquity she called a Jacuzzi, he'd forget all about this silly attraction to his best friends' little sister. Maddie could talk all she wanted about partying, but she was a settle-down kind of girl. And he would never be the settle-down kind of guy. He'd simply watch her to make sure she didn't screw up the job.

Maddie watched Chase leave with Daphne and sighed, taking a deep breath to stifle the tightening in her lungs. Good grief, she must have lost her breath running inside. Why else would she have this weird achy feeling in her chest? It certainly wasn't because Chase had left with that other *person.*

"She's a looker," Reid said.

Maddie frowned, glancing down at her own neat suit. Try as she might, she'd never be a sex siren like that cantaloupe woman. If Delilah, or whatever her name was, was Chase's typical kind of date, no wonder he hadn't commented on her inexperienced kiss. She was surprised he hadn't laughed his head off. Her brothers were drooling.

"What a bod," Lance said.

"Do you think—"

"They're not real," Maddie interjected, guessing her brother's comment by the enamored look in his befuddled eyes.

Reid wrinkled his forehead in thought. "How can you tell?"

"She moves, and they don't," Maddie said matter-of-factly.

"Who the hell cares?" Lance said with a chuckle.

Maddie took a hefty sip of her drink. "You guys are hopeless, sexist—"

Reid pointed to the entrance. "Hey, isn't that your friend Sophie from the talk show?"

"Sophie Knows," Lance said wryly.

"It's Sophie Lane," Maddie corrected as she jumped to her feet to wave her friend over. "Now *she's* a real woman, not like that Daffodil girl."

"Daphne," Reid said.

"Whatever." Maddie rolled her eyes. "And brunettes are your type, Lance."

"Not anymore," Lance said in a curt tone.

Maddie wrinkled her nose, wondering why her big brother was acting so ornery. He'd been on edge for the last few weeks, but she couldn't get him to confide what was upsetting him. She'd finally decided he must be worried about the business.

Sophie saw her and grinned, making a beeline for them. "Over here!" Maddie shouted.

A couple nabbed Sophie as she passed their table, and she stopped to autograph their napkin. "What the hell's she doing here anyway?" Lance asked.

Maddie shot him a warning look. She'd secretly hoped her best friend and her big brother would hit it off, but she'd obviously made a matchmaking mistake. "She came to celebrate with me, so be nice."

Lance clamped his mouth shut, crossed his ankles and leaned back in his seat. He sipped his beer, looking unusually sullen.

When Sophie approached, Maddie quickly made the introductions and ordered her friend a drink, puzzled at Lance's near-rudeness. He was usually quieter than Reid, more brooding, but both of them had had southern manners drilled into them since they were little.

"We don't catch the show much with our schedule and all, but we did see it the day Maddie was on," Reid said. "We're working pretty long shifts to get this new subdivision off the ground."

"I heard about the complex," Sophie said. "I thought you guys might appear on the show and talk about the new development on Skidaway."

Lance set his beer mug down with a thump. "I

don't think so, Miss Lane. Humiliating myself on TV has never been a goal of mine."

Sophie's long, black eyelashes fanned across ivory cheeks. "Who said anything about humiliating you, Lance? I was talking about a serious show. I've booked the Savannah Economic Authority to talk in late March."

Lance merely grunted. Maddie opened her mouth to reprimand her brother but Sophie's grin turned devilish. "Although, we have discussed doing an episode called 'The Dating Game.' I could work you in there if you'd like, Lance. We need a couple of good-looking guys."

Reid wiggled his eyebrows and elbowed Lance. "Hey, sounds like fun, bro."

Lance stood so abruptly, his chair clattered back against the wall. "Like I said, I'm not interested." With a disapproving glare at Sophie, he tossed a few bills on the table and stalked off. Sophie's perplexed gaze flickered to Maddie.

Maddie gaped at her brother. What in the world had gotten into him? As far as she knew, Lance had never been rude to a woman in his life. Had he been humiliated by her TV appearance or was something else bothering him? Could he possibly have something against Sophie?

"I swear that's never happened to me before," Chase said, feeling all four of his cheeks burn red with embarrassment as he stood and climbed from the hot tub. Daphne had been naked and hot and willing and he'd been unable to . . . to respond.

"Sure it hasn't, honey." Pity darkened Daphne's eyes. She'd tried everything from rubbing herself all over him to downright physical teasing. The torture normally would have put him over the edge in minutes, but this time . . . no, this time he kept seeing images of his best friends' little sister and those damn innocent eyes of hers looking at him, and his libido had gone down the drain. He'd known he shouldn't be in bed, or rather the Jacuzzi, with one woman while thinking about another.

He took one last look at Daphne's exquisite double D's and prayed for resurrection. Nothing happened.

Furious and frustrated, he yanked the towel around his waist and stalked to the corner of the room for his clothes. "It must have been all those damn candles. They almost put me to sleep."

"Aromatherapy," Daphne replied.

"Limp-dick therapy," Chase muttered as he pulled on his jeans with a vengeance.

Her laughter bounced off the walls as he stormed outside. Just as he climbed in his truck, the alarm on his watch sounded. Time to meet Maddie.

His sex stirred at the thought of her.

"Hellfire and damnation," he snarled. He had to think of some way to get out of seeing her, or he was going to lose his mind. Either that or bad-boy Chase Holloway was going to blow everything he'd been working so hard to achieve in his life for a quick roll in the hay.

Chapter Five

Maddie paced back and forth in front of the real-estate office on Skidaway Island searching for Chase's truck. They were supposed to have met a half hour ago so he could show her some of the house plans for the new development. She couldn't wait to begin sketching ideas for the interiors. But Chase was late.

He probably got lost between Daphne's cleavage and couldn't find his way out. She might have smothered him to death.

Forcing her thoughts away from Chase, Maddie checked her watch for the dozenth time, shading her eyes with her hand as a black sedan wove through the azalea-lined drive. Her stomach clenched when she saw Jeff swerve into a parking spot and exit his classic BMW. Was he here to cause trouble?

She still couldn't believe he'd forced her to offer her mother's necklace as collateral. Leaving the precious heirloom in the safety-deposit box had been the hardest thing she'd ever done. Her brothers would be furious if they knew. But she would force herself to work day and night to succeed, because there was no way she'd ever lose the treasured pendant.

Jeff headed to the office door without once glancing her way. Looking impeccable in his charcoal-gray suit, his brown hair gleaming in the sunlight, he trotted inside, emerging moments later with a tall auburn-haired woman at his side. His hand rested possessively on her waist as he helped her in the car. A real-estate agent. So Jeff was househunting? Or had he already moved on to another woman?

What did she care? She had her business to start.

First, though, she had to deal with Chase Holloway. And she had to forget the kiss she'd instigated on a whim. The hot kiss that she hadn't been able to get out of her mind, which obviously had not affected Chase.

Speaking of the kissing expert, he rolled up the drive, bypassed Jeff's BMW, spitting dust on the waxed finish as he passed. She stifled a giggle when Jeff blew his horn. She half expected Chase to appear wearing a black leather jacket, an earring and that surly frown of his that spelled trouble. She was wrong on the first two counts; the third on target.

Masculinity seemed to roll off Chase in waves as he emerged from the truck. His bad attitude climbed out with him. He wore faded dusty jeans, a denim work shirt and a baseball cap turned backwards. His long, shaggy hair protruded below the rim and brushed his collar. *He must work out or swim or do something to keep his body so toned and fit,* she thought, noticing the finely honed muscles in his legs and arms as he pounded across the gravel toward her. But he frowned as he approached her, his sour demeanor throwing a monkey wrench into her excitement about the job.

"Hey." His gaze scanned the exterior of the model home temporarily housing the sales office, the wooded lots behind them, everywhere but at her. "Sorry I'm late, we had a holdup with a tile guy."

What about Daphne? Her gaze fell to his shriveled-up fingers. "Have fun in the hot tub?"

He shrugged. "Yeah, it was great." Obviously not willing to elaborate, Chase gestured toward the river. "Rick and the crew already have ten houses framed. Why don't we walk down there and take a look?"

Maddie agreed, traipsing after him as best she could wearing her heels. He was practically jogging. Next time, she'd dress for hiking. "Chase, could you slow down please? I didn't wear my running shoes."

He frowned again, but he did slow his pace, and he even took her arm to help her down the incline. Maddie tried to ignore the heat from his palm, and the fact that he jerked his hand away from her as soon as they'd reached the bottom of the hill.

The afternoon sunshine warmed her cheeks, and the smell of wildflowers and freshly cut grass permeated the air, but it was the crystal-clear Savannah River that took her breath away. Jagged rocks jutted to a vee to form a jetty that culminated with a small waterfall. The sound of rushing water over rocks sang in the background, the splash of a fish occasionally catching in the breeze. "This is beautiful," Maddie said. "A great place to go skinny-dipping."

Chase's eyes narrowed. "We're not skinny-dipping, Mad."

Maddie quirked an eyebrow. "I wasn't referring to you, Chase. I was thinking about someone who liked a little fun, the way you used to."

"Like the twenty or thirty guys you plan to date?"

"Exactly." She smiled sweetly, deciding to change the subject before he broke into another lecture. "No wonder the boys have been so excited about this project."

His shoulders lifted slightly. "Yeah, winning this bid was the best thing that could have happened to us. The Tour of Homes is the next."

"I'm excited about the home show, too." He simply frowned and Maddie scanned the lush green grass, the rippling tide, the clusters of live oaks and hardwoods shading the property, wondering if he wasn't glad she was decorating the homes. Ignoring the doubts nagging at her, she opted for optimism, "You guys will be a huge success."

Chase nodded. "Hopefully, with the Savannah Economic Development committee enticing businesses onto the island with their research facilities, we shouldn't have trouble selling the lots." He paused, and they stood in companionable silence, savoring the sounds and scents of the surrounding woods. Dusk settled over the river, ricocheting streaks of purple and orange across the grainy earth shimmering below the surface of the water.

"I wish Mom and Dad could be here to see this," Maddie said. "They would be so proud of the boys."

Chase simply nodded again, then pointed to the immaculate property designated for the recreational activities. "The golf course is almost finished. So are the swimming and tennis facilities. And all the river lots have private boat docks."

"What an incredible clubhouse," Maddie exclaimed. "I can picture a big old-fashioned southern wedding right there on the lawn."

He shifted, looking uncomfortable. "Yeah, if someone's crazy enough to get married, I guess it'd be a good place."

Maddie frowned and started to comment but Chase continued, "We built a ballroom for formal entertaining and corporate functions and some smaller rooms for private parties."

"Your design?"

Chase shrugged. "Mine and Lance's. We figured the buyers will be looking to entertain rich clients."

"Smart brother I have." She paused, then tapped his chest with her fingernail. "Oh, and you're not so bad either."

Chase looked at her long and hard, his jaw clenched. "That's not what they used to say in school."

"Well, some of those morons weren't so smart either. As I remember, you pointed out exactly how stupid they were on occasion."

The corner of Chase's mouth twitched. "I did have a way with words, didn't I?"

Maddie laughed. "Yeah, the four-letter ones. I spent hours trying to find them in the dictionary when I was eight."

A low chuckle rumbled from Chase's chest, easing the tension. "You should have checked the boys' room."

"Why didn't I think of that?"

His voice turned low, husky. " 'Cause you were too busy being a good girl."

"So I was. But not anymore."

Chase hesitated, their gazes locking for several long, tense seconds. Maddie thought he was going to lecture her about being a good girl. Instead he plastered on his business face as if a personal conversation was off-limits. "Are you ready to see some of the houses?"

"Sure." Maddie followed him up the hill, faintly aware of his musky scent as he took her hand and helped her climb over a stump. His damp palm was so large it swallowed hers as he maneuvered them through the foliage. Maddie stumbled over a tree root and almost fell, but he steadied her. She landed against his chest, the heat pouring off her in waves. One look into his eyes, and she pulled away, quickly righting herself. Although she thought she detected a spark of desire, Chase's expression had been guarded. But his touch had felt hot.

So real and hot for a moment it seared through her caution.

Play with fire, and you'll get burned.

The old childhood warning rattled through her head. But when she caught up to Chase, any trace of a reaction on his part had disappeared completely. Maddie turned sideways, trying to gracefully climb in the truck without hiking up her skirt. Chase, seeming impatient, gripped her around the waist and lifted her. Maddie's breath caught when his hands slipped to mold over her hips.

"Thanks," she said awkwardly when she settled in the seat.

"No big deal. I used to lift you all the time when you were five, remember?"

He used to ride her piggyback, too. "But I'm not five anymore, Chase."

"You always will be to me, shortstop."

Maddie frowned. The stubborn man was impossible.

He climbed in his pickup, then cranked the engine without a word and drove through the freshly cleared roads.

"How big are the lots?" Maddie asked, still seething.

"The estate lots run up to five acres, but plans include a phase with smaller lots around three acres." He pointed out four houses that had already been framed.

"I'm already thinking of ways to give each house a unique touch. I've decided to choose a theme and build around it."

Chase shot her a worried look. "Not like those themes you used to come up with when you worked on the parties at school."

Maddie laughed. "So, you remember those?"

"Who wouldn't? I don't know many proms that had a rodeo theme. Or *Star Trek* costumes."

"Well, now I wouldn't mind a broncing bull in one of the game rooms."

Chase quirked an eyebrow, studying her. "For real?"

Maddie laughed, sensing his worry. "Yeah, but that would be in my own house. I know what I'm doing, Chase."

His gaze darkened, questioning.

She shook off the desire building within her, trying to focus on work. "When is the tour scheduled?"

"Six weeks."

They passed a two-story stucco contemporary with skylights that instantly caught Maddie's attention. "These houses are so big, it'll take me a while to pull it all together. I'll be in charge of four, right?"

"Right."

"I need to start work right away then. Some of the custom window treatments and bedding will have to be rush-ordered to be ready in time."

"But you think you can handle it?"

"Of course," Maddie said emphatically. "Stop worrying."

Chase angled his head toward her, his jaw tight. "It's just this project; the tour is important to the company, Mad. Your brothers and I have put everything we own into—"

"The tour is important to me, too, Chase." Maddie folded her arms across her middle and rubbed her hands up and down her arms. "Not only do I have to prove myself to Lance and Reid, but I have a loan to pay back, too."

Chase stared at her long and hard, as if something she'd said had upset him. Finally he nodded and continued the tour. Maddie began to silently plan the themes as she marveled at a two-story Georgian home with white columns.

"That one is studded for five bedrooms, a rec room in the basement, an exercise/fitness area off the rec room, and two offices, one on the main floor and another upstairs."

"Perfect for the corporate couple," Maddie said, thinking about Jeff and his droll idea of marriage.

Chase's gaze swung to hers as if he'd read her mind. "Regrets?"

Maddie shook her head. "Heck, no, I'm excited about my new freedom. Sophie and I are going out on the town tonight."

"Barhopping?"

Maddie laughed. "Sure, I have a lot of catching up to do."

Chase's eyes widened. "Have you broken this news to your dear old brothers yet?"

Maddie winked. "No. Maybe you could tell them for me."

"Hell, no. You think I have a death wish?" When Maddie laughed, Chase gave her a dark look. "Look, Mad, you know you need to be careful—"

He was treating her like a kid again. "Don't you dare give me a lecture, Chase Holloway, you of all people should understand what it's like to want to play the field."

"What makes you think that, shortstop?"

"Daphne."

Chase shifted uncomfortably and stared out the window.

"Come on, aren't you proud of yourself?" Maddie asked.

"A gentleman never tells," he finally said in a low voice.

"I didn't know you were a gentleman."

"I'm not." He cut her a sharp look, then grinned, the jagged scar on his forehead twisting slightly in the light. "And there's a lot you don't know about me, Mad."

Maddie's stomach tickled with strange sensations. She tried to think of a comeback, but he turned away and focused intently on the drive, his smile fading. A sprawling lot with hundred-year-old oaks loomed in front of them. Chase cut the engine and leaned across the seat, his hand brushing Maddie's knee as he opened the glove compartment. A tiny shiver of apprehension darted up her spine, but all business, he hardly noticed. He pulled out a set of blueprints and unfolded them.

"This is going to be a southern plantation home, on a smaller scale, of course."

Maddie's eyes widened. "Oh, my gosh, with sleeping porches and all! Chase, it's wonderful. Whose is it?"

"It's mine."

"Yours?"

He rubbed the back of his neck as he stared at the plans. "Yeah, it's not as big as some of the others, but I figure if I can build it at cost, I'll be able to swing it." He shrugged sheepishly. "I've been saving awhile."

Maddie couldn't contain her surprise. "How did you manage, going to school and working?"

Chase frowned as if she'd chartered into unwelcome territory. "You know I like to work on old cars."

"Yeah, I remember you hot-wired that one you stole—"

"Yeah, well, I grew out of stealing." He scratched his jaw. "I've been buying 'em cheap, fixing 'em up, then selling 'em. Making a good profit."

"Amazing." Maddie studied the massive oaks, the view of the river, speculating on a perfect spot for a gazebo. "The lot is beautiful. Will your house be finished for the tour?"

"If things go according to schedule."

Excitement budded in Maddie's chest. Decorating ideas sailed through her head—an antique four-poster bed in the master suite draped with French lace and white linens, black-and-white tiles in the master bath, a bidet . . . She had to decorate this house—his house.

Now, if she could only convince Chase.

Lance gave the final instructions to the electrical crew and hoped they would get the details right. He and Reid had planned an innovative kitchen with the most recent technology available, but he was worried the actual workers hired to install the technology weren't as advanced as the technology itself. He sure as hell didn't need any problems on the job. Having Maddie underfoot was bad enough; thank goodness Chase had agreed to babysit her.

He climbed in his Blazer and headed toward home, deciding a hot shower and cold beer would make him feel better. So would a woman, but he had no prospects in that category. Chase was lucky he had no scruples when it came to women, that he bedded them and shed them like a rattlesnake shedding his skin.

But Lance was too serious; always had been, always would be. And if he wasn't careful, he *cared* about people. Not like Chase. Chase would never have trouble keeping that bachelor pact. Lance had actually avoided relationships in order to keep it—he'd had to so he could take care of his family. Still, sometimes at night or in the early-morning hours, he longed for the feel of a woman's soft curves pressed up next to him.

An image of Maddie's friend, Sophie, with that short spiked black hair and that petite little body sprang to mind. He shifted uncomfortably at his body's arousal. Just the sight of that woman's long black lashes and creamy skin tore him into knots. He'd spent more than one lusty evening imagining her in his bed, tormenting himself with that sassy little twitch of her mouth and those voluptuous hips of hers.

But Sophie Lane was one woman he had to avoid.

Because she might know his secrets. And she was just the sort of woman who'd use them.

Sophie Knows. He could never admit to Maddie or the guys that he watched the show regularly, that he had secretly harbored a thing for the woman for ages. But that stupid show of hers could cause all kinds of trouble for him and his family. Was that the reason she wanted him to come on her show—did she already know the truth about his father?

He didn't want to hurt Maddie's feelings or ruin her friendship with Sophie, but if the woman got too nosy, he'd have to dissuade Maddie from seeing her.

Maddie and Reid would be devastated if they knew their father wasn't the loyal family man they believed him to be. They'd all thought their parents had the perfect marriage. Lance shuddered as he remembered finding the odd box in his father's things. The letter from the woman named Maria, saying how much she cared for him, how much the years with him had meant. The catalog with all those pictures . . .

Secrets.

His father had had lots of them. And Lance intended to keep them until he went to his grave.

Chase watched the different emotions play across Maddie's face and knew something was up. Some kind of Maddie scheme. Maybe she hadn't been teasing about that Trekkie stuff or that broncing bull . . . He didn't want to hurt her feelings but he'd be damned if he'd let her ruin everything he and her brothers had worked so hard to accomplish.

"Chase, I was thinking—"

"Uh-oh, sounds like trouble."

Maddie laughed. "If you let me decorate your house, it would prove to the others that you have faith in me."

Did he?

"You do have faith in me, don't you?"

"Uh, yeah, sure."

"Then you'll let me do it?"

Chase opened his mouth to cite all the reasons it was a bad idea—friends working together, mixing business with . . . business, her brothers. And their tastes were entirely different. She liked wild, flamboyant color; he liked calm, neutral earthy tones that reminded him of the outdoors. She liked noise, he liked quiet, she liked—

"Chase, oh, please, this would mean so much to me."

Steeling himself against the tide of her disappointment as he formed the word *no,* he mumbled a reply, but the word he muttered sounded like a yes. He blinked, wondering if he'd heard himself wrong.

"Oh, thanks, Chase! You're wonderful!"

Before Chase could retract his misguided reply, Maddie threw her arms around him, drove her mouth over his and kissed him senseless.

She tasted like strawberries and wine, and he had the insane urge to ask her who she'd been drinking wine with, but her hands snaked up to cup his face and the erotic pull of her body lulled his brain until he found himself curving his arm around her tiny waist and drinking from her sweet mouth. She'd said he was wonderful. No one had ever told him that before. His hands dropped to her waist, then her butt, and he cradled her in his palms, rocking himself against her. The sound of the raging river rushing over the rocks served as a perfect backdrop for the lust pooling in his loins, and mimicked his raging heartbeat. God, when had little Maddie become such a passionate woman?

Maddie—a woman?

Dear God, no. He was doing it again, kissing his best friends' sister, and he was supposed to be her baby-sitter!

He jerked away, stared at her stunned face, her swollen lips, the red flush to her cheeks and saw in the depths of those chocolate eyes a hunger unlike any he'd imagined coming from little Maddie Summers. Reflected in the startled wide-eyed expression, he also saw his own raw desire blazing like a beast unleashed, searching for innocent prey.

Disgusted with himself and completely rattled, he

stalked to the other side of the trail, jammed his hands on his hips and tried to calm his labored breathing.

Leaves rustled as she walked up behind him. He broke out in a sweat as her sweet perfume wafted toward him. "Chase?"

He flipped his hand up to stop her. "Don't say anything, Maddie. That was a huge mistake."

"I-I'm sorry I was just so grateful—"

"It's all right. It was all my fault."

"Your fault?"

Funny, her voice sounded edgy. Angry.

He decided not to be a coward and faced her, wincing at the slight scrape on her jaw. She'd gotten the abrasion from his whiskers. The image was titillating, but a flashback of her in pigtails and cutoffs fishing by the bank when she was ten swept through his mind, and his guilt doubled. Geez, what had he been thinking?

He hadn't. The tornado moment had snatched the sense from his skull and dropped all his reasoning abilities to his groin.

"I know you were just thanking me, shortstop. I took it a little farther. Just a male response." He kicked a pinecone into the river. "Better remember that before you go thanking anyone else thataway."

An acorn suddenly hit him in the stomach. "What the hell?" He jumped back. A little lower and the nut would have hit his—

"You are infuriating, Chase Holloway. You're acting like that kiss was . . . wasn't . . ."

"Wasn't any good?" Chase laughed bitterly. "Listen, Maddie, you don't have a problem with your technique, so no more lessons or tests, okay?"

She simply glared at him.

"Got that?" He stalked toward her and gripped

her arms. "And you can't go around kissing guys like that or they're going to get the wrong idea."

Maddie tipped her chin defiantly. "Exactly what idea is that?"

"You know what idea. That you want to sleep with them!"

"And what if I do?"

He couldn't have been more shocked if she'd hit him with another acorn. "Then you have to control yourself. You're on the rebound from the wuss. And your brothers would be disappointed if you jumped in the sack with some guy right now."

The mention of her brothers seemed to squelch the last remnants of hunger from her eyes.

"This is about them, isn't it?"

Chase released her, picked up a twig and snapped it in two. "They're my best friends, Maddie, and you're like family to me."

"That wasn't a sisterly kiss, Chase."

"No, but it should have been. And you can't use me to irritate them. Just because you want to rebel—"

"What?" Another acorn slammed against his stomach. "Of all the pig-headed, arrogant, stupid things to say!"

He broke the twig in his clenched fists and watched it fall into dozens of pieces, scattering in the wind. Broken and damaged, just as he'd always felt when he was a kid. Somehow, he had to make her understand. "Listen, Maddie, I didn't mean to hurt you. Lance and Reid are the only friends—no, *family*—I've ever had." He raised his gaze to meet hers, steeling himself against any emotions he might see shining in her eyes. "And I'm not going to mess up that for anything, Maddie. Especially for a quick roll between the sheets."

"How about on the ground?"

He shook his head at her attempt at humor and strode back to the truck, then waited silently for Maddie to join him. His blood drummed hot in his veins, his heart raced painfully. When she jumped into the truck and slammed the door, he knew he'd made himself clear.

He just didn't know why he felt so crummy about it.

Chapter Six

"So, here we are dateless, together, on a Friday night," Sophie said.

"At least we're out, not sitting at home eating a gallon of chocolate-fudge ice cream and watching TV with my cat." Maddie winced as unbidden images of Chase Holloway rushed into her mind. She wondered what he was up to, then wanted to kick herself for even thinking about him. He'd embarrassed her beyond words and now she was going to avoid him until she absolutely had to see him. She'd deal with him for work, and work only. Tonight she'd decided to start her romp into singlehood with a vengeance. She'd worn her shortest, tightest black dress and let her hair down so it flowed around her bare shoulders and curled around her face.

Sophie laughed and gazed around the crowded dance floor, looking dynamite in a red tube top and black skirt. "The other day when you invited me to meet your brothers, I was hoping . . ." Sophie blushed and looked into her drink, letting her sentence trail off.

"That my brother might have some sense and ask you out." Maddie sighed and sipped her vodka tonic. "I swear, I think my brothers must still be living in the dark ages. Reid called and lectured me for half an hour about going out. And I don't know what in the heck's gotten into Lance. He's been so moody lately, I think he needs hormone therapy."

Sophie laughed. "You mean it wasn't me? I thought I just wasn't his type."

"You're exactly his type." Maddie tapped her foot to the loud music rumbling through the crowded room. "Maybe he's stressed from work, although having me helping out should make him feel better."

"Yeah, it should." Sophie smiled, seeming slightly appeased, and Maddie vowed to have a long talk with Lance about her friend.

"Hey, I know those guys from art school," Maddie said, waving at two handsome Italian men approaching them. She introduced Sophie, and they spent several minutes catching up with casual conversation. Finally Antonio asked Sophie to dance. Maddie found herself being escorted to the dance floor by Marco, his brother. The rest of the night passed in a whirlwind of dancing and laughter and heated innuendoes. Sometime around midnight Maddie forgot about Lance's stupidity where Sophie was concerned.

"We would like you beautiful ladies to come visit our resort," Marco said to Maddie.

Antonio gave Sophie a glittering smile. "Yes, you would enjoy the comfort."

"Tell us more about this place," Maddie said,

thinking a weekend vacation would help her forget that Chase had humiliated her.

"The resort is rather small, tucked away for privacy off the Isle of Hope." Marco squeezed Maddie's hand. "It is quite modern also. The people are most friendly. They have what you call your Southern hospitality."

Maddie laughed. "You mean we'll be served a big dinner at a round table with lots of relatives?"

Antonio threw his head back and laughed. "Lots of food and some relatives, yes. And a big heated pool and horseback riding and golfing. Whatever is your fancy."

"And we'll have our own place?" Maddie asked.

"If you desire," Marco murmured, his dark eyes raking over her as if to say he'd like more but would be patient. "I can phone ahead and make the reservations."

"I can't believe I haven't heard of this place," Sophie said. "What did you say the name of it was?"

"Open Arms Resort." Antonio slid his hands into the pockets of his pleated chinos. "They have all-night dancing. And tomorrow we can go bareback riding."

"I haven't been horseback riding in ages," Sophie said.

"I've heard of the Open Arms." A distant memory nagged at the back of Maddie's mind. "I think I read an article about the resort in the paper a while back."

Marco nodded. "Yes, the Sunday edition featured a piece on it last month in its Leisure section. We can relax at the beach tomorrow and have breakfast on one of the fishing docks."

Maddie grinned. "We're going to powder our noses and discuss it."

They scurried to the ladies' room to talk. "What do you think?" Sophie asked.

"The guys are gorgeous," Maddie said. "And the resort sounds like fun."

"It does, doesn't it." Sophie pulled out her compact. "I could use a weekend away. But I'm not getting in the car with them."

"No way," Maddie agreed. "We'll follow them in my convertible. And when we're ready to leave, we go."

Sophie laughed and gave her a thumbs-up. "Right, and I'll call and make the room reservations just to be on the safe side."

"We have to stick together until we check out of the place, too." Maddie traced a ruby line over her lips with her lipstick. "Lance and Reid would die if they thought I wasn't coming home tonight."

"Serve them right for being so overprotective."

"And rude to you," Maddie added.

They both laughed and headed back to the table, weaving their way through the smoky room.

"Okay, we're going," Sophie announced when they found the men waiting. "But we're driving. And we'll make our own reservations."

Antonio gave them both a knowing look. "That is fair. We are honored you've decided to visit the resort. Our uncle is one of the owners."

Marco gave Maddie a long, sultry look. "And our other brothers will be envious when they see your long, wild hair. The color is so different, so vibrant."

Maddie shivered at the huskiness in his voice. The men escorted them to the car, then climbed in a new black Jaguar. With the top down, the wind felt heavenly as Maddie maneuvered her convertible along the ocean. Salt air and the scent of sand and water beckoned her, excitement building as they neared the island.

Maddie turned the radio to a local rock station, and they sang "Wide Open Spaces" with the Dixie Chicks as they flew across the bridge and drove along the bay. Finally they veered off toward a less inhabited part of the island.

Maddie squinted through the window until her eyes found a rustic sign half-hidden in the bushes bordering the resort property. A string of small white lights illuminated the sign. She followed Marco's car to the entrance and stopped behind him as he entered his code. In the distance she spotted a deer, a golf course, a few cabins.

"Wow, this place is secluded." Sophie leaned forward, gazing through the trees.

Maddie gasped, her stomach plunging to the floor. "Now I know why the name sounded so familiar."

Sophie paled. "Oh, my heavens, that woman is naked."

Maddie pointed toward the porch. "The Open Arms Resort, it's . . ."

"*Eew!* It's not a woman, it's a man. And he has hair on his . . . his back!"

They were all naked. "It's a nudist colony."

They exchanged stunned looks as Antonio approached the passenger side of the car. Sophie sank lower into the seat. Maddie's gaze swung to Marco as he sauntered toward her. No wonder he'd said his brothers would be excited to see her.

"We are here." Marco gestured toward an older couple who Maddie now realized were standing in their birthday suits on the wooden porch of the office, waving at the men as if they couldn't wait to greet them.

Maddie clutched the steering wheel in a sweaty panic. "I . . . I don't know about this."

Marco's dark eyebrows formed a vee. "But I thought you understood the concept of the Open Arms, you said you read an article about the resort."

"I read the part about bareback riding. I thought the article meant riding a horse without a saddle."

"Yes, we do that, too."

Maddie lost coherent thought at the image that flitted through her mind.

He gestured toward a raised pavilion to the right, and Maddie's eyes widened at the dozens of people, lounging and walking around the well-lit deck. Others gathered around long tables, eating dinner, chatting, dancing. Totally relaxed. Totally in the buff!

His voice sounded tender, "Ahh, *chèrie,* you said you were always up for an adventure. This is an adventure, yes?"

"Y—I guess." She gulped in horror. "But I didn't mean this kind of an adventure."

He truly looked puzzled. "You, um, do not think the human body is a beautiful form of art?"

"Well, yes."

"Hmm. You are not a prude?"

"Yes . . . I mean, no I'm not a prude."

He lifted his hands in question. "Then you are shy now?"

"Not . . . not exactly."

"You are not comfortable with your own body as it is? It is not, how you say, stacked properly?"

"I didn't say that."

"Cause let me assure you, love, you are quite spectacular with your fair skin and flaming hair. Everyone will be looking at you."

That's what I'm afraid of. "Thank you, Marco, but you see . . ." Maddie stuttered. "It's just taking off my clothes, it's . . . it's a private thing."

His eyes widened. "You have never . . . um, let anyone see you naked before?"

Maddie winced. "That's not what I meant."

He exhaled and seemed to relax, his voice teasing. "Then you have some, um, how you say, extra-hideous body part no one else has?"

She glared at him. "No, of course not."

"I don't understand, cheré." His voice softened. "You are so lovely. You aren't one of those American women obsessed with not having big—"

"No!"

His smile wilted completely, and Maddie noticed a group of tall, dark-haired Italian men sidling toward them. They looked suspiciously like Antonio and Marco.

"Ahh, these are my brothers," Marco said with pride.

The men who couldn't wait to see her.

She wished she could voice the same sentiment.

Three very tall, athletic men approached the car. Maddie smiled through gritted teeth, her heart racing as she tried to keep her eyes trained on the men's faces, a difficult task as their height lended to a very awkward and prime positioning of body parts. Boy, she certainly had been missing something with Jeffrey. And she'd needed this place years ago when she'd taken her art lessons. Talk about proportioned . . .

Not that size mattered.

But she couldn't help but wonder how Chase Holloway would compare.

Chase Holloway wanted to be naked with a woman, but he didn't have a date. Or a single, living, willing prospect in sight.

Friday night alone didn't bode well.

He'd actually considered trying Daphne again or one of the other women in his black book, but after that humiliating experience with Daphne, he wasn't sure he was up, literally and figuratively, for another trying experience. What if he couldn't perform again?

Of course, he hadn't had a problem reacting physically to Maddie—the one woman he couldn't have.

He'd tried to forget her and work on the house plans for the subdivision but every time he did, he kept seeing Maddie's face and the excitement in her eyes when he'd agreed she could decorate his house.

Just because she takes in stray animals doesn't mean she'd take in you.

Chase told himself it didn't matter and forced himself to read the note he'd taped to the wall of his garage so he could read it over and over while he worked. The Bachelor Pact.

Bachelors Forever.

Lance. Reid. Chase.

They'd each signed their names in blood when they'd been twelve years old. They'd renewed the agreement when they'd finalized their business deal. They hadn't used blood this time, but the sentiment had been the same. And he intended to keep his end of the agreement.

Just as he intended to keep the business safe by watching Maddie at work.

But he couldn't touch her—ever again.

Full of pent-up energy, Chase swiped at a gnat as he cleaned the engine of the fifty-seven Camaro. He'd bought it as a junker, taken the last six months to replace all the engine parts, and had finally finished the basic repair work. Now, he had to smooth out the body. Getting the dents out would take some time, and he'd definitely have to replace the front fender, but he welcomed the distraction from his work and from the woman dogging his memory. Maddie Summers.

He rammed his hand through his hair, smearing grease on his forehead, but not caring. Maddie's face had looked so lovely in the shadows of the wooded lot, the way the fading sunlight had highlighted that wild auburn hair of hers with streaks of gold and red, and she'd felt . . . God, she'd felt like sweetness and sex and sin all heaped together in the most fiery tantalizing kind of way. The sound of the water in the background mingled with her breathing had just about brought him to the brink, leaving him with no choice but to push her away. He'd used the only excuse he could think of and told her she was nothing but a kid to him.

Damn, he hated the hurt that had darkened her eyes. But if he allowed this crazy attraction to spiral out of control, he'd hurt her even more. Then he'd lose his job with her brothers, and their friendship would be over. Now, if only he could get the rest of his body to listen to his brain before he had to see her again, he'd be fine.

He picked up a mallet, sprawled down on the man crawler and angled himself so he could work from the underside of the left back bumper. With the precision of a master mechanic, he began to pound at the dented metal.

He only hoped the metal wasn't as hard or unwilling to cooperate as his head. His big one and his little one.

An hour later, he'd made very little headway when he heard the phone peal through the open window of his duplex. He checked his watch and realized it was past midnight. Who the hell would be calling this late?

Rolling out from beneath the car, he jumped up and ran inside, snatching the receiver on the fifth ring. "Hello."

"It's Lance. You don't know where Maddie is, do you?"

Chase leaned against the kitchen counter and wiped the dirt and sweat from his forehead, frowning at his friend's tone. "No, why should I?"

"Blast it to hell. I was hoping maybe you did." Lance breathed heavily into the phone. "She hasn't been home all night."

Chase winced at the obvious. "It's Friday night, Lance, maybe she had a date."

"She broke up with Oglethorpe, remember?"

"Yeah, well, maybe she found someone else." *After she kissed me.*

"Reid said she might be going out with that Sophie Lane woman."

"That Sophie Lane woman?" Chase stared at the phone, confused even more. "What do you have against Sophie Lane?"

Lance muttered a curse. "I just don't think she's a good influence. She's nothing but a gossip. For cripes' sakes, she may be trying to get the scoop on the family right now."

"What scoop?"

Silence descended on the line.

"What scoop, Lance? I've known you guys most of my life. Is there some dark secret about the Summers family I don't know about?"

"Hell, no," Lance bellowed. "I just don't trust the woman, that's all."

"So, no one's forcing you to spend time with her."

"You're damn right they aren't. And they couldn't even if they wanted to."

"I didn't know anyone wanted you to."

"They don't."

"Then what's the problem?"

"The problem is that Maddie is missing."

"Maddie is not missing, Lance, she's simply not home yet. Maybe she went to dinner with a friend or to a movie." Chase shook his head at his friend's exasperated sigh. "Lance, where are you?"

"Sitting in front of Maddie's house."

"Do you think that's a good idea?" Chase closed his eyes and pictured Maddie going ballistic when she saw him, especially after Chase had given her a big-brother lecture today when she'd kissed him. Was her late night somehow his fault? By chastising her about the kiss, had he set the wheels in motion and sent Maddie out on some wild night to prove a point?

Lance whistled between his teeth. "I know. But I was worried about her."

"Look, I understand, man. But if you don't want to get your butt kicked, leave her a note to call you and go home."

After several minutes of arguing, Lance finally agreed and hung up. Chase ran some tap water, washed his hands and face, then filled a glass and drank deeply as he contemplated Lance's odd behavior.

He stalked outside, grabbed the hammer again and went back to pounding the Camaro, irritated that Maddie might be out with another guy—one of those twenty or thirty men she wanted to meet. He could see her at a bar, a dozen men ogling her, a half-dozen getting up the nerve to approach her, one or two crossing the line, becoming overly friendly—

He cursed and slammed the hammer down so hard, a piece of metal broke off and went flying across the yard.

Other images followed, each more tawdry and painful: Maddie kissing another man, a tangle of arms and legs, his hands touching her in places Chase could only dream of touching . . . He slammed the hammer down again as anger churned through him.

Anger that had nothing to do with being brotherly.

Exhausted, Maddie crawled into the hotel bed late Friday night, although the party outside remained in full swing. She turned on the bedside lamp and cuddled beneath the covers, feeling satisfied and elated. The shower kicked on and she heard her roomie singing. With a few minutes to herself, Maddie grabbed her new journal, glad that after its recent purchase she had accidentally left it in her car. She had decided to record all of her dates so she could look back and compare them. She especially didn't want to forget this evening with Sophie and Marco and Antonio. Her brothers would have a fit if they knew about her date. It would serve them right if they did find out. Chase Holloway, too. But she didn't want them to worry, so she dialed Lance to let them know she'd gone away for the weekend. The last thing she needed was for her brothers to come searching for her. Lance didn't answer, so she simply left a message, saying she'd be home on Sunday, that she was sleeping over with a friend, then hung up with a grin. There, the phone call should satisfy her brothers that she was safe. And they'd never know about Marco and Antonio.

Marco's too-wet kiss sprang to mind, and she shivered.

An unbidden memory of Chase's less-than-chaste

kiss followed, mind-boggling in comparison. The mere memory sent a tingle through her. Would Chase Holloway still call her a kid if he'd seen her at the nudist colony?

Chapter Seven

"I can't believe I let you talk me into coming to this . . . this *nudist* resort." Chase shielded his privates with splayed hands and peeked from behind a bush near the party deck, unable to believe he'd allowed his buddies to talk him into walking into this place butt naked to search for Maddie. Saturday morning Lance had found the message from Maddie and seen the number on his caller ID. He'd completely freaked out, yelling that he couldn't believe his baby sister had actually gone to the Open Arms Resort, a nudist colony! They'd forced Lance to calm down, and he'd waited all day, praying Maddie would come home. When she hadn't, Lance had decided to drive up and drag her little butt home.

Of course, that meant Reid and Chase had to go with him.

Now they were hiding in the bushes with nothing on but their birthday suits, planning their strategy and becoming dinner for the bugs. And while they were swatting, other guests were swinging, having a grand old time. It was almost midnight. Nude people were everywhere, dancing on the deck, strolling in the moonlight, cuddling in the gazebo. Of course, right now, Maddie might be tucked in bed with another naked man and they'd never find her.

Chase's stomach churned at the thought.

A weed clawed at his bare leg and Chase scratched his calf, wishing he could at least have kept his socks and boots! Poor Lance had almost decked the guard when he'd explained that they couldn't enter without taking off their clothes. But Reid had spotted a pretty blonde, shucked his clothes without an argument and followed her onto the party deck. An older man, obviously her husband, had joined her, and Reid had suddenly run for the bushes, claiming he'd simply been asking directions!

Lance plucked a leaf from a nearby bush and placed it strategically over his lower extremities. "*I* can't believe Maddie let her date bring her here. What was she thinking?"

"She said she wanted to have fun," Chase said. He spotted a grove of trees bordering the trail that led from the party deck and wondered if they could find cover between them.

"She's not old enough to have fun like this," Reid muttered.

"You don't know for sure if Maddie is here." Chase made a run for it and dove behind the red tips just as a group of guests strolled by, laughing and talking as they headed toward the lake.

Reid and Lance trotted behind him, ducking down low. Still, with the three of them being more than six feet, their heads protruded from the tops of the shrubbery like turtles. "Well, if we see her—" Lance whispered, his face turning red, "You'd better keep your eyes on her *face*, Chase."

Chase glared at him. "I didn't come here to leer."

Reid's gaze followed another buxom blonde who perched herself on a flat rock on the grassy embankment, propped a guitar on her hip and began to strum. "Hey, guys, maybe this place isn't so bad."

"We're here to find our little sister, not enjoy ourselves," Lance snapped.

"Who says we can't do both?" Reid squared his shoulders and stood upright as if to leave the safety of their hiding spot. "I'm not afraid to show myself. I've been working out."

Lance gave him a warning look. "Stay put. We have to find Maddie and get her out of here."

"I doubt Maddie will be too thrilled with your plan," Chase said, scanning the crowd. A middle-aged man with a potbelly, an elderly woman with sagging breasts and wrinkled knees and an overweight couple with dimpled buttocks caught his attention. He shuddered. Now he knew why clothes were invented—some people looked better with them.

"Who cares what Maddie wants," Lance said. "This guy's probably a pervert."

"You don't have to be perverted to enjoy nudity," Reid pointed out.

He obviously hadn't seen the people Chase had spotted.

"We're talking about *Maddie,*" Lance said. "What if he tied her up and forced her to come along—"

"Stop it, Lance. You said she came with Sophie, so she's probably safe."

Quiet voices in the distance drifted to them with the faint breeze. A long trail through the woods loomed ahead. Chase parted the shrubbery enough to peer in the other direction.

"*That's* supposed to make me feel better?" Lance growled. "That woman's the root of all evil. She's going to totally corrupt Maddie. Just look where she brought her!"

Reid pointed to a half-dozen people of varying ages and sizes, playing volleyball. "Whoa, look at that redhead. She's a natural, too."

Chase gave her a sideways glance, unimpressed. "Do you see Sophie?"

Lance scowled. "No, do *you?*"

"No." Chase frowned, wondering why Sophie Lane set his friend off so badly.

"I haven't seen Maddie either," Reid said, his face flushing. "Not that I want to see my own sister—"

"This was a bad idea." Chase ducked his head as a young couple walked by, hand in hand. How the heck was he supposed to handle the situation? If Maddie was here, he didn't want to see her—yet, he did. Only he didn't want everyone else seeing her.

Besides what would they do when they found her? The whole situation would be awkward—would they walk up to her in their birthday suits and tell her to leave?

Chase remembered Maddie's reaction to her big brothers' overprotectiveness and to his big-brother routine—and they'd all been dressed. His stomach quivered. "Maddie is going to kill us if we crash her date."

A muscle ticked in Lance's jaw. "I don't call a night at a nudist resort a date. I call it a-a—"

"A crime," Reid supplied. "She's barely old enough to drive, let alone spend the night with a man in a place like this."

"She's twenty-six," Chase pointed out. *And you'd call it a lucky night, if it were you.*

But it wasn't one of them—they were talking about Maddie. Maddie with the pigtails and braces and knobby knees who used to ride piggyback on his shoulders . . .

Who the hell was he kidding? Maddie no longer fit that description at all. She was . . . gorgeous and desirable, and she'd been coming apart in his arms. Only he'd turned her away, right into the arms of another man. Just the thought of seeing her here nude with some lust-struck Romeo made his blood boil. "Shit."

"What? Do you see her?" Lance yanked off a chunk of leaves as he pivoted to search the area behind them.

"No." He hadn't realized he'd spoken out loud. Suddenly Chase felt a tap on the back. He whirled around, hoping to see Maddie and hoping not to.

Instead the security guard stood glaring at them, his arms folded across his chest. "I think you guys had better leave. We don't like Peeping Toms around here." He gestured toward the clump of leaves in Lance's hand. "And we don't appreciate folks destroying private property."

Chase's stomach did a U-turn against his ribs. How dare the man call them Peeping Toms.

Lance opened his mouth to explain, but the guard pointed over his shoulder to the entrance. "Out, now."

Reid lowered himself to hide behind a tree. Chase thought he saw a head of wild, curly russet hair coming near and panicked. Maddie! What if she saw them getting thrown out?

He lunged forward, trying to shield himself in the overgrown bushes. Maybe he should make a run for it. But a tree branch flew up and smacked him in the eye, and he fell on a pine cone. "Oww!" He grabbed his face with one hand and covered his crotch with the other as the guard yanked him up and pushed them toward the exit.

"But what about our clothes?" Lance asked, reaching for another leaf.

The guard slapped his hand away from the bush. "Maybe it'll teach you guys a lesson if you have to go home without them."

Maddie steered the convertible into Sophie's apartment complex Sunday evening and turned off the engine. "Thanks for forcing me to go out Friday night."

"It was fun, wasn't it?"

"It did me a world of good."

Sophie gathered her purse. "Are you going to see Marco again?"

Maddie sighed. All weekend she'd compared him to Chase. "I doubt it."

"I don't know about Antonio either." Sophie opened the car door. "Hey, did you hear about those guys in the woods Saturday night?"

"No, what guys?"

"The security guard caught three men lurking in the bushes at the nudist colony. They were just hiding out, gawking at the guests." Sophie laughed. "Can you believe it? They didn't join in any of the festivities, they only wanted to leer at the ladies."

"Perverts." Maddie frowned, a sudden suspicion gnawing at her. No, her brothers wouldn't be caught dead in a place like the Open Arms. "What happened to them?"

Sophie laughed. "The guard threw them out—*without* their clothes."

Maddie doubled over with laughter. "I wish I could have seen that."

"Me, too." Sophie laughed so hard tears dribbled down her cheeks. "I heard one of the guys stole some of the leaves to cover himself."

"I hope the creep gets poison ivy." Maddie shook her head.

"And one of the others tried to run away but a tree branch hit him in the eye. Gave him a real shiner."

"Serves them right." Maddie laughed. "One thing is for sure, you'd never catch my brothers there."

"Too bad," Sophie said. "I wouldn't mind seeing Lance naked."

Maddie patted her friend's back. "Maybe one day he'll come to his senses."

Sophie climbed out. "Thanks for driving, Mad."

"No problem." Maddie stretched her arms above her head. "This has been the nicest weekend I've had in a long time. And the best part is that my nosy brothers don't know where I've been."

Chapter Eight

It was the worst weekend The Terrible Three had ever had. Saturday night they'd driven home butt naked, praying the whole way they wouldn't get stopped by the cops, seen by a group of nuns or accused of being flashers when they'd had to wait at a red light and an old woman had spotted them and started screaming. Even worse, Lance had developed a rash from the leaves he'd used to cover himself. And Chase's eye had swollen and gotten infected so he'd had to visit the emergency room, and now he was wearing a patch. The doctor had said the tree branch must have scratched his cornea.

It was late Sunday, and they still hadn't heard from Maddie. If she didn't call or come home soon, Chase was going to have to commit Lance and Reid to the psychiatric ward.

"When she comes back and I know she's safe, I'm going to kill her," Lance mumbled.

Reid paced the front porch. "And if that guy's with her, I'm going to pulverize him."

Chase stared broodingly at Maddie's empty parking spot, wondering where she was and why she hadn't at least called. Had she stayed at that nudist resort all night, all weekend? Slept with a strange guy after kissing Chase? Had the guy taken advantage of her?

Or had Maddie been willing, hot and passionate, the way she'd been with him?

No, he wouldn't allow himself to think about Maddie and passion . . . especially with another man. Not that it mattered—he couldn't have her.

"Shit."

"What?" Lance asked.

He didn't realize he'd spoken aloud again. "Nothing. I was just thinking that Sophie and Maddie couldn't have gotten into too much trouble together." Although they were both beautiful women—beautiful, single, desirable women in a town, a resort, filled with testosterone-driven, sexually depraved naked men like . . . like themselves.

Lance scratched at his crotch. "I have to convince Maddie to stay away from that damned Sophie woman. She's totally corrupting her."

Worry knotted Chase's stomach. Something was bothering his best friend, something more than his rash and his anxiety over Maddie not coming home. Lance really despised Sophie Lane. And Chase couldn't figure out why—Sophie was exactly the kind of woman his friend usually drooled over. He wished he'd confide in him but Lance seemed determined to remain tight-lipped.

The sound of an engine jerked up his head. Red flashed in front of his eyes, the sporty new convertible Maddie had bought sliding into her parking spot.

"Thank God," Reid said.

Lance clawed himself one last time. "Remember, not a word about us going up there."

As if they'd actually brag about their visit. Chase and Reid nodded. The brothers raced off the porch, practically catapulting themselves at Maddie as she strolled up the sidewalk. Her windswept auburn hair curled wildly about her flushed face, her rosy mouth widening at the sight of her brothers converging on her.

"Where the hell have you been?" Lance bellowed, wriggling his hips as another itching attack began.

"Why didn't you call us, Maddie? We've been worried sick," Reid said.

"We almost phoned the police—"

Maddie silenced her brothers with a wave of her hand, narrowing her eyes at Lance when he couldn't resist and scratched himself. "You two, on the porch now." Chase caught a hint of anger in her voice and saw fire flash in her eyes when she spotted him sitting on the porch swing, then a surprised look as she zeroed in on the black eye patch.

"What happened to you?"

"Just a little accident," he said, squirming. Lance stiffened, and Chase hoped he didn't give them away.

Her eyebrows shot up. "Playing in the woods?"

She couldn't know, could she?

"Uh, no."

"Gives you a pirate image, Chase. Maybe you should keep it."

The image of him dressed in a pirate costume dragging her aboard a ship to make love filled his mind. His stomach twisted again, only this time because he was aroused. And he was so glad to see that she was safe, he didn't give a rat's ass where she'd been. She looked so damn sexy. . . . On the wheels of that image, another set in. Her date rubbing suntan lotion all over her naked body. On parts no man should touch but . . . him.

No, he couldn't touch her there either.

And why should it bother him if another man rubbed lotion on her body? He'd never had a steady girlfriend or been jealous of a woman in his life. He stood, ready to leave.

Maddie pointed to the rocking chairs. "Sit, all *three* of you."

Maddie glared at him, and he took the swing again. Did she know they'd been up to the resort—had she seen them get thrown out in such an undignified manner?

"Maddie, we—"

Maddie snapped her fingers, cutting him off midsentence.

Chase pushed the swing back and forth, watching in amazement as Lance and Reid did as she said. But he knew his buds well; they folded their arms defensively, their tempers barely in check.

Maddie dropped her purse on the floor of the porch, then planted her small hands on hips encased in a black stretch skirt that hugged her curves, sending his body into arousal again. A dark purple T-shirt molded over her breasts, leading his mind astray with wicked thoughts. He couldn't keep his eye off those long, slender legs. But the sound of her clunky high heels clicking on the wooden slats of the porch brought him back to the moment and the mess they were in.

"I'm sorry I worried you, guys, but I did call and leave a message that I was sleeping over at a friend's."

The three of them simply glared at her.

"I'm a grown woman now, not a little girl, and I can go and do whatever I please."

"The hell—"

"Shut up and listen, Lance."

Chase slowed the swing at the sound of Maddie's husky, angry tone.

"I know you guys care about me, but you're smothering me to death. You don't tell me every time you go off with a woman for the night."

Chase's stomach rolled.

Reid cursed.

Lance's face paled. "You spent the weekend with a guy?"

"I didn't say that!"

Reid and Lance exchanged hopeful looks. "Then who were you with?" Reid asked.

Chase could have sworn he saw steam coming from Maddie's mouth. "That's none of your business. What's important here is that I need some space."

Two male mouths opened to argue but Maddie's quick shush snapped them shut. "I'm not sixteen anymore, I live alone, I make my own money, I'm on my own. I don't have to ask your permission to go out."

"But overnight!" Lance said.

"Without even calling again Saturday," Reid mumbled.

Maddie hitched out her hip and shook her head. "You're impossible."

"We're your brothers!" Lance shouted.

"And we care about you," Reid added.

Maddie's temper faded slightly, but her resolve didn't budge. "Okay, let's set some rules here, boys." She shot Chase a venomous look as if to say he was intruding, but he'd better listen, too. He remembered his comment about her being like a kid sister and figured he deserved her scorn, but he didn't like it any more than Lance. No one had to point out the fact that he wasn't family; the knowledge that no one had wanted him, not even his own mother, had been burned in his brain with his mother's searing parting words. But Maddie and her brothers had always treated him as such and being a part of the The Terrible Three had saved his sorry butt more times than he could count. The very reason he had to control his male hormones around Maddie.

Sometimes being a responsible adult sucked.

"I promise to let you know if I'm going out of town again, but you have to promise not to call or drop by unexpectedly and check on me every day like you've been doing the past week. What if I'm entertaining?"

"Just what kind of entertaining do you plan to do?" Lance snapped.

"Yeah, you planning on having a naked orgy?" Reid asked.

Maddie's eyes widened, and Chase's stomach dropped to his toes. Reid was going to give them away.

"That's none of your business," Maddie said in a strained tone.

Reid leaned forward as if to stand. "But—"

"No buts. You're driving me crazy, you can't call every day. And if I do decide to have a naked orgy, I'll have one."

Chase moved to stand. "The—"

Maddie slashed her hand across the air. "Stay out of it, Chase."

Chase's mouth closed into a tight line.

"I am not your little sister at all, Chase, and I'm

not your little sister anymore, Lance—"

"You'll always be our little sister," Lance muttered.

Maddie pounded her fist over her chest. "Maybe so, but I'm also a grown woman with a right to make my own decisions, to go out with whomever I please, whenever I please, and I intend to do so, no questions asked." Maddie paused to grab a much-needed breath. "Do you understand?"

Lance and Reid simply glared at her.

Maddie's voice rose an octave. "I said do you understand?"

"Yes," Lance mumbled.

"But we don't like it," Reid added.

"I didn't say you have to like my rules, but you will abide by them." With a stern glare, Maddie shifted sideways to unlock her front door. "So you're just going to have to learn to live with them." With one last determined look, she swung open the door, sauntered inside and left the three of them sitting on the porch.

Lance and Reid immediately turned to Chase. "This is worse than we thought," Lance said.

Reid stood. "Yeah, man, you have to do something."

A splinter jabbed Chase's palm as his hands tightened around the wooden arms of the swing. He'd already gotten in over his head by committing to babysit Maddie on the job. What in the world did they want him to do now? Tag along on her dates?

Monday morning Maddie was still shaken from her confrontation with her brothers—the next thing she knew they'd be tagging along on her dates. She patted herself on the back for not giving in to temptation and revealing any details about her side trip with

Sophie. Although she had a nagging suspicion Chase and Lance and Reid were the three men who'd sneaked into the resort and been thrown out. They'd looked so damn guilty the whole time she'd lectured them. Plus, Lance had scratched himself silly and Chase's eye patch, his little accident, was all too coincidental.

Even if they had been there, they had no idea what she'd been up to. She laughed wickedly.

Let them all wonder what really happened.

She loved her brothers dearly, but she had to assert herself, or they'd suffocate her. Just the thought of Chase Holloway sitting there on her porch with that patronizing attitude infuriated her. Why, they'd probably all three had dates *and* sex Friday night while they expected her to play the good girl. And that patch—fantasies of Chase wearing nothing but that patch, making love to her had haunted her all night.

Damn man.

It wasn't fair Chase saw her as a kid sister when she'd been lusting after him all weekend. Dreaming of him naked and hot and irresistibly aroused. And bigger than both those Italians put together.

Determined to banish Chase from her mind until she was forced to meet him later to discuss the designs for the model homes, she steered her new decorating van into the subdivision on Skidaway Island to meet her first client, mentally ticking off the questions she needed to ask. Armed with carpet, flooring, tile and fabric samples, along with dozens of catalogs of furniture styles, accessories, window treatments and her laptop, which virtually allowed her access to any and everything a customer could possibly want, she felt prepared to deal with whatever arose.

Until she met Nora Ledbetter; her three-year-old

terror, Jake; and their Saint Bernard, Lulu.

Three hours later, she exhaled in exasperation, determined to make a sale no matter the consequences. Noisy Nora, she dubbed her because she had on so many bracelets she clanged and banged every time she moved, had the attention span of a gnat. Maddie settled herself on the corner of the brick hearth. She'd been trying to discern the woman's tastes so she could steer her into a few decisions today, but so far the only decision Nora had made was that she was undecided on everything. She didn't even know what color scheme she wanted to use.

Which virtually affected every decision they needed to make.

"Look, I'm Jake the Snake!" The redheaded little boy plopped onto the floor of the half-finished den and slithered through the array of fabric swatches Maddie had so carefully displayed. Lulu lay her head on Maddie's lap and drooled. Maddie pushed Lulu's head away, swiped at the wet spot on her skirt and tried to grab the swatches before Jake smeared them with his jelly-crusted hands. She salvaged most of them but Jake scooped a red velvet one in his mouth as if he meant to eat it.

Maddie strove for a calm voice and reached out as if to pet the pretend snake that was Jake. "Jake, honey, give me the material."

Jake wobbled his head back and forth. "I slither and slither and . . ." He raised his head and stuck out his tongue, dropping the soggy material to the floor. "And hiss." A loud hissing sound punctuated the air. Lulu barked like mad and tried to crawl under Maddie's legs to hide, nearly knocking her off the hearth. Maddie shot Nora a pleading look, but Nora seemed engrossed in a corner of the room that housed the floor-to-ceiling fireplace.

"I just don't know about this place." Nora rubbed her hands up and down her arms. "It feels cold in here."

"I gotta go potty," the little boy yelled.

"I wonder if someone died on this property," Nora said, once again ignoring Jake.

"No, no one died here," Maddie said. Lulu howled and started to run in circles as Jake bounced up and down. "And I'm sorry, Jake, the plumber brought the wrong toilets so they had to be returned. Can you go outside?"

"Not by himself," Nora said. "There might be snakes in the woods."

Maddie nodded.

The little boy grabbed his crotch, crossed his legs and rocked himself back and forth. "I gotta go bad."

"Mrs. Ledbetter, maybe we'd better—"

Nora waved her off. "He'll be fine. I'll take him in a minute. Now, one thing I do want is a canopy around the bed, you know with lots of fringe." She opened a catalog and pointed to a collection of French furniture. "And I want the lamps to have fringe also."

Jake yanked at his OshKosh overalls. "Mommy, I gotta go!"

"So you like the Victorian designs," Maddie said, grateful they were finally getting somewhere but worried when she saw the toddler's face turning red.

"Not particularly," Nora said to Maddie, oblivious to her son's distress. "But we are in Savannah, you know, and I heard the fringe scares off the evil ghosts."

"I don't believe there are any ghosts here," Maddie said. "This is a new subdivision."

"They're everywhere," Nora said, shivering. "And

I do think someone died here, I can feel it. A soldier, maybe from the war."

"I gotta go bad!" Jake whined.

"In a minute, Jake," Nora said, turning back to Maddie. "Besides, I have a ghost named Peter who follows me everywhere I go," Nora said. "I buy an extra copy of the newspaper every day and leave it out for him to read. He especially likes the comics." She studied the windows. "In fact, I may bring him the next time we meet and see if he likes the house."

"Mommy!"

A gust of wind suddenly blew through the open window frames.

"There is a ghost here!" Nora shrieked. The Saint Bernard tried to jump onto Maddie's lap, then covered his ears and howled. Jake screamed and promptly wet his pants.

Chase handed the set of blueprints to Lance and watched him drive away. Then he turned to examine his latest design, a reproduction of a Greek Revival mansion.

Waiting inside this first model home for Maddie, he studied the brickwork, the finished wood floors, the imported marble in the foyer. He'd been reluctant about combining innovative modern technology with traditional architecture, but the polished wooden bookcases, which housed the sound system, alarm and remote controls for heating and lighting, camouflaged all the electronic gadgets that were appreciated in the new millennium. In the end he was quite proud of how well he had managed to incorporate old-style charm with all the comforts people expected in a twenty-first century house. The wall-wide theater screen hidden behind retractable oak paneling would definitely fit the lifestyle of the modern family.

Now, he had to see what Maddie had in mind for decorating the interior.

This was the first home on the tour, the first impression the tourists would have of the development. It had to be spectacular. Lance and Reid were worried Maddie would get a wild hair and add psychedelic colors or art-deco furniture and ruin the effect they'd created. They also wanted him to babysit Maddie *personally.*

And not in the hands-on way he'd like. Hell, he'd spent half the night thinking of Maddie walking around naked, the other half thinking of some other man watching her walk around naked.

How the heck had he gotten himself into this mess?

A few months ago Maddie had been at school, stuck like glue to Jeff Oglethorpe, he had finally finished his degree and joined forces with Lance and Reid, they'd renewed their bachelor forever pact—life had been perfect.

Now, everything had gone to hell in a handbasket.

The sound of an engine broke into his thoughts, and he spotted a minivan with the words MADDIE'S—MADE FOR YOU—DESIGNS written in bold red on the side. *Made for You*—the slogan gave him an uneasy feeling for some reason. Or maybe it was just Maddie that did. She opened the door of the van and slid down to the ground, gracing him with a tantalizing view of her long, shapely legs. He sucked in a harsh breath and told himself to remember her in pigtails with her two front teeth missing and mustard smeared all over her face.

It didn't work. She was still just as beautiful as he remembered.

Although as she entered the house, he did notice an odd odor clinging to her clothes, a purple stain smeared on her white blouse, something brown on her shoe and a damp spot on the front of her black skirt.

"What happened to you?" he asked as she limped inside the curved doorway.

She rolled her eyes. "Don't ask." With a weary sigh, she sidled over beside him, swung her briefcase onto the cherry desk in the foyer and dropped into a chair, her gaze scanning the interior of the home. Even rumpled and smelly, she stirred his loins. And she was studying the house, *his* design, as if she were scrutinizing every feature.

His breath caught in his chest. What would Maddie think of his work?

"This place is fabulous," she whispered in awe. "You are one talented man, Chase Holloway."

His chest swelled, along with the rest of him. *More talented than you know.*

He bit back the reply, refusing to voice the double entendre less she see it as an invitation. "Thanks. I put a lot of time into this project."

Her vibrant smile lit up the room like a hundred twinkling stars lighting up an inky sky. "I'd say you succeeded."

Chase shifted, feeling his face flush uncharacteristically at her praise.

"You know, I want to tour the house, then I'm going to do some research, and I'll put together a plan."

"Sounds good."

Maddie rose and walked around the room. He watched her hips sway beneath the black form-fitting skirt and gulped, grateful when his cell phone pealed and distracted him.

"Chase, it's Lance. We've got trouble."

But Maddie was with him. Reid maybe? "What kind of trouble? Is it Reid?"

"I can't find him anywhere."

That didn't sound like Reid.

"I can't talk about it over the phone, Chase, but I'm worried. I think you'd better get over to the clubhouse right now."

Chapter Nine

Trouble, trouble, trouble. Everywhere they turned.

Reid Summers only hoped he could keep the worst of it from Lance and Maddie.

He wasn't ordinarily a religious man. In fact, he'd been known to take the Lord's name in vain more times than he had turned to Him in prayer, a sin he now wished he could recall, since he needed all the help he could get on this latest development. If he hadn't been such a hellion when he was a kid, he'd try to cash in some favors, but he doubted he had a prayer to spare.

Even so, he stood at the threshold of the Trinity Methodist Church, figuring the significance of the oldest Methodist church in Savannah had to hold some special spiritual resolution. The Savannah gray brick-and-stucco finish was impressive as were the wall plaques immortalizing the pastors who died while serving the church. He felt like a peon-nothing in comparison.

He started to turn and leave, but organ music drifted through the church, beckoning him, so he shuffled in, astounded by the serenity of the building. Pausing to absorb the peace, his problems collided in his head. Not only was his company having more trouble—they'd had two contractors pull out this morning on the project—but Lance was having fits and acting abnormally tense. Probably because he shouldered most of the responsibility for the financial side of the company; Reid tended to deal with hiring the contractors and overseeing them on a daily basis.

But other problems weighed on Reid's mind. Recently he'd found a file in some of his parents' things that had upset him immensely. A file and some other pamphlets. He and Lance and Maddie were a close bunch, but so far, he'd been able to keep the news he'd discovered from them. His older brother and younger sister thought they had had the perfect parents, the perfect family. But Reid knew differently.

They would be devastated if they learned the truth.

He shuffled down the aisle, his head bowed to avoid recognition, although only two people were sitting in the church, both several rows away. He took a seat on the fourth row from the back, keeping his head lowered as he tried his best to remember how to pray. A childhood blessing raced through his mind, although distorted. And bits and pieces of the Lord's prayer resurfaced, although he'd forgotten how it started.

At a loss, his gaze zeroed in on a Bible, and he picked it up and thumbed through the pages, hoping for some inspiration. But he got sidetracked when he noticed the structural details of the flooring. Virgin longleaf Georgia pines were hand-hewn; he'd read they'd also been used for the framing and wainscoting. The Corinthian architecture exemplified the type of quality historic work he and Lance hoped to copy. Then he noticed a wad of gum on the underside of the bench. He used to stick his gum there when he was a kid. Couldn't be the same piece of gum after all these years, could it?

A chunky man wearing a dark raincoat slid into the pew beside him, jerking him from his jumbled thoughts. Knobby Smaltz, the P.I. he'd hired. Reid glanced up and saw the man's bushy eyebrows raise. He smelled like stale cigars and Old Spice, but Reid nodded and accepted the envelope the man thrust toward him. Feeling like a spy out of some low-budget TV drama, he carefully tucked it inside his jacket. "Did you find out anything?"

"The information confirms your suspicions," the man murmured.

Where was God when he needed him?

Reid silently cursed, then cursed himself again for forgetting he was in a holy place. Somewhere in the back of his mind, he knew it was wrong to come to church when you *needed* something, and he vowed to do better, then realized he was still trying to bargain his way out of his problems. He handed the man the payment they'd agreed upon and watched as he shuffled from the sanctuary. His heart pounding, Reid opened the envelope and pulled out the neatly typed information.

What in the world had his father been thinking?

The church pulpit swam in front of him as he tried to digest the truth. Lance and Maddie would be shocked. Especially Maddie; she was so young and innocent. With shaky hands, he refolded the envelope, tucked the papers back inside his jacket, and closed his eyes. Lance shouldn't have to deal with this right now. And thank goodness his bud Chase was watching out for Maddie. He could strike one problem off his mind.

He and his siblings didn't keep secrets, but he had to keep this information to himself—just this once so he could protect them.

Maddie knew she should have stayed behind and gotten started on the research for the Greek Revival house, but one look at the worry on Chase's face, and she insisted on going with him. If her brothers needed her, she'd be there. After all, they were family and had no secrets. Well, except for the little trip to the nudist colony and the one *she* harbored about their mother.

"What did Lance say the problem was?" she asked as she climbed in Chase's pickup.

"He didn't. He just said for me to come over there."

"Some problem with the building?"

"I don't know." Chase sped out of the circular drive, careened over a pothole and swore when the jolt sent Maddie bouncing over beside him. "Fasten your seat belt."

Maddie shoved a mass of hair from her eyes and glared at him. "I was trying to do that when you hit that hole."

"Well, hurry up. The last thing I need is for you to get hurt and your brothers to blame me."

"Then slow down," Maddie snapped, irritated he felt so *responsible* for her. Responsibility wasn't the same as attraction, and a one-sided attraction wasn't fair. Why couldn't he see her as someone other than Lance and Reid's kid sister? Marco certainly had.

She considered telling him just that, but his surly expression didn't invite conversation. He slowed the truck though, his knuckles turning white around the steering wheel. As soon as they parked at the clubhouse, Chase jumped from the truck and hurried up the walkway. Maddie stumbled along behind him, trying to jog in her high heels. Still Chase's long legs made double time compared to her shorter stride.

The minute Maddie stepped inside, she knew the source of the problem. It was almost as if Nora Ledbetter's ghost had found the place and decided to haunt it. The lights flickered like strobe lights on an eighties disco-dance floor.

Chase stood in the foyer with his hands on his jean-clad hips, his feet spread wide. "Try the dimmer."

Lance pushed a remote-control button. The air-conditioning kicked on.

"Blast it to hell," Lance muttered. "Let's try the stereo system."

Chase pushed another set of buttons, and the lights flickered off. In the kitchen, Maddie heard the dishwasher whir on, grinding and spitting empty air.

Another try, and the room was cast in a greenish, ghoulish tint.

"This is a mess," Chase muttered. "They're going to have to completely rewire the place."

Lance raked his hand over his chin. "It's going to put us behind schedule. I've already arranged for the floor and cabinets to be installed. And we want this place completed before the tour so we can have the open house here."

"We'll just have to reschedule and push the crew," Chase said.

"I don't understand how they could mess up the wiring this badly." Lance stalked over to examine the controls. "I gave the electrician specific instructions, and he assured me he understood. It's almost as if he intentionally botched the job."

Chase shook his head. "Seems like you can't find good help these days."

"There's more," Lance muttered, sounding discouraged.

Maddie glanced at Lance, then Chase, and saw Chase stiffen, bracing for bad news.

"The masonry crew laid the wrong kind of bricks at the Swanson place. And someone mixed sawdust in the cement so they couldn't pour the foundation on Lot 21B. Ruined a whole ton of good materials." Lance flicked the remote again, this time triggering the lights in each room to go off intermittently almost as if they were synchronized to the tune of "London Bridge Is Falling Down." "If I didn't know better, I'd think someone was sabotaging our plans."

Maddie felt the hair on her neck prickle. The livelihood of her brothers' company depended on this development and the tour of homes, and so did hers. But who would want them to fail?

Chase fought off the urge to hit something in response to the problems that had arisen. This development, this job, meant everything to him—it was the one chance he had to prove to the folks of Savannah that Chase Holloway, illegitimate orphan, the kid nobody wanted, could be somebody.

And no one was going to ruin it.

Reid sauntered up just as they stepped outside. His gaze flickered from Lance to Maddie, almost guilty. Chase frowned. "Where've you been? We've been hunting for you."

Reid's gaze swung to his battered boots. "I had some stuff to take care of."

Lance immediately explained the situation.

"I'll wait for you at the truck," Maddie said.

Chase nodded, letting Lance and Reid pull him aside.

"How come she's with you?" Reid asked.

"You've been watching out for her, haven't you?" Lance said.

Chase swallowed, regretting the agreement he'd made. "Yes. We met at the Greek Revival house to discuss the design."

Lance patted him on the back. "Good, I feel better knowing you're taking care of our little sister. She hasn't been too difficult, has she?"

Chase winced, remembering the heated kiss. To be exact, the *two* heated kisses. "No, not at all." *Handling her was the problem.*

"With these problems at work," Reid said, "it's good to know Maddie's under control."

I wouldn't exactly call things under control. Chase winced again, but tried to focus on the construction setbacks. Lance and Reid had never had trouble with a project before, at least not that he knew of. But he'd made a few enemies over the years, some of them troublemakers. If someone was sabotaging their business, could it possibly have something to do with him?

"I'm thinking of touring some of the historical sites this afternoon to refresh my memory of Savannah's historic district," Maddie said a few minutes later as they left the site. "I haven't done anything like that in ages. When I was growing up, I didn't pay much attention to Georgia history."

"Sounds like a good idea, I'll tag along," Chase said, shocking Maddie. "It'll help us both with the historical aspects of the projects."

"Can you afford to take off that much time?"

"Looking at the ironwork and other details of the

historic homes will help me double-check some of my own work," Chase explained.

"All right." *Heck, she'd take any excuse she could to be with him.*

How pathetic was she, she thought morosely.

Thirty minutes later, they bought tickets for one of the walking tours. It began at Factors Row, a unique range of red-brick buildings named for the cotton factors and brokers who brought fame to Savannah for their cotton commerce. They covered Bay Street, then cut through the wharf area to River Street, enjoying the overhanging iron-railed balconies and soft, old brick. Maddie noted several restaurants and shops she wanted to visit later. They passed the train museum, then the group divided up when they came to Emmet Park, some people choosing to explore the many statues and memorials on their own. Chase and Maddie opted to tour some of the historical houses, starting with the Eppinger House.

"He built this almost entirely out of heart-of-pine timbers," Chase whispered.

Maddie grinned at the boyish excitement in his voice as he dropped in tidbits about the other details of the house. He did the same when they passed the Pink House, then the Herb House.

"They painted the shutters blue to ward off ghosts in the Herb House," Chase said.

"I have a client who'll be glad to know that fact," Maddie said wryly.

"You have a client who believes in ghosts?"

"Oh, yeah. Nora Ledbetter."

Chase chuckled. "Right, the bracelet lady. I'm surprised her clanging jewelry doesn't scare off spirits."

Maddie laughed. "Frankly, I'm shocked her terror of a little boy doesn't scare them off. If I had a kid like that, I'd probably send him back."

Chase's smile faded. "Maybe he needs some extra attention."

Maddie immediately realized what she'd said and silently chided herself for sounding so callous. "I'm sorry, Chase, I didn't mean that I'd really send him back. That was awful of me to say. His mother was ignoring him—"

"Forget it, Maddie."

"No, really." She grabbed his arm and forced him to look at her. His musky scent enveloped her, the pain in his eyes so intense it nearly took her breath away. "I was only joking. Sometimes I forget . . ."

His jaw tightened, but his husky voice reverberated with emotions. "That I came from the orphanage."

"Yes."

"I never forget, Maddie. Not even for a minute."

Her heart aching, she released him, and they walked in silence for a minute. Finally he ushered her toward the Pirate's House. "Why don't we get something to eat in here."

Maddie agreed, noticing the way Chase self-consciously adjusted his eye patch. His reaction to her earlier comment stuck with her as they were seated. She tried to remember growing up, what Chase would have been doing when she and her family had celebrated holidays together. A wave of sadness washed over her. She missed her parents terribly but at least she had precious memories of them—what did Chase remember? Being abandoned? Not being wanted? Spending Christmas in the orphanage with sixty other homeless boys?

"This place has a ghost all its own," Chase said.

"Tell me about it," Maddie said, although she really wanted Chase to tell her about the ghosts in his past.

* * *

While the waitress set bowls of gumbo and plates of fresh bread on the table, Chase poured them each a glass of wine, forcing his gaze away from the tantalizing trap of Maddie's eyes. He shouldn't have grown defensive over her comment about the boy.

But he couldn't help it. She'd only been joking, but memories haunted him day and night. And for a moment, he'd felt a strange connection, as if she wanted to hear his thoughts. He'd been tempted to unburden himself, too. He didn't want Maddie's sympathy though. He wanted her . . . her body. No, her friendship.

Hell, he'd have to settle for friendship. Lance and Reid would kill him if he took anything else. *Even if Maddie offered?* a little voice inside his head whispered.

"Chase, I thought you were going to tell me about the ghost."

He nodded, pushing his private ghosts away in lieu of the pirate's tale. At least the legend was a safe topic. "There's an opening in the Buccaneer Room. It leads to the hidden tunnel underneath the Captain's Room. Legend says that when sailors would come in to port, the townspeople would get them drunk here, then spirit them away through the tunnel to the Savannah River."

Maddie sipped her wine, a frown marring her face. "That's awful. I thought you were going to tell me some romantic tale."

"Sorry." Chase laughed, unable to keep himself from teasing her. "I forgot you're a romantic, Maddie."

"A lot of women have pirate fantasies," Maddie said in a low voice.

Chase shifted, touching his eye patch awkwardly.

Did Maddie have fantasies about a pirate?

"You look good in that patch, Chase. Every woman in here is staring at you."

But *she* was the only one he had noticed.

And she was definitely a woman.

"How did you say you hurt your eye?"

Chase's hand stroked the black triangle, heat climbing his neck at the memory. "I . . . uh, a branch flipped up and hit me when I was walking the property."

Maddie's gaze locked with his and for a second, Chase thought she'd caught on to his lie. Then she bit into a chunk of bread, the dim light creating shadows around her lovely face, and he completely forgot about his discomfort. Candlelight flickered, highlighting her coffee-colored eyes with hints of gold that reminded him of caramel. Chase hadn't thought the atmosphere of the restaurant, with its fishing nets and dark exposed beams, would be especially romantic, but with Maddie sitting across from him in a slinky top, her hair spilling wildly about her face, those kissable lips begging for his mouth, they could have been in a dungeon and the place would have seemed romantic.

Hell, he was in big trouble.

"I bet the sailors weren't the only ones who used the tunnel." Maddie licked a drop of wine from her upper lip, sparking his body to arousal.

Think aromatherapy, he silently ordered himself. *It worked with Daphne, it might work with Maddie.*

"The tunnel would have been a a perfect meeting place for lovers."

Chase shifted uncomfortably. He'd thought the story of the tunnel was a safe topic.

"Especially couples who were forbidden to be together," Maddie murmured wistfully. "A British soldier maybe and a young girl from one of Savannah's founding families. They slip out and meet in the tunnel at midnight—"

Think about all those sweet candles, the heat, the hot bubbling water. You couldn't get it up.

"They'd meet in a dimly lit corner so no one could see them, hold hands and kiss in the dark."

Damn, it wasn't working! He was getting more and more aroused. He had to stop Maddie from any further musings. "You've got some imagination, don't you?"

Maddie blushed. "Sorry to get carried away. Touring the town reminded me of all the ghost tales and stories of star-crossed lovers in Savannah. Like the one about Nellie Jordon sliding down the banister and crushing that man's velvet hat. It must have been destiny for them to meet like that, then marry."

Chase attacked his gumbo, hoping to at least sate one of his appetites. "I don't believe in any of that nonsense, romance or ghost-wise."

Maddie ran her finger along the stem of her wineglass. The glass would feel smooth and cold and slick—how would Maddie's skin feel if he traced his finger along the edge of her cheek?

"You mean you don't believe in love, Chase?"

He nearly choked on a piece of okra. "Hardly."

"I do. Maybe you should think about putting a tunnel or secret room in one of your designs. Someplace the couple could escape for a secret rendezvous."

"The war was over a long time ago, Maddie."

"Yeah, but there's all kinds of distractions for a couple. Who knows, maybe when they're having a dinner party or their nosy family drops in, they could sneak away for a quickie."

Chase coughed and downed his wine, wondering

if she was referring to her nosy, protective brothers.

He'd build that tunnel, take Maddie down inside where it was cozy and dark, strip her naked and love her until she screamed her brains out.

Of course, if Lance and Reid discovered he'd done it, the tunnel would be the perfect place to bury his body after they murdered him.

The next day Maddie glanced up from her computer and rubbed her tired eyes. Her sleep had been less than restful the night before, filled with romantic dreams of making love in a tunnel with an illusive pirate, a man who smelled and tasted like Chase Holloway. A man wearing nothing but a black eye patch over one eye.

T. C. purred, looking at her as if she'd neglected him, and she reached down and rubbed his belly, laughing when he rolled onto his back and shined his jewels. Typical male.

To release her sexual energy, she'd jogged three miles before breakfast. All afternoon, she'd been researching the history of Savannah, documenting some of the more famous mansions and their furnishings, hoping to create a classy decorating scheme for the replica of the Elizabeth Henry house. She'd also been putting off calling Noisy Nora to set up another meeting. And she'd been trying not to think about Chase all day.

Why had he rushed away from the Pirate's House so quickly? He'd acted as if he'd been called to an emergency. As if he couldn't escape from her fast enough. Did he know she suspected the truth about the way he'd injured his eye?

Or had all that romantic gibberish disturbed him? Chase had said he wasn't a romantic. She believed him now. Or maybe he just couldn't see *her* in a romantic way. Just as his kid sister.

The sooner she accepted it, the better off she'd be.

The wind chimes on her decorating den door clinked as a knock shook them. Probably Lance or Reid coming by to check—although they hadn't been by in two days. Maybe they were actually taking her seriously and going to give her some space. And maybe Chase had decided to pick her up here instead of meeting her on the square as they'd planned. To wind up their little historic tour, they were taking one of the famous carriage rides tonight. A flutter of excitement tickled her stomach at the thought of the moonlit ride. Yesterday she'd felt as if she'd grown closer to Chase, as if he'd allowed her to peek at the emotions he tried so hard to keep hidden. Tonight . . .

The knock sounded again. She rose and rubbed her neck. "Who is it?"

"It's me, Madison."

Jeff? What was he doing here?

He opened the door, lowered his head to enter and gave the inside of the van a quick perusal. Maddie pursed her lips, biting back a reply when she saw that little vee of disapproval crinkle between his eyebrows.

"Jeff, what are you doing here?"

"I came to see how you were doing." His eyes flickered warily. "After all, I did help you get set up."

And took her mother's pendant. "You aren't here to remind me of that, now are you?"

The groove deepened between his eyes as his right eyelid twitched. "I didn't mean it like that, Maddie. I just . . . I don't really know why I came."

The honesty in his admission surprised her. "All

right. Then come on in, but I don't have long. I have a meeting in half an hour."

He made a point of checking his watch. "A business meeting so late?"

"I'm trying to put together this Tour of Homes. There's a lot to do, Jeff."

"So you still intend to drive this decorating van around town?"

Maddie's hand closed around her briefcase. "Yes, of course I do. I've invested a lot of money as well as my mother's heirloom in this, as *you* know."

He ignored her barb. "Who are you meeting?"

"Not that it's any of your business, but I'm meeting Chase Holloway to gather research for the project."

The frown on his face resembled jealousy. "Holloway, that . . . that derelict boy from the orphanage. Good grief, Maddie, he has a bad reputation—"

"He's not a derelict anymore, Jeff. He graduated from college and is an architect now."

"Well, as long as you aren't involved personally."

Maddie bit back a reply.

"Well . . ."

"Well, what?"

"I miss you, Maddie." He shrugged sheepishly, that boyish smile she'd always loved twitching at the corner of his mouth. "I've been thinking about us, about all the good times we had. I never realized how much I needed you until you walked out of my life."

"We did have some good times, Jeff," Maddie conceded, fond memories suffusing her. "But things have changed. We're not the same people we were in college."

He fiddled with a tray of floor samples. "It doesn't have to be that way. Have dinner with me, Maddie. Let's see if we can work things out."

"Dinner?"

"Yes, we could talk about a reconciliation."

"A reconciliation?"

"You sound like a parrot, Maddie. I simply wanted us to talk. Get back to where we used to be."

She gathered her briefcase and a notepad. "I'm sorry, I can't afford to take the time, Jeff. I have a lot at stake here." *My mother's pendant for one. My independence for another.*

"I realize now how important your business is to you." He brushed a tendril of her hair away from her face. "I'm sorry I didn't understand before."

"I always told you I had dreams, Jeff. And I intend to see them through."

"I know, and I was being selfish." He reached out and traced her jaw with the pad of his thumb. "I really care about you, Maddie. You just took me off guard that day. I'm sorry I acted like an ass. I should have been more understanding."

Maddie hesitated. He sounded so sincere. "I . . . I don't know what to say, Jeff. But I do need to go."

Jeff moved his legs sideways as she bent to retrieve her shoes. She'd kicked them off hours ago when she'd sprawled on the floor to survey her fabric samples.

He looked crestfallen. "I guess I'll leave then. Just promise me you'll think about it."

"I'll think about it, "Maddie said quietly.

He nodded, then climbed from the van, and Maddie followed, sliding her feet into the pumps when she made it to the ground. Jeff grabbed Maddie's hand and squeezed it, then leaned over and kissed her on the cheek. "I'm not giving up on us."

Maddie nodded mutely, then watched him walk to his BMW and drive away, stunned. Did Jeff really want to go back to the way things were? And if he did, was it really possible?

Chapter Ten

"You're late," Chase said when Maddie rushed up to meet him by the City Market.

"Sorry." Maddie smoothed a lock of her windblown hair back into the clip at the base of her neck, drawing his attention to the pale skin beneath her earlobe. Tender, delicate skin he'd like to touch . . .

"Jeff stopped by. I was trying to get out the door—"

"That wuss came to see you?"

Maddie paused, a small grin tugging at her mouth. "Wuss?"

Chase shrugged. "Sorry, I never did like Oglethorpe much."

"Really?"

Chase realized he'd said too much and pointed to the horse and buggy. "I already bought our tickets. I think they're waiting for us."

"Oh, right." She sashayed toward the buggy, leaving him to stare at the curve of her hips swaying beneath the short navy skirt she was wearing. When she raised her arm to wave at him, her bright red T-shirt rose above her navel, giving him a tempting view of smooth stomach. The heat suddenly seemed oppressive, like steam rising from the bayou. He pulled at the buttons of his polo shirt and exhaled, wishing the spring weather didn't remind him of long, lazy days by the river, days where he and the guys would strip and go swimming in the buff, hoping to catch a glimpse of a young girl doing the same.

Maddie should wear more clothes, and he had half a mind to tell her so. Maybe some pants instead of those short skirts. And a long-sleeved shirt. With a high button-up neck.

Maddie stopped. "Aren't you coming, Chase?"

I'd like to.

"Chase, why are you looking at me like that?"

He'd been so completely dumbfounded by her sexuality that he hadn't actually moved. Mentally cursing himself, he jogged over to the buggy. Just in time to see her climb up the steps, he received a tantalizing glimpse of her luscious bare legs.

Remember those knobby knees when she was ten. Those bruises she always had from climbing trees and tagging along after The Terrible Three. The time she had chicken pox and red splotches all over her face.

Thankfully, the tour guide, a college student named Tonya, who had more earrings in her nose than he could count, took over the conversation when he arrived at the carriage, and he was saved from speaking. For the next hour Chase and Maddie relaxed in the carriage and let the guide lead the way through the historic tour. Moonlight played across the streets, the ironwork of the historic homes, and danced along the river, spilling its radiance across Maddie's features as she oohed and aahed over the scenery. Maddie was totally animated and seemed enthralled in the ghost stories and legends, as if she'd never seen Savannah before, while he found himself enthralled with *her*.

"You mean the people back then actually considered the staircase like welcoming arms?"

"Yes, that's what they were called," Tonya explained. "The ladies entered and exited one side, the men the other. They weren't allowed to come down together. Women also used their fans to indicate their availability. A lady placed her fan to the right side of her face to indicate yes, to the left side to indicate no."

Maddie laughed. "I guess we have come a long way. I'm certainly glad I didn't live back then."

"Might have been easier on your brothers," Chase said. "Those arranged marriages."

Maddie rolled her eyes. "Just what I want, Lance or Reid to pick out a husband for me. He'd probably look like one of those monks from the monastery."

The only safe place for a sexy woman like Maddie.

"On your right you'll see the historic Colonial Graveyard where many soldiers are buried," Tonya said, going on to tell about a few of the specific burials.

Chase stared at the Colonial Graveyard and started counting tombstones, trying to direct his thoughts from Maddie. But the whisper of a breeze brought the scent of her delicate perfume and the carriage rocked, knocking her bare knee against his jean-clad one, torturing him.

"That orange house is—"

"The Pumpkin House," Chase supplied.

"Right," Tonya said. "And there's the Juliette

Lowe house where the founder of the Girl Scouts lived."

"I was a Girl Scout," Maddie said. "Chase, did you—"

"No, Maddie, I was never a Boy Scout," he said in a husky voice. "They didn't have a troop at Bethesda. Remember I was a troublemaker."

Maddie grinned wickedly. "You still are, aren't you?"

He cocked his head sideways and lowered his voice. "I could be."

Maddie's sympathetic look tore at him. He was tempted to tell her the truth, how he laid awake on rainy nights, all alone, and dreamed of being something other than a troublemaker. That he wanted to show all those kids who'd made fun of him that he could be successful. That one of his ex-buddies might be the person causing trouble for Lance and Reid. But Chase Holloway had never spilled his guts to a woman, and he certainly wouldn't start now. Not even to Maddie.

The echo of loneliness in Chase's voice tugged at Maddie's heart. She wanted to wrap her arms around him and soothe all his old hurt feelings. She wanted to admit how much she admired him for putting himself through school and overcoming all the disadvantages of his past to build a successful career for himself.

But judging from the fierce expression on his face, he would never let her.

Maddie he would let her soothe him in other ways, Maddie thought wickedly. She'd been shocked back at the town square when she'd turned to see him watching her with heat in his eyes. She'd never expected to see hunger like that from any man, especially Chase. Ever since they began the tour, she'd barely heard a word the guide had said for thinking about how she'd like to follow through on that desire in his eyes. Thank goodness, she'd covered her reaction by babbling along with the guide, as if she was interested in history!

"We're back." Tonya jumped down and patted the huge horse's mane. "I hope you've enjoyed the tour. If you want another tour sometime, just let me know."

"Thanks, we learned a lot," Maddie said.

Chase tipped Tonya and stroked the horse's back. "You gave us a good ride, boy."

Maddie watched his big, gentle hands move across the mare's neck and wondered how they would feel stroking her own body. "Where did you park, Chase?"

"Over by the city market. Why, you want a lift?"

Maddie gazed up at the sky, admiring the twinkling stars and the full moon. "I thought I'd walk. It's such a pretty night."

"A little hot," Chase said in a husky voice.

"Yes, but the jonquils are in bloom and all the other flowers in the gardens. You can even smell the honeysuckle."

"I thought it was you." He cleared his throat. "I meant your perfume."

Maddie smiled and grabbed his hand, tugging him playfully. "Come on, it feels good to be outside, breathing in the life of the city."

Chase shrugged and followed her down Bay Street, then along River Street. The sights and sounds of the city strummed in the background like music as they strolled across the cobblestone street, along the riverbank. Music and voices drifted out from local bars and kids ran by, chasing one another and laughing.

Couples huddled beneath the live oak trees by the river, cuddling and holding hands while others shared ice cream from a vendor or relaxed on the open balconies of *Teddy's Tank House*. Bringing the scents of salt and the ocean, a breeze ruffled Maddie's hair. They walked in silence most of the way, tension thrumming through the air.

"I plan to have sketches for you on the first two houses by Friday," Maddie finally said when they reached her porch.

"No leopard-skin furniture or lava lamps?"

Maddie grinned. "You like lava lamps?"

His eyelids lowered to slits. "Yeah, but I don't think they fit with the historical society's code."

Maddie hitched out her hip, unable to resist teasing him. "But your subdivision isn't monitored by the historical society, is it?"

"No, but the designs are based on replicas of the homes built in the 1700s. I'd think the furniture should go along with it."

Maddie pretended to pout. "Then I guess the cowhide sofa is out. And the disco dance floor?"

He stared at her, a muscle ticking in his jaw. "Maddie, the people looking out here want old town Savannah, upscale—"

"I know," Maddie said softly, patting his arm. "I was teasing, Chase. Don't worry so much, I know what I'm doing."

He leaned against the steps, still looking doubtful. "Good. I hope we can stay on schedule. This tour is important, Maddie. Your brothers—"

Would die if they knew she'd used their mother's heirloom as collateral. "I know, Chase. Don't you trust me?"

His dark gaze trapped her. A loaded question, and one to which she hoped he'd answer yes, but he simply lowered his eyes and let the silence stand between them, like a brick wall that couldn't be scaled. She studied his profile in the moonlight. He was so big and strong, his long raven hair brushing his collar, his eyes dark and heavy in the shadows. She remembered how he'd always stood like that, in the edge of the doorway at their house, looking lost and alone, like he wanted someone to invite him in, but he wasn't sure he'd say yes if they did. That hollow loneliness that always seemed to shroud his good mood and shadow his words with a huskiness sent heat spiraling right through her. She'd felt it when she was a teenager and had had a crush on him. She'd thought she'd outgrown him while she was away at school.

But she hadn't. Maybe she never would. Maybe he was waiting on her to make the first move. *But he turned you away after that kiss,* she reminded herself. *Because you're like a kid sister to him.*

Only he wasn't looking at you like a sister back in the street before the tour.

"I'm sure you'll do a good job," he finally said in a husky voice.

And he isn't looking at you like a sister now.

"It's just—"

"Shh." She took his hand and pulled him up the steps so he was standing only a hairbreadth away. "You don't have to say anything else, Chase. Just shut up and kiss me."

The raw desire that darkened his eyes burned through any reservations she might have had. With a low groan, he cupped her chin in his hands, tilted his head and yanked her against his hard chest. His thighs felt hot as her body molded against his strong corded muscles. And his big hands felt like heaven as he stroked her back and drove his mouth over hers. He teased her lips apart with his tongue, then nipped at the corner of her mouth with his teeth before he plunged his tongue inside her mouth and swept her away with desire. His breath fanned against her cheek as he whispered her name on a husky sigh. Sweet fire rose within her. Hot and hungry and desperate.

She had never wanted anyone so badly in her life.

Maddie tore at his shirt, trying to drag it from his jeans. He walked her backward, pressing her back against the hard wood of her door, his hands snaking up her thighs, pushing up her skirt to rub her bare legs. She grabbed his buttocks and dug her hands into the clenching muscles as he ground his sex into her heat. Moisture pooled in her abdomen and dampened her center, sensations spiraling through her so quickly she thought she was going to scream with pleasure or die if he didn't take her right there on her porch.

Good heavens, they were right there on her porch.

Trying desperately not to destroy the moment, she ran her heel up along his leg and lifted her hands to his back, then she stroked his jaw and slowly broke the kiss, growing even more excited by the sound of his ragged breathing penetrating the silence. "Chase, let's go inside."

He rained kisses on her neck, licking the sensitive skin beneath her ear. God, she wanted him now.

"Chase, come on, let's go inside. Someone might see us on the porch."

A long moan escaped him, and he dropped his head against her cheek, his heavy body stiff and obviously aroused as his thick shaft wedged between her thighs. Her words seemed to slowly seep in, though, and she felt him start to pull away. She held him with her foot, but he lowered her skirt, dragging his gaze up to meet hers. His eyes were heavy and filled with hunger, his black lashes lowered, his jaw clenched for control. Heat swept through her again at the intensity of his passion. It would be so good . . . so incredible. . . .

"Jesus, Maddie, I'm sorry."

Her breath hissed out as if he'd slapped her. "Don't, Chase. I want you to come in. To . . . to finish." She indicated the sexual hold he had on her body, the way her leg was wrapped around his, the way the bulge of his sex fit so intimately with her body. "I want you."

The passion she'd seen earlier slowly dissipated as he set her aside. "No, Maddie. We can't do this."

She was cold now and shivering, so she wrapped her arms around her middle, missing his warmth. "But . . . but why? We're good together. I feel it, and so do you."

She indicated his arousal, refusing to allow him to throw the blame off on her or say the attraction had been one-sided.

He backed toward the stairs, lingering at the post again. She stepped forward, her heart in her eyes, and traced a finger along the scar on his forehead. "Chase, don't—"

"Don't what? Stop us from doing something stupid."

"Don't shut me out. I . . . I like you, and . . . and we've known each other forever and—"

"Maddie, stop. You're Lance and Reid's little sister." Chase pulled away from her, ran a hand through his hair, and dropped his head forward, his face twisting with emotions.

"Chase, I'm not anybody's kid sister."

"The hell you aren't."

Maddie swept her hand down her body. "Forget

them for now. Just look at me and tell me what you see."

Chase raised his gaze to hers, his eyes stormy. "All right. I see a beautiful, desirable woman who's looking for a man."

"Not just any man, Chase. *You.*"

A muscle ticked in his jaw, almost as if her admission hurt. "Maddie, you think that now, just because you got all fired up, but tomorrow you'd regret it if we made love. And I'd regret it."

Maddie swallowed, fighting tears, determined not to shed them in front of him. She already hated herself for begging, but she had to make one last attempt. "What if I said I wouldn't regret it tomorrow?"

He hesitated, fisting his hands by his side as if he wanted to reach for her. Or maybe he wanted to push her away. "There's too much at stake here, Maddie. The job, my friendship with Lance and Reid, our working relationship—"

"We can deal with all that."

"Trust me, Maddie, I'm not the man for you."

"Why don't you let me decide that."

His eyes flickered with doubts, turmoil written on every feature of his face. Finally, he exhaled, rammed his hand through his hair again and backed down the stairs. "It's not going to happen, Mad. You're just going to have to accept it."

Without another word, he turned and stalked down the sidewalk, leaving Maddie alone and frustrated. She watched him move into the shadows of the street and fumed, wondering what she had done to deserve this humiliation, wondering if the excuses he'd given were just that—excuses—because he didn't want her badly enough.

She pressed herself against the wall and struggled

to breathe normally. The strong scent of his cologne mixed with his musky masculine smell and lingered on her clothes, the rough texture of his lips still burned her mouth. Her heat still ached for his touch. But he didn't look back. And when he finally disappeared around the corner, she unlocked the door and went inside, vowing it would be the last time she would ever throw herself at Chase Holloway.

Chapter Eleven

What if I don't regret it tomorrow?

Maddie's words were burned into Chase's mind as if they'd been seared by a branding iron. What if . . . No, he could not even think it.

He would have regretted it enough for both of them.

He had signed that bachelor pact, because he liked his life and he wanted to stay single. Making love with Maddie would be almost like a proposal. Lance and Reid would hate him. And his whole life would go to hell.

His father had let a woman ruin his life, and Chase didn't intend to fall into the same trap. Lust wasn't worth it.

He turned on his power sander and began to work on the rusty edges of the Camaro, hoping the physical labor would ease the tension from his knotted muscles. He'd already tried sleeping, but images of

Maddie's desire-slitted eyes had come unbidden in the dark, hacking away at his resolve. The delicious taste of hunger on her lips, the purr of passion rumbling from her whispered pleas, the perfect way his sex had fit between her wet, willing thighs . . .

Ouch! He sanded his nail down to the quick, the end of his thumb raw. He sucked on the tip to ease the pain, determined to forget the way his libido acted around Maddie.

The machine whirred as he aligned it with the fender and gently guided it along the rusty spots. He'd worked too hard to earn his degree, to stay out of trouble, to perfect his architectural skills so he could work with his best friends. He was so close to making it, he could almost taste the heady nectar of success. He couldn't possibly jeopardize his own future for sex. Not even the hottest, most fiery, dynamite sex he might ever have in his life.

But it wouldn't simply be sex with Maddie.

Hell, nothing was simple where Maddie was concerned.

What if I don't regret it tomorrow?

What had she meant by that? Sure, she'd regret it. Tomorrow, she'd wake up and see the orphan bad boy who'd spent half his time in detention, the other half scraping himself out of trouble with the law. The man no one had wanted when he was a kid because he was so damn mean.

Maddie deserved better.

She was just acting this way, because she was on the rebound from the wuss. She wanted to rebel against Lance and Reid, and he was the perfect man to flirt with to rattle her brothers.

She was damn sure rattling *him*.

Ouch.

He'd done it again, only this time he'd sanded his

whole thumb. Yanking a handkerchief from his pocket, he tried to blot the blood oozing from the broken skin, and turned off the sander. And what if she did put leopard-skin furniture or lava lamps in his antebellum homes? What if she completely went retro and turned off buyers?

He stumbled sideways, stepped on a nail and swore again when the broom handle slapped him in the head. Limping to sit down, he dug the nail from his boot and blinked but felt his eye, which had finally started to heal, already swelling shut. He slowly rose and groped to find his way inside, deciding he'd better quit for the night before he killed himself—which absolutely proved his theory one hundred percent—just thinking about Maddie Summers was dangerous.

"Look, you can't pull out now," Lance said. "We'll get back on schedule—"

Viranda Roth, millionaire and owner of several Italian restaurants across the states, tossed him a look of disdain, ranking him somewhere among the rats crawling underground in the city. "I'm sorry, Mr. Summers, but time is money. I want to move in *this* year. I've decided to settle on Hilton Head instead."

"I'm afraid at this late date, you'll lose your down payment, ma'am."

"That little paltry amount hardly matters." She wrapped her silk scarf around her platinum-blond hair and waved him off, then sauntered out of the door.

He silently wished revenge, something that would really get the snotty lady's goat—maybe for her hairdresser to screw up and turn her beehive some hideous orange the next time she went in for a dye job.

The minute her Ferrari drove away, Lance spun around, studied the planning board filled with pegs he used to indicate pre-sold lots and removed a peg, growling in frustration. They couldn't stand to lose another sale. They'd counted on the capital from the sales to get them through the first phase of building. Losing the Rothchild account meant an immediate cash loss as well as losing the chance at having one of the Roth restaurants located in the hub of the development. The business would have added a continental flavor to the area, enticing prospective buyers.

"What's that growl for?"

Wheeling around in his chair, he spotted none other than Sophie Lane standing in the doorway. Sunlight danced across her ivory skin, streaking her short black hair with golden light that shimmered and made the vibrant dark ends shine like silk. A short blood-red dress hugged every feature of her petite body, outlining her curves and accentuating her generous breasts. His body hardened and began to throb.

He forced his brain in control, reminding himself he had his family's reputation at stake. And this was nosy Sophie of *Sophie Knows*. "What do you want?"

She hitched out a hip and planted her small hand on the curve of her waist. Even her fingernails were painted blood-red. He wondered about her toenails. "Is that the way you greet all potential buyers, Mr. Summers?"

He swallowed his surprise at her comment. "No, but then I didn't realize you were interested in buying a house."

"Why? Did you think I came—to see you?" Her green eyes glittered with emotions—interest, mischief, amusement maybe? Or was she mocking him, because she already knew his secret?

"Show must pay you well," he said.

A smile tugged at the corner of her mouth. "Enough."

He frowned, even more disturbed by her cheerfulness. "Somehow I don't see you as the traditional settle-down type of woman."

"And you have to be this type to own a home?"

He shrugged. "No, but I'd think an apartment in the city would be more your style."

"Oh? So you have me all figured out, huh?"

"Pretty much." He crossed his legs at his ankles, leaned back in his chair and studied her. "Art-deco style, ultramodern furniture, maybe chrome and glass. One of those icelike statues in the foyer."

Sophie tossed her head back and laughed. "Maybe I'll invite you over sometime and let you see if you're right."

His body stirred again, painful and hard. Grateful for the desk shielding his burgeoning arousal from her, he leveled his gaze straight into her eyes. He had to ignore her comment, to find out what she had in mind. Nothing like the direct approach.

"What do you want, Miss Lane? Looking for another hot scoop for your show?"

Her teasing smile widened. "As a matter of fact, I still haven't filled the spots for that 'Dating Game' show."

"I told you I'm not interested."

"So you said. Your brother seemed like he'd enjoy it though."

So, she'd use Reid, too. Or maybe she'd spill the truth to him before Lance could. He couldn't allow it. "I don't think he has time right now."

Her eyebrow quirked in challenge. "Maybe you should let your brother speak for himself."

Let her charm the pants off Reid? No way. "He's

not here right now, but I'll pass along your message."

"You do that." She moved around the room, her gaze straying to the different floor plans, the layout of the lots. "Business going well?"

"It's all right. We're keeping busy."

"So your sour mood must be related to something personal?"

Yeah, you. A pang of regret hit him for his rudeness; he'd never in his life treated a woman the way he'd treated this one. But she snuck under his skin like nobody else ever had, and he could not, *would* not allow her to use him to find out the juice on his father. The whole thing was too . . . too embarrassing. He had to protect Maddie and Reid.

"I'm sorry, I didn't mean to be rude, but I've got stuff to do." He stood, gesturing toward the displays. "Are you really househunting?"

She turned and walked over to him, her small chin tipped up so she could see in his eyes. He suddenly realized how small she was, five-feet-two at the most. He was a good foot taller, dwarfed her by at least a hundred pounds. Funny, she seemed so spunky and full of energy, he'd never imagined how fragile she'd seem beside him. And heaven help him, she smelled sinful. Like roses, all delicate and sweetly pungent, the way the front porch of his mother's old farmhouse had smelled when her climbing roses bloomed. The same scent his first serious girlfriend had worn, the girl he'd given up to have more time to take care of Maddie.

"Yes, but not one of these," she said, gesturing toward the lots. "I don't quite have that much to invest. But I did buy one of the old homes in the historic section at an auction, and I want to restore it."

The renovation project sparked his interest. He loved the older homes and couldn't wait to see them refurbished. "You already bought one?"

"Yes," she said softly. "Maybe you could look at it with me sometime and help me decide what to do with it."

Spend time with her? No, that wasn't a good idea.

"Well, I'm pretty busy right now. We have this Tour of Homes coming up—"

"Too busy to turn down a business deal?"

He bit the inside of his cheek. *Sounded like a challenge.* "Well, no, I guess not."

"You could have your brother Reid help me."

He felt a muscle tick in his jaw. Reid was too gullible. A cunning woman like Sophie would wrap him around her little finger in a minute. "That's not possible. Reid likes to stay on site with the contractors."

"Good, that means we'll be working together." She smiled, reached for his hand and braced it between both of hers. His earlier arguments flew out of his head at her touch. Heat spiraled through him, thrumming his blood to a fever pitch. His knees suddenly wobbled.

"Right, we'll be working together," he heard himself say in a weak voice.

She gave his hand a firm shake, then released him as if she were unaffected.

"I'll get my thoughts together and be in touch." With a fluttery wave, she turned and flitted out of the door.

Lance stared, dumbfounded by desire as she glided to her car. His gaze swept toward the hidden safe where he kept the box he'd found of his father's. The box of . . . no, he couldn't even think about the sordid contents.

He had to figure out what Sophie Lane wanted

from him. To know what he'd just agreed to. Was the beautiful talk-show host really interested in restoring a house or was she digging for a story—a story that might destroy his family?

Determined to prove she was a professional, not just a fly-by-night decorator as she'd been with other interests in her life, Maddie spent the week completing mock-up boards for the first three model homes, ordering basic furnishings, and shopping for accessories to complement the color schemes she'd chosen. The Internet expedited her workload, but only door-to-door legwork could take her into the small specialty shops to unearth the unique touches she envisioned. By Friday afternoon, she was exhausted but proud of her progress.

Her obsession with work had also enabled her to put Chase Holloway out of her mind. At least for ten or fifteen minutes at a time. Still, on those long lonely nights, she'd sink into bed and images of him, naked and *willing*, danced through her head. And in none of her fantasies did he ever once refer to her as Lance and Reid's kid sister.

But she'd die before she'd offer herself to him again. Pirate eye patch or not.

She settled the roses Jeff had sent her earlier into a vase and studied the card.

"I miss you, Maddie. Call me. Love, Jeff."

She couldn't decide whether to call him or not. Could they really renew the old spark? She wasn't sure what to make of his new attitude toward her career. Could she trust him?

The phone pealed, interrupting her thoughts, and she jammed a stack of paint chips back onto the shelf of her cluttered office and reached for it.

"Maddie, you have to come with me to this party

tonight," Sophie said, her voice bubbling with enthusiasm.

Maddie leaned back in her chair and rubbed her aching foot. "I'm really wiped out. I think I'll settle for a bubble bath and pizza—"

"No," Sophie declared. "This party is going to be wild. The director of a new sci-fi show, *Invisible Izzy,* which is supposed to air next week—"

"*Invisible Izzy,* what kind of name is that?"

"It's about this invisible female warrior from the planet Sexton who's into bondage—"

"Bondage?"

"Yes, you do know what bondage is, don't you, Maddie?"

Maddie flushed. "Of course I do."

"Anyway, the show is supposed to be great," Sophie continued. "And the director, Greg Pugh, is going to be there. He's one hottie. I think he'd be perfect for you."

"If he's so perfect, why don't you go out with him?"

"Because I'm still working on your brother." Sophie paused. "Besides, he loves redheads."

"I don't know—"

"You have better prospects? A hot night with Nerdy Ned, that computer geek you met Monday at Kinko's?"

"No."

"Barry, the bisexual antique dealer you met Tuesday?"

"No."

"Cameron, the control freak you met Thursday?"

God, no. He'd sauntered toward her bedroom, announced that he wanted to pick out her outfit for the night, then ordered her to change. She'd kissed him off before they'd made it to the front door.

But a man who directed a show about invisible female warriors who were into bondage.

She should call Jeff, she thought, glancing at the roses again.

"Maddie, you're not still upset over that Holloway man, are you?"

"No," Maddie said emphatically, forcing herself to remember Chase's attitude. "He's just as overbearing and old-fashioned as Lance and Reid." And he'd never send her flowers.

"Let me guess, he's not the settle-down type either?"

"Hardly."

"And if he did, he'd probably want some Stepford wife who'd be at his beck and call while he cavorted around with other women."

Like her mother.

"Yeah, probably." Maddie saw the hollow loneliness in Chase's eyes and wondered though. Would he? Or once a woman snagged his heart, would he be forever loyal to her? Passionate beyond control?

No . . . she couldn't think about passion—

"Maddie, you have to come. I've already told Greg you'll be there."

Maddie twirled the phone cord around her finger. When Sophie made up her mind to do something, she didn't give up. And she wasn't ready to talk to Jeff again yet. "All right. I'll go."

Sophie laughed. "Good, I'll pick you up at eight. Oh, and wear that black leather skirt with the silver tube top."

Maddie agreed, frowning as she hung up the phone. Should she bring a whip and handcuffs, too?

Chapter Twelve

"Look, you guys, we've got trouble on all sides." Lance shoved his hand through his hair in frustration and ordered his second beer.

Chase leaned back on the bar stool and studied Lance's worried expression. "That Roth woman backed out?"

"Yeah, and two more buyers canceled today."

"Our flooring contractor showed up with the wrong kind of materials, too," Reid added. "He has to reorder, which will set us back a few days."

"Blast it all to hell." Lance closed his eyes and pinched the bridge of his nose as if he had a headache.

"So, a couple of days won't matter, and you'll find new buyers," Chase said, striving to remain calm.

"Does Maddie know about the problems?"

"No, and she's not going to," Lance growled.

"We don't want to worry her," Reid said. "Besides, she's been busy all week shopping."

Chase frowned, wondering why they felt they had to shelter Maddie. "You know Maddie's a lot tougher than you think. She might be able to help."

Lance and Reid looked at him as if he'd lost his last little bit of intelligence.

"We don't need her help," Lance said.

"Yeah, we have things under control," Reid added.

"It didn't sound like it a few minutes ago," Chase said.

An angry scowl darkened Lance's eyes. "We'll decide whether or not to tell Maddie about our problems. Have you been keeping tabs on her like we asked?"

Yes, and I kissed the hell out of her the other night, and I almost made love to her on her front porch. Chase swirled his mug around, staring into the rich amber liquid, contemplating how to answer. After the way they'd parted, he'd been afraid to call her this week. She might be out every night nude dancing for all he knew. Or picking chinchilla carpet or leopard-skin couches for the tour.

"Chase?"

"She's been working on the designs," he said, praying he was right.

Reid winked at a pretty brunette who waved to him from across the room. "Good."

"Yeah," Lance said. "Maybe this job will be good for our little sister."

"Keep her too distracted to date?" Chase asked.

Lance laughed in agreement.

"I tried to call her earlier," Reid mumbled, still eyeing the woman. "But she wasn't home."

"Probably shopping for the houses," Lance said.

On a Friday night? Chase frowned, remembering

Maddie's comment about dating at least twenty men before she settled down. Was she out working on house plans or working toward her dating quota?

No, surely Maddie had been joking about that list. And Lance was right, the job was good for her. The perfect venue to keep her out of trouble.

"This party is great," Maddie admitted. "To think I planned to stay home and work tonight. Music, champagne, sexy men, what more could a girl ask for?"

Sophie's eyes twinkled with laughter as she grabbed one of the lobster hors d'oeuvres from the metallic table. "That one of those sexy men would be a keeper?"

Maddie laughed, gobbling down a raw oyster and sipping her fifth soda of the night. She'd started with champagne, but realized she wanted her wits about her so she'd switched to diet cola after the second glass.

Sophie gyrated her hips to the beat of the song and scanned the crowd. "I think everyone from the station came tonight. And all these reporters, it's great for Greg."

"He is racking up publicity," Maddie agreed.

The crowd had thinned in the past hour but still several of the producers, directors and stars from some of the locally produced shows lingered, sipping drinks and enjoying the elaborate appetizer spread and pulsating music. Kicking off his sitcom's debut with this press-covered event, Greg had chosen a retro theme related to the sci-fi show. Reporters and photographers mingled through the crowd, interviewing the cast as well as jazzing up Greg's genius in producing the innovative program. Maddie had watched him pose for photo after photo. Poised.

Handsome. A Tom Selleck look-alike, he was definitely an eye-pleaser with the female crowd.

Izzy, the white-blond femme fatale of the show, exuded power, strength and beauty. Maddie could imagine her brothers drooling over the woman. Of course, they'd want to get her in the sack. Would Chase go goo-goo-eyed over her, too?

Forget Chase. Greg Pugh was a handsome, successful doll who obviously liked independent modern women or he wouldn't be producing a show featuring one. She'd have a little fun tonight, go back to work tomorrow and see Chase in a whole different light.

A tall blond man with a Brad Pitt face played the leading male role on the show. He pulled Sophie to the dance floor. Maddie laughed as her friend engaged in a bump-and-grind routine that had the man salivating. Greg approached, a reporter dogging him, and gestured toward the dance floor.

"Come on, I've been wanting to get you alone all night."

Maddie waved toward the crowd. "Alone?"

Greg laughed. "We can pretend."

Maddie accepted his hand, aware his palms were smooth and not callused like her brothers' and Chase's. Because the man was a producer, not a construction worker, she reminded herself. A more exciting kind of guy. Classy, not that rough-hewn macho type. And he could dance, Chase probably couldn't even two-step.

Greg swayed seductively to the music, and Maddie slipped into the rhythm, playfully maneuvering her hips in sync with his, the crowded room fading from view. For the next hour, she felt almost smothered by his warm attention, stripped naked by his twinkling green eyes and suggestive smile. A fast beat bled into a slow song of seduction, and Maddie reluctantly allowed him to pull her in his arms.

"You're fabulous," he whispered near her ear. "I'm glad Sophie insisted I meet you."

"Thanks." She rested her hand against his chest and felt his heart beating rapidly. "She had a lot of nice things to say about you, too."

His hand stroked the small of her back, pulling her tight against his muscled body until Maddie felt the undeniable evidence of his arousal pulsating against her. The lights seemed to dim, the couples each gliding into a different, more intimate plane, but Maddie felt crowded, as if she couldn't breathe. As several couples left, Greg's gaze intensified. Uncomfortable with the lusty edge to his eyes, she tried to pull away slightly, but he accidentally stepped on her toe.

"Ouch." *His shoe must weigh a ton.*

"I'm sorry," Greg murmured, concern softening his voice. "Are you all right?"

"Yes," Maddie whispered. "But I need to powder my nose." And go to the bathroom. Suddenly all the Diet Coke she'd drunk was pressing on her bladder.

A grin slid onto his face. "Sure. Maybe this crowd will leave and we can really be alone."

Maddie winced but hobbled away, her toe throbbing. Did the man have lead weights inside those designer shoes?

Sophie seemed enthralled with the blonde so Maddie didn't disturb her. She darted toward the bathroom alone, but several women had gathered, obviously waiting in line. Geez. She crossed her legs and swayed from side to side. She really had to go to the bathroom now.

A quick trip up the spiraling staircase, and she found the guest bath also occupied. She cursed. She couldn't wait!

She tiptoed down the hall, deciding she'd slip into the master suite and out before anyone knew she'd been there. Chrome and glass caught her eye as she opened the door. Steel-gray carpet covered the floor and a black lacquered bed dominated the room. A picture of a nude woman, blindfolded and chained to an iron bedpost, hung dead center above the modern-sculpted headboard. A basket of condoms sat on the nightstand with several tubes of body gels beside it. Nude figurines embraced in sexual poses graced an entertainment center, and videos were stacked neatly on the shelf below. *A Tongue Lashing by Tiffany*, *Betty in Bondage*, *Danny for Dessert*, *The Twin Orgy . . .*

Maddie rolled her eyes and studied the other furnishings, expecting to see a blow-up doll pop from the ceiling any minute with sexy music and strobe lights accompanying it, but footsteps sounded on the staircase. She didn't want Greg to find her near his bedroom. Panicking, she darted farther into the room, closed the door, and leaned against the wall to catch her breath. The footsteps grew louder, and the urge to go the bathroom hit her harder as a man's voice boomed from the hallway. Laughter followed. Greg's. Then another male voice. Good heavens, they were coming into the bedroom!

"I saw you talking to that redhead. You have plans for later?"

"I hope so," Greg said. "She sure is hot."

Maddie crossed her legs again, anger brewing, her bladder aching.

"Maybe I can talk Sophie and her into a threesome."

Maddie's mouth dropped open.

"Or better yet, maybe I can talk Izzy into joining us, and we can have a party."

"Tell her to bring her whip and chains, and I'll bring my camera."

"We'll have a marathon night of it."

The other man laughed. "I don't know how you do it, Pugh."

"Viagra," Greg said with a masculine chuckle. "I'm going to take some right now."

Maddie curled her fingers into fists, her heart racing. The doorknob began to turn. She couldn't let him know she'd overheard him!

Or worse—what if he thought she'd come in his bedroom to wait for him? To seduce him? Oh, God, she had to hide!

Her heart pounding, she glanced at the bed, but it was so low to the floor she couldn't crawl beneath it. No large chair or screen to hide behind. Not even a blow-up doll!

The bathroom.

The door squeaked open, and she raced to the bathroom, scanning the huge room. The walk-in closet—no, it was too open. The tub, no, he would see her. The shower? Frosted gray glass shielded the black tiles. Maybe he wouldn't notice her through the muted glass. Sucking in a frantic breath, she slipped inside and leaned her head back, wincing when the door squeaked.

Had he heard her?

When she realized something sharp jabbed her ear, she pivoted. An oddly shaped massage tool dangled from the shower head, and a small camera was wedged in the corner of the ceiling. Above the mirrored wall floated a chrome shelf, overflowing with various body paints, jellies, handcuffs and a dildo the size of a banana that looked painful. Obviously Greg Pugh liked kinky sex.

The footsteps grew louder. He was coming nearer.

She closed her eyes and prayed he didn't have to use the bathroom.

She was wrong. Seconds later, his hard shoes clicked across the tile floor. She pinched her eyes closed, stuck her fingers in her ears and silently hummed her own made-up version of "You Won't Get Any Tonight." But she had to go so bad herself, she had to bounce up and down in place to control herself. Seconds later, she paused to see if he was finished, but he was still going. Damn. He was like the Energizer bunny. He just kept going and going.

Finally, she heard the toilet flush. She opened one eye and peeked through the tiny crack in the door. He kicked off his shoes and began massaging his feet and she realized the man had metal lifts in his shoes. No wonder he'd clobbered her toe. And without the lifts, he was two inches shorter than her. Then she watched in shock as his hand swept along his head and removed a wig. A slick, shiny head appeared—the man was completely bald!

A bridge in his mouth came next. He scrubbed the front two teeth, gargled with mouthwash, then beamed a smile at himself in the mirror. "Gonna have a party tonight, Pugh."

That's what you think.

Maddie was so furious she backed up, but she bumped the tray of gels and a bottle of lime green goop toppled over. She reached out to grab it before it hit the floor, but the gel splattered all over her head, dripping down her face. The sticky mess was cold and . . . and fluorescent. Her tube top glowed with tiny bright green dots, her fingers, her hands, and most likely her hair and face! Geez, how would she return to the party now? She couldn't let Greg see her, or he'd know where she'd been.

Greg began to whistle, and she grabbed a dry washcloth from the corner of the shower to wipe the gel from her forehead, wincing in horror when he used a small pair of scissors to trim his nose hairs.

Then he splashed aftershave on his cheeks, reached inside his slacks and adjusted himself, and jammed a handful of condoms in his pocket. The weasely, toothless bastard!

With quick, confident movements, he slipped on the loafers, settled the dark crop of fake hair back on his head, then inserted the bridge that formed his front two teeth. Smiling at himself again in the mirror, he opened the chrome medicine chest, pulled out a bottle of what she supposed was Viagra, opened the cap, and swallowed a pill.

Maddie held her breath until he left the bathroom. She waited for what seemed like forever, then stepped from the shower. A peek into the bedroom revealed the coast was clear. Maddie quickly relieved her poor bladder, praying the whole time Greg wouldn't return. Then feeling five pounds lighter, she stepped into the bedroom. Her top glowed neon green in the dark. Frantic for a disguise, she ran to his closet and jerked out the first thing she came in contact with—his black silk bathrobe. Footsteps padded nearby. Darn it. Someone was coming in the bedroom again.

She had to get out of there!

Yanking on the robe, she searched the bedroom for an escape. No back door or adjoining room. The window would have to do. Heaving in frustration, she jammed up the frame and slid onto the balcony. Her heart pounded as she slowly climbed over the trellis and dropped to the ground. A dog growled, Pugh's watchdogs obviously, and she ran for the car as fast as she could with the hounds from hell right on her heels.

Once she made her way safely home, she'd call Sophie and tell her that her handsome friend and the director of the new hit show, which had all the press and women in Savannah drooling, was a toothless, bald, impotent, complete male fraud.

Chase lay in bed, listening to the early-morning rain splatter against the roof and hoped the bad weather moved on by lunchtime so the work crews could stay on the job. He rubbed a hand over his face, shaking his head at the black patch he had over his eye. He felt like an idiot. And if Maddie ever found out the truth . . .

Thunder rumbled outside, and through the window and his one good eye, he spotted dark clouds rolling above the oak trees surrounding his apartment. Spanish moss draped the branches, creating shadows that framed the window like long bony fingers. As a child, he'd often had nightmares on stormy nights, had imagined those fingers were real, that they were going to reach out and strangle him because he was such a bad boy.

He'd wake up shaking and scared and alone.

Now he was simply alone.

Not that he minded it, he thought, forcing himself to gaze at the Bachelor Pact he'd photocopied and hung in every room of his house. But he couldn't help wondering if Maddie had gone out last night. He'd driven by her house after leaving Lance and Reid and had seen her car parked in front, but her lights were off, so he'd assumed she was in bed or had a date. He hoped she was not in bed with her date.

Had she gone back to that nudist colony?

Rolling sideways, he shoved back the covers and pushed himself out of bed, ignoring the way his muscles protested. He needed a quick run, some exercise to relieve his pent-up stress. And his unsatisfied libido.

Maybe he could run with one good eye without bumping into something and killing himself.

Yanking on a pair of shorts, a T-shirt and tennis shoes, he stumbled toward the den and opened the front door, but a flash of lightning streaked the sky, and he decided he'd have to wait until things settled down. The morning paper lay on the stoop so he knelt and retrieved it, tucked it beneath his arm, then went to get some coffee. Several minutes later, he relaxed on the sofa with a cup of hot brew, opened the paper and gaped at the front page in surprise.

A picture of Maddie wearing some shiny slinky aluminum-foil type top and a short leather skirt caught his eye. But her outfit didn't disturb him half as much as the rest of the picture. She was plastered all over a tall suited man whose hands were cupping her butt while they performed a bump and grind.

He saw red for a minute before he refocused and his eyes zeroed in on the article. *Greg Pugh, director and originator of the new innovative show*, Invisible Izzy, *which features a woman superhero heavily into bondage, hosts a gala celebration to kick off the show. His house certainly reflects his modern philosophy and the theme of the sitcom, leaving fans to wonder—does his own personal life and sexual preference provide the inspiration for the show? And who is his latest conquest?*

Chase cursed at the same time the phone rang. He didn't even have to answer to know the caller would be one of his buddies, wondering what the hell was going on with Maddie now, and why he hadn't been watching her. He had no idea what he was going to tell them.

Chapter Thirteen

"Are there any normal, single men left in Savannah?" Maddie cradled the phone to her ear, juggling the coffeepot. "You should try that as a topic for your show."

Sophie laughed. "I can't believe Greg is such a phony. He has everyone at the station completely fooled."

Maddie filled her cup and emptied a packet of artificial sweetener in her coffee, then stirred as she grabbed a bagel from the toaster. "So, are you going to expose him?"

"I don't know." Sophie made a tsking sound. "I hate to ruin the guy; he has worked hard to get this show going, and it's supposed to be the best comedy of the new millennium."

"He's a pervert," Maddie said matter-of-factly, jumping when a roar of thunder rent the air. It had been raining all morning, so she'd slept in and still wore her pajamas—boxer shorts and a T-shirt. "He wanted the two of us *together*, Soph."

Sophie laughed again. "A lot of men fantasize about having more than one woman at the same time," Sophie said, obviously unimpressed.

Maddie opened her mouth to bite into the bagel but accidentally bit her tongue instead. "So, you're saying you'd . . . you'd participate?"

"That's not what I meant," Sophie said quickly. "I interviewed a sex therapist on the show last year, and he said having more than one lover is the most common fantasy men have."

"He wanted to video us, too. And you should have seen his shower."

"You were in his shower?"

"Long story, but yeah. I was hiding out there." Maddie tucked her feet beneath her and rubbed her hand over the black silk robe lying next to her on the couch, wondering how she'd get it back to Greg without revealing herself. "Anyway, this guy had enough gels and body paint in there for an orgy. I'm wearing the evidence of it—my hair still shimmers with neon-green sparkles."

"Sounds interesting," Sophie said. "Wonder where he bought it?"

"Sophie!" They both burst into laughter. Finally, when they calmed down, Maddie said, "Maybe you can help me get his robe back to him."

"You stole his bathrobe?"

"I had to wear something to cover my neon glowing top." The doorbell rang, and Maddie set her cup down, almost spilling her coffee in her lap. "Uh-oh, someone's here. I hope it's not my brothers checking up on me."

"If it's Lance, tell him I'm going to drop by and see him later today."

Maddie hung up, then tucked her feet in her fuzzy bedroom slippers and hobbled to the door, cursing Greg for nearly breaking her toe with his weighted shoes. One glance outside, and she knew her brief reprieve was over—Lance and Chase stood on her doorstep, hunched over in the rain. Lightning illuminated the porch, highlighting her brother's fierce scowl. Chase kept his head tilted downward, raindrops sliding off his jaw and plopping onto his worn boots. She had a good mind to leave them both outside and let them drown.

Lance reached up and pounded on the door, though, and she realized her neighbors would be complaining if she didn't answer. Heaving a sigh, she brushed her hair out of her eyes and opened the door. Lance pushed past her, dripping water all over her floor as he strode in. Chase hesitated, then wiped his feet and followed. Without waiting for an invitation, Lance poured himself a cup of coffee and handed one to Chase. While Lance searched for the sugar dish, Maddie stared at Chase. He was still wearing his eye patch, which reminded her of her erotic dream—he was a pirate in a secret tunnel, wearing nothing but that patch—

Obviously aware of her gaze, his hand adjusted the black triangle. "Uh, I have to wear it a few more days," he mumbled sheepishly.

She quirked an eyebrow, trying to remind herself to treat him like a big brother. Nothing more. But her traitorous tongue betrayed her. "After that visit to the Pirate's House, I thought maybe you decided you liked it."

His gaze latched with hers, dark and dangerous, and she saw when he caught the connection. His mouth quirked sideways in that sexy half-smile, but his good eye strayed and landed on the couch. More exactly on the black silk robe she'd stolen from Greg Pugh. Greg's initials seemed to glare back at her.

Chase's half-smile evaporated. Panicking at the thought of Lance seeing the man's robe, Maddie grabbed it and shoved it beneath the cushion, then sat down on top of it just as Lance turned, slowly sipping his coffee.

Who sent the flowers, shortstop?" Chase asked.

Maddie bit down on her lip. "Jeff."

Chase raised a brow.

Lance pushed the paper toward her. "Explain that."

"What?" Maddie opened the paper and stifled a gasp when she saw the front page. Remembering Greg Pugh and his toupee and bridge, laughter bubbled up inside her and spilled out.

"What the hell's so funny?" Lance asked.

Maddie shoved the paper toward him. "This."

"I don't see the humor." Lance paced across the floor. "What were you doing at this weirdo's house like *that*? And what does this mean—you're his latest conquest?"

She couldn't argue with the weirdo part. But his conquest? "I wasn't his conquest."

Chase snarled. "Well, hell you're all over each other—"

"We were just dancing, Lance."

"How did you meet him?"

Maddie felt the first embers of her temper flare, but ignored them, reminding herself she'd extricate herself from the situation faster if she offered a quick explanation. They didn't have to know everything. "Sophie introduced us. She works with him at the station."

Lance cursed. "I should have known that woman had something to do with this."

"That woman?" Maddie's control snapped. "That woman has a name—Sophie Lane. She's my friend, Lance. I don't know what you have against her, but I expect you to be nice to her." She swung her hand toward the door. "Now, if you can't respect me and my friends, get out."

Lance's eyes widened in alarm and shock. Chase sat stoically, his one-eyed gaze level with the sofa. Maddie glanced down in horror and realized the black belt was dangling from the cushion like a snake, almost touching the floor.

She raised her head a notch, pleading with Chase to help her out. "Chase, can't you make my macho, pigheaded brother understand that I'm a grown woman now?"

"She's a grown woman now," Chase said in a curt voice, his gaze locked to that black belt. "Besides, we have work to do, Lance."

Lance and Chase exchanged looks Maddie didn't quite understand, but Maddie was grateful when Lance conceded to Chase.

Chase sipped his coffee, staring at her over the rim of his mug. "It's raining, so I thought maybe we could look over the designs you've done so far." His shoulders lifted in a small shrug. "I want to make sure we're on the same track."

Maddie's temper deflated. "You're really interested?"

"Of course." He snatched a bagel, bit into it and gave Lance a pointed look. "This project's got to be the most important thing to all of us right now. More important than our personal lives."

Maddie nodded. "At least we agree on something."

"Mad, listen, I'm just worried." Lance's withered expression tore at Maddie. "It can't look good for your business to be associated with this character, Pugh. Do you know what his show is about?"

Maddie refused to tell him she knew a lot more about Greg Pugh than he did. "Yes, I know."

He frowned, but lowered his voice to that concerned, protective tone that always mellowed her anger. How could she stay mad at him for loving her? Heck, she was mad at Chase, because he *didn't* love her.

"So, are you serious about him?"

Laughter swelled in her chest, but she bottled it. Let them think the guy was a catch and that he was interested in her. "It was just a party, Lance." Lance stood to get more coffee, and she quickly stuffed the robe belt under the cushion, then placed her coffee cup on the counter. "Now, I'm going to shower and dress so Chase and I can get to work."

She felt Chase's eyes watching her as she left the room. And she couldn't help but wonder what *he* had thought of the picture.

Three hours later. Chase had reviewed all the mock-up boards Maddie had made and somehow let her talk him into accompanying her on a buying trip. Just to make sure he approved of things for the model homes, she'd said. Plus, she wanted to get an idea of his tastes and maybe select a few items for his house. Heck, there wasn't much he didn't approve of—except the fact that the night before while he'd been lying in bed alone, she'd had some other man's hands crawling up her skirt.

But her work had really poleaxed him—while he'd expected outlandish or eclectic, she had practically reproduced the original furnishings of some of the antebellum homes. He nodded as she pointed to a painting of a Roman goddess she wanted for the dining room of the Italian Renaissance house, barely cognizant of her chattering away about furniture and accessories and color choices. Not her choice in men. She'd been treating him like a big brother ever since that pirate comment. And she hadn't ventured onto the topic of the photo or the robe. He hadn't dared to mention them either for fear she'd think he cared.

And he didn't. Did he?

Ever since he'd seen that damn picture, he'd been battling the oddest feeling. A twinge that kept nagging at him like a bad headache coming on, but it pressed against his heart and burned up through his throat, then sank back down to his gut and made his stomach feel like it was on fire.

A feeling he thought might be jealousy.

But how could a man be jealous of something he'd never had? Or never had the right to have. Or didn't even really want.

Or did he—did he really want Maddie?

Ye—hell, no.

He was glad she'd suddenly started treating him like a friend again. That was exactly what he wanted. An uncomplicated personal life so he could concentrate on business. He would not wind up ruining his life for a woman like his old man had, especially if Maddie only wanted to date him as a rebellious act against her brothers.

He wanted to be successful, to show the folks of Savannah he wasn't just a poor white trash, orphan little boy. Nothing else mattered. So, he'd never had family, well, except for Lance and Reid. They were all he needed. *The Terrible Three—bachelors forever.*

"Chase, what do you think about this vase? It's imported—"

"It's fine."

Maddie planted her small fists on her hips. "But you didn't even look at it."

"I guess you convinced me you know what you're talking about."

A pleased, almost grateful smile spread on her face. "Really?"

He made a gallant effort to avoid her gaze. Something magnetic about her eyes . . . "Yeah, really."

"Oh, Chase, I'm so glad." She blushed. "For some reason I was afraid you were actually coming along because you didn't trust me. I even . . ."

"Even what?"

"Even wondered if my brothers put you up to it, you know, made you baby-sit me in case I screwed up. But even they wouldn't do something so devious, now would they?"

He winced inwardly, a mountain of guilt welling in his chest.

She indicated her briefcase. "Thank heavens I'm wrong."

But she wasn't. And she would be crushed if she discovered the truth.

"Now, follow me. There's this divine four-poster bed I want to show you."

A bed? Had Maddie just said she wanted to take him to bed?

"Come on, old man. See if you can keep up."

Old man?

She talked nonstop about furniture and bedding and vases and crystal while they walked, the earlier intimate flirting vacant from her eyes and voice. So, she was going to treat him like a pal. Great.

Good. Fine. That was exactly what he wanted.

She grabbed his hand and led him out of the store, down two blocks to a small antique mart. When he walked inside, he felt as if he'd stepped back in time.

Antiques and period pieces filled the store along with collector's items, French tapestries and a corner full of Revolutionary War paraphernalia. Maddie dragged him upstairs past Belgium lace canopies and ornate antique mirrors to a section of period bedroom furniture. When Maddie explained she was a decorator and planned to make several purchases but wanted time alone to study the merchandise, the saleslady excused herself to let them browse.

Suddenly, Maddie sprawled on top of the white lace-draped mattress, waving a hand at the ornately carved headboard and explaining the time period. "It's a replica of the bed Duncan Phyfe made for his daughter. It'll be perfect in the Georgian estate, don't you think?

Chase nodded, his gaze glued to Maddie's body stretched seductively on the pristine comforter, her long legs beckoning from beneath that slinky black skirt. As she reached above her to point to the carving, the satin fabric of her sleeveless blouse hugged her breasts and slid over the generous mounds, tightening across the peaks with every breath she took.

His own breath collected in his lungs.

She seemed oblivious.

"Just imagine how romantic this will look by that circular fireplace you designed, Chase. Whoever buys the house will love it." She propped on one elbow, her gorgeous hair tumbling around her shoulders. "With firelight glowing all around, the golden grain of the wood will sparkle."

Just like her eyes.

"I'd put an antique clawfoot tub in the master suite."

For a nice warm bath in the evening. He'd dribble water over her breasts, then lick the moisture away with his tongue.

"And a Victorian dressing table for the lady with decorative perfume bottles arranged on a silver tray," she murmured.

He'd squirt the bottled fragrance behind her delicate earlobe, then nibble at the soft, sensitive column of her neck.

She continued, not bothering to wait for his reply. "A gentleman's wardrobe in the corner, a lady's lacy chemise and garter scattered at the foot of the bed."

The garter he'd just removed from her long legs. He'd trail kisses all the way up her thighs.

"So, what do you think? You think I should buy it?"

God, she was killing him.

"Chase?"

"Oh, yeah."

"What kind of bed would you like in your house?"

Any bed with her on it. "I don't know, I can't really think right now."

"Well, let's pick some other things first then." Maddie sprang up and pointed to a bearskin rug in the corner. The rug seemed decadent, out of place with the antique furnishings.

"You want to put that rug beside the Duncan Phyfe bed?" Chase's voice squeaked.

Maddie shook her head. "No, the owner bought this at a flea market and planned to take it home for himself, but I thought it might go in your house, Chase. I figured you might want to buy a little more contemporary furniture. Wouldn't it look great next to the Jacuzzi, especially with the black-and-white tiles?"

The guys would laugh themselves silly if he put that bearskin rug in his house.

"Chase?"

"Uh, yeah." *But he would love it.*

She lay her hand on the soft white fur and began to stroke it up and down with her long red fingernails, eliciting tempting mental pictures of her stroking his back, his chest, his . . . "You could also put it in the bedroom. It would be nice for long, cozy nights by the fire. You could stretch out after a hard day's work."

And let her massage his aching muscles.

She ran her fingers over the white pile, stroking the fur so it fluffed up and down. "You should try it out. It's so soft and thick and plush, it feels wonderful next to your skin."

Just like she would.

"Go ahead, take off your shoes and walk on it."

He shrugged off his boots, and tested the rug with his feet, smiling at how his toes sank into the thick pile.

"What do you think? You want me to ask the lady to put it on hold?"

Oh, yeah. And, if she'd just sprawl out there naked with him on top of it, everything would be perfect.

"So, what do you think, Lance?"

"It's nice." Lance tried to concentrate on the house Sophie had just shown him, but it was damn difficult when she was standing in front of him looking as sexy as a centerfold—and she was completely dressed. Sophie tucked a stand of her short, spiked hair behind an earlobe, her silver earrings dangling with the movement.

Why did she have to have those jet-black eyelashes and those emerald-green eyes, which sparkled like stones covered in soft raindrops? And that innocent little look that wasn't innocent at all?

"Nice?" Sophie laughed, a soft musical sound that stirred his nether regions. "It's in pretty bad shape,

Lance, but I bought this house for a bargain, and I figure you can help me restore it."

Lance ran his hand along the paint-peeled walls. "You've talked to Mrs. Howard at the historical society?"

"Yes, she's a doll. I've gotten information on the original owners and photos of the woodwork, flooring, moldings, even the tapestries that covered the walls. I'm going to copy as much as I can." She sashayed toward him and placed one clunky heel on the bottom step of the staircase. He couldn't help but notice the way her short maroon skirt hugged her butt and rose to reveal the sexiest little knees he'd ever seen. And he could span her waist with both his hands.

"I just love the Victorian era," Sophie said. "All the attention to detail, the fretwork, all the curved windows and doorways."

Lance shifted onto the balls of his feet, forcing himself to study the grainy wood of the stairwell. "You know they say this house is haunted?"

Sophie glanced at the banister and ran her finger along the slick surface. "I've heard the stories." A dreamy look settled in her eyes. "Something about star-crossed lovers never being able to be with each other because of the war."

Lance nodded. "A British soldier was wounded. When he was injured, the young woman who lived here took him in and hid him, but once he recovered, he had to return to battle. He probably went back to England or died in the war."

"They say her spirit lingers here, waiting for him to return," Sophie said in a low voice. "It's so incredibly sad."

Lance jammed his hands in his pockets. "You don't really believe in that nonsense, do you?"

Sophie quirked an eyebrow. "You mean in true love?"

He would not discuss the *L* word with this woman. Why, she'd already started corrupting his little sister. He certainly wouldn't let her sink her claws into him. "I mean in ghosts."

Sophie leaned against the weathered paneling. "Yes, I believe in ghosts."

This time he raised a brow.

"I think we all have things in our past we want to keep quiet. Issues unsettled, problems that haunt us." Her gaze became hooded, those long eyelashes curling along her ivory skin. She continued in a soft, husky voice, "Secrets that we don't want anyone to know. Wouldn't you agree, Lance?"

Lance's heart thudded to a painful halt, then resumed double-time. He wanted to trust her, but the person he'd trusted the most, his own dad, had deceived him and his family. His dad hadn't been the loyal husband they'd thought; he'd had habits that would have shocked his patients and Reid and Maddie. Had his mother known?

Sophie was still smiling at him, waiting expectantly, hoping to lure him into her trap. She loved hot topics for her show, he still remembered the one about the transvestite Methodist ministers, and then he'd seen the tail end of a volatile episode where several wives had announced on the air they were lesbians.

No, he couldn't get close to Sophie, he couldn't trust her.

In fact, after learning about his father, how could he trust anyone again? Why, he barely trusted Reid and Chase. But they were his blood brothers—they would never let him down or keep anything from him. Thank God.

The serious tone of her voice, the way she kept watching him with those intense liquid eyes—what had she meant? Did Sophie Lane have secrets of her own? Or was she trying to get him to reveal his family secrets?

Or maybe she was hinting that she already knew them.

Chapter Fourteen

Maddie sipped her cappuccino, trying to decide why Chase had been looking at her so oddly while they'd been shopping. At first, she thought he'd been bored to death, but he'd perked up when they'd toured that last antique shop. He'd really liked that four-poster bed and the bearskin rug. What other kinds of things did he like?

She gazed across the river, enjoying their view from the outdoor cafe where they'd stopped for lunch. She had to do something to avoid watching Chase. Sightseers and locals strolled the riverfront edge, lingering to taste the Savannah delicacies or bask in the beautiful spring weather. Tulips sprang up along the shore edge and colorful pansies lined the flower boxes along the storefronts while the breeze from the river fluttered the budding new leaves.

Chase cut into the piece of chocolate pie he'd ordered, lifted the fork to his mouth and made a soft little moan of pleasure, drawing her gaze to his lips, which of course, made her remember their last mouth-watering kiss on her porch. His gaze caught hers, and she instantly glanced at the table, wiping at the perspiration beading on her forehead. Springtime temperatures were always comfortable, ranging from the low sixties to the seventies. But working in close quarters with Chase seemed to jack the heat index up to the hundreds.

Think of him as that other big brother. Focus on work.

"Chase, if I'm going to decorate your house, I really need to know your tastes. Do you have anything specific in mind?"

Like her stretched across that bearskin rug? Sex and sin and a night full of passion they'd both always remember.

There went that odd look again.

He let the pie slide into his mouth, chewed thoughtfully, then swallowed. "Not really."

Maddie licked a dollop of foam off her coffee, her gaze riveted to Chase's when she noticed him follow the movement. "What? Do I have cream on my nose?"

He swallowed audibly. "No."

"Then what? Why do you keep staring at me like that?"

This time he looked away, focusing on a ship docking at the harbor. "No reason."

Maddie sighed. He really didn't want to get personal with her, did he? Oh, well, two could play that game. "I'm simply interested in knowing what kind of furniture you want, Chase, so when I'm shopping, if I spot something you want, I can make a deal."

He ate another bite of the dark-chocolate pie, licking his lips at the rich, sweet taste, making Maddie almost groan. She'd always believed chocolate was a sexual experience when *she* ate it, but she'd never imagined watching someone else consume a slice of pie could be so titillating. Of course, she'd never watched Chase eat before. He might not be the flower-sending kind of guy, but he devoured the dessert slowly, seeming to savor each bite, the rich, delicate flavor, the fluffy almost erotic texture, as if he wanted the pleasurable sensation to last. Would he treat a woman the same way in bed?

She forked a spoonful of her own chocolate sundae, licking the dark syrup with her tongue.

"I just want some basic stuff," Chase finally said.

Basic, as in him on top, her on the bottom?

"Not antiques or anything fancy or impractical. I want to be able to sit on the couch, not show it off."

Maddie blinked, trying to remember what she'd asked him. Oh, yeah, the furniture. "You have a color scheme in mind?"

His sideways frown made her laugh. "Sorry, I guess I should rephrase that. What is your favorite color?"

"Brown?"

She narrowed her eyes. "Brown?"

"Uh, I mean blue. I . . . I was looking at . . . nothing."

"You were looking at what, Chase?"

"At your eyes," he said sheepishly. "They're so dark brown sometimes, just like that chocolate syrup on the corner of your mouth." He reached out and wiped the drop off with his thumb, then sucked the tip of his thumb clean. A tingling sensation started in the pit of Maddie's stomach and swirled through her abdomen. "Then other times when the sunlight plays off your eyes, they turn a lighter shade, like caramel candy."

The heat spread through her body, settling in her thighs. Now, she understood that look—lust. On some primal level Chase didn't want to admit because of her brothers, he did want to sleep with her.

Only he'd been right in calling a halt to their lovemaking the other day.

If she made love with him, she'd probably fall for him and wind up getting hurt, then their working relationship would be ruined. And her brothers . . . whew. They'd have a fit. No—getting involved with Chase wasn't a good idea. Besides, he was too much like her brothers and she wanted . . . she wanted independence, to enjoy her freedom. Not to fall in love with an overprotective, macho ladies' man, die-hard bachelor.

She'd just have to look for someone else—

Had Jeff been serious about a reconciliation? Should she consider seeing him again? He did have some romantic tendencies, but . . .

Maybe she'd keep looking.

"Sorry," Chase mumbled. "That was out of line."

"No problem," Maddie said. "You were right the other night, Chase. Us being together would have been a big mistake."

His dark eyes locked with hers, forceful and penetrating. That lonely, emptiness that seemed to haunt him returned with a vengeance.

"So, let's talk furniture. Do you want fabric for your sofa or leather?"

"Leather."

"Dark colors or light?"

"Dark."

"How about the kitchen? Wallpaper? Paint?"

He shrugged. "Plain white walls."

"What? Not even a stripe or maybe a hunter green?"

"I'm a plain kind of guy, Maddie."

Maddie sipped her cappuccino, trying to let that comment slide. But she couldn't resist. "Plain isn't so bad, Chase."

His dark eyes fell to his coffee. "But you like the exciting type, don't you, Mad? That TV producer? The wuss with his pansies?"

"They were roses."

Chase harrumphed. "Or the guy who took you to the nudist colony?"

Maddie flushed. "How did you know about the nudist colony?"

Chase's face suddenly paled. "Uh . . . oh, your brothers were worried and actually the name of the place showed up on Lance's caller ID."

Maddie's eyes narrowed to slits. "You guys didn't come up there, did you?"

Chase sipped his drink, looking shocked. "Of course not."

Maddie continued to stare at him, wondering why he refused to meet her eyes. She had a feeling she knew—he was feeling guilty about spying on her.

"Okay," he finally admitted. "Lance and Reid wanted to, but I talked them out of making the trip. I wouldn't set foot in a place like that."

"What? I didn't think you were shy, Chase."

He glared at her. "I'm not, but I like nude parties to be in private."

Maddie nodded, deciding to go along with him. "Well, Chase, thanks for not coming. I can't tell you . . . well, how awkward and embarrassing it would have been if they had charged up there after me."

Chase nodded but shifted nervously, downing his drink, confirming her suspicions.

Maddie drummed her fingers on the table and almost burst into laughter at his reaction—Chase Holloway was a rotten liar. The Terrible Three had snuck into that nudist colony, had gotten caught with their pants down, literally, and had been thrown out for acting like Peeping Toms!

She sipped her drink, stifling laughter, but the door behind her opened, and she saw Chase's shoulders stiffen. Following his gaze, she pivoted in her seat, surprised to see Jeff walk in with a young brunette. Jeff's eyes widened when he noticed her, his lips pursing together tightly a fraction of a second before he gathered his composure. With a stiff nod of his head to acknowledge her presence, he leaned over and spoke to the woman beside him. Then they headed their way. Maddie turned back to Chase, hoping Jeff would bypass them and not make the situation awkward.

"How about your bedroom and the master bath? Some kind of paisley or navy?"

"Whatever goes with the rug," he said in a husky voice.

She and Chase, naked and writhing on top of it.

"I've always pictured—"

Jeff paused by their table, interrupting Chase. "Maddie, how nice to see you."

She pasted on a gracious smile. "Jeff, what a surprise. You know Chase Holloway, don't you?"

Jeff offered Chase a tight hello. "How could I forget, the troublemaker from Savannah High. How many times did you get arrested in high school?"

Maddie's hands tightened around her cup.

A vein pulsed in Chase's clenched jaw.

"He's an architect now," Maddie said pointedly. "We're working together on the Tour of Homes."

"Oh, right."

The woman beside Jeff cleared her throat as if she suddenly realized she was being left out of the conversation. "Mr. Oglethorpe, is this the interior decorator you said you were going to introduce me to?"

Jeff finally dragged his gaze from Chase. "Yes, Cynthia. This is Maddie Summers."

The woman's smile seemed sincere. She reached out and shook Maddie's hand. "Nice to meet you, Maddie. I'm the new loan officer with the savings department. Mr. Oglethorpe has been showing me the ropes."

Maddie heard Chase mumble something that sounded like, "I'll bet he has."

"Anyway, Mr. Oglethorpe mentioned he had a friend who was in the decorating business, and I just moved here so I'm looking for a decorator."

Maddie twisted her napkin in her lap. "Have you purchased a home?"

"Yes, my first, and I'm so excited! It's a little town house off Baker Street, but I do want to fix it up, and I'm color-blind. Would you mind helping me out? Jeff . . ." She hesitated and blushed. "I mean Mr. Oglethorpe has raved about how talented you are."

"I'll bet he has," Chase mumbled again, this time not bothering to muffle his comment.

Maddie quirked a brow at Jeff, shooting a dark look at Chase. He leaned back in his chair and folded his arms, looking perturbed. "I'd love to," Maddie said sincerely. She pulled out a business card and handed it to the woman. Jeff shifted sideways, waving at the maître d' that they were ready to be seated.

"I'll call you for an appointment," Cynthia said.

Maddie nodded. "Jeff, thanks for the recommendation."

"I do want you to succeed, Maddie." Jeff flashed

her a brilliant smile as the maître d' approached. "Well, we have some business to discuss so we'll let you get back to your . . . whatever."

"Maddie and I were talking about my bedroom," Chase said.

Jeff's mouth snapped tight. He quickly turned and followed Cynthia and the waiter.

Maddie gaped at Chase. "I can't believe you said that."

Chase scowled. "I can't believe you fell for that wuss's nice-guy act. And what was he talking about—he meant what he said the other day? And he's going to call you?"

"Why do you think he was acting?" Maddie asked, avoiding his question.

"Because he was," Chase mumbled. "He's up to something; I just can't figure out what it is."

"Maybe he really wants me back," Maddie said. "Some men find me attractive you know, Chase. And he has been sending me gifts."

"You are attractive, Maddie, but you deserve better than some sneaky wuss." Chase rammed his hand through his hair. "Are you going to talk to him when he calls?"

Maddie lifted one shoulder non-chalantly. "Why not? You keep pushing me away."

"That's because I don't want you using me to rebel against your brothers," Chase hissed.

Maddie balled her napkin onto the table. "You're so suspicious, Chase. Don't you trust anyone?"

His troubled gaze fell to his hands, answering her question. She barely resisted the urge to tell him he could trust her.

But she didn't know if she trusted herself where Chase was concerned. And Jeff?

Maddie glanced over her shoulder, remembering

Jeff's invitation the other day to see her again. Had he really changed his mind about her career? Did he really want her back, or could he have some sort of secret agenda?

Reid couldn't believe he'd nixed a date with Tracy, the sexy blond secretary from Wade's Roofing Company, for a meeting with Jeff Oglethorpe, but for once, his family had to come first. Maddie was out of control. Going to nudist colonies, cavorting with producers of S & M shows. Their mother was probably rolling over in her grave.

She'd wanted the best for Maddie—a secure family life and husband like she'd had. Or like she'd thought she had. A seed of guilt nagged at him—had their mother known about their father's little indiscretion? Not that he'd been unfaithful exactly but well, the . . . no, he couldn't bear to think about his father doing such . . . such tawdry stuff. He still remembered his dad as the respected, distinguished doctor everyone admired, exactly the memory he wanted to keep. Images of him involved in the elicit behavior suggested in the file he'd found were unthinkable. Fathers just didn't do stuff like that.

Maddie and Lance would be shocked.

Determined to do all he could to make sure his mother's wishes for Maddie came true, he stepped inside the Shrimp Store and scanned the room for Oglethorpe. The spicy scent of Creole and fishy scent of shrimp, clam chowder and other seafood permeated the air, making his stomach growl. He'd missed lunch on account of battling with two painting contractors over a bungled job, and he was a man who had to eat, or he got ornery. He ran a hand through his hair, weary. Every day this week had been filled with problems on the job. He was almost convinced someone was trying to sabotage their success. As soon as he left Oglethorpe, he was going to phone Smaltz and ask him to investigate the problems.

He allowed the waitress to seat him at a corner table and nursed a beer while he waited. Twenty minutes later, he ordered an appetizer of fried shrimp and oysters, wondering if Oglethorpe would even show. Of course, he wouldn't blame the guy after their last encounter. They had been pretty rough on him following that TV disaster. He'd probably have to suck up big time.

He'd just polished off the hush puppies and the last of the shrimp when he spotted Oglethorpe walking in. The man's stiff posture and stony gaze did not look promising. And Reid instantly realized he should have changed from his work clothes. Next to Oglethorpe's designer suit and neat haircut, he resembled a field hand, or a construction worker . . . which he basically was.

"I can't imagine why you wanted to see me." Oglethorpe stopped beside the table, narrowing his eyes in disdain. "I thought I'd seen the end of you Summers boys."

Reid clamped his mouth shut to control his temper. Did the guy have to sound so condescending?

"I'll have a bourbon," Oglethorpe told the waitress. "On the rocks."

She nodded and bustled away while Jeff planted himself in the chair.

"I appreciate you coming," Reid said.

"Make it brief, Summers. I'm a busy man."

As if he really wanted to do this. He didn't especially like this man, he realized. *But he's successful and respectable, the type of man Mom would have wanted Maddie to marry. Just suck it up. Maddie must have been in love with him, or she wouldn't have given him that ultimatum on* Sophie Knows.

"Listen, man, we got carried away that day after the show. We were worried about Maddie . . . we've always been protective of her."

Oglethorpe's steady gaze didn't waver as he accepted his drink.

"You can understand, right? With our folks being gone, we've always had to take care of her."

Oglethorpe's expression softened slightly.

"And we're still worried about her."

The ice in Oglethorpe's drink clinked as he raised his glass.

"I guess you saw the newspaper picture?"

A pained look crossed his face. "Yes."

"Maddie's been dating around," Reid admitted.

"You mean she's become loose?"

Reid's fingers curled into fists. "No, of course not."

"But you're worried she will?"

He contemplated his dad's secret side. What if Maddie had a secret side just waiting to emerge? "We want what's best for her."

Oglethorpe traced a finger along his glass. "So, why did you call me?"

Reid's throat burned with the effort to speak. "Because you may be it."

"I may be what?"

"What's best for Maddie."

Oglethorpe leaned forward, his eyebrows climbing his forehead. "Let me get this straight: One day you want to kill me, the next you're giving me your approval." A sarcastic laugh escaped his thin lips. "I might be grateful, except you've forgotten one thing. Maddie broke up with me."

"Only because you didn't want her to work."

"I wanted us to discuss the situation." Oglethorpe

stiffened, adjusting his red tie. "But I've changed my mind. I've already talked to Maddie, and I've been trying to make things up with her. I've sent her flowers and gifts every other day."

Reid shrugged. "Sounds like a plan."

"Exactly."

"Then maybe you and Maddie could work this out. She's impulsive, always hopping from one thing to another. This decorating thing may just be another one of her whims."

"You think she'll give it up—"

"I don't know. I hope Maddie's found her calling, and if she has, maybe you could compromise. You could always have your parties catered. And Maddie's a great conversationalist."

"That's true." A smile finally lifted Oglethorpe's mouth. "In fact, I've been thinking along those lines myself. An attractive, successful woman can be an asset to any man in the business world."

Reid tipped his drink back, feeling smug. After all, he really did want to see his sister happy. And even though he'd never be best buds with Oglethorpe, he supposed women thought him a good catch. And if Maddie did decide to drop the business, he'd done her a favor by smoothing things over with her old boyfriend. Better to have her safe with Oglethorpe than running around nudist colonies with naked strangers or cavorting with producers of S & M shows.

Chapter Fifteen

"I love my business," Maddie told Sophie over coffee two days later. "I already have color schemes planned for all four houses, and I've ordered the window treatments and most of the furnishings. Plus I have two clients that aren't a part of the Tour of Homes."

"Who?"

"Noisy Nora, that lady who believes in ghosts. I'm meeting her later today. Actually her house is in the same subdivision as the tour, but she purchased on one of the other streets."

"Sounds like things are going great."

"And Cynthia, a new loan officer who works with Jeff."

"The old boyfriend?"

Maddie nodded.

"You aren't interested in reconciling with him, are you?"

"I'm not sure." Maddie blotted a drop of white powdery sugar from her pastry and licked it off her finger. "I'm trying to keep an open mind. Especially since Chase keeps me at a distance."

"So, has Jeff changed?"

"He says he has. He recommended my services to his co-worker, so maybe he's decided to respect my work. And he's been sending me flowers and romantic cards almost every day. He even sent me imported perfume today."

Sophie squeezed lemon in her tea. "He sounds determined."

"I still haven't forgiven him for making me put Mom's jewelry up for collateral though, and I haven't told the boys, so I have to make enough to recoup my investment and get it back before they find out."

"Sounds like you're off to a good start."

The rich scent of chocolate drifted toward Maddie from a neighboring table, and Maddie thought of Chase, then instantly forced him from her mind. "So, what's up with you? Been seeing that hunky blonde you were dancing with at the party the other night?"

Sophie tapped her fingernails on the table. "No, turn's out he's gay."

Maddie sighed dramatically. "What a waste."

"Then Thursday night I went out with this guy named Rob."

"A hopeful?"

"Not even close." Sophie laughed, propped her elbow on the table and leaned her chin on her hand. "Get this—I was really impressed at first. When he showed up, he was wearing an Armani suit and arrived in a Porsche. And he brought me imported chocolates."

"Wow."

"But the suit belonged to his roommate. Then I found out he works for a candy company. He keeps all the leftovers and outdated candy in his apartment and gives them as gifts. He had a huge box of chocolate-covered cherries in his trunk."

Maddie chuckled. "Chump."

"Tell me about it. Chocolate had melted all over the floor of his car. It looked like a puddle of . . . you know."

Maddie laughed again. "What about the Porsche?"

"A loaner." Sophie shook her head in disgust. "He was trying to make a good impression."

"Another case of male fraud."

"Definitely." Sophie snapped her fingers. "Which reminds me—what did you do with Greg's robe? I heard him telling someone in the green room it was missing."

"I'm still trying to figure out how to return the danged thing without him knowing I took it."

Sophie chewed the tip of her fingernail. "I certainly don't want to go to his house again."

"Maybe I should mail it."

"I have a better idea—keep it as a souvenir. Or you could lay it across your bed to make other men jealous."

Maddie remembered Chase's reaction. No, he couldn't have been jealous—he was too adamant about his brotherly relationship. "I don't know, Soph. I had a heck of a time keeping the truth from Lance. My brothers would totally freak if they knew about that night. When I think of hiding in that man's shower . . ."

They both burst into laughter. Finally Sophie said, "I'm beginning to think you're right. There aren't any normal men left in Savannah."

"Except for my brothers." And Chase. "And they've got this moronic bachelor pact they made when they were younger that they claim to live by. I don't know who thought of it, but I'd like to ring all their necks."

"So they've sworn never to marry," Sophie murmured miserably.

Maddie made a face. "I was hoping you could change Lance's mind, Sophie. He needs a good woman to add some excitement to his life. He's way too serious."

"I don't think Lance and I will ever happen, Mad." Sophie frowned in thought. "When I showed him the house the other day, I got the distinct impression he didn't trust me."

"Why wouldn't he trust you?"

"I have no idea. But he definitely acted as if I had the plague or something. I guess he just doesn't like me."

Maddie covered her friend's hand with her own. Although Sophie didn't whine or complain about her past, Maddie knew it hadn't been a happy one. Still, she was the most upbeat person she'd ever met. "How could he not like you, Sophie? You're smart and talented and gorgeous. Half of Savannah's male population drools over you every day when they watch your show."

Sophie's mouth twisted. "Your brother certainly isn't one of them. He must not find me attractive at all."

Maddie stewed over Sophie's comment. Sophie would be perfect for Lance. Why wouldn't he at least give her a chance?

Lance studied the layout of Sophie's house and all the renovations needed, jotted down the estimated costs, and made a note to call her and set up a meeting. He ran a hand through his hair and sighed, dreading the conversation already. If only he didn't find the woman so damn attractive, he'd be able to turn this deal down and tell her where to go. But he'd better meet with her and try and find out what she knew about his family. Reid was too gullible and might be swayed by her sexuality. Besides, his younger brother still thought of their dad as some hero; destroying that boy's image of his father didn't sit well with Lance at all. And Sophie could do just that if she aired their dirty family secrets on TV.

He gathered his files and hurried to his Blazer. Fifteen minutes later, he rushed into the town planning meeting, grateful to see Chase and Reid already seated. The committee had phoned him, asking questions about two of the restoration projects, griping about the moulding they'd chosen for the parlor, the flooring for one of the kitchens, even the stones they'd used to build the mantel. The guidelines were stringent, but Lance figured they'd been lucky to win five of the ten accounts, and he planned to make the citizens of Savannah proud of the fact they had shown faith in their company. Only judging from the expressions on Chase's and Reid's faces, things weren't going well.

"We expect every detail to be put before the committee," Ross Pierceson, the head of the committee said. "Maintaining the history of Savannah and the original architecture is our prime concern. We will not allow structural changes that interfere with the basic lines developed by our ancestors."

"We're not talking about changing historical details," Chase said in a patient voice, "but for safety reasons, the foundation of the Rhinehold house has to be redone. We'll make every effort to restore—"

"I want to see each change detailed in writing and be kept abreast of your plans every step of the way." Mr. Pierceson interrupted.

"You've seen our plans," Reid snapped. "You know we will adhere to the committee's restrictions. Why are you being so difficult?"

"Those lights at the Butler mansion are the wrong style," Elvira Huddle said.

"And I believe you should have used granite in the entryway of the Hudson room, not Italian marble," Bobby Bruins added.

"Lord only knows what that Maddie Summers will do when she starts decorating the beautiful mansion," Lilith Palmer said. "She didn't do well in history in high school."

"What does that have to do with anything?" Reid asked.

"Maddie knows what she's doing," Lance said.

"He's right," Chase agreed. "Besides, I researched those houses myself. According to the files I found on the history of the Butler house, every detail is correct."

Paulette Rhoder patted her funnel silver hair. "Gentlemen, you don't need to be rude. Need I remind you, this project can be turned over to someone else?"

"I don't understand why they were given the job anyway," Marvin Mullins mumbled. "Bunch of troublemakers."

Chase and Reid both stiffened, squaring their shoulders as if for combat.

"Did you see the front page?" Lilith murmured. "Maddie Summers draped all over that TV producer like some two-bit saloon girl."

"Even worse than that TV debacle where she embarrassed that nice Jeffrey Oglethorpe. His mother still hasn't recovered from what that hussy did to her son."

Chase slammed his fist on the table. "Maddie is not a hussy!"

Lance stepped forward, his hand held up in warning. "We'll follow your guidelines, but I don't want to hear another defamatory comment about our character, especially my sister's."

The room fell into a strained silence. Reid was the first one out of the door, Chase on his heels. Lance followed, surprised at the vehemence Chase had used to defend Maddie.

Then again, why should he be surprised? They had asked Chase to watch out for Maddie—his reaction simply proved his best friend was doing as they'd asked.

Chase leaned against his pickup, pinched the bridge of his nose and bowed his head, trying to calm himself. How dare those old biddies talk about Maddie like that.

If they wanted to criticize him, well, let them go ahead. He was used to it. He'd heard their gossip all his life. Their hurtful words rose to haunt him. *The little orphan boy. His mama didn't want him. He's mean just like his daddy. Won't never amount to anything. Won't no good girl in town ever want to marry him. Can you imagine if he did get married and have kids—what would he do? Take them to see their granddaddy in jail every Sunday? His kids would be ashamed of him.*

"Chase, Reid, come here. We have to talk." Lance's voice barely cut through the noise cluttering Chase's mind. But Lance patted him on the back, and Chase winced at the odd expression in his eyes. Had Lance sensed Chase's real feelings for Maddie?

"Thanks for sticking up for Maddie like that." Lance nodded at Chase.

"Yeah," Reid said in an unusually gruff voice. "Can't say how much that means to us."

Guilt once again weighed on Chase. If they knew his unbrotherly thoughts, they'd kill him.

"We can't let this group of busybodies affect our work," Lance said. "We're going to prove they're wrong about all of us."

Chase nodded. Exactly what he intended to do—prove them wrong. He had to keep his goal in mind—making sure the company succeeded so every person in that room would eat their words. They'd been right about him and marriage though—he wouldn't want to have a kid and make him suffer through the ridicule he had. Forget a personal life.

Work was the only thing that mattered.

Work was the only thing that mattered—Maddie mentally repeated the sentiment over and over while Jake curled into a ball and bounced across her wallpaper books.

"*Booooing! Booooing! Booooing!* Look, Mom, I'm a rubber ball."

Nora Ledbetter settled the rocking chair in front of the window. "I see, Jake."

Maddie massaged her right temple where a headache had started to form and pasted on a smile as the three-year-old demolished Maddie's hard efforts in record time. Fabric samples for the window coverings were scattered in a dozen different directions. If ever Maddie wanted to reconsider her career choice, now would be the time.

Just what her brothers would expect her to do—quit. Like she always had before.

Not a chance.

Jake really wasn't a bad little boy, but he needed to be on a playground with other kids, not dragged around and made to sit idly while grown-ups discussed decorating plans. Nora seemed oblivious—she was too busy settling her ghost, Joseph, who she'd brought to see if he approved of the new place, into a corner with the rocking chair, a pipe and the business section of the daily paper.

Maddie had thought she was prepared for today's visit with Nora and her entourage, but first thing, Nora's Saint Bernard, Lulu, had bolted in and pooped on the brand-new white carpet. Then Jake had bounced in, knocking Maddie sideways so she'd stepped in the mess. The day had gone downhill since. From now on, she'd stick an extra pair of shoes in the trunk of her car for emergencies.

"Look, I'm skating." Jake shucked his sneakers in record time and began gliding across the slick floor, swinging his arms and swaying back and forth as if he were on ice skates, singing at the top of his lungs. Nora turned her back on him and pointed to the vibrant walls in the study.

"Joseph doesn't like the teal color so you'll have to change it. He prefers mustard." Nora's bracelets clanged like wind chimes. "And he wants the study furniture to be cherry wood, just like his was when he was alive."

Maddie made a note of everything Nora said, drawing little crazy faces out by the margin. "And what does Mr. Ledbetter want?"

Nora waved a manicured hand. "He doesn't care. He said to do whatever I wanted."

"What does Mr. Ledbetter think about Joseph?"

"Oh, he wants Joseph to be happy so he'll leave us alone at night." Nora's face turned animated. "You see we have a deal with Joseph that if he's happy he doesn't just walk through the walls anytime he wants to—he burst in one time right when . . . well, let's just say, he scared the life out of Mr. Ledbetter, if you know what I mean."

Maddie tried not to imagine the specifics. "I suppose having a ghost in the house would be difficult."

"Look, I'm an airplane!" Jake stretched his pudgy arms out by his sides and began to zoom across the room, making crashing noises each time he banged into a wall.

"Go play your silly games upstairs so we can hear ourselves think," Nora snapped.

Jake's small mouth dropped, but he zoomed even louder as he soared up the steps. He pretended to crash and burn on every other step, prolonging the agony.

Maddie checked her notepad to see what else she needed to discuss with her client. The master bedroom and bath, the dining room and parlor, the five suites upstairs . . . it would take forever. Maybe Jake would play upstairs, and she'd have a few minutes of peace and quiet to get things decided. She reached inside her purse to search for some aspirin but a knock sounded at the door, and she glanced up to see Chase entering the foyer.

Nora's face lit up. "Well, Mr. Holloway, what brings you here?"

Chase nodded in greeting to her, his eyes narrowing when he noticed Maddie's missing shoe. She mouthed, "Don't ask."

He nodded, then smiled at Nora. "I was checking the progress on some of the other houses and noticed you two here. I thought I'd drop by and see how things were going."

Nora began to gush about the house. "The skylights are simply wonderful, and my husband is going to love that hi-tech entertainment system in the basement rec room Maddie suggested. Suspending that wide screen TV so that the screen rotates and you can watch it from anywhere in the room was ingenious."

"I'm glad you—"

"Zooom!" Jake suddenly flew down the stairs, arms extended, *"Zoooom!* Watch out, engine's out of control, I lost a wing!" He careened through the stack of wallpaper books Maddie had brought, sending them flying. Lulu raced behind him, knocking Maddie with her tail. Maddie staggered backward, and Chase reached out to catch her.

"Whoa, partner," Chase called to Jake as he released Maddie. "Better check your pilot's license before the air-traffic police haul you in for reckless driving."

Jake halted and stared at Chase wide-eyed. "You're bigger than my daddy. How tall are you anyway, a hundred feet?"

An amused, almost tender expression crossed Chase's face. "No, I'm six-four."

And every bit muscle, Maddie thought, distractedly.

Jake grinned, shining a hole where his front tooth was missing. Maddie thought of Greg Pugh and his bridge.

"Wow," Jake said. "And you got big feet, too."

Maddie checked her watch, trying to avoid thinking about what other body parts might be big. She'd always heard foot size was proportional to . . .

"Jake, leave Mr. Holloway alone. We're talking."

Jake's excited face fell. Chase ruffled his hair. "It's okay, sport. You made a great airplane."

His tender way with the boy touched a chord inside Maddie, but she refused to think about the reason. She had business to finish. And other houses to decorate for the tour. "Mrs. Ledbetter, if you want the house completed before your husband returns from Europe, we really need to discuss the wall coverings."

Jake tugged at Nora's arm. "Look at me, I'm a power saw." Jake held out his arms and began to make loud buzzing noises.

Nora frowned and picked up a book of wallpaper samples, exclaiming over the floral designs. Maddie saw spots behind her eyes, indicating a migraine. She pressed her fingers to her temple and began to rub in slow circles.

"Hey, bud, you want to come outside with me." Chase scooped up the child and shifted him for a piggyback ride. "I have a bunch of scrap wood and some tools. You could build something while your mama finishes in here."

Jake clasped his arms around Chase's neck. "Can I, Mom?"

Nora rolled her eyes. "Sure, why not. Then maybe I can get something done."

Maddie caught the disapproval on Chase's face and the disappointment on Jake's and realized the woman had once again ignored her son the entire time they'd been there. Chase had been right, the boy simply needed some attention. Or maybe some parenting. He would probably be a different little boy if Nora spent time with him.

Judging from Chase's reaction to the boy, he'd make a good father. But what kind of mother would she make?

She'd heard kids were a lot like animals. Her cat had certainly changed since Maddie had taken him in. When she'd first found him, he'd been mangy and injured and too frightened to let her even touch him.

He'd been hiding in the bushes by her house, mewling and crying, starved and hurt. Was that how Chase had felt when he was little and his mother had abandoned him?

Maddie remembered how long it had taken her to win T. C.'s trust—she'd set out food daily, and had waited until he was ready to accept her touch. It had taken more than three months for him to warm to her, but each day he'd inched a little closer until one day he'd stopped to sniff her feet, and he'd actually let her touch him. From then on, he'd been beside her every minute. Her love and patience had won his devotion. And it had all been worth it.

If she was patient, would Chase learn to trust her someday, too?

Chapter Sixteen

Chase watched Jake hammer the two pieces of wood together, grateful he'd suggested the idea when he saw the excitement on the little boy's face. Where was the child's father? Jake acted as if he'd never been around a man. Did he ever spend time with his dad?

Not that he had any right to judge. He hadn't seen his own dad since he was two. He didn't even remember what he looked like.

"It's an airplane," Jake said, proudly holding up the simple structure. "Thank you, Mr. Hawoway."

"You're certainly welcome, sport."

Jake suddenly threw his arms around Chase and hugged his leg. "You're the bestest."

For a brief moment, Jake's face faded and another child's face slid into view—a little boy who looked up at him with admiring eyes and called him Daddy. A glimpse of a little boy with russet-colored hair and big brown eyes like . . . Maddie's?

He shook himself, jerking his thoughts back to reality. He wasn't husband or father material. His own family had taught him that. Maddie must know it as well.

"Look, it can fly." Jake took off running, holding the crude plane above his shoulders as he made flying sounds. "Up, up and away."

"You're a good builder," Chase said, remembering the first time he'd hammered two pieces of wood together in a similar fashion—the day Lance had let him tag along with him and Reid behind their house. The boys had built planes. Then their imaginations had taken over, and they'd formed the club, The Terrible Three. The following week they'd built a clubhouse for themselves and used it to hold their club meetings. Of course, Maddie had often begged to join them, but her brothers had excluded her, claiming the club was for boys only. Years later, they discovered Maddie had sneaked in and hidden behind one of the wooden boxes and listened to almost everything they'd said.

Precocious, pigtailed, knobby-kneed Maddie—who'd grown up to be the sexiest woman in Savannah.

"I wanna build somefin' else," Jake said. "How about a machine gun?"

"No, no guns," Chase said, glancing up when he noticed a shadow behind him. Maddie and Nora had emerged from the house, laughing and chatting.

"Look, Mommy, see what Mr. Hawoway helped me build."

Nora barely glanced at the boy's creation. "That's nice. We need to go, Jake."

Once again Jake's smile drooped.

Maddie paused and ruffled Jake's hair. "Good job, there."

Jake's little chest puffed up with pride. "Can I come and play with you again sometime, Mr. Hawoway? I'm going to ask for a tool set for my birfday."

"Sure." Chase shifted uncomfortably when he noticed Maddie watching him. But when Jake threw his arms around him again, he knelt and patted his back. "See you later, sport."

Nora and Jake climbed in the car, Jake hugging his new toy tightly. Maddie walked over beside him. Dusk had started to settle, the faint purple and orange lines of the sun streaking the sky with an ethereal glow, highlighting her oval face.

"That was really nice of you to take time with him, Chase. We accomplished a lot."

He shrugged. "He's not such a bad kid."

"I know," Maddie said gently. "Nora really should leave him with a sitter or a play group while we meet."

Chase nodded agreement. Their gazes locked, and he wondered what she was thinking, if she remembered how scraggly and homely he'd looked when he'd tagged along behind her brothers. If she remembered the names the other kids had called him. The image of that little boy's face, *his* son's face, flitted through his mind though, and his heart squeezed in his chest.

"I saw you helping him; you were so patient, Chase," Maddie said. "You'd make a good father someday."

Chase fisted his hands by his side. How could he when he had no example to follow? And how could he have a kid and let him grow up in his tainted image? How could he tell his son his grandpa was in jail for murder?

No, he was never getting married. *He was a bachelor forever.*

"I'm not ever having kids," he said. Before the image of that little boy could return to haunt him or Maddie could reply, he turned, stalked to his truck and drove away.

Maddie watched Chase drive away and dug her heel in the dirt. Chase's truck roared out of the subdivision, lights flickering in the distance like twin dots growing smaller and smaller until they disappeared out of sight.

Chase had looked so damn lost and lonely for a minute, like he needed someone to wrap her arms around him and cuddle him and love him forever. She'd been tempted to fill the bill, but she'd also seen that shuttered look in his eyes, that untouchable warning sign that flashed caution—stay away. So she'd held herself back, played it safe. Something Maddie had never been known to do in her life.

Or had she?

Hadn't she stayed with Jeff to be cautious, to please her brothers and her mother?

She was starting to sound melodramatic, she realized, the same way she had as a teen when she'd gotten hooked on soap operas. Acting—another career she'd wanted to try. No wonder her brothers hadn't believed she'd follow through with this decorating career. But she would show them.

Chase was a different story.

He thinks of you as a sister. And he's never going to come around. Even if he did, you aren't the person he'd turn to—he's too loyal to your big, dumb brothers.

Determined to forget Chase, she climbed in her van and headed toward town to meet with the curator she'd consigned to locate some hard-to-find antiques for the tour. According to her notepad, she needed to check on several houses to see if the painting was finished, the carpeting laid, the wallpaper complete. Next she'd check to see if the furniture she'd custom-ordered was ready for delivery. Chase's house was first on the list. Since he wanted simple furnishings and clean living space, his house had been easy to furnish and decorate. If things went as scheduled, she'd have it finished before the end of the week. A sudden idea for his study hit her and she quickly tried to figure out how to put her plan together. A surprise she had a feeling Chase would like. Something personal for his office.

She frowned. Good heavens—there she was doing it again. Thinking about Chase Holloway.

Oh, well, it's okay this time, she decided. She wasn't really thinking about *him*. She was simply doing her job—decorating his house. And soon, when the tour was complete, she could go her own way with her business, and they would never have to work together again. Then everyone would be a whole lot happier.

She blinked, irritated that her eyes were suddenly watering. What in the world was wrong with her? She must be getting sappy at the thought of the project being complete, all the excitement was making her sentimental. Her tears certainly had nothing to do with Chase Holloway and the fact that soon he would no longer be a part of her life, except as her brothers' best friend.

Lance rubbed a callused hand over his forehead, still reeling from the day's problems as he settled into the armchair in his bedroom to rest. Why the hell couldn't something go right on this project?

Today the real-estate agent manning the front office had quit, he'd discovered low-quality materials had been sent in place of the expensive wood he'd ordered, and two of the near-completed houses had suffered water damage from hot-water heaters that had burst in the night. The carpet, which had just been laid the day before, would all have to be replaced as well as the wallpaper Maddie had just had hung. And his company would eat the money. It seemed they were either jinxed or doomed to miss their deadlines, and the tour was creeping up on them. Could their problems be a fluke or was something else happening? Sophie's talk of ghosts flitted through his head. Maybe the project was haunted.

Really, he must be losing it.

His hand fell on the wooden box he'd found in his father's things, and he grimaced, deciding he might as well open it and see what he had to deal with. When Maddie had moved into her own apartment, she'd plowed through the attic of their old home, searching for some old folk art for her new apartment. The pieces she'd selected were so garish, no wonder he doubted her judgment as a decorator. While helping her search through their parents' belongings, he'd discovered some interesting things as well. Things that had shocked him. The letters from Maria. The catalog. And this box. The box he'd avoided opening until now.

With sweating fingers, he jammed the key inside the lock and slowly lifted the lid. His eyes widened at the sight inside. An assortment of *Playboy* magazines. No big surprise. His dad had been a healthy male, albeit a respectable doctor. But he'd been young once.

Bottles of body gel in fluorescent colors. Scented, edible undies?

Sweat pooled on his forehead and rolled down his jaw.

A black silk mask. Feathers. A red silk jock strap with a picture of a devil on the crotch. A book of naughty sex games. A video entitled *Deep Throat and Peter the Pumpkin-Eater*.

Jesus, what was his father doing with all this . . . this stuff? Had he been into weird, kinky sex with this woman Maria?

The phone rang, and he nearly jumped out of his seat. He slammed the box lid and stared at it guiltily.

The noise trilled again, and he contemplated letting it ring. But he remembered all his problems at work and reached for the handset, knowing if something had gone wrong that required his immediate attention, he couldn't ignore it. "Hello."

"Hey, there."

Sophie Lane's sultry voice spilled over the line. What the hell did she want? He dropped the box on the floor, shuddering when the top flew off and a vibrator rolled across the floor. He jerked up the plastic dildo, locked it in the box and quickly shoved the offensive treasure chest out of sight, unable to imagine his father with the sex toys.

"Lance?"

"Yeah?"

"I didn't catch you at a bad time, did I?"

No, he was just holding a long plastic penis. And she sounded so innocent. "It's been a long day."

"Problems at work?"

How would she know about his problems? "Sort of."

He raised up, trying to think of a reason, a connection, but couldn't come up with anything to link Sophie to his bad luck. Unless the show was doing some kind of *Candid Camera* thing . . .

"Lance, if I'm disturbing you, I can call back."

"No, what made you ask if I had problems?"

"The sound of your voice." She paused, her voice mellow, her breathing like a soft, feathery whisper over the line. "You sound tired, like you've had a long day."

"Building requires long hours," he said curtly.

"Well, then I won't bother you."

Curiosity got the best of him. Or maybe it was her sexy voice. And the fact that she sounded slightly hurt at his tone. "No, it's okay. What can I do for you?"

"I wanted us to get together to discuss the renovations for my house."

"Oh, yeah." He grabbed a pencil and looked at his calendar. "What day did you have in mind?" A month from now? No, a year would be better. When this whole project was over and he'd figured out what to do about his family life. And when he'd demolished that damn box.

"How about tomorrow night over dinner?" Sophie asked.

"Why not tonight?" Lance said, wanting to find out what she was up to.

Light laughter tinkled back. "I can't tonight. I'm already ready for bed."

Lance groaned. Why did she have to go and tell him that? Now, he'd lie awake imagining what kind of nightgown she wore to bed. Or if she wore one at all . . .

"Lance, is tomorrow all right? It'll be my treat."

Her treat? "Fine. What time?"

"Why don't you come by my place at seven?"

"I'll be there." Lance hung up and stared at the phone, his head beginning to pound from the day's revelations. First the work problems, then the box, now an invitation for dinner with Sophie Lane. He guessed he should make some reservations someplace. Not too fancy of a place though—if the classy talk-show host wanted to dine with him, she'd have to make do on his budget. No, she'd said *her treat.*

The gall—as if he couldn't afford to entertain a woman like her.

Just what was she up to now anyway? Could she possibly have found out about his father's clandestine meetings with Maria?

The Boar's Back was filled with patrons drinking and enjoying themselves, but Chase and Reid had met to commiserate over the day's problems. The waitress deposited steaming bowls of gumbo, a platter of raw oysters, and a stack of hush puppies on the table, along with a pitcher of beer. Chase attacked his gumbo while Reid filled him in on the day's events, listing snag after snag with the sites.

"I keep wondering why all this is happening," Chase said, chasing a spicy bite of the thick soup down with a sip of beer.

Reid finally lay down his pen and bit into a thick crab cake. "Yeah, me, too. Seems like someone doesn't want us to succeed."

Chase had been thinking the same thing. "You financed the company with Waterbyrd, right?"

Reid leaned back in his chair, half gazing off to the side. Chase had the sneaking suspicion Reid was avoiding answering him. "Right?"

Reid's wary gaze finally cut back to Chase. "Partly. But we had to turn to the Savings and Loan for help, too."

"You mean Oglethorpe had a hand in this?"

Reid shook his head. "Not exactly. Middlemyer runs the company—we only dealt with him. It's all on paper, legit, not one of those personal loans. We didn't want to put Maddie in a compromising spot."

All sorts of possibilities raced through Chase's mind. "Hasn't it occurred to you that Oglethorpe might be a little pissed at being dumped on TV and decided to take his animosity out on you?" He groaned, suddenly remembering the way the two brothers had gone after Oglethorpe the night of the TV debacle. "Especially after you two scared the shit out of him."

Reid's chair thunked down on the wooden floor. "There's no way that could happen. We dealt strictly with Middlemyer. Oglethorpe couldn't possibly benefit by messing with us."

"Maybe not financially. But if you can't make your note, he'll sure as hell enjoy watching you fail."

Reid's jaw tightened. "Oglethorpe wouldn't do that, Chase. I know you don't like him, and he's not my pick either, but he's a stand-up business guy. He has to uphold his family's reputation."

"But he can undermine—"

"He won't." Reid shook his head emphatically. "He's still interested in getting back with Maddie. He won't jeopardize his chances."

A knot of gumbo suddenly stuck in Chase's throat. "He told you he wants to get back with Maddie?"

Reid turned up his mug and took a swallow. "Yeah."

Chase's eyebrows climbed his head. "Even if she keeps her business?"

Reid laughed. "It seems he's changed his mind. Now he thinks a successful businesswoman would be an asset for him."

Great, Chase thought sourly. So, Oglethorpe had been sending her all those damn flowers to woo her.

Why couldn't he think to do something like that?

Because you're not that romancy type. You're a glorified construction worker who likes football and old cars and hot women . . . well, lately he'd only liked one hot woman, but hell.

Suddenly nauseous and angry with his best friends and himself and the wuss, Chase pushed his bowl away, disgusted that their company was even remotely associated with Jeff Oglethorpe. And even more frustrated at the thought of Reid supporting the man. On some level, he realized it was illogical for him to care so much. Business was business. And Maddie could do whatever the hell she wanted with her personal life. But if he wanted to prove to anyone in the town he could be successful, Oglethorpe was one person he wanted to show more than anybody.

He refused to examine the reason.

But he'd die before he'd let his friends' company go down in front of the man. And Maddie, well, hell. She deserved a real man, someone better than that pansy-sending weasel. . . .

Chapter Seventeen

Reid barely tasted his pecan pie, his absolute favorite dessert, because he was so damn nervous. The waitress delivered a pot of coffee, and he stirred creamer in his, jabbed a toothpick in his mouth and studied the private detective he'd hired, grateful Chase hadn't lingered for dessert. The beefy man spooned up a hefty bite of peach cobbler loaded with ice cream and devoured it, lapping up the double dish as if he hadn't eaten in days. Knobby Smaltz, he called himself. Sounded like something out of a cheesy porn movie to Reid.

Reid had phoned the P.I. after Chase left and told him to meet him at the River House, not wanting to take a chance on being seen with him at the Boar's Back and open himself up to questions. He hated like the dickens to keep these secrets from Maddie and Lance, but he was doing them a favor. He wished to hell he'd never opened that file and seen that stuff himself, had never unearthed this . . . this sordid information about their father so he wouldn't have to sneak around and hide it from them. But some things were better left in the dark, like his father's hobbies and . . .

If the news ever leaked out, if these . . . these *others* ever came seeking something, *anything*, from them, he needed to be prepared. And he couldn't help but wonder if one of them had already discovered the Summers kids, knew about their company. If one of them might be sabotaging the business for revenge.

Or maybe because they wanted in on the company.

He'd heard of corporations, slick entrepreneurs, ruining a company, then buying it up for a song and dance while the poor owners were still trying to figure out what had gone wrong.

Knobby indicated the file, the hospital name to be specific. "Anyone from this place ever contacted you?"

Although they'd been seated in the back corner, Reid angled his head to shield his face from any patrons who might wander by. "No. And I don't want them to know I'm looking."

Knobby grinned, shining a gold tooth as he scraped his bowl clean. "But you want to know if there are any other k—"

"Shh," Reid snapped. "Yes, I have to know, but keep it quiet. I need to be prepared in case any of them show up at our door." His stomach somersaulted every time he imagined innocent little Maddie's reaction. And Lance would go ballistic.

"It ain't like your folks were millionaires or anything," Knobby said in a low voice. "What could they get from you if they did show up?"

"They could mess up everything," Reid said. "Ruin my dad's reputation. Shame my mother's memory. Embarrass my brother and sister. The others might want a piece of our business." If they aren't already plotting to steal it.

Knobby bobbed his chunky head up and down and waved the waitress over for another piece of pie. Coconut cream this time. "All right, then. I'll get right on it." He picked up his fork and dug in to the rich dessert. "Just as soon as I finish this pie and order me up a dish of that chocolate mousse."

Reid paid the bill and hurried away, hoping Knobby didn't eat so much he couldn't walk away and do the job. Which proved what a sorry state he was in—he was actually depending on the man to help him protect his family. They all stood to lose so much both personally and professionally.

All week Maddie had literally shopped until she dropped, but she'd made a tremendous amount of progress toward furnishing the homes for the show, and barring a few accessories, which had yet to arrive, Chase's house was almost complete. Tonight she intended to buy him dinner and unveil the results of her first completed project.

A jittery sensation rippled through her. What if he wasn't pleased?

He'd given her full reign, and she'd run with it.

He actually trusted her decorating sense with his own personal home, a revelation that meant more to Maddie than she'd ever imagined. He hadn't just been tagging along to make sure she wouldn't screw up as she'd first suspected—something her over-protective skeptical brothers might have done. No, Chase had faith in her.

Something she wasn't sure Lance and Reid or Jeff had.

Stripping off the suit she'd worn all day, she glanced at the latest present Jeff had sent—chocolates and an expensive bottle of wine—and remembered how she was once touched by his gestures.

Had Chase ever thought about sending her flowers or candy? Or even asking her on a date?

No, because he didn't want her, not in a relationship anyway.

Greg Pugh's bathrobe was lying across the chaise in the corner, mocking her, as if she needed a reminder of her failure to find the right guy. Greg was strange but wanted her. Jeff hadn't wanted her, and that had hurt. Now he seemed to want her back, but he didn't set her heart racing like Chase. Chase who was normal, caring, and passionate didn't want her. She wadded the robe up and decided she'd put it to some good use—she'd make a pillow out of the fabric for her cat.

After a quick shower, she dressed in a simple short, black knit dress with sandals, donning a pair of blue opals to dress up the ensemble and pulling one side of her hair up with a matching clip. T. C. swaggered in and meowed, climbing onto the foot of her bed. She paused to give him an affectionate hug. "I'll be back later, Kitty. Keep my pillow warm."

He purred contentedly and snuggled into a ball in the center of her bed as if pronouncing her entire bed his domain. Maddie laughed. "Just like a man, you'll probably demand sole possession of the remote control next."

A few minutes later, she picked up Chinese takeout and headed toward Chase's house to set things up before he arrived. Candles, a little wine, the built-in stereo system strumming soft music—they'd christen his house tonight, and tomorrow she'd show him the other three houses she'd finished.

Chase arrived about ten minutes after Maddie, just as she broke open the wine decanter and placed the crystal glasses on the wet bar. If he didn't want to keep them, he could return them. And since he wasn't moving in until after the tour, she'd have time to redo any item or area if he was displeased with her choices. Still, she found herself holding her breath as he walked toward the front door, praying for his approval.

Chase wrestled his hands out of fists into a more relaxed position as he approached the house, still agitated from his meeting with Reid. The business might be in trouble. And Oglethorpe wanted Maddie back. Hell, he was romancing her like some Romeo out of the dark ages.

Whereas *he* was running like a deer caught in a pair of headlights.

What else could go wrong?

He held his breath as he opened the front door of his new house, praying Maddie hadn't done something outlandish with the decorations, something to cause them another setback. For some odd reason he really wanted her to prove her brothers wrong and stick with the job. He felt disloyal for being annoyed with Lance and Reid, but they should show a little faith in their baby sister.

The polished brass doorknob felt slick to his hands. His stomach quivered as he realized that this house, this antebellum beauty was actually his. Back at Bethesda when he was little, he used to lie awake and dream of having a real house someday, of having a winding staircase, a fireplace, a place to call home.

He spotted Maddie standing in the foyer, the crystal chandelier dappling soft light around her russet hair. She looked incredibly beautiful, her voluptuous body molded into a short black dress that accentuated her long legs and curvy backside; a simple dress, but it radiated femininity and flattered her every feature.

God, he could get used to her greeting him every night.

Especially if she was naked.

"Chase?" She smiled, filling the room with warmth. "You want the fifty-cent tour?"

He nodded and let her lead him through the rooms. She remained silent most of the way, occasionally pointing out the reason for her choices. He thought he detected a slight quiver in her voice and twice, noticed her gnawing on her lower lip.

He'd seen the flooring, the carpet, had approved of the neutral palette she'd chosen earlier, the soft grays and blues and touches of maroon, so why should she be so nervous? Unless she'd added something wild to surprise him.

"I tried to keep it basic like you asked," she said softly when he ran his hand over the buttery soft leather of the L-shaped sofa. The den consisted of mellow heart pine and oak and quarry tile adorned the modern kitchen with a skylight, center island and breakfast bar, which opened up to a sunny screened-in porch. A bluestone floor, fieldstone fireplace and wet bar created a cozy family room, natural light spilling inside via the surrounding palladium windows.

The furnishings and accessories Maddie had chosen—the comfortable leather sofa, the wooden rocker, the collection of antique cars situated on the bookshelves, even the formal dining room set, which wasn't formal at all, but consisted of a clawfoot oak table with shaker chairs—everything seemed perfect, yet not exactly perfect. She'd coordinated everything so the areas appeared to flow from one to the other, but none of the rooms seemed stuffy or looked as if a decorator had furnished them. The house felt comfortable, homey.

The first home Chase had ever known.

And those antique cars—the collection seemed so personal, private, as if Maddie sensed some of the inner feelings he shared with no one.

A lump grew rapidly in his throat, and he blinked,

unnerved at the sudden welling of emotion. What the hell was happening to him? He'd never grown sappy over a house before, and he'd designed hundreds, at least in his mind.

"I have a surprise," Maddie said, dragging him toward the master suite.

Uh-oh.

Seconds later, he stared in awe of the impressive four-poster oak bed, which dominated the room. Immediately memories of Maddie sprawled on top of this very same bed the day they'd been shopping taunted him with elicit thoughts. A navy comforter artfully covered with dark red and navy throw pillows created an inviting den for nighttime, and a wardrobe to house his clothes stood adjacent to the full-length window. His gaze strayed to the corner where Maddie stood smiling.

"Ta da." She waved her arms and removed a sheet, which had been draped over an odd-shaped colorful structure. Unveiled, the unusual structure resembled a big bird. A hawk. "It's muffler art," Maddie explained. "This hawk is a one-of-a-kind piece. Since your hobby is working on cars, I thought you'd appreciate the craftsmanship."

Chase grinned, stunned at the interesting piece. He moved closer to study it in detail. "The artist used the muffler from a fifty-five Corvair to make the wings."

"Right." Maddie laughed. "I hope you like it."

"It's great," Chase said. "I've never seen anything like it."

"I saw a special report on unusual kinds of art on the *Today* show and when they interviewed the artist who specializes in muffler art, I instantly thought of you."

The lump grew back in his throat. No one had ever thought of him so personally before, had ever given him such a gift.

"I put all the receipts in the office so you can look over them," Maddie said, interrupting his thoughts. "If there's anything you don't approve of, we can return the items and replace them with something else you prefer."

"No, the house looks great." What was he thinking? She hadn't given him a gift—the art had been a decorator's choice—a business decision, nothing personal.

Feeling shaken by his own stupidity, he turned to retreat to the den.

"Chase, I hope you're pleased."

He paused, surprised by the hesitancy in her expression. Then he remembered her brothers' teasing, the way they'd doubted her abilities. "The house is great, Maddie. You've done a super job with everything."

Her brilliant smile made him forget his own silliness. "Really? 'Cause if there's anything, I mean *anything* you don't like, we'll take it back, Chase. And after the tour, if you want to change something, just let me know."

He pressed his finger to her lips to quiet her. "I love everything."

Her big eyes flickered with uncertainty. "Honest?"

He honestly wanted to kiss her. "I swear."

She wet her lips with her tongue, eliciting silent fantasies for Chase, then broke into a big smile. "Good. Then come on, I can't wait for you to see the study." She sashayed past him, and he followed along like a dog in heat, unable to resist watching her lithe body twist and turn in its own unique feminine way. Bare legs. A tight, firm butt. Slender arms. That narrow waist.

His body thrummed with arousal.

She stopped in the doorway of the den, and he was so distracted he ran into her.

"Oh, sorry." He grabbed her by the waist so he wouldn't knock her facedown.

Oblivious to his turmoil, she laughed, placed her hands over his, and turned in his arms. For a brief moment their gazes caught. Heat rippled through the air, hunger surged from deep within him. Then she swallowed, her breath hitching out, and spoke in that soft, sexy drawl that tied him in knots, "I have a surprise in here, too. I think every man's study should be his private room, his place to unwind. His special place to hibernate."

Her voice was quivering again. He wasn't sure if it was because of nerves or because of the heat racing between them. And the words she'd said, she'd described his feelings about a man's study. So what had she done in here?

He summoned amazing strength and pulled away, then walked past her into the room. Library paneling, wide windows with custom wood shutters, and a stone fireplace offset a massive oak workstation with a drafting board, extra lighting and storage compartments for supplies. A free-standing globe and wall map occupied one corner but his gaze was drawn to the opposite wall, the sitting area where a cozy leather wing chair in navy resided by a tan loveseat and recliner. The only pictures in the room hung above this comfortable furniture—an arrangement of photos framed in black leather—photos of Chase and Reid and Lance growing up.

His throat completely closed this time.

"I found most of the photos in the attic. If you don't want them all on the wall, that's fine, or if you have others or would prefer—"

"They're perfect." His gaze swept the candid shots, all the memories of growing up bombarding him. Years of being The Terrible Three, of being a part of a gang, a home, the Summers family. He and the boys camping. Hiking in the mountains. The afternoon they'd gone rafting down the Chattahooche. The clubhouse they'd built together. Maddie lingering in the background, hiding behind the wooden planks, trying to sneak in.

"Chase?"

Maddie was standing so close to him he inhaled her sweet perfume, the erotic scent of her skin. But now she was all grown up, and he wanted her so badly he could hardly breathe. He couldn't be disloyal to her brothers though, could he?

He stared at the photos again. He'd made a deal—he'd watch out for Maddie. He squared his shoulders and inhaled, praying he could keep his promise. But every moment he spent with Maddie seemed to test his endurance—to test whether he really was a bad boy at heart. The wuss offered her romance and money and prestige—what did he have to offer?

The hottest, sexiest night she'd ever had. Shit, he could not think like that.

"I brought Chinese and wine." Maddie said, handing him the corkscrew. "You want to celebrate?"

Good. Food, a perfect distraction. "Sure." He followed her back to the breakfast bar, opened the wine and helped her empty the Chinese onto paper plates.

"Oh, one more surprise."

"I'm not sure I can take any more tonight," Chase said.

Maddie laughed. "Well, it's not really a surprise since you've already seen this piece. But I wasn't sure it would be delivered today." She hurried into the laundry area, dragged out a rolled-up bundle and tore at the plastic covering. Chase helped her, laughing when she unveiled the contents.

"The bearskin rug. Isn't it gorgeous?"

"Yeah." *And so are you.*

"Let's put the rug in front of the fireplace in the

family room for now. You can move it into the bedroom later." Together they stretched out the thick white fur, then brought their plates over and sank down on the decadent rug to eat in the family room.

"I really hope you like the way things turned out, Chase."

He made a grand effort to eat instead of looking at her. "I do. The place looks even better than I expected. It's homey, too, not stuffy like most of those decorator homes."

"That's what I'm aiming for in my business—a house that's a home, a place that reflects the individual person, not a room that looks sterile like a magazine photo."

"With that philosophy, you should have a booming business."

Maddie grinned and raised her glass for a toast. "I managed to stay in budget, too."

"The best part." He clinked his glass with hers, thinking what a remarkable woman she'd turned out to be. Her brothers should be proud, not trying to hold her back.

Maddie nibbled a water chestnut off her chopsticks, and he bit into his spring roll to distract himself, mesmerized by her luscious lips. With a flick of her tongue, she licked a drop of sweet-and-sour sauce from the corner of her mouth, then sipped her wine, making a small moaning sound of pleasure at the sweet taste.

Chase sipped his own, wondering if Maddie had any idea how much she was torturing him. Or if she simply looked at him as a big brother. Maybe she'd finally gotten the message. He'd certainly pounded it into her head enough.

The realization should have pleased him. Instead, it made his stomach twist into a knot. With Oglethorpe trying to woo her, was she interested in reconciling with the wuss?

Chapter Eighteen

As the sun faded and dusk fell, hazy shadows from the live oaks outside cast faint shadows around the family room, creating a sultry atmosphere that hinted at long, lazy romantic nights. Maddie wondered if Chase realized the effect. The mood was certainly wreaking havoc with all her good intentions. She wanted to rip off Chase's clothes, throw him down on the rug and extinguish the fire that had burned between them ever since he had arrived. She wanted to make love with him until he could no longer possibly think of her as a kid sister or a kid *anything.*

Surely the tension between them wasn't a trick of her imagination or one-sided.

Forget the romantic cards and flowers and chocolates—she'd rather have Chase.

Chase had been looking at her with hunger in his eyes all night. Hunger and lust filled with a strong dose of wariness, as if he knew he'd be jumping into the abyss of an inferno unprotected if he even touched her. She'd heard that sometimes fire could be so enticing, so captivating and alluring and downright enchanting that the heat sucked you into its vortex before you had a chance to escape.

Maddie had never felt or even believed in that kind of heat before tonight. But the minute Chase walked through the door, she'd felt it spark. And when he'd praised her work and stretched out beside her on the rug, the flame had grown even stronger.

The chemistry had never been this strong with Jeff.

"Thanks for all the hard work you did." Chase's denim shirt stretched taut across broad shoulders as he poured them both another glass of wine.

"You're welcome. I hope you like the way I put the other houses together just as much. Although I have to admit your house was the most fun. It's always easier when you really know someone, then you can choose more personal things."

"Like that muffler art?" The slight bristle of a five o'clock shadow darkened his jaw, making her fingers itch to reach out and touch it, to see if his face was both as rough and smooth as she'd imagined.

"Right."

Propping himself on one arm, he leaned sideways on the floor and traced one finger along the stem of the wineglass. It was almost as if he was avoiding looking at her. Maddie wondered what it would feel like to have that finger running along the column of her neck. Her bare breasts. Her back.

"I can't wait till it gets cold and I can light a fire in here," Chase said, gazing at the stone hearth.

As if he hadn't already lit one. "It will be nice," Maddie murmured. "You are really talented, Chase.

This place may not be as large as some of the others, but it's extraordinary."

He rubbed a hand along his forehead, wiping away the perspiration. "Of course it's hard to believe it'll ever be cold in here; it's so hot right now."

"That's true." Maddie's face flushed when she realized she'd spoken out loud.

His crooked smile appeared, the scar on his forehead glinting in the light floating in from the window. Maddie couldn't resist. She reached out and touched the jagged puckered flesh. "I remember the day you got that scar."

"So do I." Chase glanced into his wine, his breath hissing out. "I never could back away from a good fight."

Maddie laughed. "Turn one down? I thought you started it."

His big shoulders lifted into a shrug. "Everyone thought I always started all the fights." His gaze slowly rose to collide with hers. In his dark eyes, she saw the bad memories, the pain he must have felt as an orphan. "It doesn't matter anyway."

"No, it doesn't," Maddie said softly. "Just look at you now—you're a great architect. You should be proud of yourself."

An emotion she couldn't quite read flickered in his eyes. His hand reached out to toy with a tendril of her hair curling around her cheek. "I think that's the first time anyone ever told me I was good at anything."

Maddie's heart raced. "It's true, Chase. I really admire the way you put yourself through school, the way you worked to make it—"

"Maddie, don't—"

"Don't what?"

A crooked smile crept onto his weathered face. "I'm not used to talking like this."

"What? You're not accustomed to compliments?" Maddie waved her hand around the room. "Well, you'd better get used to it, Chase. When the tour opens and everyone sees what a great architect you are, you'll be so booked up, you won't have time for anything but work."

"I hope I always have time for something besides work," he murmured in a husky voice.

Maddie's gaze locked with his, the tension and passion exploding. On some level, she knew there was a good reason she shouldn't be here like this with Chase, a reason she'd promised herself she wouldn't throw herself at him, but for the life of her, she couldn't remember it. All she could think about was wiping that sadness out of Chase's eyes, of seeing that haunting anguish vanish and his desire sated.

She placed her glass on the floor, then gently reached out and lay her hand along his cheek. The texture of his beard was coarse, rough, his jaw tight as he clenched his teeth. His dark eyes turned a darker hue as if he wanted to say something, to deny the lust between them.

As if giving in would hurt him. But not relenting to his hunger would be even harder.

"Maddie, we—"

"I know, we shouldn't." She lowered her head, flicking her tongue along the edge of his mouth, inhaling his husky male scent like an aphrodisiac, then nibbled at the tender skin along his earlobe. "But I don't care. I want you, Chase, like I've never wanted a man in my life."

His quick intake of air sounded full of pain and desire and finally, of surrender. With a harsh, low growl, he tunneled his fingers through her hair, covered her mouth with his and jerked her to him.

"God, Maddie." A battered sound of defeat rasped from deep within his throat as he hugged her to him, pressing her breasts against his chest in a fierce hold that made her cry out his name.

"Chase, please, I want you, now. Let us be together."

He drew back, looked into her eyes, whispered her name on a heady sigh, then cupped her face with both his big hands. "Maddie—"

"Shh, don't talk." Gently she pressed her lips to his to silence him. He tasted of spicy food and wine and dark desire. "Just hold me, Chase. Feel the way I want you."

She pulled his hand to her chest, lay it gently across her breasts so her racing heart pounded against his fingers. The turmoil in his face flickered into excitement, surprise and finally acceptance. "Lie down with me, Maddie."

She swallowed, lost at his command. He covered her body with his, as he swept his hands over her face, across her nose, her lips, through her hair, over her shoulders. Each hungry touch felt desperate, as if he wanted to memorize each part of her, as if he wanted to touch every sensitive bit of flesh and couldn't complete the task fast enough.

Maddie responded in kind. She'd never wanted anyone as much as she wanted Chase at that moment. With a low growl that sent a shiver up her spine, he ravaged her mouth, plundering the inner recesses with his tongue, and cradled her limp body in his arms. His hands were everywhere, on her breasts, her hips, her thighs, pushing up her dress, teasing the soft skin between her legs, his fingers exploring the tender folds of her womanhood. She clung to him, caressing the taut muscles knotting in his back, grasping his hips as he pushed her farther into the plush rug and thrust against her.

Dizzying sensations spiraled through her, sweeping all common sense from her mind, and she tore at his shirt, popping buttons in her haste to touch his bare skin. Seconds later, his clothes lay discarded in a heap by the fireplace, and he stretched beside her wearing nothing but a pair of dark briefs that barely contained his bulging sex. Maddie was stunned by the sight of his near-naked body, the strong, rippling muscles of his chest and shoulders, the firm, flat washboard stomach, the dark hair tapering from his chest toward the burgeoning erection pressing against her leg. Another scar puckered along his side, running a jagged path around his back, but each imperfection only served to remind her of the power and strength within the man.

Gently, he stroked her arm, ran his finger along her throat, let her look her fill. "Are you sure, Maddie?"

His low, husky voice sounded unsure but oddly tender. She felt herself smiling from the inside out, the lust and hunger she'd felt earlier heightened by the emotional bond she felt drawing her closer to him. Hesitation had no purpose. She lay her hand along his jaw again, one thumb stroking his bottom lip. "I've never been more sure of anything in my life, Chase."

He closed his eyes momentarily, breathing out a sigh that pulsed with heat and hunger. His gentle caring and passionate body made the moment even more seductive, and when he opened his eyes and gazed into hers, she saw no trace of hesitation, only the quiet acceptance that for this moment in time the two of them should be together.

Slowly, he raised his hand and traced circles along

her breasts, lowering his head so he nipped at her neck. Tracing a path along her body with his mouth, he gently bit her ear and laved her throat until she moaned and writhed against him. As if he understood her fierce need, his hands swept down to gather her dress and he lifted it over her arms, then tossed it aside.

"God, you're so beautiful," he said, his breath whispering against her skin.

She reached for him, and he came into her arms. Tongues mated, bodies surged and pressed together, legs entwined, their kisses escalated as the passion overrode all coherent thought. He unfastened her bra and shoved the lace aside, feeding on her breasts with such hunger that Maddie felt her whole inner core churn with desire. Passion exploded within her, sensations spiraling out of control, wickedly playing havoc with her senses until she was pulling his hips into hers. He rocked against her, his straining sex begging to be freed, and she clawed off his briefs, pulling his shaft between her thighs as he rose above her.

Bracing his weight on his hands, he rose above her and stared into her eyes, his own face glazed over with desire. Sweat soaked his skin, and his breath panted out as he shifted and moved so his sex pressed at her damp opening. She clung to him, a wanton smile lifting her lips as he thrust inside her; then she braced herself for the moment she would feel the small shock of pain, the triumphant giving of her first time.

And she finally remembered the reason she shouldn't be doing this. Because giving Chase her body meant she'd given him her heart. She gazed at his face, tight with passion, and realized that it was the very same reason she wanted to give herself to Chase.

Because she'd already fallen in love with him.

What the hell?

Chase froze, the heady scent of Maddie and sex almost overpowering the realization that Maddie was so slick, so hot, so . . . so incredibly *tight.* As if she'd never . . .

Anguish and fear suddenly jerked him to a halt, and he used every last ounce of restraint to pull back and look into her eyes. He searched her face, his gut clenching as her passion-glazed eyes played up and down his chest while she actually looked at their joined bodies and smiled in wild abandon.

"Maddie?"

"Don't stop, Chase," Maddie whispered. "*Please* don't stop."

His heart clamored for words even as his body sank deeper within her. His hands braced his body weight so he wouldn't crush her. Because he was going to hurt her if he continued. And dear God, the last thing he wanted was to hurt Maddie.

"I want you, Chase." She glanced at their joined bodies again, sending a shudder through him. "Like this, the two of us."

"But why . . ." His voice grew gruff, thick with emotion. "Why me?"

The sultry, loving smile that encompassed her face tore through his resolve. "Because you're special, Chase. You've always been special to me. And I want you to be the first."

He'd never been anyone's first.

Chase hesitated, his breath locking in his chest while Maddie slowly reached up and cupped his face tenderly in her hands, drawing his mouth to her for the sweetest, most erotic kiss he'd ever experienced in his life. Could he do this? Take Maddie's virginity?

Be the bad boy everyone believed him to be? Be her first.

Maybe her *only*.

No, he couldn't think in terms of only.

She ran her hands down his naked buttocks and pulled him toward her, reaching down to touch his sex.

Now, he couldn't think at all.

Heat and fire and hunger bordering on pain rippled through him. His sex throbbed inside her, begging for completion, begging for the salvation Maddie offered. Willpower—where was it when he needed it?

He should have lit some candles, tried that damn aromatherapy.

Maddie rocked her hips against him, her tongue flicking out to lick at his tight nipple. "Chase, please, I need you now."

The soft pleading in her voice, the passion-crazed look in her eyes, the tightening of her sex around his, the fact that out of all the men she could have slept with, she'd chosen him to be her first destroyed every last ounce of his good intention. He was lost.

"This might hurt," he whispered hoarsely, gently moving inside her.

"It can't hurt, it feels too wonderful."

Without giving him a chance to withdraw, she lifted her hips and suddenly surged herself against him until he broke through her barrier. She cried out, but the whimper sounded so full of excitement, so full of rapture, he gathered her in his arms and sank into oblivion. "God, Maddie."

"You feel wonderful, Chase, so good."

Her words were like an erotic striptease, shredding him of his senses. He told himself to give her time to adjust to his body, but Maddie didn't want time. She wanted him, strong and powerful and full of force, and he gave, finally allowing the sensations ravaging his body to block his conscience from his thoughts. Her hands begged for him to fill her, her mouth devoured his, her whispered erotic words and little moans robbed him of all caution. He surged inside her over and over, building a rhythm that rocked them both to the core, and when their releases finally swept through them, they came together in a kaleidoscope of colors and thrashing sounds that completely stole his sanity.

Several minutes later, Chase rolled off Maddie, their sweat-dampened bodies entangled, Maddie's perfect round breasts nudging his side as she cuddled in his arms. His breath slowly returned to normal, but he realized the rest of him would never be the same. He had taken a precious gift from Maddie, a wondrous gift that he didn't deserve. He'd have to tell her they'd made a mistake—

"Chase, don't go thinking now, okay?"

A low chuckle rumbled from deep within his chest. "You do know me pretty well."

Maddie rolled to her side, threw her bare leg across his, trapping him, and played with a damp strand of hair that had fallen in his eyes. "Damn straight." With a sultry smile that made his sex twitch back to life, she scraped her nails down his stomach, then lower to the inside of his thigh. His stomach clenched, and he sucked in a sharp breath.

"Maddie—"

She lifted herself on top of him and taunted him with her naked breasts as they swayed above him. "Yes, Chase?"

"What are you doing?"

A grin lit her eyes. "I thought we'd christen the house now."

He laughed slowly, pinching one of her nipples between his fingers. "I thought we just did that."

She dropped her face forward and kissed his forehead, tracing her tongue along the scar. "I meant every room in the house."

Then she jerked him to his feet, dragged him butt naked to the master suite where they began to do as she'd said. Hours later, they ended up in the bath, where Maddie bathed his sex with her tongue, accompanying each stroke with a sound of hunger so intoxicating, Chase thought he might die from the pleasure. He dug his hands into her tangled hair and groaned, finally reversing positions so he could treat her to the same sweet bliss she'd given him. Finally she climbed above him and impaled her lovely body on his, drinking in his every thrust with her hot, tight center.

Chase moaned in ecstasy and fondled her breasts as she brought him to the brink again—nothing could keep him from wanting Maddie. And tonight, she seemed bound and determined not to let him forget it.

Chapter Nineteen

Lance parked his Blazer in front of the apartment number Sophie had given him, reminding himself to be on guard all night in case Sophie tried to worm some information out of him. Thank God Reid had stayed to iron out their problems with one of the contractors who'd caused a delay. And Chase was meeting Maddie tonight to check out furniture, so she was in good hands. One problem off his mind—he could always trust Chase to do him a favor.

Sophie greeted him at the door. Dressed in a dark green halter top with slinky black pants that clung to her hips and those clunky shoes that seemed to be so fashionable these days, she looked absolutely gorgeous. Hell, he wished he did prefer blondes, but he'd always liked black hair. And porcelain skin. And ruby-red kissable lips.

Still, he had to resist her.

"Hi, Lance, come on in."

He'd get right down to business. "Are you ready to go?"

She arched one of those black eyebrows, drawing attention to her huge green eyes. His gut clenched. "In a hurry?"

He shrugged. "Just thought we'd get dinner over with so we can talk business."

A smile tugged at the corners of her pouty bow-shaped mouth. "Actually, I thought we'd eat in. I cooked dinner for us."

He couldn't have been more shocked if she said she'd invited him to sleep over. "You cooked?"

"Yeah, gourmet cooking is a hobby of mine."

For some reason, he hadn't pictured her as the domestic type.

His expression must have given away his surprise because she suddenly laughed, a soft, wispy sound that reminded him of wind chimes.

"I suppose you thought I had my food catered every night or ate out."

"I . . ." Exactly what he'd thought.

"Don't sweat it, Lance. There's a lot about me you don't know." She gestured for him to enter. He did so, taking in her small apartment in surprise. Stuffed bears filled a window seat below a gingham curtain, a collectible brown bear with tiny round glasses propped in one of those useless antique wicker baby carriages. An outdated plaid sofa and a worn leather recliner occupied the small den, the only other furniture was a battered pine entertainment unit with a CD player situated on it. Splashes of yellow and blue made the room feel fresh but airy, and a blue braided rug gave it a down-home country feel. All in all, a comfortable homey-looking room.

Not at all what he'd expected.

"Let me see, you thought I'd have all chrome and

glass, black lacquer furniture, an ice statue in the formal living room—isn't that what you said?"

Momentarily speechless, he simply stared at her like an idiot.

Her laughter startled him. "Everything isn't always what it appears to be on the surface, Lance."

Exactly what he was afraid of—hidden agendas.

Her gaze drifted toward a wooden trunk that had seen better days. "I've been saving my money for the house," Sophie said, for the first time not quite meeting his eyes. Something about that moment of vulnerability tugged at Lance, making him want to know more about Sophie Lane, and making him want to pull her in his arms and comfort her. But then the moment passed, and he wondered if he'd imagined it.

"I guess I was wrong. But your place, it's nice. Comfortable."

"Well, if that's an apology of sorts, then I accept it." She indicated a small white pine table in the tiny kitchen nook. "Dinner's almost ready. Why don't you sit down, and we can talk while I finish the pasta. There's wine on the counter, beer in the fridge. Make yourself at home."

Again, not at all what he expected. What was she up to? Trying to get him relaxed, ply him with liquor, then sneak in her questions?

She busied herself slicing bread and slathering butter on top, tossing the salad and stirring pasta, occasionally sipping her wine while she talked about the house. Strains of a jazz CD played softly in the background. Lance nursed a beer and listened to her plans.

"I don't think I can do everything I want upfront, but I'd like to get started, at least make the house livable," she said, pausing to taste the pasta. Obviously deciding it was done, she dished it up on a huge blue platter, then dribbled a white sauce over the top. His stomach growled, reminding him he hadn't had time for lunch. The dish smelled like clam sauce and wine and looked delicious.

"Then you'll want to check out the heating, wiring, plumbing, all the basics."

"Since I'll be the only one living there for a while, I'm going to redo the kitchen, bedroom and living area first."

"Sounds practical." Or was that her way of subtly telling him she didn't have a live-in?

She added some kind of homemade dressing to the salad and placed it on the table. His mouth watered. "I'm sorry. I didn't mean to start right in on business. I should have given you a little time to unwind." She turned and toyed with her wineglass, studying him. "How are things, Lance? Business going okay?"

Here she goes with the drill. "Yeah. We've had a few minor delays but minor problems always go with the territory."

Sophie smiled as she set a yellow plate in front of him and gestured for him to serve himself. "Maddie's so excited about the Tour of Homes. It must be wonderful to have such a close-knit family."

An odd expression darkened her eyes. Envy? Or was she priming him to find out about their father? "Yeah, we stick together," Lance said warily.

Her green eyes flitted over him. "Maddie brags about you all the time, Lance. How you've taken care of her and Reid since your parents died."

His chest wanted to swell with pride. If only he could trust her. "We're family, I couldn't do anything else."

"Well, I want you to know I think it's remarkable. Not every young man would have done the same thing at your age. You must have had to make some sacrifices."

Was she talking from experience or trying to butter him up to find out information on his family? "I couldn't let my folks down. And I intend to continue taking care of the family." She glanced up, her eyes huge beneath those long black lashes, and he realized his voice had sounded harsher than he'd intended. But his words were meant as a warning; he only hoped she accepted his wishes and didn't press the issue. "What about your family, Sophie? Do they live around here?"

Sophie pushed the pasta around on her plate. Interesting that she didn't like being put on the hot spot. "No, they're kind of scattered. I don't see them much."

"Aren't you close?"

"No, not at all. I've been on my own for a long time." Her small shoulders lifted slightly as if to indicate her strained family relationship was unimportant. The gesture made her appear delicate, vulnerable again. And more than a little bit lost.

Whoa, where had that thought come from?

He was doing it, letting her pretty face and that vulnerable look crawl under his skin.

"Look, Sophie, I'm not here to chat or talk about the family." He grabbed a chunk of bread and bit into the grainy thickness. "I think we'd better stick to business."

The warm smile she'd greeted him with instantly disappeared. She rose, then brought some crude sketches to the table. The rest of the dinner they focused on her plans for restoration. When he'd polished off his last bite, she offered him coffee and a slice of the best lemon meringue pie he'd ever tasted. But the conversation remained stilted, and Sophie looked strained and aloof, barely sampling her own dessert.

"I'll work up an estimate for you right away," he said, standing to leave.

She stood also, her petite body moving gracefully across the kitchen to place their dishes in the sink. "Fine. I'll wait on your call."

When she walked him to the door, he lingered for a moment, studying her small apartment, trying to figure her out. She clutched the doorjamb with her dainty fingers, her wide green eyes locking with his. "I appreciate the business advice, Lance."

"No problem."

A whiff of her perfume wafted toward him, sending his body into arousal.

"I didn't mean to upset you earlier, Lance. I meant what I said, that I admired you for taking care of your family. Not everyone is lucky enough to have an older sibling there for them."

His body hardened at the sound of her husky voice, angering him. The only way to *not* be attracted to Sophie Lane was to avoid her. He might as well be straightforward.

"Sophie, I don't know what you're up to, but if you intend to nose around in my life, you can forget it. I don't like the way you exploit other people's lives for TV ratings and parade their secrets in front of the world just to make a buck. It's a sleazy way to make a living, and I don't intend to let my family be a part of your dog-and-pony show."

Her sharp gaze made his gut clench, but he steeled himself against those mesmerizing eyes. "How do you know what my show is like if you don't even watch it?" Sophie asked, her voice a soft, hurt whisper.

Heat suffused Lance's face. He'd never admitted

to anyone how many times he'd sat in front of that tube and gawked at her like some silly adolescent boy. Could she possibly know?

"I just know," he said gruffly. Without another word, he said good night, then left with a stack of notes in his hand and a bad case of indigestion that had nothing to do with the gourmet meal he'd consumed.

And everything to do with the fact that he felt like a heel.

He should have felt relieved, he'd skirted her questions and avoided letting his family be caught in a revealing exposé on her nosy *Sophie Knows* show.

But her lights flickered off as he drove away, and he had the oddest feeling he'd just screwed up in some major way, that he'd lost something important tonight. Only he had no idea what it could have been and how it might be related to Sophie.

When Maddie said they were going to christen every room of the house, she meant every room. Including the breakfast bar, the hearth in the master suite and the staircase.

Chase climbed into the hot tub, sinking into the bubbles, and prayed his body wouldn't fail him. So far, it hadn't, but he was getting older, and he'd never had this much sex in one night in his entire life. He'd also *never* had sex this sensational. All because of Maddie.

"You don't mind me taking control?" Maddie asked in a husky whisper.

Chase threw his arms to his side and grinned. "Have your wicked way with me, woman."

Maddie slipped beneath the soft spray of water and bubbles, sliding her leg in between his. "Then put your leg over here. No, turn that way."

Water sloshed over the side of the garden tub as he obeyed.

"Scoot back just a little."

A stream of soapy water trickled across the brand-new floor.

"Here, let me get on top."

The hot tub whirred, spinning frothy water at Maddie's back.

"Oooh, don't move, Chase, that feels good."

Bubbles dotted her pert nipples, peaked and formed a cradle where Chase's hand rested between her thighs. "Oh, Maddie."

"Wait, I can't reach you—"

"Lean back."

"Oooh, let me turn around . . . yeah, just like that—"

"I can't believe you were a virgin less than three hours ago."

"Faster, Chase. Faster."

Chase gripped Maddie's hips and thrust inside her. "Where did you learn—"

"Magazines." Maddie dipped her head to kiss behind Chase's ear. "Now, shut up and love me."

Chase covered her mouth with his, and did as she asked, until the world exploded into starlight fragments that tore erotic sensations through him.

Maddie leaned her back against him, panting. "I think I'm having a stroke. My whole body's going numb."

"Should I call the doctor?"

She reached behind her to pull his face toward hers and kissed him. "What are you going to tell him—that you gave me a stroke orgasm?"

Chase chuckled. "That would be a first."

"Good, I'd like to be your first something."

Chase swallowed, guilt beginning to wear down on him.

Maddie's hand snaked beneath the water to cup his sex. "You're doing it again."

"What?"

"Thinking." She traced a line down his damp chest, drawing circles along his inner thigh. "Don't think, Chase. Not yet, anyway."

Chase groaned with pleasure. "Oh, Maddie."

"How about we try—"

He threaded his fingers through her hair. "Again?"

Maddie arched a brow. "What, you're too tired?"

He chuckled and swatted bubbles at her, laughing in delight when she stood, giving him a spectacular view of soap-slicked naked thighs. And he was at just the right level . . .

With a growl of pleasure, he raised himself on his hands and knees just as she lifted her leg and placed a dainty foot on the side of the tub. Wow, another position came to mind. "Maddie, don't move."

A wicked grin met his gaze. He tried to turn but his hand slipped, his body slid, and he sank beneath the water. Soapy water sloshed into his eyes and onto his face, and he closed his mouth, holding his breath, grasping for control. He reached for something stable, caught Maddie's leg and felt her weight collapse on top of him. Seconds later, he came up sputtering, and heard Maddie laughing as she clutched the tub and stood. Feeling playful, he tried to turn to dunk her, but a sharp pain suddenly exploded in his back.

He let out a yell, clutched his lower spine and clung to the side of the tub, spitting bubbles.

"Chase?"

Sharp pain knifed through his body, shooting down his leg. "Shit, Maddie. I can't believe this."

She sank to her knees beside him, her hand automatically stroking his tense muscles with concern. "What's wrong?"

He groaned as the pain intensified, almost blinding him. "I threw out my damn back."

Three hours later, Chase groaned and sprawled awkwardly in the backseat of Maddie's car, barely cognizant of his surroundings and the fact that Maddie had helped him from the hospital bed to the wheelchair to the car, and he'd almost crushed her in his drug-induced stupor. Thankfully, the pain pills were dulling the blinding ache in his back, but he'd lost all control of his faculties.

Of course, he'd done that earlier with Maddie when he'd made love to her in every room of his house. And that was *before* the pain pills.

He moaned and tried to mumble an apology, but wound up muttering something incoherent that vaguely resembled "Sorry."

Maddie tried to scoot her arm from behind him and nearly fell on top of him. "Easy, Chase. I just want you to be comfortable."

"Sorwe, so sorwe," he mumbled again.

Maddie patted his arm sympathetically and shut the door. He winced at the movement, gritting his teeth as she opened and shut the front door on the driver's side. They'd had a harried trip to the ER, Maddie in a panic, him in excruciating pain. Now reality had set in.

He had slept with Maddie Summers. Not just slept with her, but repeatedly had wild and crazy sex with her. And he had not only had wild and crazy sex with her, but he'd taken her virginity.

Worst of all, he had betrayed his best friends' trust.

He deserved a fate worse than a back out of whack.

Maddie cranked the car and shifted into gear, jolting the car forward. He dropped his hand over his forehead to shield his eyes from the lights outside and his mind from remembering. The effort proved fruitless.

"Oh, sorry," Maddie said. "Just try to relax, and I'll have you home and in bed in no time."

Wasn't that how he'd wound up in this position?

No, they'd been in the hot tub.

Great. How was he going to explain this to her brothers?

"Are you okay, Chase. Please tell me you are. You look so pale, I'm getting worried."

He tried to wave and tell her it was all right, but his hand flopped up, then down, and he hit himself in the face. And his stomach was suddenly climbing to his throat.

God no. He couldn't humiliate himself by throwing up now, too.

The hospital visit had pretty much already shredded his dignity. He needed to keep what little he had intact. All that poking and prodding. Nurses taking off his clothes and handling him. He hadn't slipped a disc or done any serious damage, for which he was grateful. But no, the doctor had said he'd had too much strenuous exercise. As if he was too ancient and out of shape to be having so much sex. He'd felt a hundred years old in front of Maddie.

She swerved, and he swallowed, clutching his stomach and praying for control, at least until he could make it to his own bathroom and find some privacy. Thankfully his whole body was going numb.

She hit a pothole, and he swore, his stomach lurching.

"We're almost there, Chase," Maddie sang.

He closed his eyes and must have drifted in and out of sleep because all he remembered after that was Maddie half-dragging him inside his apartment. Then he flopped onto his bed and smiled like a fool as she stripped off his clothes. Moments later, he sank into oblivion with dreams of Maddie's sweet little tush tucked up beside him. He had two thoughts before he finally gave himself up to the darkness of sleep. One, the next day he had to find a way to end this madness with Maddie and grovel forgiveness from her brothers.

And two—if he had just died, how had bad-boy Chase Holloway ended up in heaven?

Maddie lay snuggled with Chase, her own heart aching at the pain she'd seen etched on his face the last few hours. Poor baby. She ran her hand along his bare chest, memorizing every detail of his body, trying to imprint the memories into her mind in case he woke up and decided they'd made some kind of monumental mistake in making love.

Not that she wasn't having doubts herself.

She was already in love with him, a foolish thing to give her heart to a man who seemed dead-set on not becoming involved with her. Tonight, the time she'd spent in his arms had been the best night of her life, but would he want another woman tomorrow?

She winced as her aching muscles protested. Deciding a cup of hot tea might calm her after the hospital ordeal, she eased herself from bed, slipped on Chase's denim shirt, inhaling the masculine scent clinging to the fabric as she padded to the kitchen. A flick of the light switch, and her gaze zeroed in on the front of his ancient avocado refrigerator, so different from the one in his new house.

Her stomach plummeted when she saw the paper lodged with magnets in the dead center of the fridge.

Bachelors Forever.

Signed in red—blood—by Lance and Reid. And confirming her fears, she saw Chase's name scrawled at the bottom in big bold letters.

Maddie couldn't believe her eyes. Not only was the juvenile pact she remembered from when her brothers and Chase were younger—the one signed in blood—floating before her eyes, but at the bottom of it she saw all three of them had resigned the paper in pen. And the new date was less than a month ago.

Chapter Twenty

Lance was in a foul mood. All night he'd obsessed over the evening with Sophie and still couldn't put his finger on what was bothering him. She'd seemed so . . . so sweet, so interested in him. So damned complimentary of him, as if she sincerely admired him for taking care of his family.

He'd noticed this soft, vulnerable womanly side of her that in no way fit with the glitzy, glamorous talk-show host everyone gawked at on daytime TV.

Was her vulnerable sincere act just a ruse? Or could she possibly be for real?

It didn't matter. He had to be cautious. And if she was sincere, well—no. Blast it all to hell, he didn't have time for a personal relationship. A woman would only complicate his life right now. Forcing himself to put the striking brunette and her cataclysmic emerald-green eyes out of his mind, he'd phoned Reid and Chase and insisted they meet for breakfast to double-check that things were back on schedule.

Only Chase hadn't answered the phone.

Swerving his Blazer into Chase's apartment complex, he noticed Maddie's sporty new convertible parked in front and slammed on his brakes. What the . . .

He checked his watch. Seven A.M. What was Maddie doing here so early?

Could Chase and Maddie . . .

No, *never.*

Laughing at the irony, he threw the truck sideways into a parking spot, killed the engine and climbed out, then stalked to the front door. She'd probably wanted a breakfast meeting, same as him, to finish some of her decorating stuff—that is, if she still was in the business. He'd thought her interest would have waned by now, but Chase seemed to think she was going to stick with it. At least until the project was finished. At this point, he hoped so. It was too late to hire someone else to decorate the homes for the tour.

As much as he hated to bust up their meeting, he had to get Chase over to meet with Reid before their session with the planning committee today. Wiping the sweat from his brow, he raised his hand and pounded on the door.

Maddie had just poured herself a cup of strong coffee when she heard someone at the door. The loud knock startled her, and she accidentally spilled the hot liquid on her hand. Who the heck would be knocking on Chase's door so early in the morning? Should she answer the door or not? No, she'd ignore it. It might be Lance or Reid. Or that Daphne woman!

Lord, she needed some sleep, not to have to explain why she was here or meet one of Chase's other lovers. *Other lovers.* Is that what she had become? One of his many women?

That bachelor pact had started the wheels of doubt spinning in her brain last night, and she'd chastised herself a dozen times for making love with Chase. Then she'd restlessly roamed his house, and to her consternation, had seen copies of the bachelor pact tacked up in every room.

His mumbled, "Sorry"—had he been apologizing for ruining the evening by throwing out his back or for making love to her? Was he already regretting their evening together, afraid she'd get territorial and start making demands?

The knocking grew louder.

Irritated and more than a little dizzy from exhaustion, she cradled her cup in her hand, tiptoed to the window and peeked out, slapping one hand to her mouth to stifle a gasp. Good heavens.

Lance, was standing on the doorstep.

She glanced down at Chase's wrinkled, denim shirt and her heart thundered in her chest.

What in the world should she do now?

Chase clutched his aching back, ran a hand through his sleep-tousled hair and staggered out of bed, determined to tell the neighbor next door to put the damn jackhammer away for a while. Nothing else but a jackhammer could make that awful pounding sound so early in the morning. They must be working on the roof.

Slowly managing to put one foot in front of the other, he swaggered into his den and headed straight to the door. So groggy he was oblivious to anything else around him, he swung open the front door with a curse and ran straight into Lance.

His buddy stood in the middle of the doorway, a frown on his face. "The jackhammer?"

"That was me knocking." Lance planted his hands on his hips. "What's wrong with you—hangover?"

Chase rubbed a hand over his face, still clutching his stiff back, then turned to hobble to the sofa—where Maddie stood, cradling a cup of coffee with her hair mussed and wearing his denim shirt.

Dear Jesus. Maddie.

Reality crashed back like a keg of dynamite exploding into his brain. He groaned, swaying dizzily and blindly reached for the wall.

"Chase?"

"Maddie?"

"Lance?"

Out of the corner of a hazy, swollen eye, he momentarily caught the questioning looks shooting across the room between his best friend and his lov—best friend's baby sister. Guilt and pain and the pills collided, turning his brain into a hazy mush. He might as well go ahead and tell the truth, rescue Maddie before her brother jumped down her throat. He would take full blame, tell him he seduced her, say anything so Lance wouldn't fuss at her.

He opened his mouth to confess, but saw Maddie's concerned look and swayed again. Maddie and Lance both ran for him. Grabbing him on opposite sides at the same time, they helped him to the couch where he sprawled down, flopping his legs in front of him like a rag doll. He wished he could just lose consciousness and wake up when this terrible, awkward morning-after was over.

"Some hangover?" Lance muttered. "What'd you drink—a fifth of Wild Turkey all by yourself?"

Chase shook his head, aware the room was still spinning. "No, pain pills."

"He threw his back out last night," Maddie explained.

Through a slitted eye, he saw Lance turn a questioning expression toward Maddie, then back to him. "How did you do that, Holloway?"

Just spit it out and let him kill you while you're still too numb to feel it. "We . . . uh, went to my house—"

"We were moving . . ." Maddie said, looking panicky.

Apparently she wasn't ready for her brothers to know about him. A pang of hurt hit him, though he didn't understand why. "Boxes," Chase finished.

"Last night we met to view his house, and he had to move some boxes of furniture and he threw his back out—"

"Maddie drove me to the ER."

"And back home."

Lance's frown darkened. "And?"

"And he was in so much pain I was worried—"

"She stayed on the couch—"

"To make sure he was all right."

They both finished, blankly staring at each other. Lance's head titled sideways as if he considered the story and wasn't sure he bought it. Chase's chest tightened with guilt.

He hated lying to his best friend. Not that he usually spilled his guts about women or his sex life, but he'd vowed to protect and watch over Maddie.

Not seduce her.

She'd been an innocent.

He would take full blame.

Lance suddenly burst into laughter. "Gosh, for a minute I thought . . ." He rubbed his chin, chuckling.

"Thought what?" Maddie asked.

"You wouldn't believe it."

"Try me," Maddie said, folding her arms across her chest. Chase thought she sounded irritated but he wasn't sure.

She sure did look beautiful though.

Lance laughed even louder, sending the drums beating in Chase's head again. "Naw, that would be ridiculous." He walked over to Chase and sat down beside him on the sofa. "I know you'd never do anything like that."

Black spots danced in front of Chase's eyes. He figured it was the guilt sending him a message.

"But blast it all to hell, Chase. What rotten timing. We have a meeting with the planning committee today at noon, and I need for you to be there. Do you think there's any way—"

"I'll be there," Chase said, knowing he couldn't let his buddy down anymore than he already had. He tried to stand but pain knifed through him, rocking his world sideways.

"Uh, the pain pills are on the counter in your bathroom. I'll get you one," Maddie offered.

"Thanks."

He shot her a grateful look and saw hurt darken her eyes. What did Maddie want?

He searched for some kind of cue.

She bit down on her lip, and he didn't know whether she wanted him to keep silent or spill his guts.

Hell, he had no idea what to do. His brain was too foggy and so full of pain and guilt, he couldn't possibly read her mind. So he said nothing. Instead he hobbled off to the other room, silently cursing himself for being a coward and a screw-up.

"I really screwed up big time." Unable to hide her misery, Maddie sank onto one of the seats in the back of her van where she had created a small makeshift office.

Sophie handed Maddie a cup of hot tea. "Come on, Mad, it can't be that bad."

"I slept with Chase."

A wide grin split Sophie's face. "Ooh. Good."

"No, it was awful."

"A disappointing lover, huh?"

"Hardly. I mean the sex was wonderful . . . mind-boggling."

"I'm not following. So why was it bad?"

Because I'm in love with him. Unable to voice her feelings yet, Maddie sipped the tea, wincing when it burned her tongue. "I just think sleeping with him was a big mistake."

"Is that what he said?"

"Not exactly. He was too doped up on pain medication to say much when I left."

"Wow, you must have had some wild sex."

Maddie laughed, remembering the innovative position they'd been trying when Chase had popped his back out of whack. "Yeah, but then he messed up his back, and we had to go to the hospital and then I saw all those stupid bachelor-pact signs."

"Whoa, bachelor-pact signs?"

"Remember how I told you that Chase and my brothers had made a "bachelor forever" vow when they were younger? Well, it turns out they renewed the pact a month ago. I still can't believe they are so immature! Anyway, they all signed a sheet of paper vowing to be bachelors forever. And Chase hung copies of that juvenile sign in every room of the house as if he wanted a constant reminder not to get involved with anyone. And then Lance showed up—"

"Lance showed up?"

"Yeah, the next morning." Maddie blew into her tea to cool it. "I didn't know what to do."

"Did he say anything about me?"

Maddie squinted at her friend. "Why would he say something about you?"

Sophie shrugged, a forlorn expression on her face. "I don't know. I suppose he wouldn't."

"Sophie, is there something you're not telling me?"

Sophie thumbed a strand of hair behind her ear, her tortoiseshell earrings clinking. "We had dinner last night."

Maddie pushed to the edge of her seat. "You have been holding back, girl. Come on, I want all the details."

Chase struggled to remain upright, wincing with every movement. He'd tried not to take the pain pills because they made him groggy, but his whole body felt like Gingsu knives were stabbing at his skin, and he was either going to pass out from the pain or float through the meeting with a goofy grin on his face. He'd figured the latter was the best choice. Only now, he felt dizzy again, and the room kept slipping in and out of focus. Sometimes there were two Lances, sometimes Reid was upside down . . .

"So, Mr. Holloway, you've agreed to stay on with the project if we decide to expand?" Thornton Wainright leaned his bony face on his bony hand, and Chase decided the man reminded him of an ostrich. An anal, uptight, bony ostrich. He couldn't help but laugh at the image.

"Chase?" Lance's growl cut through his blurry euphoria.

"Yeah." Reid scowled, and Chase tried to sit up straighter. "Uh, yes, sir. I plan to stay on." *If I can just hold my head up.*

"And you're familiar with the lay of the land, the price range, the type of clientele we're targeting."

Chase nodded, gripping the desk with white knuckles when the room swayed.

Lance picked up the conversation. "You can look at the homes Chase has designed so far and examine our work, and you'll find we've used top-notch materials and come in with a fair price."

"Yes, well . . ." Mr. Wainright shuffled his dark glasses down on the bridge of his nose, glaring at Chase. "I have heard rumors about problems on-site. And we all know Mr. Holloway is fairly new at this business. As you gentlemen are."

"We can handle the project," Lance said. "Check out our work for yourself."

"And I've dealt with the contractors we were having problems with," Reid assured him. "Everything's back on track. We should have the first set of homes ready for the tour next week."

Wainright tilted his head sideways, studying Chase. "Are you all right, Mr. Holloway?"

Chase leaned in the same direction, trying to focus on Wainright's face.

Wainright's eyes bulged in his head. "Mr. Holloway, have you been drinking?"

The pain pills must have been stronger than he remembered. Or had he taken two instead of one? Let's see, Maddie had given him one before she ran out, then he'd taken another one when that one hadn't worked. . . .

Lance's hand tightened around his arm. "We're sorry, Mr. Wainright. Mr. Holloway threw out his back last night and is taking pain medication."

"Oh, I see," the man said, disapproval still edging into his voice.

Chase pivoted to apologize himself but lost his balance. The room spun like a Ferris wheel, and Chase saw black just before his head landed in his soup.

"I'm afraid there's nothing to tell." Sophie blinked, and Maddie realized her friend's eyes looked suspiciously moist. "Your brother simply doesn't like me. I think it's time I accept it and—"

A rattling at the door interrupted Sophie. Someone was knocking.

Maddie rose and opened it, surprised to see Lance and Chase standing outside.

"Come on in," she said, her teeth clenched at the thought of her brother hurting Sophie.

Lance gave her an odd look, then ducked his head and climbed inside. Chase wobbled in none too steadily, a sickly pallor to his face. She instantly gave him her chair and ordered him to sit. He didn't argue, but dropped into it, a testament to his pathetic state of health. Or was he yellow from being a coward—too afraid to tell Lance about the two of them?

"What are you doing here?" Maddie asked Lance.

Lance's gaze flashed to Sophie, the tension palpable between them.

"I came to drop these off." He handed her the keys to the Victorian home.

"How did the meeting go?"

"Fine until Chase passed out."

Maddie frowned and saw Chase sink lower in his chair as if he were a child being reprimanded. She wondered if he'd mentioned their relationship and was waiting for the ball to drop. Instead Lance turned on Sophie.

"What are you doing here, Miss Lane? I thought we understood each other last night."

Sophie twisted her hands on top of the small table.

"I understood you perfectly, Mr. Summers. But Maddie's my friend."

His scowl said it all.

"Lance, what in the devil is wrong with you?" Maddie asked, suddenly furious at the entire male race. "I've never seen you be so rude to anyone in my life!"

"I don't like nosy busybodies."

Red flashed on Sophie's cheeks.

"Of all the nerve!" Maddie swatted her brother.

Sophie stood, her small fists on her hips. "I'm not a busybody, Mr. Summers. I bring the news to people, provide entertainment—"

"And—"

"That is quite enough, Lance Summers." Maddie pounded her fist on the table. "I think you'd better leave."

She glanced at Chase who'd remained suspiciously silent. The big chicken. Obviously he hadn't told her brother about them, or Lance would have said something.

She didn't know whether to cry or to hit him. She spied a carpet sample and almost reached for it. Maybe she could beat some sense into both of them. But Lance was already backing out of the van. Sophie folded her arms and stared after him, anger flashing in her vibrant eyes. "Under the circumstances, I think it would be better for all of us if I took my business someplace else, Mr. Summers."

"Fine." Lance dropped to the ground and stalked toward his car.

"Don't worry, Soph." Maddie wrapped her arm around Sophie. "We'll find another builder to help you. And we'll go down to that voodoo shop on River Street and buy a Lance doll and stick pins and needles in it tonight."

Chase stood, weaving sideways, and clutched the door to climb out, pausing to stare at her. Maddie's gaze caught his, questions thrumming through the air. Was he going to tell Lance about the two of them? Was it over between them before it had really even started?

Then the moment was lost, and he staggered out of the van, leaving all of the questions behind.

"Make that two voodoo dolls," Maddie muttered. "One for each of those stubborn, dumb men."

Chapter Twenty-one

That night Chase took a muscle relaxer and crawled in bed with a heating pad, determined to banish the horrible day from his mind. Seeing Maddie after they'd made love, after the humiliating experience at the hospital and the meeting, had his emotions skittering in a dozen different directions.

And seeing Lance had brought on the guilt. His best friend trusted him and he'd let him down. No question about that.

The bigger question now—what was he going to do about his deception?

Break things off with Maddie? Never touch her again?

He groaned in misery and twisted in bed as the erotic images from their lovemaking taunted his mind. Even in pain, his body hardened with want at the memories.

Why Maddie? Why couldn't he have felt this kind

of heat with Daphne? Or some other anonymous woman who simply wanted sex with no strings and no relationship. A woman he wouldn't have to face at work, a woman who wasn't connected to Lance and Reid, a woman who wouldn't mess up his life . . .

A woman who wouldn't eventually want all that romance garbage. How did she stand all those flowers in her little van anyway; they'd practically made him nauseous.

Finally the pills worked, and he floated into a restless sleep. But the next morning, he woke, feeling irritable and disjointed, the dreams that had dogged him all night haunting him. Dreams of Maddie.

Maddie's pleased smile when he'd praised her work. Maddie's spunk and determination to succeed. Maddie's struggle to be independent in spite of the odds, in spite of her brothers' overprotectiveness. Maddie's sexy eyes whispering erotic promises to him in the dark, telling him he was wonderful. Maddie loving and giving herself to him, climbing on top of him, offering her virginity . . .

Him being smothered by a truckload of those damn roses.

He bolted upright, a sickening realization dawning. Maybe he was actually falling in love with . . . no.

Not Chase Holloway. He was a man who liked to be alone, a man who needed no one and wanted no one to need him. A bachelor forever.

A man who literally owed his life to Maddie's *brothers*.

The rest of his dreams rushed back to slap at him, knocking some much-needed sense into his befuddled brain. The horrible fight his parents had had the night before his father had gone berserk and killed that man. The day the sheriff had carted his father off to jail for murder. The night his mother had dropped him off at the orphanage. The way she'd coldly walked away and never looked back. The day he'd gotten into a fight at school and wound up on the bottom of ten boys. The ugly names they'd called him. Lance and Reid dragging the boys off his battered body, defending him.

Feeling weary and confused, he crawled from bed, climbed in the shower and dressed for work, deciding he needed a firm wake-up call. He'd drive by the orphanage today to help himself refocus. Seeing where he'd come from would put where he was going back into perspective.

A half hour later, he drove down the long winding drive, parked in front of the ancient cold structure, and stared at the building that had been his home more than ten years. The house he'd shared with sixty other homeless, faceless, boys whose parents had either died and left them without relatives or anyone who wanted them, or abandoned them because they didn't care. Painful memories rushed back. His father and mother fighting, his dad in a rage, ruining his life because he'd been obsessed with Chase's mother, his mother saying she'd grown tired of them both . . .

He couldn't become that obsessed with Maddie. He couldn't let his emotions and feelings and lust for her control his future.

And he refused to give in to his emotions and feel sorry for himself because of his past.

Instead he let anger at the circumstances, at the other kids who'd been cruel to him, drive him forward. He'd planned to prove to them he could be somebody, and he damn well was going to do that. The company, his business was the key.

His determination renewed, he shifted into gear and headed toward the subdivision. First, he'd meet Maddie and explain that any kind of physical relationship was over. She'd certainly understand—after all, he couldn't imagine her telling her brothers that she'd slept with him. They'd both let the moment—the atmosphere with that damn decadent rug, the wine, the close proximity in which they'd been working, the mood—get out of hand. Their libidos had done the talking.

But not anymore.

Now, common sense would bulldoze right over those hormones.

Yes, he'd tell Maddie it was over, then he'd find Lance and Reid, apologize for passing out at their meeting the day before, tell them Maddie had the decorating thing under control so they needn't worry and pour himself into drawing plans for the next phase of the development.

After all, in the cold light of day, Maddie was probably thinking the same thing.

Maddie shivered, surprised at the chilly spring morning. Unusual. Normally by 11:00 A.M., the temperature in March had risen to the sixties, maybe seventies.

Or maybe her anger at Chase and Lance was making her cold.

Angling her clipboard on her hip, she breezed through the Greek Revival mansion, checking off the furniture and accessories she'd ordered, making sure everything was in place. Only a few more days until the tour. Excitement bubbled inside as she imagined a stream of people admiring the exquisite homes and the furnishings she'd handpicked herself. Wall coverings, window treatments, antiques . . . She was proud of the results.

She hoped her client list would explode after the tour. Then she could pay off her loan and retrieve her mother's pendant without her brothers learning she'd used it as collateral.

Determined not to neglect a single detail, she tagged the items to indicate where they'd been purchased in case a potential buyer expressed interest in acquiring an item with the home. The task had taken her the entire morning. Just as she was winding up in the downstairs exercise room, she heard footsteps above.

"Maddie?"

Chase?

Excitement warred with anger. How was he going to act today?

He'd been in pain the day before, and the medication had affected his behavior, but she'd half-hoped he'd call this morning. When he hadn't . . .

No, maybe today they'd talk, they'd make love again, everything would be perfect. . . .

"Downstairs, Chase. I'm in the weight room."

She heard his boots pounding on the floor above, the steps creak, the sound growing muffled as he walked across the carpeted basement rec room. A knot of anxiety pressed against her chest, her breath whooshing out when she saw him lean inside the doorway. Just as he had when she'd first met him, but he was even more endearing now than he had been then.

He looked even taller today, his shoulders broader, the overly long strands of his hair still damp from his shower. She could smell his soap and aftershave all the way across the room, or maybe the scent had been imprinted in her memory forever.

A sheepish grin curved the corner of his wide mouth. "Hey. What are you doing down here?"

"Just making a list, checking it twice," she said, indicating her clipboard.

"Everything looks great."

"This house is all ready for the show. I'm starting to get excited about the tour." Her stomach fluttered. "And a little nervous, too."

"You don't have any reason to be nervous," he said in a husky voice. "You've done a super job. Lance and Reid are going to be proud of you."

His praise thrilled her, reminding her of the conversation they'd had the night they'd make love. God, she wanted him again.

His eyes seemed to pick up on her feelings, and she silently cursed herself for being so transparent. But why hide—why not go after what she wanted?

Because he might not want you.

His smile faded into seriousness. "I, Maddie . . . we need to—"

Lord, she wasn't ready to *talk*. "Have you seen the exercise room?" she asked instead, moving toward him. "The weight set, treadmill, StairMaster—everything you need to get your heart rate going is right here in this room."

His gaze tracked the contents, then rested on her, that loneliness she'd sensed calling out to her. Then hunger flickered across his face, and his voice dropped to a husky whisper. "Yeah, everything I needs right here all right."

She gently lay her hand on his heart, her own heart racing when his pulse quickened. His chest felt so strong, so solid, so masculine, so hungry. Her body responded with a tingle of want that rippled through her, settling in a pool of heat at her very core.

"Are you feeling better today, Chase—up for a workout maybe?"

Chase stared at Maddie, the words he'd practiced saying on the way over evaporating into thin air at her breathless invitation and the desire written so plainly on her face.

Desire for him.

Her finger traced a teasing path along his neck, down the center of his chest, to his groin where she reached down and boldly cupped him. "I missed you yesterday."

"I . . ." What was he supposed to tell her? "I missed you, too."

No, that wasn't what he meant to say.

But he couldn't find the words. Or the determination to think of them. Or the willpower to resist her and walk away.

The allure of her deep-set dark eyes, the flicker of her tongue, the way she wrapped her leg so seductively around his thigh and tucked her womanhood into the heart of his sex . . . his body thrummed with instant arousal, and all his reservations died. Lights dimmed in his brain, and he forgot where he was or why he shouldn't have this woman—because everything seemed so right. So perfect.

With a moan of pure primal lust, he grabbed her to him. His tongue beat a foray along her body as his hands stripped her clothes and tossed them aside. He took her fast and hard and deep against the mirrored wall, against the barbells, on top of the exercise mat where she sprawled, her legs spread in invitation, her whispered moans and pleas orgasmic in themselves. And when she cried out his name in a thunderous sound of rapture, he growled and let his release spill into her depths, grinning as her hands clawed down his back, pulling him so deep inside her he thought he might be lost within her warm, loving chambers forever.

Lying sideways, she draped herself across him so he received the most tantalizing view of naked butt and cleavage, and his breath rasped out, his sex straining for her again. His heart was beating so fast he swore it sounded like horse hooves all around him.

No . . . footsteps.

"Maddie, Chase?" Voices drifted from the floor above, in the foyer.

"Dear heavens, it's Lance and Reid," Maddie said in a panicked whisper.

He took one look at their naked, sweat-slicked bodies, Maddie's panties still around her ankles, his underwear and jeans hanging on to one boot, Maddie's hair tousled and wild around her face, the bite marks on her neck—had he put them there?—and totally freaked.

"We have to hide!"

Jerking her up, he yanked his pants up to his waist and raced to gather their clothes. Where was her bra? Had she even been wearing one? He couldn't remember taking it off. And his shirt, where had she thrown it?

Maddie grabbed their shoes, frantically searching for a place to hide. "In here, the closet."

He nodded, spotted one of his socks dangling from the treadmill, yanked it down, then ran into the closet with her.

"Hurry, get dressed in case they find us," he whispered.

"I think they're going upstairs first."

"How did they know we were here?"

"They probably saw our cars."

"Good grief, I can't see, it's dark." Maddie grabbed her bra and slipped it on, her elbow jabbing his face. "I can't get the clasp," she said, pivoting so her bare back brushed his chest. His sex automatically jutted toward her backside, and he groaned in agony.

"Shh," Maddie whispered.

He fumbled with the clasp. "I can't get it!"

"Just give it to me." She yanked off the bra and dropped it to the floor. He stuffed the lacy contraption in his jeans pocket while she dragged on her silk blouse and began to work the tiny buttons.

"Some of the buttons are missing," Maddie whispered.

He winced, remembering he'd popped them in his haste to get her naked, and tried to help her fasten the few remaining little pearls. God, he'd been like an animal. The buttons were probably on the floor. Or the exercise mat. What if Lance or Reid found them?

His leg hit a paint can, making it rattle, and his heart nearly stopped. He halted the can's movement with his foot, then reached out to hand her the hair clasp. Unfortunately she reached for the clasp at the same time, jabbing her finger with the end.

The whites of Maddie's eyes shone in the dark as her eyes widened. "Oww!"

He covered her mouth with his hand. "Shh."

She nodded, then grinned devilishly and licked at his hand.

He yanked his hand away. "Maddie, stop that!"

Footsteps and voices sounded again.

"They're coming down here!" Maddie whispered.

He stuffed his arms in his shirt and tried to zip them.

"Chase?" Lance yelled.

"Maddie?" Reid called.

His damn zipper was stuck! Maddie noticed him tugging and reached down to help him, but her hand brushed his fledging erection, stirring it to life again. He swelled against his fly just as she tried to zip his pants.

Owww!

Maddie stifled his groan by planting her mouth over his with a firm kiss.

He doubled over as far as he could inside the tiny space, but pain shot through his back, his head connected with Maddie's breasts, and his mind turned traitorous again, conjuring images of naughty things they could do in the closet, with Maddie's brothers right upstairs. Of course, first he had to get his sex uncaught from his zipper.

Maddie's brothers were right upstairs! He must be losing his mind!

The footsteps grew closer, louder, hit the creaking steps, then grew softer on the carpet.

"Where do you suppose they are?" Lance muttered from near the doorway.

"Beats me," Reid replied. "I don't get it. Both their cars are out front."

"Maybe they took a walk around the property."

Maddie massaged Chase's aching sex, only adding to the problem. He pushed her hand away, willing his manhood to go down and his body to stop screaming in pain and arousal.

"Let's see if they walked down by the river," Lance suggested.

"Good idea. They're probably surveying the property line."

He should have been surveying the property, Chase thought in remorse. Not surveying every inch of Maddie's body.

Finally, the stairs creaked as Lance and Reid walked up the steps. Chase said a quick thank-you to the man above, then cursed himself for his foolishness. As soon as the boys left, he would have to explain things to Maddie, end this crazy affair.

"I'm sorry, Chase. Are you all right?" Maddie whispered.

The concern in her voice only heightened his arousal. Grinning like a she-devil, she dropped to her knees, whispered an erotic promise that sent a shudder through him, then placed her mouth above his swollen shaft and licked the tip. His knees almost buckled.

"Let me kiss it and make it all better," Maddie whispered.

Chase shook his head no, but Maddie's hot mouth closed around him, and he lost his voice. Unable to fight the temptress Maddie had become, he shut his eyes and gave in, momentarily forgetting his guilt and the snagged zipper as Maddie replaced the pain with sweet oblivion.

Chapter Twenty-two

He was out of control, Maddie was out of control, *everything* was freaking, completely out of control.

"Stay here, Maddie. I'll go head the guys off by the river."

"No, let me come with you, we'll explain—"

"No." Chase grabbed her hand, forcing her to look at him. "Not now." He indicated their disheveled state of dress, then brushed his fingers tenderly along Maddie's whisker-burned cheek. "I'll tell them but . . . not like this, Maddie."

She stared at him long and hard, questions and uncertainty in her eyes. Chase felt like the worst kind of lowlife, torn between hurting Maddie and losing his best friends' friendship. Still, if or when he did tell the guys, he didn't want to confess with the scent of his sex still lingering on Maddie's body as if he'd intentionally seduced her to throw the affair in their faces.

He suddenly felt sick to his stomach. "Please, let me handle this," he said gruffly.

She finally nodded, then reached up to gently trace a finger over his lips. "All right, Chase. We'll do it your way."

The trust he saw in her expression only compounded his turmoil.

He'd already broken her brothers' trust—could he do the same to Maddie?

With a sigh of contentment, she reached up and kissed him on the mouth, then patted his butt and smiled. "Go on now before they come back. I'll slip out the front."

His stomach churning, his back throbbing, he nodded and hurried away, slipping out of the back basement door and scooting through the woods. Seconds later, he jammed his hands in his pockets and ambled up the path toward Chase and Reid.

"Hey, we were looking for you," Lance said, waving him over to the clearing.

Reid leaned beneath a maple tree. "Where's Maddie? We figured you two were down here together?"

If they only knew *how* together, they'd have a fit.

"We were." His throat burned with the lie and he could barely stand up straight for his backache. "I was showing Maddie the property, but she had an appointment and headed back. I guess you just missed her on the trail."

Lance narrowed his eyes, studying him. "You all right, Chase? You look kind of funny." Lance's gaze dropped to his pocket. Chase glanced down guiltily, grimacing when he noticed the edge of Maddie's bra peeking out from his pocket.

"Well, you must be feeling better," Lance said with a chuckle. "Daphne again?"

Chase nodded, mumbling that he was fine, the lies

and guilt growing. He couldn't even use the pain pills as an excuse for his crazy behavior today.

And no, he wasn't all right. And he wasn't sure he would be ever again.

After changing her clothes, Maddie hurried toward town, remembering she'd promised Cynthia, Jeff's coworker, she'd meet her at her new town house today for a consultation, worry nagging her. Had Chase been slightly distant when he'd left? Was he mentally withdrawing from her?

Or had her imagination been going wild?

He had said he'd handle things, right—meaning he would tell Reid and Lance about the two of them?

Would he tell them the sex had been cataclysmic?

It certainly had been to Maddie. Euphoric beyond anything she'd ever dreamed. Passionate, hot, exciting. Even their first kisses had been full of fire and erotic promises.

Nothing like the humdrum kisses she'd shared with Jeff.

Of course, now she realized the reason why. She'd never been in love with Jeff, not the wild, have-to-have-you sexy kind of love she felt with Chase. Not that her feelings were all about sex; she admired Chase. He was a self-made man, a talented architect, and he'd risen above a rotten childhood to make something out of himself, had overcome obstacles Jeffrey Oglethorpe knew nothing about. Roses and candy be damned.

Chalking her worries up to anxiety over the coming tour, she parked in front of Cynthia's house, killed the engine and grabbed her notepad.

Cynthia greeted her with a glass of sweet iced tea and a plate of sandwiches.

"Thanks, what a relief. I'm starved," Maddie admitted.

"I'm so glad you agreed to help me," Cynthia said, brushing a wrinkle from her pale green suit. "I'm not very good with colors but I do so want to have a nice place."

"Hoping to impress someone?" Maddie teased.

Cynthia blushed. "Well . . ."

"You don't have to answer that." Maddie said, snatching a sandwich. "Just tell me what you have in mind, and we'll go from there."

They spent the next twenty minutes chatting about Cynthia's likes and dislikes while they ate. During the conversation, Maddie learned Cynthia was the daughter of an orthodontist from Raleigh, had recently ended a bad relationship where her boyfriend had actually stolen most of her furniture and she had dreams of becoming president of her own company someday. Maddie liked her.

She drained her tea and placed the glass on the small glass-topped kitchen table. "Okay, so you want something elegant and modern but not so outlandish and pricey that your place doesn't feel homey?"

"That sounds vague, doesn't it?" Cynthia asked, looking unsure of herself.

Maddie patted her hand. "Don't worry. I think I know what you mean." She studied the small living space and began to sketch a few ideas, asking questions as she drew.

"If you go with a neutral palette, you can always add splashes of color in the accessories to liven up the place. What kind of art do you like?"

An hour later, Maddie had outlined several ideas, and Cynthia had narrowed her selections down to two choices. She wanted to think about them overnight.

"You know, you're really easy to talk to," Cynthia said. "I'm glad Jeff . . . I mean Mr. Oglethorpe recommended you to me."

Maddie folded up her sketchpad. "Cynthia, is Jeff one of the people you want to impress?"

The young brunette fluttered a manicured hand over her chest. "Maddie, I'm sorry, this is awkward, isn't it? I know the two of you were involved—"

"Don't worry about that," Maddie said, waving her off. She ignored the fact that Jeff still seemed to be pursuing *her*. Chase was the only man for her. And she wanted Jeff to find someone who would really love him. "If you like Jeff, then go for it, Cynthia. Just because he and I didn't work out doesn't mean I don't want to see him happy."

Cynthia's light blue eyes twinkled with surprise. "You really mean that?"

"Absolutely. As a matter of fact I'm kind of involved with someone else myself."

"Really? Who?"

"This guy I work with."

"That handsome man you were with at the restaurant?"

"Yes, things are pretty hot with us right now." Maddie's face heated as she remembered her earlier encounter with Chase in the exercise room.

"Oh, wow," Cynthia said. "He was buff. I bet he knows how to please a woman."

"He sure does," Maddie said with a laugh, deciding she'd better not say too much. Suddenly anxious to see Chase again and find out how her brothers had taken the news of their relationship, she stood and thanked Cynthia for lunch, promising to bring back full-color sketches when Cynthia called with her decision on the fabrics.

As she drove back toward the subdivision, Maddie found herself smiling like a schoolgirl. While she and Cynthia discussed window treatments and furniture, she hoped Chase had been explaining to her brothers the wonderful bond the two of them shared. Lance and Reid might be upset at first, but then . . . they'd understand. They'd have to.

Chase would make certain they did.

They'd probably even be happy for her since they loved Chase so much.

Memories of that stupid bachelor pact rose in Maddie's mind to taunt her, threatening to destroy her hope, but she shoved her reservations aside. Surely after their wild coupling today, Chase would have to tear up that stupid piece of paper, too, and admit he cared about her. Maybe even that he loved her.

Reid's beeper chirped. He glanced at the number and frowned. Knobby Smaltz. What had the P.I. discovered?

Only one way to find out.

He made a token excuse to Lance, saying he had to meet with a plumbing subcontractor and hurried toward his truck. The radio blared an old country-and-western tune "Crazy," as he drove a safe distance from the complex, veered down an old dirt road by the inlet and parked in the shade of a live oak dripping with Spanish moss. What better place to hide while he carried on his clandestine conversation. What better song to indicate how this whole thing with his father made him feel. Crazy.

He hated all this lying and sneaking around.

How had his father handled it? Had their mother

known the secrets his father had harbored?

And what if Knobby had discovered another Summers, one who wanted to meet them, to be part of the family.

No, he wouldn't allow the situation to come to that.

If Knobby had discovered someone, Reid would find them and head them off before Lance or Maddie ever had to know.

Gripping the phone with sweaty hands, he punched in Knobby's cell phone number and waited. Seconds later, the man's rough-hewn voice echoed over the line.

"It's Summers. What do you have?"

Knobby wheezed through the phone. "The nurse at the hospital said there have been several inquiries, all anonymous. But one of the calls was a repeat, a woman."

"And?"

"And she's not at liberty to give out any information regarding your father."

"That's a relief."

"Don't relax too soon."

A bad feeling twisted Reid's stomach. "Why not?"

Knobby's rusty breath rattled over the line. "There may be a hitch here."

"Go on."

"Someone broke into the files about a month ago."

"Shit."

"She isn't sure what the person was looking for."

"Were any files taken?"

"No, but the intruder could have photocopied files." Knobby whistled through his teeth. "Looks like the kind of thing that could mean trouble. I guess you'll just have to wait and see."

Several minutes later, Reid dropped his face into his hands and groaned. He had to think.

The first step. He'd ask Knobby to find out if his father had any accounts set aside that they didn't know about. Maybe his dad had taken precautions or set up some kind of fund in case this . . . these others ever came back to haunt him.

He thought of his and Lance's fledgling business and silently cursed a blue streak—they were finally so close to making a success of their company.

Surely, his father had anticipated problems and set up accounts for emergency's sake. If not, he . . . he didn't know what he was going to do.

He racked his brain to remember if there'd been any strangers lurking around asking questions about the family lately. Suspicions gnawed at him—the only person he could think of was that TV talk-show host that had invited his brother over for dinner. Lance had said she'd been asking him about the family, that he didn't trust her, that she liked to sneak into other people's lives for a story.

And Knobby had said the repeat caller had been a woman. Could the caller have been Sophie Lane? If so, was she after a story or something else?

After getting away from Lance and Reid, Chase spent the afternoon and evening locked in his office, drawing up blueprints for a new colonial home he hoped to add to the next phase of development. He avoided calling Maddie. He also avoided her calls.

Only two more days until the tour. If he could wait until the tour was over, he could break the news to Maddie calmly, reasoning that close working conditions had prompted their affair and that they would no longer be working together, so it would seem natural to end their . . . their physical relationship.

Sex, lust—that was all their relationship was anyway. He did not, was not, could not be in love . . . with anyone. After all, this was the new millennium, not the dark ages. Just because he'd taken Maddie's virginity didn't mean he had to marry her or fall in love with her. She hadn't mentioned commitment or love; in fact, she'd been adamant about dating different guys. And as far as falling in love; well, what did he know about the emotion, except that it was another four letter word? He'd never had it from the people who should have loved him. Maddie knew he would make a sorry excuse for a husband.

But then again, she had chosen him as her first, and he did feel territorial. She was his, no one else's but *his*. She never had been, and she never would be. . . . Besides, wasn't she really the first woman he'd felt . . . emotionally involved with during sex?

No, eventually this emotional connection would dissipate, and he'd go on to someone else and so would she. They'd both be grateful they hadn't complicated things by telling Lance and Reid.

He only felt an emotional attachment to Maddie, because he'd known her so long, and because of this insufferable guilt. Yes, Maddie would find some nice guy and settle down one day.

As long as that guy wasn't the wuss.

A thick burning sensation rose in his throat as the image of Maddie with Oglethorpe or any other man passed through his brain. He balled his hands into fists and pressed one over his chest, reminding himself not to eat that spicy Creole again. On top of everything else, the damn woman had given him heartburn.

The phone trilled, and he glanced at the caller ID, breathing a sigh of relief when he noticed the number didn't belong to Maddie.

His relief was short-lived. A disgruntled-sounding client's voice echoed on the line. "Listen, Mr. Holloway, I'm going to have to tear up that contract."

Dammit, more trouble. "That's within your rights and the grace period," Chase said, fighting the edge to his voice, "but do you mind telling me why you changed your mind? The other day you seemed impressed with my work and the Summers developers—"

"Money," the man admitted in a sheepish voice. "I can't possibly stick with you when I was promised a lower interest rate if I go with another developer—"

"A lower interest rate?"

"Yeah, it'll save me thousands of dollars."

"Who offered you the better deal?"

"The Savings and Loan. I just finished speaking with the manager, and he promised to take care of me personally."

"Martin Middlemyer?"

"No, that nice Mr. Oglethorpe."

That sneaky, weaselly wuss! Anger churned in Chase's stomach. "Oglethorpe promised you a lower interest rate if you signed with another developer?"

"Right. Well, thanks for understanding."

The man hung up, and Chase pounded his fist on the desk, a sudden uneasy feeling rolling through him. He'd been suspicious of Oglethorpe before. If the wuss had promised this man lower interest rates, had he offered the same deal to the other three clients who'd reneged on their contracts? And what about the contractors? Oglethorpe and his family had connections all over town. Had he also cut a deal with them?

Furious, he fumbled through his rolodex, grabbed

the phone, and punched in the number for the Savings and Loan. It was about time he had a little talk with Jeffrey Oglethorpe, the back stabber. And he wouldn't leave his office until he had some answers.

Chapter Twenty-three

Maddie tucked her feet beneath her bottom in the chair and glanced at the door for the hundredth time. She'd been expecting Lance and Reid to call or stop by all night, especially if Chase had told them the truth about the two of them, but she hadn't heard a peep from any of them. Including Chase.

Had Chase confessed? Had the boys beaten the sense out of him? Were they laughing over the fact that the two of them had finally gotten together, deciding it had been destiny?

So, why hadn't she heard something, *anything?*

Determined not to be paranoid, she shrugged off the anxiety knotting her insides. Maybe the boys had accepted the news easily and were busy finishing up last-minute plans for the tour.

Or maybe Chase hadn't told them at all?

Maddie refused to think about it anymore. Instead, she turned her attention back to her best friend.

"Cheer up, Sophie. Just because my brother is a stupid dweeb doesn't mean there isn't a wonderful guy out there somewhere for you."

Sophie sighed, running her finger around the rim of her margarita glass. "I know. But for some reason, the first time I saw your brother I felt this connection with him. Sounds corny, doesn't it?"

"Not at all, Soph. I had a crush on Chase when we were kids. I'll never forget the first time Lance brought him home." Maddie laughed and twirled her straw in her drink. "I got all nervous, thought he was a hellion."

"There's something about that type, isn't there?"

Maddie nodded. "But there was more than that—he always had this kind of sad, lonely look about him. Like my cat had when I found him." Maddie smiled wistfully at T. C. who lay snuggled in her lap, purring. "I never dreamed Chase would wake up one day and see me as something other than a little girl."

"I'm so happy for you, Mad."

"You know what the best part is?"

"What?"

"He not only supports my work, but he appreciates my talent, too. He told me what a wonderful job I've done on the project, and he means it. And we work great together."

"That's so cool, Maddie."

Maddie grinned, thinking of her mother and wishing she and her father could have worked out their differences. "Sophie, I have something I've never shown anyone. You want to see?"

"Something about Chase?"

"No, just wait, and I'll explain." Maddie settled T. C. on the sofa, ran to her bedroom, and hurried back, a book clutched in her hand.

Sophie turned a questioning look at Maddie, her

voice squeaking out, "*Erotic Body Desserts.* Wow, I guess sneaking into Greg Pugh's shower opened up a new side of you."

"It's not mine," Maddie confessed with a sly grin. "The book belonged to my mother."

"Your mother?"

"Yes, I found it in the attic a few weeks ago." Maddie rubbed a thumb over the spine. "I never told Chase and Lance but I heard Mom and Dad arguing the night before the accident. Mom said she was tired of being a doctor's wife, that she had dreams of her own, and she didn't want to live in his shadow anymore. She wanted to start a catering business, but my dad didn't support her decision."

Sophie's gaze fell to the book. When the implication dawned, her mouth gaped open. "You don't mean . . ."

Maddie shrugged. "I thought she meant a regular caterer until I found this book. At first, I was so embarrassed and appalled that my own mom was so . . . so—"

"Hip?"

Maddie laughed. "Sexually oriented. I mean, you don't usually think of your *parents* having sex lives."

Sophie nodded, biting down on her lip.

Maddie opened the page and smiled when Sophie gasped. "It was hard for me to believe anyone would make stuff like this at first, but now I've been with Chase, I can understand."

"Oh, my gosh," Sophie exclaimed. "Look at the icing—it's covering that man's . . ."

"Looks good enough to eat, doesn't it?" Maddie said.

Sophie laughed. "You're a wicked woman, Maddie Summers."

Maddie flipped the page. "I know. Now help me

pick out a dessert I can make for Chase."

"You're going to decorate him?"

"No, I'm going to decorate me." Maddie pointed to a photo of a naked woman adorned in cake icing, cherries and whipped cream. "Chase loves sweets. After the tour, I'm going to surprise him with a sexy confection he can't possibly resist."

Chase entered the Savings and Loan the next day, his mind a whir of confusion. The sleepless night had done nothing to alleviate his anxiety about Maddie; the empty bed had only made him miss her. Her warm, sensual body, the soft curve of her hip, the rapturous way she moaned in ecstasy when he made love to her.

How could he possibly miss someone so much when he'd only slept with her twice? Well, technically not twice, several times actually, but they'd only slept together on two separate days, not that they'd actually slept. . . .

Taking a deep breath to focus, Chase paused and studied the surroundings. The pristine bank with coat-and-tie executives sitting behind shining glass-door offices sent a tremor of unease up his spine. He felt out of place, reminding him of his teen years when he'd been an awkward street kid invited to someone's upscale suburban home. Of course, those invitations had been almost nonexistent.

But he had to deal with Jeff Oglethorpe today and find out if the wuss had been backstabbing them the last few weeks, accounting for all the setbacks they'd incurred. He'd phoned Lance and Reid and asked them to meet him here so they could confront Oglethorpe together. Where were they?

"Can I help you, sir?"

He adjusted his tie, hating the choking knot at his

neck, and smiled at the receptionist, a thin, wiry woman in her early fifties. "Chase Holloway, I came to see Mr. Oglethorpe."

"Do you have an appointment?"

Her condescending tone irritated him. "Yes."

She indicated a chair, and he took it, scanning the spacious front area. To his surprise, Maddie's friend Sophie exited Oglethorpe's office. A dynamite little woman with jet-black hair, exactly the dark-haired type Lance usually liked. He was surprised his friend hadn't already had a fling with her.

"Chase?"

"Yeah. Hi." He stood, shaking her hand when she offered it.

"It's good to see you. I saw Maddie last night, and she told me how excited she is about the project."

Guilt over not calling Maddie suffused his conscience. "Yeah, she's done a great job. I think she'll probably be swamped with clients after the tour."

"Good, Maddie really wants this business to work." Sophie's eyes twinkled as if she knew something Chase didn't. "So, how are things with the company?"

He shrugged. "Okay, we've had a few glitches. I'm trying to work out last-minute problems." Curiosity got the better of him. "Lance said he was helping you with that house you wanted to restore?"

Her smile faded. "I met with Lance, but things didn't work out between us. I decided it would be better if I found another builder for the renovations."

"Another builder?"

"Yes, that's why I'm here. Jeffrey Oglethorpe had recommended someone else when I took out my loan but I was hoping, well . . . since Maddie and I are friends, I wanted to use her brothers."

"Oglethorpe recommended someone else to you?"

Sophie nodded. "Yeah, as a matter of fact, he quoted me a better interest rate if I worked with this other builder." She shrugged. "I guess I'll have to now."

The receptionist cleared her throat. "Mr. Holloway, Mr. Oglethorpe will see you now."

"Well, I'll let you go," Sophie said, waving as she sauntered out the door.

He said good-bye, scanned the front in search of his buddies but came up empty. He had no choice but to face the weasel by himself. He stepped into Oglethorpe's office, his anger growing by the minute. Cynthia, the young woman he'd seen with the wuss at the restaurant, stood in the office looking over Oglethorpe's shoulder.

Oglethorpe's bony face twisted with agitation when he spotted Chase. Chase could not see Maddie with this man. "We'll finish up later, Cynthia," Oglethorpe said. Placing a ballpoint pen that probably cost more than Chase's Timex into a leather pencil holder, he steepled his fingers and gestured toward the expensive chair across from him.

Chase took a seat, refusing to let the man's wealth and social station intimidate him. He cut straight to the point and asked about the offers for lower interest rates.

"I have a deal with this other builder," Oglethorpe said snidely. "It's strictly business, Mr. Holloway, all on the up-and-up, I can assure you. He's a much bigger builder with a long-standing reputation, so he can afford to offer lower rates. Of course if you were more experienced, you'd know—"

"I'm experienced enough to know a backstabbing jerk when I meet one."

Oglethorpe's eyes bulged. "I should have expected you to try to strong-arm me. How like you, Mr. Holloway. Can't quite shed those street gang ways, can you?"

Chase ground his teeth together. "Just tell me what you want, Oglethorpe. What's in this for you?"

"I don't know what you mean. I'm simply a business—"

"Cut the crap. You're mad at Maddie for dumping you on TV, and you're getting revenge by sabotaging her brothers' business."

"And you know this because you're the brains of the bunch?"

"I know this because I put two and two together."

"While you were cavorting around with Maddie trying to seduce her?" Oglethorpe sneered. "Didn't your plans work, Mr. Holloway? Did Maddie turn you down?"

"No, as a matter of fact . . ." Chase caught himself, horrified at his almost-blunder. He had to control his temper. Besides, how did Oglethorpe know about their affair?

Oglethorpe rose stiffly. "Don't bother to deny it; my coworker told me all about you. I'm sure Maddie's family will be thrilled to find out—"

"Your coworker is wrong. There's nothing to find out," Chase snapped. "Maddie and I have a working relationship, period."

Oglethorpe raised a skeptical brow. He might as well have called Chase a liar. What exactly had this Cynthia woman told him; was she a spy for Oglethorpe? Had she been hiding out somewhere, watching them?

"In that case, I'd like you to know that I am going to get Maddie back. And her brothers approve."

Chase swallowed, his throat thick. Why would his best friends approve of a guy like this for Maddie? But not him. Just because they thought he was a ladies' man, that he'd had a lot of women. This guy was a jerk. And if Oglethorpe and the guys had discussed a reconciliation, it would seem the wuss would want to help Lance and Reid? "If you really want Maddie, then why sabotage her brothers' company? Hurting the company won't win you any points."

"I'm not sabotaging their company." Oglethorpe ran a hand through his oil-slicked hair. "And I will have Maddie back."

"The hell you will." Maddie wouldn't go from his bed to this bony ass's.

Oglethorpe planted his skinny hands into fists on his credenza. "Holloway, you may have Maddie snowed right now, but she'll realize what a low-life piece of scum you are, that I'm the man for her. I care for Maddie and want to give her a good life, a stable marriage. What are you offering?"

Nothing, Chase thought sourly. Exactly nothing.

But he'd never admit it to this man. "This isn't about me and Maddie," Chase said, pounding his fist on the desk for emphasis. "It's about you and what you've been up to. I don't understand your logic, but I'll figure it out and then I'll—"

Oglethorpe laughed viciously. "Stay away from me and stay away from Maddie or I'll ruin you for life, Holloway, and I'll see to it that the Summers boys never get another job in Savannah."

Chase cursed. "You sneaky, conniving—"

"I'm calling security, Mr. Holloway. I suggest you leave and take your threats with you."

Chase flew around the desk, jerked Oglethorpe's shirt in his hands, bunching the collar in his fists. "Not before you admit you've been undermining—"

"Chase, what in blazes are you doing?"

Chase froze, his hand still clutching Oglethorpe's

neckline as Lance and Reid walked in the door.

Oglethorpe tried to yank his shirt free. "Thank God you're here. Your friend is a maniac. Will one of you please take him back to his cage?"

Chase tightened his hold. "Tell them about the loans."

Oglethorpe's ears turned red. "I don't know what you're talking about."

Chase raised his fist to pound some sense into the man. "Tell them—"

Lance grabbed his arm, tugging him away. "Chase, what's wrong with you?"

"Yeah, man, we don't need this," Reid said. "We've got enough problems already without you making the situation worse."

"Worse? I'm trying to help."

"Well, you're not helping anything right now," Lance said. "We got a reputation to uphold."

"You weren't worried about your reputation the day Maddie was on TV."

"We made a mistake," Reid said, his forehead puckered with a frown. "The tour's tomorrow, and we're trying to keep clean—you know how important this tour is to the company."

It could make or break them. Chase spoke through clenched teeth. "Listen to me, this turd's been offering lower interest rates to people if they use other builders. Just ask Sophie Lane."

"What's she got to do with this?" Lance asked, looking thunderous.

Reid gave Chase a suspicious eye. "And why have you been talking to her?"

"She was here, right outside," Chase said.

"He's a lunatic," Oglethorpe snarled. "I've been recommending you guys to everyone who asks. I can't help it if someone chooses another builder."

Oglethorpe rattled off several clients who had bought from Lance and Reid. "And Warner signed with you, didn't he?" Oglethorpe said. "You guys wouldn't have half the business you have if I hadn't recommended you. And I did it all for Maddie."

"That the truth?" Reid asked.

"Of course," Oglethorpe replied.

"He's lying," Chase said.

"I don't know, Chase. I can think of at least two folks who signed with me after coming from here," Lance verified.

"But that was before Maddie broke up with him," Chase argued. "He's trying to trick her—"

"I don't have to trick her, I love her! And he just wants Maddie for himself," Oglethorpe shouted. "Just ask him. Ask him if he hasn't tried to get her in bed. My coworker said Maddie as much as admitted things were hot between them."

Maddie told Cynthia they were hot?

Lance and Reid both turned on him, their expressions a cross between shock and anger and betrayal. Chase's stomach lurched to his throat. He should fess up. But not now, not like this.

Not in front of the wuss.

"You know I'd never hurt Maddie," he said instead. "I've just been watching out for her like you guys asked." While the wuss was sugar-coating his act with gifts and flowers.

"He's a violent, crazy man exactly like his father, and he ought to be in jail," Oglethorpe said.

"I'd be a hell of a lot better for Maddie than you," Chase said.

Oglethorpe's nostrils flared. "If you don't haul him out of here and get him under control, I'm calling security and pressing charges for assault."

Chase reached for him again but Lance and Reid

grabbed him and dragged him out of the door.

"What the hell's going on?" Lance bellowed.

Chase swallowed, ready to confess, but everyone in the bank was watching, and he still wasn't sure whether Maddie wanted her brothers to know the exact nature of their relationship. He motioned for them to step outside. "Look, guys, Oglethorpe saw Maddie and me having dinner, a business dinner, that's all. He's blowing things out of proportion to get revenge on you for that scare tactic you pulled after the show."

"What did you mean you'd be better for Maddie than Oglethorpe?" Reid asked, raising a suspicious eyebrow.

"I don't like the guy. Anyone would be better for Maddie than him," Chase said through gritted teeth. "You guys surely don't believe Oglethorpe over me."

Lance ran a hand through his hair, glancing around at the crowded street. "Of course not. You may be a ladies' man, but you'd never seduce our baby sister."

An hour later, Chase sat in his dark apartment, the lights out, nursing a beer. His whole world was falling apart. His business, his friendship with Lance and Reid, his reputation—and all because of this crazy attraction to Maddie.

An attraction that could go nowhere.

And now he'd lied to Lance and Reid. How would he ever fix things?

Maybe Maddie was enjoying this . . . this wild fling with him. But she'd been a virgin for Christ's sake. She had no other experience. She'd been on the rebound from Oglethorpe, looking for someone to assuage her pride or sow a few wild oats with. But one day he'd disappoint Maddie just like he had everyone else. She would grow tired of his wild-ass ways and want more. A family. A man with a name she could be proud of. Not a jailbird's son with a bad reputation in town. And after today, Oglethorpe would no doubt spread the news of their encounter and rip what little bit of respect Chase had earned to smithereens.

He pulled out an old worn photo of his mother and stared at the faded image. She was young, about twenty-two when she'd given him away, long, straight, brown hair; thin, hollow face; gaunt-looking, shadowed eyes as if she'd lived beyond her years. Her face floated like a distant memory in his mind.

But her parting words were just as sharp as if she'd said them yesterday. "You're just like your no-count daddy. You make me miserable."

Chase's chest tightened.

No, he wasn't cut out to be a family man or a husband.

He had no idea how to make a woman happy, not in a long term relationship. He didn't think to buy fancy gifts or use flowery words, all the things women desired, or eventually desired once the hot lust died down.

Hell, his own mother hadn't wanted him. And she hadn't loved him. How could anyone else?

Chapter Twenty-four

The tour was set to begin in two hours, but desperation forced Reid to find out the scoop on Sophie Lane now. Wiping the sweat from his brow, he pulled up to the model home where he was supposed to meet Lance and Chase, punched in Knobby's number and waited. Three rings, four, five . . .

On the sixth ring, Knobby's churly voice echoed on the voice-mail system. "Smaltz here. You know the drill."

"This is Reid Summers. Listen, about that problem we've been discussing. I have a name—Sophie Lane. She's that pretty talk-show host on *Sophie Knows*. Her show airs every day at three on NBC." He paused to catch his breath, hoping the machine's tape held out. "I heard she's been asking around about our family. She even cozied up to my sister the minute she got to town. Check into her. I want to know everything there is to know about her."

Feeling slightly relieved to have made the call, he hung up, frowning when he saw Lance staring at him through the window. Had he heard?

Lance pecked on the glass. "What are you doing?"

Reid opened the truck door and climbed out, his knees wobbling. "Just checking on some last-minute details."

Lance's face crinkled with worry. "Don't tell me, more problems? It's almost time—"

"Don't worry." Reid patted his big brother on the back. "I've got everything under control." At least he hoped he did.

Lance breathed a sigh of relief, and Reid followed him inside the model-home office. He would just have to wait for Knobby to investigate Sophie Lane and discover whether she was someone from his father's checkered past. Someone who was only pretending to be Maddie's friend—someone who'd come to wreak havoc in all their lives.

Maddie paced the foyer of the Greek Revival home, her stomach in knots. She'd checked everything in every home twice, had her business cards in place, the greeters for the homes all lined up at their stations, but she was supposed to meet Chase before the tour and he hadn't showed.

She was so nervous she'd been biting her acrylic nails.

He'd finally phoned her this morning, claiming he had to see her before the tour, there was something important he wanted to tell her. Jeff had also phoned, saying he really wanted to see her tonight, too.

She had to see Jeff eventually, but first, she needed to talk to Chase. Would he announce his love tonight? End their wonderful affair? Suggest they go together to tell her brothers about their involvement, then see how their relationship developed? Or maybe he was going to propose?

No, Chase was a confirmed bachelor.

Excitement stirred along her nerve endings though at the possibility of a future with him. She and Chase had great sex, they worked well together, and if they decided to marry someday, they'd make beautiful babies. A little boy who looked like Chase, that dark hair, those big, dark eyes. She could already picture Chase teaching him how to build, constructing a treehouse for their son. . . .

Reservations kicked in, replacing her daydreams. She hadn't seen Chase since that day in the exercise room. According to Lance and Reid, he'd locked himself in his office to finish some work for the next building phase, but they'd acted funny when they'd talked to her. And they hadn't once mentioned the fact that she and Chase had made love.

He had told them, hadn't he?

If not, maybe he was waiting for the tour. Or maybe he had never intended on telling them; maybe he planned to show her the bachelor pact and send her packing.

In the background, she heard the tour guide rehearsing her notes, practicing her spiel. Maddie's hand flew to her throat, automatically feeling for the missing heirloom. She'd frozen up yesterday when Lance had asked her if she was going to wear it to the open house. Finally, she'd had the good sense to tell him she was having the necklace cleaned. Soon she would have it back. Very soon.

Another motor rumbled, and she recognized Chase's truck through the branches lining the drive. He swerved into the driveway and climbed out, looking handsome and powerful in a dark blue shirt and khakis. Had he dressed for the tour or her?

Sunlight glinted off his bronze skin as he stepped onto the covered portico and opened the door. Maddie's heart raced, her stomach fluttering.

"Hey," she said, unable to hide the smile that slipped onto her face.

His gaze raked over her, hungry and dark, and maybe a little bit troubled.

"Chase?"

"Can we talk?"

"Sure." *Maybe he wanted a quickie before the tour. Arousal sparked, hot and exciting, throughout her body. She'd be more than happy to accommodate him.*

Instantly hungry for his touch, she dragged him upstairs to the master suite, and then to the master bath where she eyed the Jacuzzi with interest.

He didn't mince words. "You all set?"

Maddie twisted her hands in front of her, wanting to touch him, but hoping he'd make the first move. "Yeah. I think so anyway."

"The house looks great, Mad. You should win a lot of clients from this tour."

"Thanks. You and the guys are going to impress everyone, too."

He leaned against the tub, shuffling as if he were nervous, then jammed one hand in his pocket. Maddie's heart thumped with anticipation and dread.

"I . . . we need to talk, I was going to wait till after the tour, but . . ."

"Chase, what is it?" Maddie reached for his hand and held it between both of hers, tracing lines across his dark skin. Her fingers burned from the erotic chemistry spiraling from the innocent contact. "Just say what's on your mind. You can tell me anything, you know that?"

Surprise registered on his face. "I went to talk to Oglethorpe yesterday."

Maddie sucked in a breath. "You talked to Jeff?"

"Yeah, did Lance or Reid tell you?"

"No." Maybe that was the reason they'd acted so odd on the phone. Her hand flew to her neck again. "It's about the necklace, isn't it? Jeff told you?" She sank onto the side of the tub, dropping her head into her hands. "Lance and Reid know, don't they?"

Chase shook his head. "What necklace?"

"My heirloom." Maddie shook her head. "I didn't want the boys to find out."

Chase sat down beside her, tipping her chin up to look at him. "I'm not sure we're talking about the same thing, Maddie. What's going on?"

"Then they don't know?"

"Know what?"

"That I put Mom's heirloom up for collateral to back my decorating business."

"You mean Oglethorpe actually took your mother's necklace?" Chase asked in an incredulous voice.

Maddie nodded miserably. "I was surprised, too, but he said I'd made the rules. I wanted a business loan so that's exactly what he gave me." She tucked a stand of hair behind her ear, relieved to have the secret out in the open. "That's why this tour's success is really important to me. I have to make money, make a go of my business so I can get the necklace back."

"I don't think your brothers have a clue," Chase said, massaging her back.

Maddie frowned. "I hope not. They'd be disappointed, and I really want to make them proud. This heirloom means a lot to all of us. It's the only thing I have of my mother's." *Other than that strange rec-*

ipe book, and I certainly couldn't have put it up for collateral.

Chase's gut clenched at the misery on Maddie's face. "I can imagine, Mad. Your mom was wonderful."

"She was, wasn't she?" Maddie said.

"Yeah, a hell of a lot better than mine." He could kill the man for taking the prized piece of jewelry from Maddie. Did Oglethorpe think that if he made their business fail, Maddie's would also fail, and she'd come running back to him?

A twisted, selfish plan, but one he could imagine the wuss conjuring.

Unfortunately, one he doubted he could ever prove. Oglethorpe was the type to hide his sneakiness in legalities and well-chosen syntax, covering his bony ass all the way.

On the ride over, Chase had debated how to handle the situation with Oglethorpe. And what to do about Maddie. He'd planned to end their affair before the tour, but he couldn't stand to upset her or add to her worries now. She looked so sweet and vulnerable. . . .

He reached out just to comfort her, to hold her. But holding Maddie led to other things. Things that were supposed to be off-limits.

No, he had to break it off. Maybe if he told her about his own mother, she'd be so repulsed she wouldn't want him either. He screwed up his courage, but his voice still quivered, "Maddie, I always admired your mom. My mother hated me. The day she left me, she said she was glad to be rid of me, that I was so mean I'd tear up a rock."

"How awful." Maddie's hand gently cupped his jaw. "Little boys are supposed to tear up rocks, Chase. That's why they're little boys."

This wasn't going as he planned.

Her tender concern made his throat tighten. "I didn't tell you to gain sympathy, Maddie, I only wanted you to know how lucky you were to have a mom like yours. So, don't worry, honey, the tour will be a success, and you'll have the necklace back in no time."

Maddie's face split into a radiant smile that sent a tingling feeling all through his body. "You're wonderful, Chase." She threw her arms around him and hugged him, her breasts pressing against his chest in an erotic tease. "I've missed you so much. I'm so glad you're here now."

Suddenly her lips found his, her hands tunneled through his hair, and he forgot all reason. He swept her into his arms, his body aching and hard, his sex swelling painfully against his slacks. She arched into him, her nails scraping his back, drawing him closer as she suckled his lips and plunged her tongue into his mouth.

"God, Maddie, the tour."

"We'll make it fast," she whispered hoarsely, already tugging at his shirt. "But I have to have you, Chase. I've been so empty without you."

Her words destroyed any lingering reservations.

"And I have to have you, Maddie." *Just one more time.* He dipped his head to lick her neck. "I've never tasted anything as sweet as your body."

She caressed his chest, then dipped her hand lower into his slacks and stroked his sex, freeing him from his underwear and into her hand. He moaned and snaked his arm around her to lift her onto his aching shaft.

"Yes, Chase, oh, yes." She spread her legs, straddling him as his hands worked the front clasp of her bra. Her beautiful breasts spilled forward in his hands, and he cupped her weight, bowing his head to suckle her. The sounds of his mouth feeding on her echoed in the empty room. He didn't care.

He pushed her skirt up further, groaning at the sight of her garter. With a devilish, teasing grin, she impaled herself on him.

Footsteps clinked on the hardwood floor downstairs.

"Chase, Maddie?"

"Damn," Chase whispered hoarsely, "your brothers are here!"

"Oh, my God!"

Maddie jumped up to grab her clothes and banged him in the eye with her elbow. He moaned and reached for his pants.

"They have the absolute worst timing." Maddie quickly fastened her bra, righting her shirt just as her brothers appeared in the doorway.

Chase was trying to fasten his pants, but they were caught on his boot!

"What—" Lance's words died in his throat as he summed up the scene.

Chase fisted his hands by his sides. Shit. There'd be no denying it this time.

Maddie had missed a button on her shirt, making the ends hang askew. And he'd been caught, literally, with his pants down.

Chapter Twenty-five

Maddie was prepared to stand up to her brothers and confess everything, especially since her brothers were glaring at Chase if they planned to murder him. "Lance, Reid—"

"The tour's here!" the real-estate agent announced from downstairs. "Maddie, hurry so you can greet them."

Chase, Lance and Reid exchanged labored looks. "This isn't over," Lance snarled.

Chase leaned closer to Maddie and whispered in her ear, "Don't worry. I'll take care of things. And we'll get your necklace back."

The real-estate agent rapped on the staircase. "Maddie, they're coming up the sidewalk!"

Maddie inched to the edge of the window and peered out. "Oh, my goodness. There are so many people. I have to go." She turned and saw her brothers yanking Chase toward the door. He was still trying to buckle his belt.

"We're going to have a little talk," Lance said in a growl.

"Guys, wait!" Maddie yelled.

"It's okay, Maddie," Chase said in a low voice. "I'll see you after the tour."

"Like hell you will," Reid snapped.

"Boys, don't you dare—"

"Get downstairs, Maddie." Chase jerked free of her brothers. "This is what you've been working so hard for. Go on."

Maddie glanced back and forth between her brothers and Chase, torn. "You guys have to take your places, too."

"We'll do what we have to do," Lance said.

"Maddie!" the real-estate agent chirped. "Hurry! You should be here to greet them!"

Chase nodded for her to go ahead, and she brushed down her skirt, rebuttoned the front of her blouse, patted her hair into place and raced down the stairs. She heard the men's footsteps following but didn't have time to pause as a steady stream of people came flooding through the front door.

Three and a half hours later, Maddie sank onto the Chippendale sofa and breathed a contented sigh of relief. The first phase of the tour had been a success. So successful in fact that the real-estate agents had decided they would keep it open all week. Potential buyers had seemed to jump out of the woodwork. Maddie had a pocket full of business cards from prospective clients, buyers had expressed interest in two of the houses she'd decorated, and she'd heard nothing but praise for her brothers' work and Chase's designs. Jeff and his mother had even come.

Her chest swelled with pride for all of them even as her stomach fluttered with nerves. She had to find the boys and talk to them. And Chase. It was better everything was out in the open.

But her earlier conversation with Chase nagged at her; he'd planned to tell her something important. Was it that he'd seen Jeff or had there been something else on his mind—as in a breakup?

Or had he already explained things to her brothers by now, smoothed things over?

A girl could hope, couldn't she?

Unease pressed a fiery path down her throat. What if Chase wanted to end things? He'd always been fiercely loyal to Lance and Reid, but how did he feel about *her?*

"Maddie, I'm glad I caught you here alone for a minute." Jeff Oglethorpe coasted up beside her, sipping champagne from one of the flutes that had been set up at the celebratory table. He handed her a small jewelry box.

Maddie's heart raced—was it her mother's heirloom?

"Hi, Jeff." Maddie stood, feeling anxious.

"Congratulations on the success of the tour. Mother was impressed as well." Jeff's smile radiated warmth. "Go ahead, open the box."

Maddie's fingers trembled as she lifted the lid. A stunning cameo pin lay on a square of red velvet.

"I picked it out just for you," Jeff said, his voice thick with emotions.

Maddie's gaze rose to meet his. "But Jeff, I . . . I can't accept this."

"Sure you can. It would mean a lot to me, Maddie. I want you to have it to commemorate your new career."

Maddie blinked back tears. Jeff took the oval cameo out and pinned it to her collar. Then he brushed a kiss on her cheek. "The tour was really impressive, Maddie."

"Thank you." Maddie pulled away slightly, still uncomfortable with the gift. "I'm glad you thought so, Jeff. We all worked hard on organizing the show, but Lance and Reid have been especially diligent about checking their contractors' work."

"Their efforts obviously paid off." He gestured around the room with a wide sweep of his hand. "You definitely have a talent for decorating. A couple of Mother's friends are interested in buying one of the tour homes. Furnishings and all."

"That's wonderful," Maddie said, her smile sincere. "There was so much interest, we've decided to keep the tour running all week."

"Superb." He clasped her hand in his, pulling her nearer. "Your houses drew a lot of comments, Maddie. I'm proud of you."

Maddie patted her purse. "I did pick up a lot of contacts. Hopefully, I can pay back my loan soon and get back my mother's necklace."

Jeff nodded. "Yes, of course." He reached out and caressed her cheek with the palm of his hand. "Can we go someplace and talk?"

"Er—"

"Come on, let me buy you dinner. I want to make things up to you. You have received all my gifts, haven't you?"

"Yes, and they were all very thoughtful. But I can't go right now," Maddie said. "I have to meet Lance and Reid about the tour."

"Later, then?" He stroked her cheek again. "Maybe we could celebrate together. Go out to the river like we used to do. Maybe take a boat ride."

Maddie took a step backward, her pulse clamoring as if she were being disloyal to Chase. Silly, since he'd never said he wanted a commitment. "I'll call you later and we'll talk, but right now I really have to go."

With a quick good-bye, she turned and fled to find the boys. She hoped Chase had already explained their relationship, so she and *Chase* could go celebrate together. That is, if her brothers hadn't tied him to a tree with his own belt and lynched him.

Chase shook hands with the last guest, a physician from New York who had decided to relocate to the sunny South, and jotted a note about the meeting they'd scheduled for the following week in his calendar. He should be excited—the tour had been a bigger success than any of them could have imagined. He had retainers from two customers, five others interested in custom-designed homes and a few more calls to return.

But he still had to deal with Lance and Reid and explain about his relationship with Maddie.

They'd temporarily called a truce when the tour had begun, all three of them turning to business, acting the professionals he'd thought none of them would ever be. But with each passing second, his anxiety grew. Reid and Lance had avoided looking at him at all—a testament to how much they hated him. He'd helped them intimidate Oglethorpe after that TV debacle. And now, he'd acted far worse than the wuss. He'd seduced their baby sister—they'd probably kill him.

Just at the time his business was finally panning out, his dreams for making something of himself and showing Savannah he wasn't a nobody, the rest of his world was falling apart. Crumbling in his hands so fast he wasn't sure he could save it.

"Looks like everything was a success," Lance said

as the door closed behind the last visitor. The three of them converged around the round oak table in the breakfast nook, sipping on coffee.

"Yep. I'd say we're in good shape," Reid added with a grin. "And I heard several people raving over Maddie's decorating. Sounds like our little sister's found her calling."

Chase squared his shoulders and faced them. Might as well act like a man. "I told you she had things under control."

Both his friends' faces twisted with emotions—anger, hurt, disbelief.

"Yeah, and we thought *you* had things under control with her," Lance said.

"We trusted you," Reid said in a gravelly voice.

And therein lay the crux of the problem, Chase thought. He'd betrayed his best buddies' trust, the guys who'd helped him all his life. And the only way he knew to fix the problem was to let go of Maddie.

Maddie slipped into the model-home office, pausing when she heard voices. Her brothers' voices, Chase's. Hesitating by the kitchen doorway, she twisted her hands together and leaned next to the doorjamb beside the built-in bookshelves.

"We asked you to do a simple favor," Lance said. "To watch out for Maddie and make sure she didn't go wild with this decorating gig of hers, and look what happens."

Chase was supposed to be watching out for her?

"All we wanted was a baby-sitter so we could get our work done," Reid added.

Maddie clutched her stomach in misery. *A baby-sitter?*

"And, you agreed," Lance snapped. "You didn't think she'd succeed or even stick with this design idea any more than we did. And what did you do—you tried to seduce her!"

They didn't think she'd succeed?

"How far has it gone?" Reid asked. "How long have you been—?"

"Shut up," Chase growled. "I . . . I mean . . . it was just today."

A tear rolled down Maddie's cheek. *What? Just today?*

"Look, guys, I take full responsibility. Maddie was excited about the tour, we've gotten to be good friends—"

Good friends?

"That's all. I let the situation get out of hand today, and I'm sorry. It won't happen again."

Maddie bit back a sob. *It wouldn't?*

"I should never have touched Maddie; I was a—"

"Jerk," Lance supplied.

"SOB," Reid said.

Scumbag coward.

"You're right," Chase said in a low voice. "I was wrong, and I'm sorry."

"Think about Maddie," Lance said. "She's not the screw-around type, Chase. And you're not the marrying kind. You go through women like some men go through cars."

"Yeah, remember that bachelor pact," Reid added.

"I know," Chase said harshly. Maddie heard the chair scrape across the hardwood floor, heard Chase's boots clicking on the surface as he paced. "Don't worry, I'll explain things to Maddie and apologize. I won't . . . I won't touch her again. You have my word."

Maddie pressed her hand over cheek, wiping at the tears. What a fool she'd been—she'd secretly hoped he might confess his love, even talk about a commitment.

The sound of chairs moving startled her, and she realized they were all leaving, coming toward her. Her heart breaking, she tiptoed in the opposite direction and let herself out of the French doors, then hurried around the front to meet them on the doorstep.

Chase had broken her heart, but she'd be damned if she'd let him mangle her pride. She'd bid him good-bye before he had a chance to tell her their relationship was over.

Chase's feet felt heavy as he walked to the front door, but his heart was aching so much he couldn't seem to find the energy to make his body move any faster. Telling Maddie wasn't going to be easy, but he had to face her. He'd broken his promise once and look where it had gotten him. He'd lost the respect of his two best friends—no, his *only* friends. Now, he'd given the guys his word, and he had to keep it, no matter how much it hurt.

He had never hurt over a woman before, not since his mother.

Lance and Reid stepped outside, and he followed on their heels, shocked when he saw Maddie flying up the steps. "Hey, you guys," she sang cheerfully. "How'd the show go on your part?"

Lance and Reid exchanged confused looks.

"The tour?" Maddie said, shrugging as if none of them had any sense. "Everyone seemed pleased, didn't they?"

"Oh, yeah," Lance said. "We made a lot of good contacts."

"Me, too," Maddie said, barely looking at Chase. "I have a folder full of business cards. I'm probably going to be so busy the next few months I won't have time to breathe."

And so would he. But he would still miss her.

Chase fisted his hands by his side at the realization. Maddie was like a burst of fresh summer sunshine in a world that had been dark to him for ages. Now that he'd seen the light, had felt how incredible it was to be warm and . . . and loved, even if only physically, for a little while, how was he going to walk back through that tunnel of darkness?

He jerked when Maddie touched his arm, and realized Lance and Reid were leaving.

"See you later," Lance said, giving Maddie a quick kiss on the cheek. "We're proud of you, sis."

"Yeah, you surprised everyone," Reid said.

Maddie frowned at her brother. "You didn't think I'd succeed?"

Reid looked sheepish. "Sorry, Maddie. I admit we were a little nervous, just because you used to jump around a lot." He hugged her. "I guess we underestimated you. I'm glad we were wrong."

Maddie's smile seemed a little tight, but then Chase was having a hard time forcing one on his own face, so he figured his perception was completely distorted. Lance and Reid gave him a pointed look as they left. He nodded, gesturing that he understood.

Maddie grabbed his hand and squeezed it. "Chase, I want you to know—"

"It's over, Maddie." Chase stared at his boots. "Our, uh, affair, I mean."

He heard her inhale sharply and expected to look up and see hurt on her face. Instead, she smiled, her dark eyes glistening with emotions he couldn't quite read.

"I know. I came to tell you the same thing."

His breath whooshed out in surprise. "You did?"

"Yes," Maddie said gently. "The sex has been great, Chase. You were a fabulous lover. You taught me how to loosen up, let go of my inhibitions." She laughed, releasing his hand. "Why, next time I'm with a man, I'll really know how to please him. And I have you to thank for being such a good teacher. Just like you taught me how to throw a baseball."

She was comparing their lovemaking to playing baseball—as if there had been no emotion or meaning? And he'd simply been her teacher?

"But like I said, I'm going to be so busy, and well," she hesitated, her voice softening, "Jeff's asked me to go out and celebrate and I told him I would." Her hand toyed with a Cameo pin, drawing his eye. "Jeff gave it to me," she said as if she realized he was staring at it. "To commemorate my new career."

So, the guy's gifts were winning her over.

Without saying another word, she pecked him on the cheek, turned and sauntered toward her sporty new convertible, leaving Chase alone with his thoughts—with images of Maddie in another man's arms, the wuss's to be specific, pleasing him the way she'd pleased him, filling his life with love and laughter and her radiant smile.

And he didn't like the image—not one damn bit.

Chapter Twenty-six

"I'm such an idiot," Maddie cried. "I should wear a big fat sign that says GULLIBLE FEMALE—SCREW ME, AND LEAVE ME."

Sophie placed a plate of frosted brownies on the table in front of Maddie, then plopped down beside her and handed Maddie a fork. "You're not the idiot, those pigheaded stubborn brothers of yours are fools."

"And Chase. Don't forget Chase Holloway."

"He's lower than an idiot—he's slime." Sophie handed Maddie a tissue. "No, roadkill."

Maddie swiped at the tears streaming down her cheeks, dug into the rich chocolate and swirled it around on her fork. "But he seemed so . . . so sincere."

"Sincerely horny," Sophie said wryly.

Maddie laughed, and licked the icing. "I can't believe I fell for him. I actually was dreaming of a church wedding and bridesmaids dresses and . . . and of having his baby."

Sophie made a sympathetic sound. "Aww, Maddie. Maybe he'll still come around, maybe he wasn't ready—"

"No, Chase has always been a fighter. If he wanted me badly enough, he would have fought for me."

"Then you have to accept that your relationship is over and move on." Sophie nibbled the end off her own brownie. "How about some ice cream, Mad? We could add some whipped cream, too."

"No, every time I think about a decadent dessert, I remember that one I was going to make for Chase to surprise him. I probably won't ever be able to eat a hot-fudge sundae again."

"There are plenty of other men out there."

Maddie remembered the nudist colony, the TV producer. "We haven't done very well so far, have we?"

"I suppose not." Sophie grabbed a bag of chips and opened a jar of salsa to go with their comfort food. "By the way, Greg Pugh's still wondering what happened to his robe."

Maddie gestured toward her cat. Even he had trusted Chase. Poor thing. "I made T. C. a pillow out of it but he shredded it to pieces."

"We could try Marco and Antonio again. Antonio's been leaving messages on my machine."

"Yeah, Marco left me one, too." Maddie sighed wearily. "I just don't think I'm up for all that charm. At least Chase was . . . was real. Macho like, not so smooth and such a pretty boy."

Sophie laughed. "I'm glad you salvaged your pride, Maddie, and didn't let Chase know he broke your heart. That's something."

Maddie inhaled another bite of her dessert. "I

can't tell you how many times I've wanted to let my brothers know I overheard their conversation. Every time I've seen them at the tour this week, and let me tell you I've seen all three of the rascals at least a thousand times, I've wanted to confront them."

"It would serve them all right if you did, just to watch them grovel." Sophie forced a smile. "So, what did you tell Chase?"

"That I was going to be too busy to see him." Maddie propped her chin on her hand. "And that I was going out to celebrate with Jeff. And I hinted that I might get back with him."

"Really?"

"Yeah, he asked me to go out. And he seems sincere, like he's really interested in my work now."

"So, did you go?"

Maddie shook her head. "No, I made an excuse. I just couldn't. He's just not . . ."

"Chase," Sophie said sympathetically. They sat brooding together for a moment, but finally Sophie broke the silence. "Look on the bright side though—your business has picked up."

"I know. I am planning to be so swamped for the next few months I won't have time to think about Chase. And when the tour's over, maybe I won't keep running into him."

"You might meet a nice single male client," Sophie suggested.

"He'll probably be a confirmed bachelor, too."

Sophie thumbed her hair away from her eyes. "That bachelor pact is so ridiculous. I can understand three goofy teenage boys making a dumb agreement like that, but now they're grown men, you'd think they'd realize how juvenile their plan was."

Maddie's hurt turned to anger. She had put her whole heart into Chase and into decorating his home. And maybe she'd secretly been dreaming of the two of them living in it when she'd chosen some of the furnishings.

But she wasn't dreaming anymore. And she wanted revenge. "I have an idea, Soph."

"Uh-oh. Planning a counterattack?"

"Maybe."

"Something devilish I hope."

Maddie polished off one brownie and scooped up another. "I was thinking about how much time and care I put into decorating Chase's new home."

"And?"

"And maybe I didn't do his house justice. Since Chase wants to be a bachelor forever . . ." Maddie tapped her fingernails on the table. "I need to rethink the furnishings for his house."

Sophie's green eyes twinkled with mischief. "Are you thinking what I think you're thinking?"

"Absolutely. Now hand me the phone. I have work to do." Maddie reached for a pad and pencil. "After all, a bachelor should have a bachelor pad for entertaining, shouldn't he?"

Chase slammed the hammer against the side of the Camaro, pounding out more dents. If only he could repair his friendship with Lance and Reid as easily as he could the damaged car. Ever since that day they'd caught him pawing Maddie like some oversexed teenager, they had been cold and distant. He'd crossed the line with Maddie and broken their trust. The Terrible Three would never be the same.

On top of everything else, he missed Maddie like crazy.

He'd been stewing over the breakup all week. Not

seeing her was for the best; they both had to move on with their lives. But he hadn't been able to look at another woman without seeing Maddie's long, wild hair or her dark, mesmerizing eyes or thinking about that sexy little walk or the way she'd parted her legs and pulled him deep inside her.

Had she already moved on to another man?

He pounded the Camaro even harder, determined to straighten the rusted piece of metal, and tried to force the unwanted images from his mind—the images of Maddie, *his* Maddie, giving herself to another man. On some rational level, he realized his feelings of possessiveness were barbaric, but his emotions had no logic or order these days.

His business was going great. The tour was almost over and had been a magnanimous success for all of them. And he should be moving into his new house.

But he couldn't bring himself to even go by the house, much less step foot inside the beautiful place—it simply didn't feel like *home* without Maddie. Every room conjured memories of their lovemaking. And in every corner of the house, he knew he'd be able to smell Maddie's sweet, erotic scent. The memory of that bearskin rug taunted him—Maddie's naked voluptuous body, those long slender legs wrapped around his waist, her sweet, erotic words, offering her virginity . . .

Forcing the tormenting images at bay, he tried to focus on the fact that he'd obtained his dream—he'd proven to all those people in Savannah he was somebody. He hadn't let a woman control his life like his father. And he'd made up with Lance and Reid.

He should be happy.

But he'd never been more miserable in his entire life. And instead of feeling as if he had it all, he felt as if he had nothing.

* * *

Maddie stood in the middle of Chase's bedroom in his new house, and motioned to the movers, her head in a tailspin. "Haul it out."

The two beefy men she'd hired gave her a skeptical look. "Everything?"

Maddie nodded. "Yep, everything goes."

The men grunted as they began to disassemble the four-poster bed, occasionally pausing to reaffirm that she really wanted the room emptied. She didn't even hesitate.

Instead she waited patiently while they cleared the bedroom, then she began to give directions where the new interior pieces of furniture and accessories would go. "Put that lamp in the corner. Don't forget the remote control."

One of the movers shoved a hand on his hip. "I hate to question you, ma'am, but do you really want to put *that* bed in *this* house?"

"Yes, right there in the center of the room."

The second man scratched a balding head. "You don't think it's a tad bit on the . . . the wild side?"

Maddie studied the red velvet comforter, anger and hurt welling inside again. "No, the new furniture is perfect. My client is a bachelor, gentlemen. He'll be doing a lot of entertaining, and this bed will come in handy."

Knowing leers graced the men's faces. "I see."

"Gotcha."

The first man left and returned, holding a box containing a life-sized, customized blowup doll. "Where do you want this?"

"I'll take care of her," Maddie said, her imagination clicking in.

The balding man clucked his tongue. "Whooee, I ain't never seen a room like this one."

"My, my, you're an interesting lady," the other man commented as Maddie situated the voluptuous plastic figure in an erotic pose in the center of the bed.

"I'm gonna have to tell my wife about this. Maybe she can buy me one of those dolls for my birthday."

"Dream on, Willie," the first man said. "Your wife would belt you one good if you asked for one of those dang things. Now, come on and help me move the rest of the stuff."

"Be careful with those mirrors," Maddie called as the men left the room. "I have a special place I want to hang them!"

"From the ceiling," one of the men suggested with a chuckle.

Maddie grinned and dragged the bearskin rug inside the room, rolled it up and stuck it in the corner like a coatrack, then placed a basket of erotic goodies at the foot of the bed, along with a silver gift bag overflowing with condoms.

A half hour later, she surveyed the room, pleased with the results.

She only wished she could be a fly on the wall when Chase walked in and saw his new custom-designed bachelor pad.

"Oglethorpe, why did you want to see us?" Lance asked as he and Reid took seats across from the man at the Shrimp Store.

"Let's order first, shall we?" Jeff said. He indicated the menus. "My treat, of course.

"We can pay our own way," Reid said.

Oglethorpe looked slightly offended but didn't argue. After the waitress came, and they ordered, Lance cut to the point. He still wasn't sure he trusted Oglethorpe, especially after the accusations Chase had flung at the man that day in the bank. But he'd totally trusted Chase, and he'd let him down, so Lance decided he wasn't exactly the best judge of character. "Okay, what's up?"

"I wanted to talk to the two of you about your sister."

Lance and Reid exchanged questioning looks. "All right," Lance said. "What about her?"

Reid broke the loaf of bread and slathered butter on a piece.

"I think I made a mistake in letting Maddie go. I want to reconcile."

"Then you aren't undermining our company?" Lance asked. "Cause if you are, and we find out or Maddie finds out, you're history, bud."

Oglethorpe shifted sideways, twiddling with his fork. "I-I'll continue to do everything I can to help the Summerses' business."

"We talked about you and Maddie before," Reid interjected, "but things have changed. I was wrong about Maddie giving up her career. She was a big success with the tour, and I think she's going to stick with this decorating business."

A wave of pride washed over Lance. "She's good at decorating, too."

"I realize she's talented and serious about her company," Oglethorpe said. "I attended the tour the first night and saw her work for myself."

Lance leaned back in his chair and folded his arms. "I thought you were against having a wife who worked."

Oglethorpe frowned and stirred sweetener into his tea. "I was at first. But . . . well, I realize now I was being old-fashioned. I can hire an assistant, and we can always have dinner parties catered. Maddie has won the respect of the businessmen in the town, and I think she'd be a great asset for me."

Lance rocked his chair back on two legs. "So, what do you expect us to do about it?"

"I've been sending Maddie gifts and flowers to romance her, but I want to do something really special to surprise her." Oglethorpe leaned forward in a conspiratorial whisper. "Now, this is what I have in mind . . ."

"You're going to do what?" Chase dropped onto the bar stool beside Lance, stunned.

"Oglethorpe wants another chance with Maddie."

Chase searched Reid's face, hoping he hadn't heard right. "And you're going to help him?"

Both men shrugged. "Not exactly help," Lance said.

"But we're not going to stand in his way," Reid clarified.

"The decision will be up to Maddie," Lance said.

"So now you trust Maddie to make her own decisions?"

Both men frowned at him. "What's that supposed to mean?" Lance asked.

"That maybe you should have trusted her in the first place." Then, he for one, wouldn't have been in this mess. He'd never have spent time with Maddie, never been tempted, never seen her lying on that bearskin rug, never fallen in l—

"We trusted *you.*" Lance pointed out.

Reid glared at him. "Yeah, at least Oglethorpe was upfront about how he felt about her job. And now he's changed his mind, he's man enough to admit it."

He couldn't believe they were defending Oglethorpe. "That wuss only wants her now because she's a success. He thinks she'll make him look good since the businessmen in town liked her work," Chase argued.

"They did like her, didn't they?" Reid said proudly.

"I keep thinking that Mama would have wanted Maddie to wind up with Oglethorpe," Lance said. "And I have a feeling Maddie's considering getting back with him."

She was? Chase opened his mouth to tell them the entire truth about the wuss, that he'd threatened to destroy Lance and Reid's business if Chase didn't leave Maddie alone, but the closed expressions on his friends' faces said it all. They no longer trusted him, and nothing he said would change things. And if they believed Maddie's mother wanted her to be with Oglethorpe, they'd support him all the way.

A hollow feeling dug its way inside him. He couldn't have Maddie—hell, she didn't even want him; she'd said so that night of the tour. She thought of him as a teacher, for God's sakes, someone to show her how to please other men.

Not one time since that night had she expressed any emotion toward him. While he'd lain awake every night, wishing he could hold her, feeling miserable and lonely without her.

But Maddie had broken things off with him. She must have realized he wasn't husband material and was ready to move on.

Just as his mother had left his father and him.

Besides if he tried to fight Oglethorpe, the wuss would ruin Lance and Reid. No way in hell could he let the man destroy their company. And if Maddie wanted Jeff, he'd have to do the noble thing and not stand in her way. But he couldn't stick around and see the two of them together and pretend he liked the guy. No, there was only one thing left to do.

He had to leave Savannah.

Chapter Twenty-seven

The next morning Chase drove north to Atlanta, determined not to dwell on all he'd lost. Surely, in the big city where construction and new developments sprang up every day, he could find an architectural firm that would hire him. Or maybe he could rent a little place in the suburbs and set up an office. Of course, he'd have to sell the house in Savannah. . . .

Skyscrapers, million-dollar hotels, storefronts and businesses flanked both sides of the highway as he wound his way through the downtown area. Traffic crawled by, and pedestrians filled the sidewalks and crosswalks during the noon hour, all rushing to and fro like ants on a big anthill. Life in the city seemed fast-paced compared to Savannah, something he supposed one day he'd grow accustomed to. A police car raced past him, blue light spinning, siren blasting, and in the distance he spotted a work crew of prisoners gathering trash along the interstate exit.

He immediately thought of his father.

He hadn't seen him since he was a toddler. Hadn't heard from him since the day he'd been sentenced to life in prison. Without realizing what he was doing, he suddenly found himself changing directions and heading toward the state penitentiary. Time seemed to drift into a fog, the minutes floated by in a hazy blur. And suddenly he was there.

Parked in front of the tall, iron-gated prison.

A short while later, he'd convinced the guards to let him see his father even though visiting hours weren't until the next day. Apparently his father had earned favors for good behavior. He almost laughed at the irony, but as he sat in the empty paint-chipped room staring at the dull and worn linoleum floors, he knew his visit wasn't anything to laugh about. He also realized he had no idea why he'd come.

"Chase?"

A tall, lean man with graying hair and a ruddy complexion appeared in the doorway. Chase's breath locked in his chest.

The guard indicated that his father could proceed, and the old man ambled over and took a seat at the scarred wooden table, his brown eyes filled with joy and uncertainty. "This is a surprise, son."

He refused to let the quiver in his father's voice bother him.

"I don't know what I'm doing here," Chase said slowly.

His father nodded solemnly, folding his big callused hands in front of him on the battered table. Chase saw the prison number on his father's faded work clothes, the fine age lines around his deep-set eyes, a scar on his arm that looked jagged and old. He smelled of cigarettes and sweat, and the unnatural pallor to his skin testified to his confinement.

"I'm glad you came anyway," his father said. "I've wanted to see you so many times. To call you on the phone."

"Then why didn't you?" Chase asked, unable to keep the bitterness from creeping into his voice.

His father shook his head, his features twisting with emotions Chase refused to analyze. "I didn't know if you'd want to hear from me."

"Did you even know where I was?"

"I knew." His father pulled a newspaper clipping from his pants pocket, a recent one that Chase recognized and read aloud, "Chase Holloway, a talented new architect, is on hand to greet visitors for Savannah's recent Tour of Homes."

A tight sensation gripped Chase's throat.

"I'm proud of you, son."

He didn't want him to call him son, but he couldn't seem to find his voice.

"It says here you're working with these builders, someone named Summers."

"I was."

His father's forehead crinkled into a frown. "Something happen?"

Chase had no inclination to tell his dad his whole life story, but he did find himself rambling on about his friendship with the Summerses.

His father simply nodded and listened quietly. "Sounds like they've been your family."

"The only one I've had," Chase admitted. He finally summoned the courage to look his father in the eye. "Why'd you do it, Dad? Why'd you kill that man?"

A sadness seeped into his father's eyes. "I was young and stupid, son. Crazy in love with your mom." He rubbed a hand over his beard stubble. "She had this boyfriend on the side, and when I saw them together, I went nuts. But look where my temper got me. Locked in these walls."

"Did . . . did my mother love you?"

"No, I don't think she ever did." His father's voice grew stronger, resigned. "That was my mistake—I picked the wrong woman to fight for. Your mama wasn't the stick-around type."

Just like Chase.

"So, you in love with this girl, Maddie?"

Chase's gaze met his father's. He saw understanding and wisdom there, knowledge learned at a painful, life-altering price. "What makes you ask a question like that?"

"She's a pretty thing. I saw the way she was looking at you in this picture. Like she thinks you're the cat's meow."

Chase laughed at the old-fashioned expression, then tipped his head to study the photograph. It was a candid shot one of the reporters had taken during the tour. He'd been so upset after the breakup with Maddie he hadn't even looked at the paper or read the articles.

"If she's a good one, don't let her slip by. You don't want to end up like your old man, aging and alone."

And locked in those walls.

Chase heard the silent message. The guard had told him his father was up for parole again soon; maybe this time the courts would release him. Of course, he'd already given up so many years. . . .

"You know what I regret most?"

"What?"

His dad cleared his throat, his voice husky, "The day the judge sentenced me, I lost a whole lot more than my freedom. I lost my son."

Moisture warmed Chase's eyes but he blinked the

offending substance away. "Maybe not, Dad. When you get out, maybe . . . maybe we can start all over."

His father stood and hugged him, the big man almost choking up. "I'd like that, son. I'd like that a lot."

Chase contemplated his father's words all the way back to his truck. In a way, he'd been in a self-imposed prison of his own his entire life, refusing to believe that anyone could love him.

Refusing to love anyone for fear they wouldn't want him.

Until Maddie.

He put the truck in gear and said good-bye to the prison walls, smiling at the sunshine slanting off the dark gray roof, grateful he'd come.

He'd go see Oglethorpe. And if Maddie hadn't already retrieved her mother's necklace, he'd get it back for her. The heirloom would be his final going-away gift, a gesture to show Maddie that their relationship hadn't been all about sex. That somewhere down the line Chase had fallen in love with her.

And that he wanted her to be happy, even if it meant he had to walk away.

Lance studied the books, smiling as he jotted down the latest figures. Business was great. In fact, if they continued to make deals the way they had this last week, they'd be able to pay off their initial loan by the end of the year.

He only wished everything else in his life was going as well. Reid had been acting oddly lately, not being where he said he was supposed to be, making phone calls from his truck that he didn't want to discuss. What was up with his brother?

He glanced back over the records one more time, turning the page to study an entry Reid had made.

Miscellaneous. Hmm, the sum was an odd amount. And he thought they had a petty cash fund for such purchases. He had no records of a KS contractor or subcontractor or potential buyer. Making a mental note to question Reid, he closed the book and stood, his thoughts turning to his best friend and his other sibling.

His friendship with Chase hadn't been the same since that night of the tour when he'd seen Chase making out with Maddie. The sight had shocked him to the core.

Chase and Maddie?

Now he'd had some time to think about it, he remembered Maddie had had a crush on Chase when she was little. Hmm, what if?

No, Chase claimed their relationship was over, and Lance believed him.

Although Maddie had been acting strange lately, and she hadn't returned any of his calls. In fact, she'd been curt with him when he'd seen her during the remainder of the tour. She'd also looked exhausted, as if she'd lost weight. Pale and peaked, her eyes puffy as if she hadn't been sleeping well. Maybe she was just swamped with work the way they'd been, but his gut feeling told him something else was wrong. He decided to give her a couple more days, then if she didn't call him, he was going to drop by and find out what was going on. Maybe she was in love with Chase.

Or maybe she was still mad at him for the way he'd treated that Sophie woman.

Come to think of it, he hadn't been sleeping too well himself. Images of Sophie's bright green eyes glittering with desire, her jet-black hair against his white pillowcase, her naked, voluptuous little body pressed into his sheets . . . the images had kept him awake constantly. Hell, why did she have to be Maddie's friend and work for that show? Why couldn't she be someone he could just bed and . . .

No, he wouldn't, couldn't think of Sophie Lane in a personal way. But she was Maddie's friend, and he did have to pay her a visit and ask her to help with Oglethorpe's surprise. He'd definitely have to suck up and offer her an apology if he wanted her help. He'd just have to brace himself against her sexuality.

Reid left the work site, climbed in his truck and snagged his cell phone, quickly punching in Knobby's number. "Did you find out anything on Oglethorpe or our business problems?" After Chase's accusations about the banker, Reid had called and asked the P.I. to look into Oglethorpe as well Sophie.

"Nothing substantial. I have heard that Oglethorpe likes to use his influence to his own gain. He's had several meetings with some contractors, off the record, of course."

"So, nothing we could prove?"

"No, the man's too smart to do anything that might be traced back to him. But I'll keep looking into it."

Maybe Chase had been right about Jeff. If so, he couldn't let Maddie reconcile with the man. "What about that Lane woman?"

Knobby chuckled. "Are you kidding? She's definitely an interesting lady."

"So I was right. The lady's up to no good?"

"I don't know about that," Knobby said. "But she's not everything she seems to be on television."

"Could she be the woman whose been inquiring at the hospital?"

"It's possible. Sophie does have an unusual past,

but I couldn't find out very much information beyond the basics."

"Her parents?"

"Didn't locate them. Seems she's been on her own for quite a while."

"I wonder why."

"Had a falling out with her old man when she was fifteen, and he threw her out. Turns out he wasn't really her old man."

Reid sighed. "Any connection to the hospital?"

"Her mama worked there right about the time in question."

Reid leaned back in the seat and frowned. Oglethorpe might be a problem. And Sophie Lane might be real trouble. He'd seen the advertisement for her upcoming shows, one of them a piece that was a little too closely related to his father's activities for comfort. Did she plan on using her own history as food for the show? Was she going to try to involve the Summers family?

He couldn't put it off any longer. Much as he wanted to protect Lance and Maddie, he'd have to break down and tell Lance everything. His brother needed fair warning to know what they might be up against. And Maddie needed to be forewarned about Oglethorpe.

"You actually want my help?" Sophie asked.

Lance almost ducked his head in shame at her condescending tone. He guessed he deserved her scorn, but . . .

Sophie leaned a sexy hip against the front of her desk, tapping a sleek ballpoint pen on her leg, distracting him. He watched the ripple of silk on her thigh, wishing he could replace the pen with his fingers.

"You haven't exactly been friendly to me, Mr. Summers. In fact, I thought you detested my show—I believe you called me a nosy busybody."

Lance shifted, forcing himself to meet her eyes. "I'm sorry, Sophie. I was out of line. I know you're . . . you're just doing your job."

She studied him warily. "Give me one good reason I should deceive Maddie and help *you*?"

Lance winced. "Because you're her best friend. You want her to be happy, don't you?

Sophie's green eyes raked over him. "Yes, of course I do."

"She seems upset lately." He scratched his chin, angling his head. "Has she talked to you, maybe mentioned something that's bothering her?"

"She's been busy with work," Sophie said in a noncommittal tone, as if she knew more than she'd ever reveal to *him*—the slime she thought him to be.

"There's something else upsetting her," Lance said. "But she won't return my calls. I'm really worried about her."

Sophie's expression softened slightly. "You really do care about your sister, don't you?"

"My family means everything to me."

Sophie dropped the pen on her desk and pivoted to look out of the window, her silence creating tension in the air. Or maybe she felt the thread of sexual energy rippling between them and wanted to avoid acting on it, the same as he did.

She spun around, crossing one delicate ankle over the other. "All right. But what makes you think Maddie is interested in reconciling with Jeff Oglethorpe? They broke up weeks ago."

Lance shrugged. "I'm not sure. She may not be interested, and if not, that's okay."

"You aren't going to interfere and push her toward him?"

"Are you saying I interfere in Maddie's life?"

Sophie rolled her eyes. "You and Reid are a tad on the sexist, overprotective side."

Lance chewed the inside of his cheek, then finally conceded her point with a curt nod. "We mean well."

"I know," Sophie said, softening. "But you won't force her to go back to Jeff?"

"No." Oglethorpe hadn't exactly confessed his love for Maddie, Lance realized. He'd called her an asset as if being with Maddie was some kind of business decision. Maybe Chase was right about Oglethorpe. And maybe he shouldn't have interfered with Chase and Maddie. . . .

No, Chase might be his friend, but he wasn't the marrying kind, and he didn't want him to hurt Maddie. Besides, Chase had been sneaky; he'd lied to him. And he'd been with so many other women. And he hadn't actually confessed his love for Maddie either.

Sophie folded her arms across her chest. "All right, I have a show already planned that might work. I'll talk to the producer and see if I can fit Jeff in."

"Thanks, Sophie. I appreciate this."

"And I'll talk to Maddie this afternoon. I just hope you know what you're doing."

Lance stood and shook her hand to thank her, his body hardening with desire at her touch, his mind racing with reservations over what he was doing for Oglethorpe. "And I promise, all I'm going to do is to set them up to talk. The rest will be completely up to Maddie."

Maddie twirled the phone cord around her fingers, shoving her sketchpad and a dozen floor samples aside so she could plop down and rest. She hadn't slept much the last few days, couldn't eat, didn't even want to get out of bed in the morning, much less venture outside. All in all, she'd never been more miserable in her life. "I don't know, Soph. I'm not sure I want to come on the show again. Last time was such a disaster. People will probably remember me."

"But this time will be totally different," Sophie argued. "This is a fashion show. Designers, fancy clothes, makeup artists—it'll be so much fun."

Maddie glanced down at her baggy sweatshirt and jeans. "I don't even feel like getting dressed up, I just want to stay home and look through my decorating magazines."

"That's the very reason you need to come, Maddie. You're depressed, and I don't like it."

"But I look terrible; I have dark bags under my eyes."

"We have a fabulous makeup artist, he can do wonders with any problem. Come on, Mad. He'll make you look like a million bucks, every man in Savannah will be calling."

Except the one she wanted.

Sure, she'd kidded about enjoying the single life, but she had to admit it—she was the marrying kind. And there was only one man for her.

Only he didn't want her.

"You can keep all the clothes you model," Sophie said. "Oh, please say you'll fill in for me. One of the models has the flu, and the show's tomorrow. I'm really in a bind."

Maddie sighed. "All right. What time?"

Sophie filled her in on the details, and Maddie reluctantly agreed, deciding a new look might help her attract a new man. Then she might be able to finally forget about Chase Holloway.

Chapter Twenty-eight

"You are going to knock his . . . I mean the audience's socks off with that dress," Sophie said.

Maddie turned sideways to study herself in the mirror. The royal-blue silk piece shimmered beneath the bright lights, the low-cut neckline and foot-long slit up the side revealing more body than she'd ever dared expose. Except to Chase.

Dammit, this show was supposed to help her forget the infuriating man.

"Are all the models wearing such provocative outfits, Sophie?"

Sophie eyed the form-fitting sheath with a gleam in her eyes. "I told you I'd pick out something special for you, something you can keep to entice the single men in Savannah. You'll have them down on their knees in no time."

Maddie laughed. There was only one man she wanted on his knees—proposing to her. But that hadn't happened and never would. "I'm through with men," Maddie said. "I really don't think—"

A knock rapped at the door, and she looked up in shock to see her brothers standing in the doorway.

Lance's smile looked fake. "Hey, mind if we come in?"

"What in the world are you doing here?" Maddie asked.

Her brothers exchanged guilty looks. Maddie's stomach suddenly contracted with nerves. "What's up, guys?"

Lance shrugged. "We heard you were going to be on the show today, and we thought we'd join the audience and watch."

Reid hooked his thumbs in his belt loops. "We've never been to a live show before."

Maddie gaped at him. "I thought you guys hate . . . didn't watch the show."

Sophie backed toward the door, shooting Lance and Reid an odd look.

Maddie's queasiness escalated. "Wait a minute, Soph. What in the world is going on?"

Sophie froze and bit down on her lip.

Reid sputtered something about seeing the models, which would have been believable if he'd been able to maintain eye contact.

Lance began to tap his heel on the floor in a nervous gesture.

Then she spotted Jeff Oglethorpe being whisked into the green room across the hall.

Maddie planted her hands on her hips. "The truth, guys? This isn't about a fashion show, is it?"

Sophie shook her head with remorse.

Maddie pointed to her older brother. "Lance, you made it plain how you feel about the show." She shot Sophie a suspicious look. "And the last I knew you two weren't speaking."

Sophie threw up her hands as if she didn't know what to say.

"We reached an understanding," Lance said.

"What?" Reid sounded surprised. He shot a nervous glance at Sophie. "Lance, we have to talk."

"About what?" Lance asked.

"We can't discuss it here," Reid said, glancing between Sophie and Maddie. "Not in front of them."

"You mean, us ignorant, helpless *women?*" Maddie asked.

Reid's face flushed, and Lance shook his head. "Look, Mad, all we've ever tried to do is take care of you—"

"I don't need taking care of."

Lance inched inside the room. "We love you, Maddie, it's natural to want to protect you."

"Yeah," Reid said. "And I wanted to protect both of you."

"You wanted to protect me?" Lance asked, clearly stunned.

Maddie folded her arms, furious. "Protect me the way you did when you asked Chase to baby-sit me, because you didn't trust that I could decorate the homes for the tour?"

Both her brothers' gaped at her. "You knew?"

"I heard you talking to Chase after the tour."

"Geez, Mad—"

Reid reached for her. "Just listen—"

Maddie backed away from both of them. "No, I told you once to stay out of my business and I meant it. You even followed me to that nudist colony!"

"Well, what in the hell were you doing there?" Lance asked.

"That's not the point!" Maddie shouted.

Reid cleared his throat. "Look, Maddie, forget about that. Just let me tell you about Oglethorpe."

"You're doing it again—interfering!" Maddie jammed her hands on her hips, pacing across the room and peering out the door. "Is Chase here, too?"

"What would he be doing here?" Reid asked, puzzled.

"Aw, blast it all to hell." Lance rammed his hand through his hair, narrowing his eyes at her. "You *are* in love with him, aren't you?"

Sophie answered for her. "She's been miserable without him."

"Maddie's in love with Chase?" Reid asked.

"So, what if I am?" Maddie cried.

The boys exchanged confused looks.

"That depends on whether or not his intentions are honorable." Reid finally answered.

"His intentions are to leave me alone," Maddie said.

"We'll talk to him," Reid began.

"No, stay out of it. You guys have humiliated me enough." Tears stung Maddie's eyes. "And now you're involving Sophie in your devious plans. How could you?"

Reid gestured toward Sophie. "I still have to talk to you about *her*."

This time Sophie spoke up. "Why do you have to talk to him about me?"

"It's family stuff," Reid said.

"We should have a private family meeting then," Lance said.

"Anything you have to say about our family can be said in front of Sophie," Maddie said.

Both her brothers stared at her in shock. "What

are you saying, Maddie?" Reid turned pale. "That Sophie is part of the family?"

Lance gripped the doorjamb as though he needed it to support himself. "Oh, Lord."

Maddie sighed in exasperation. "What in the world is wrong with you guys?"

Lance dropped into a chair, looking ill. "I was attracted to my own sister?"

"Sister?" Sophie shrieked.

"Technically she'd only be our half-sister," Reid clarified.

"You were attracted to me?" Sophie asked.

"But we don't have a sister?" Maddie cried.

"We might," Lance said.

Reid cleared his throat. "Or we might have a bunch of half-sisters and half-brothers we don't know about."

"You mean you know about Dad?" Lance asked.

"You do, too?" Reid said.

Lance cleared his throat. "I found a letter from Maria—"

"I'm not your half-sister," Sophie cut in.

"Who's Maria?" Maddie asked.

"The woman Dad was having an affair with," Lance answered.

"The nurse at the hospital," Reid said.

They looked at each other in surprise.

"Dad was having an affair with a nurse at the hospital?" Maddie asked in disbelief.

"I didn't know about the affair." Reid looked questioningly at Lance.

"Maybe I was mistaken." Lance shrugged. "I found this letter, and in it Maria said the years knowing Dad meant a lot to her."

"Yeah, she worked at the sperm bank," Reid said.

"Sperm bank?" Maddie, Lance and Sophie all said at once.

Reid spoke slowly as if he were talking to a daft person, "Where Dad donated his sperm. Maria was a nurse there. I guess they got to be friends over the years."

"Our father donated his sperm to a sperm bank and his girlfriend worked there?" Maddie said.

"Blast it all to hell," Lance mumbled. "That's why he had that sex kit."

Maddie's eyes widened. "Dad had a sex kit?"

"It gets worse." Reid groaned. "I found a picture of him wearing women's clothes."

"Our father was a cross-dresser?" Lance asked.

"He must have been into kinky sex," Reid said.

"Maybe it was some kind of joke," Sophie suggested. "Or a Halloween costume."

"Earth to maniac brothers." Maddie waved her arms as if she were an air-traffic controller. "Tell me where you got all of these crazy ideas."

"They're not crazy, they're true," Reid said in a dark voice. "Apparently during med school, Dad needed some money to help with expenses so he started donating his sperm to this clinic. I guess he enjoyed his . . . activity so much he kept donating. He might have hundreds of offspring out there."

"He did this for years?" Maddie asked.

"No wonder you said we might have a lot of siblings," Lance added.

"But why did you think Sophie was our sister?" Maddie asked.

"Because she's been asking about our family," Lance said. "And she's done family reunion stories before where surprise siblings show up unexpectedly—"

Sophie raised a brow, a smile tugging at her

mouth. "I thought you didn't watch my show, Lance."

"And she's getting ready to do a show on the ethics of sperm banks," Reid added.

"That's the reason you've been so rude to her?" Maddie asked.

"I've been afraid one of Dad's sperm-bank kids would come looking for us, wanting money or to be a part of the family," Reid said.

"I'm not your sister," Sophie said emphatically. "And I had no idea about your father's activities."

"Then why did you keep after me?" Lance asked.

Maddie swung her hands wildly. "Because she wanted a date with you, you moron!"

Lance swiped a hand across his face in shock.

Sophie's face twisted with hurt. "But you thought I knew something about your past and wanted to expose it or worse, that I wanted part of the Summers fortune."

"What Summers fortune?" Reid asked suspiciously.

Lance had the good sense to look contrite. "There is no Summers fortune."

"Rest assured, guys," Sophie said calmly, "hospitals and sperm banks don't give out that kind of information."

"How would you know?" Reid asked suspiciously.

"We did a show on it a year ago, that's the reason we've planned a follow-up episode. Medical files are strictly confidential."

"I know," Reid admitted. "But someone had broken into the hospital records; that's why I was worried."

"It probably has nothing to do with you," Sophie said.

"Maybe I overreacted a bit," Reid admitted.

"This is unbelievable," Maddie said. "Here I thought our family had no secrets and I was feeling guilty about keeping—" Maddie hesitated.

"Keeping what," Lance asked, his eyes narrowed.

"You knew about Dad?" Reid asked.

Maddie shook her head. "No, Mom."

"Mom?" Lance and Reid said at once.

"I have a feeling Mom knew about Dad's . . . habit." She held up a hand when the boys started to argue. "Mom wasn't quite as innocent as you guys thought. I heard them arguing the night before their accident. Mom wanted a career."

"Mom wanted a job?" Lance squeaked.

"Doing what? I thought she was happy being Suzy Homemaker," Reid added.

"She wanted to be a caterer—"

"Whew." Lance exhaled a heavy sigh of relief. "I thought you were going to tell me the box of sex toys belonged to her."

"It's possible," Maddie said. "She wanted to decorate erotic desserts."

"What are erotic desserts?" Reid asked.

Maddie gestured with her hands. "Naked people decorated like ice cream sundaes, cakes—"

"Oh, God," Reid groaned.

"Blast it all hell," Lance mumbled, his own face turning scarlet.

Reid dropped his head in his hands. "I can't believe it—both our parents were perverts."

Maddie and Lance nodded miserably.

"Come on, you guys," Sophie said calmly. "Your mother may have just had that book for fun; maybe she was going to cater weddings and parties. And just because your parents enjoyed sex—"

"Our parents didn't have sex!" Lance, Reid and Maddie all exclaimed at once.

The stunned silence that followed was filled with tension. Seconds later, they all burst into laughter.

Everyone but Sophie. She simply glared at Lance. "I hate to break up this family party, but I have a show to do."

Maddie gulped. "What is the show about for real, Soph?"

"Friends," Sophie said. "Forgiving them for mistakes."

"This I gotta see," Maddie said as she turned and left the room. Reid ducked his head and followed.

Sophie moved to follow, but Lance gently grabbed her wrist. "Wait, Sophie. I—"

"This isn't a good time, Mr. Summers."

Lance winced at her icy tone. "Maybe later?"

Sophie shrugged, not meeting his eyes, making Lance feel about two feet tall. He let her wrist go.

Sophie turned her head to look up at him. "Lance, why don't you go sit in the audience? I think you'll enjoy the show, it's called 'Forgive Me, I Was a Fool.' "

Then she turned and left the room in a cloud of anger, her sweet perfume lingering behind to taunt him. Lance hurried to catch up with Maddie and Reid.

"Forgive Me, I Was a Fool"—if ever there was a show he should watch, this episode would be the one. In fact, he could play the lead.

Maddie found a seat near the front and sat down, still stunned from all her brothers had revealed—and from their misconceptions. Then Sophie emerged onstage and the camera lights began to flash, and she realized that in all the chaos, she still hadn't found out why Sophie had deceived her into coming on the show. Or why Jeff had been in the green room.

Chapter Twenty-nine

"Thank you, Cynthia, I really appreciate all your help." Chase clutched the small jewelry box in his hand as he walked toward the exit of the Savings and Loan.

"I'm glad to have helped. I really want things to work out for you and Maddie."

"What?" Chase paused mid-stride. "I simply want to—"

"You don't have to explain, Mr. Holloway." Cynthia patted his hand. "Are you going to give her the necklace today?"

"Well, yes. I have a stop to make first though." For some odd reason, Sophie Lane had left a message that it was urgent she see him. Probably about her renovation project, but why would that be urgent? Unless something had happened to Maddie—

His heart thundered in his chest.

Cynthia checked her watch and frowned.

"What is it?"

"I bet she's already left."

"Left for where?"

Cynthia gnawed on her lip as if she'd said too much. "The show."

"What show?" Chase asked, trying for patience.

"Mr. Oglethorpe was going to surprise Maddie by apologizing to her on that Sophie Lane show. He wants to ask her to marry him."

Chase ground his teeth together, seeing red. Maybe that was the reason Sophie had phoned.

"The show should be starting soon." Cynthia checked her watch again, a forlorn expression on her face. "If you hurry, you might be able to catch her before . . ."

"Dammit." Chase glanced through the window at his car and groaned. "I'll never make it in time. I have a flat tire."

Cynthia smiled and flashed a set of keys. "Come on then, I'll drive. My car can do zero to ninety in six seconds."

"She really just wanted to date me?" Lance asked.

Maddie shot him a venomous look. "Yes."

"I guess I blew it big time."

"I'd say that's accurate."

"I still don't understand why you thought Sophie was our sister," Maddie said.

"I assumed Dad had had an affair with this Maria woman, so I thought maybe Sophie was our half-sister when she seemed so interested in our family."

"This P.I. I hired—" Reid started to say.

"You hired a P.I.?" Lance interuppted.

"Yeah, his name is Knobby Smaltz."

"KS," Lance mumbled. "That's what the notation in the book meant."

Maddie jerked Reid's hand. "You hired a P.I. to investigate my best friend?"

"Oww, Maddie, you're hurting me."

"Good, you deserve to be in pain—"

"Shh," several people behind them hissed.

"What did he learn?" Lance asked.

Maddie fumed at him. "You two should be ashamed of yourselves. Don't you dare ask him what he found out about Sophie. She would be devastated if she knew you were snooping into her private life!"

"I'm sorry, Maddie, I guess I overreacted," Reid said.

"Promise me you won't say anything about the P.I. to Sophie," Maddie whispered.

"All right," Reid agreed.

"How could I? She's not even talking to me," Lance muttered.

Maddie pinched his arm. "Promise me, Lance."

"Okay, I promise. If she ever speaks to me again, I won't tell her about the P.I."

Maddie released his arm. "Thank you. And you'd better mean it."

"But the P.I. thinks Chase may be right about Oglethorpe," Reid whispered.

"What about Jeff?" Maddie asked.

"Chase thinks he's responsible for our problems at the sites," Lance explained. "He wanted revenge on us for scaring him that night after you dumped him on TV."

"Or maybe he wanted you to fail, Maddie, so you'd come running back to him," Reid suggested.

Maddie wanted to scream. She would kill Jeffrey Oglethorpe. The sneaky creep had actually taken her mother's heirloom from her, wanted her to fail, then sent her all those flowers and gifts, pleading with her to come back to him. And to think, once she'd wanted to marry him! "This is unbelievable."

Lance and Reid patted her hand sympathetically.

"I have a request," Maddie said.

"What now?" Reid massaged his aching wrist.

"Could we please not keep any more secrets from one another?"

Both her brothers stared at her, then broke into grins. "Fine by me," Lance said.

"Gladly," Reid mumbled.

"Either be quiet or leave, the show's beginning!" a lady with helmet hair hissed behind them.

"Here's our host, Miss Sophie Lane," the director announced. Music floated through the speakers, and Sophie pranced in front of the audience. The stage lit up, and Maddie gaped at the title of the show—"Forgive Me, I Was a Fool."

"You guys all need to be in this one," Maddie muttered.

"Shh!" several people whispered.

Off to the side, she saw Jeff Oglethorpe hiding behind a screen. Reid and Lance both sat up straighter, looking nervous. Her stomach clenched. They obviously knew the reason she'd been asked to appear on the show, and it had something to do with Jeff.

She should have known better than to trust them. No more secrets? Ha!

Next time she asked for a promise, she'd make them sign their names in blood the way they'd done the bachelor pact. So far, it was the only promise they'd kept.

Chase slipped into the audience, his nerves tied in knots. A wide sweep of the crowd, and he spotted Maddie sitting between her brothers. A glance at the stage, and he read the title of the program and instantly knew Cynthia's suspicions had been right. Oglethorpe intended to propose.

A sick feeling rose in Chase's throat. His father's words haunted him—"The day the judge sentenced me to prison for life, I lost a lot more than my freedom. I also lost my son." Could he stand by and lose his chance for happiness, the chance for a life with the woman he loved, the chance for a son of his own?

He pulled out the bachelor pact he kept in his wallet and stared at it, his hands shaking.

"Today we have a special guest with us, Jeff Oglethorpe, one of Savannah's prominent bankers. Mr. Oglethorpe, would you like to tell us why you're here?"

Oglethorpe stood in the limelight, his perfect suit and perfect hair and perfect manicure probably intoxicating half the female population watching. Oglethorpe had no scars or ghosts in his past to deal with.

He'd also never slept with Maddie.

Oglethorpe pasted on a charming smile. "I'd like to talk to someone in the audience. Maddie Summers, will you come up here, please?"

The beam of light focused on Maddie. Chase watched her stand, saw her hands trembling by her side as she slowly walked up to the stage. She looked absolutely breathtaking in that shiny blue dress, every stitch of fabric molding to her curves, her long, wild hair curling around her face. And damn if her cleavage wasn't showing and the wuss was staring right at it.

Oglethorpe took Maddie's hand in his. "Maddie, you surprised me and brought me on this show a few weeks ago, for Valentine's Day, and I was so stunned, I didn't handle the situation very well. But

I've given a lot of thought to our relationship and that day and realize I made a terrible mistake—"

"Jeff, you don't have to do this," Maddie said in a strained voice.

"Yes, I do." Oglethorpe squared his shoulders. "So, please let me finish. I don't want to lose you, Maddie."

Chase had always called Oglethorpe a wuss but maybe *he* was really the wuss—too afraid to stand up and fight for something he wanted.

And there was no doubt in his mind now that he wanted Maddie.

Even more than he wanted his friendship with her brothers.

If they thought Oglethorpe was right for Maddie, they didn't know Maddie as well as they should. As well as he did.

He knew every sweet inch of her by heart. And he wanted to be the only man in her life.

If he had to perform a song and a dance to prove it to her, he'd damn well do it.

Oglethorpe suddenly dropped to one knee. "Maddie, forgive me I was a fool, I want to—"

"No, Maddie, forgive me, I was a fool!" Chase shot to his feet and fisted his hands by his sides as the light zoomed to him. The audience gawked and gasped.

"Chase?" Maddie whispered.

The light swung back to Oglethorpe as he wobbled on his knee. "Holloway?"

Lance and Reid jumped up from their seats. "Maddie?"

Sophie rushed forward to take control, but Maddie stopped her.

"No, wait! You two stay out of this!" Maddie held up her hand to ward them off, then stared at Chase long and hard. Tension thrummed throughout the set. The air grew tight with anticipation. Finally Maddie sighed and spoke in a low voice. "I'll hear what Mr. Holloway has to say."

Mr. Holloway? Chase swallowed, gathering his courage.

"This is an outrage," Oglethorpe wailed. "This is our moment, don't let him ruin it."

"Shut up, Jeff," Maddie hissed.

"No, listen to me. Please." Jeff thrust a huge diamond ring toward Maddie. "Marry me, Maddie."

Chase dropped to his knee. "No, marry me, Maddie!"

The light swung back to Chase. "What did you say?" Maddie whispered hoarsely.

"I said, marry me, Maddie." His voice was rough with emotions when he spoke again, "Please, Maddie."

"Why . . . are you doing this, Chase?" She glanced at her brothers, suspicion darkening her tear-filled eyes. "Did they make you come here, are they forcing—"

"Nope, my interfering days are over." Lance rocked back on his heels with a goofy grin. Reid was staring at Chase as if he'd morphed into an alien.

"Chase?"

"No one's forcing me to do anything, Maddie." Chase's gaze locked with Maddie's, his eyes pleading. He'd always fought for what he wanted. First, with his fists when he was a kid. Then, with his head when he'd worked his way through school. Now, it was time to fight for his woman with words.

"I'm doing this because I love you, Maddie. I . . ." His voice broke, but he didn't care; he cleared his throat to continue. "I love you with all my heart."

Oohs and aahs rippled through the room, but

Maddie's soft cry of joy echoed above the noise. "Oh, Chase, I love you, too."

"This cannot be happening." Oglethorpe waved to the cameramen. "Will someone get him out of here? He's ruining everything!"

Instead, Lance and Reid rushed onstage, hooked their arms under Oglethorpe's and hauled him aside. Cynthia raced over to console him.

Maddie had already left the stage and was running toward Chase. The crowd clapped and cheered as Maddie flew into his arms. She covered his mouth with a kiss that was deep and tender and sweet and so erotic that Chase had to fight the urge to throw her down on stage and have his way with her. Later, he would. . . .

Finally, when they pulled apart, tears glistened in her eyes.

"You didn't answer me," he said in a husky voice. "Will you marry me?"

Maddie toyed with the hair at the nape of his neck and cocked her head sideways with a grin. "What about your bachelor forever pact?"

Chase kissed her neck, then held up the sheet of paper and ripped it in two. "I'll trade it in for a *husband forever* one if you'll have me."

"Oh, yes, I'll have you." She kissed him again. "Now and forever." Then Maddie turned to Sophie. "Hey, Soph, you wouldn't happen to have a preacher in the audience, would you?"

Chapter Thirty

"Ladies and gentlemen, we're here live, bringing you the wedding of Maddie Summers and Chase Holloway." Sophie smiled radiantly, and the cameras zoomed to the centerstage where Sophie had had the staff throw together a small wedding set during the commercial break. She had even managed to find a wedding dress for Maddie from props, complete with veil, and a tuxedo for Chase.

"Here, this will have to do as a bouquet." Sophie grabbed the silk flower centerpiece off the set table and stuffed it into Maddie's trembling hands. Maddie giggled and whispered, "Thanks."

Both her brothers stood beside her to give her away, tears glistening in their eyes. Sophie took her place as Maddie's bridesmaid, Lance as Chase's best man.

The justice of the peace held up an open Bible. "Mr. Holloway, please repeat after me . . ."

Chase squeezed Maddie's hand. "I'd like to say my own vows, if that's okay."

The justice of the peace gestured toward Maddie, and she nodded.

A flush crept on his tanned face, but his gaze never wavered. "Maddie, I met you when you were just a little girl. I watched you tag along after your brothers when you were a knobby-kneed kid, and I saw you turn into a spunky teenager."

Maddie laughed softly, aware her brothers and the audience were also chuckling.

"Then suddenly you turned into this incredible, beautiful creature right before my eyes." He hesitated, his voice growing thick with emotion. "Most of my life I hung around your house trying to fit in, just wanting to be a part of the Summers family, feeling I didn't belong. Not thinking I deserved anyone as wonderful as you."

Maddie's chin quivered as she brushed at the tears seeping from her eyes.

"But you made me feel welcome, and for the first time in my life, you made me feel loved." He thumbed a strand of hair away from her cheek. "You've given me light when the world looked dark. You took the hollow place in my heart and filled it with love and hope and all those things I was too afraid to admit I even wanted. . . ." He cleared his throat. "I may not always remember to be romantic or give you gifts and flowers, but know this, Maddie—" He placed their joined hands over his heart. "—I love you now and will love you forever."

Maddie sniffled, then brought his hand to her mouth and gently kissed his palm. "Chase, what you don't seem to realize is that without you, the world is a dark place. Without you, the Summers family would never have been complete, because we needed you as much as you needed us." She took a deep breath, her chest swelling with love and affection. "I admire your strength, your strong will, and the determination and grit it took for you to overcome the obstacles in your life." She pressed their hands to her heart. "Chase Holloway, forget the roses and gifts; I'd rather have you. I loved you when you were a wild little boy, I loved you when you were a bad-ass teenager, and I love you more with every passing day. Now and forever."

The justice of the peace completed the ceremony, and there was an awkward moment when he asked about rings.

"Here," Sophie said, thrusting two simple gold bands at them. "I found these in props, too. You can get the real ones later."

Maddie and Chase laughed, then exchanged rings, their hands intertwined just as strongly as their lives would be from this moment forward.

"I now pronounce you husband and wife," the justice of the peace announced.

Chase cupped her chin in his hand, lowered his mouth and kissed her.

Applause rang through the crowd.

Lance and Reid pulled them apart and pounded Chase on the back.

"Congratulations, man," Lance said.

"Too bad you've fallen from the pact though," Reid added.

"But at least now we'll know Maddie's taken care of," Lance said.

Maddie slugged Lance on the arm. "I plan to take care of *him* guys."

"You were right about Oglethorpe. I'm sorry I ever doubted you, man," Reid stuck out his hand for a shake. "Welcome to the family."

Chase nodded and accepted the gesture.

Lance's expression turned serious, and he pulled Chase into a hug. "I can't think of a better man to be my brother-in-law." He brought her into the circle of his arm as well. "I should have known the two of you belonged together."

"You said no more interfering," Maddie whispered with a warning look.

Lance and Chase both laughed.

Jeff approached, looking oddly remorseful. "Maddie can I talk to you for a minute?" Chase glared at him and threw his arm protectively around Maddie. "We're married now, Oglethorpe."

Maddie rolled her eyes. "It's okay, Chase. I'd like a minute with him."

Chase hesitated, and Lance stepped forward, as if to back up Chase.

"Look, guys, I can handle it," Maddie warned.

Chase nuzzled her neck, smiled at Oglethorpe as if he'd publicly laid his claim, then let Lance pull him aside.

"Before you say anything, Jeff," Maddie said, hands on hips. "I know that you sabotaged the boys' business."

"I'm sorry, Maddie." Jeff shoved his hands in his pockets. "That was wrong. I shouldn't have taken your mother's pendant as collateral, either. I guess letting you go was harder than I thought it would be."

Maddie bit down on her lip. "I'd like us to be friends, Jeff. I want you to be happy." She gestured toward Cynthia. "I think she really likes you."

"Yeah, she's pretty nice." A blush stained Jeff's face. "I want you to be happy, too. You deserve it. Even if Holloway was a hellion—"

"Watch it, Jeff. You're talking about my husband now."

They both laughed, then Maddie hugged him. Sophie came up and Jeff left to meet Cynthia. "God, I'm glad that worked out today," Sophie said with a whistle.

Maddie laughed. "Thanks to you, Soph. Hey, I saw you talking to Lance. Will my brother be the next one to walk down the aisle?"

Sophie winked at Lance. "I don't know, but at least he's talking to me now instead of treating me like a leper. And he agreed to come on the 'Dating Game' episode to make things up to me."

Lance and Chase moved closer. "Blast it all to hell," Lance mumbled. "I figure I've got a one-in-three chance that I won't get picked for the date." Maddie exchanged a knowing grin with Sophie. Her poor dumb brother had no idea Sophie would be the contestant, and the show would be rigged. Sophie would finally get her date with Lance.

"I'm sorry we didn't have time to send for a wedding cake," Sophie said.

Maddie hooked her arm through Chase's. "Don't worry, Soph. I think I can rummage up something at home to make us a dessert. I have this incredible recipe book."

Maddie leaned on tiptoe and whispered in Chase's ear, telling him about the erotic dessert cookbook.

"Time for our honeymoon," Chase growled.

"Wait, I have to throw the bouquet!" Maddie waved her arm for the single women to form a line. Several of the stagehands appeared, but Sophie lingered in the background, looking sheepish. Maddie turned and tossed the silk flowers over her shoulder, then spun around at the sound of laughter and squeals. Sophie stood, holding the bouquet, a shocked expression on her face. Maddie glanced at Lance and saw him staunchly avoid looking at Sophie. She laughed in delight. Maybe Lance would be the next man to fall from that bachelor pact.

"Let's go." Chase scooped her into his arms and carried her off the stage, the audience whooping and hollering.

In the limo on the way to his house, Maddie told Chase all about the secrets she and her brothers had been keeping. "So, you see, our family wasn't the perfect family we thought it to be."

Chase tipped her chin up with his hand. "Honey, I don't think there's any such thing as a perfect family. I certainly didn't have one. That's what scared me the most." Chase's voice grew serious. "I'm not sure I know how to be a part of one, Maddie."

Maddie traced a finger along his jaw. "Oh, Chase, you know more than you realize. Look how hard you fought to stay loyal to my brothers."

Chase shrugged. "But I couldn't let them pair you up with Oglethorpe. And did you know, he's really not a descendant of the Oglethorpes who settled here?"

Another case of male fraud, Maddie thought. She rubbed a finger over Chase's lips. "I wouldn't have gone back with him anyway, Chase, because I was so in love with you. But he did apologize for what he did to the business, so he's cool with us."

"Good, I don't want any problems, or any man coming after *my* wife." Chase dipped his mouth for a tender kiss. When he pulled away, he suddenly felt in his pocket. "Oh, gosh, Maddie, I almost forgot." He lay a velvet box in her hand. "This belongs to you."

Maddie's chest tightened as she opened the box.

"Oh, Chase. You got my mom's heirloom back. Thank you, thank you, thank you."

Chase lifted the delicate pendant from the box and fastened it around her neck. "Now, the necklace is where it's supposed to be."

"And so are we," Maddie whispered. "Let's promise not to have any secrets from each other, Chase."

"Okay." Chase grinned and pulled her to him, winding a strand of her hair around his finger. "As long as we're being honest, sweetheart, there is something I've been wanting to ask you."

"What is it, Chase? You can ask me anything."

Chase held her face in his hands and looked deep into her eyes. "Did you really get naked at that nudist colony?"

Maddie laughed, climbed in his lap, then looped her arms around his neck, and crossed her fingers behind his back. "Oh, honey, of course not. You're the only man who's ever seen me naked."

Chase smiled smugly. He'd figured as much.

The limo pulled up and parked at his house, and the driver opened the door. Chase lifted her in his arms and carried Maddie up the sidewalk. "This happened a little too fast for me to plan a honeymoon," Chase whispered. "But maybe we can plan a trip to Cancun or something in a couple of weeks."

Chase paused at the entryway to his new house and gazed into Maddie's eyes. "After we broke up, I couldn't bring myself to come back in here, Maddie. I knew every room would make me remember you."

Speaking of remembering—Maddie suddenly remembered her little revenge ploy and realized he hadn't seen the changes in his bedroom yet. "Uh, Chase, maybe we should go to a hotel for the night."

"No way." Chase unlocked the door and carried

her straight to the bedroom. "I've been dreaming about making love to you on that four poster bed ever since that first time."

"Um, about that four poster bed . . ." Maddie closed her eyes as he flicked on the light.

Chase gasped at the sight of the red velvet, heart-shaped bed, and blinked at the strobe light flickering with psychedelic colors. "Oh, my God, Maddie. What have you done?"

An hour later, they both lay sated and content and happily married in the middle of the plush, heart-shaped bed. After the first time they'd made love, Maddie had fixed them a special dessert, and they'd eaten it in bed. Literally off each other.

Chase nuzzled Maddie's neck and pulled her on top of him, his body hardening at the sight of her naked breasts. "So, you wanted me to have a bachelor pad, huh?"

"Well, I thought *you* wanted to be a bachelor. So I figured you might as well have a proper love nest for entertaining your love bunnies." Maddie nibbled at the sensitive spot just below his ear where the scent of whip cream still lingered.

"My love bunnies?" Chase sighed with a grin. "So, are you going to dress up like a bunny for me?"

Maddie rolled her eyes. "In your dreams, honey."

Chase laughed. "Seriously, you're the only love bunny I want, sweetheart. You fulfill my every fantasy."

"Speaking of fantasies?" Maddie quirked a mischievous brow. "Do you still have that black eye patch?"

Chase's laughter rumbled deep from his chest. "Oh, yeah, you did mention you have a thing for pirates." Chase felt for his shirt, unearthed his black eye patch, and winked as she tied it around his head. "I did vow to love, honor, and cherish now, didn't I?" He began by stroking his fingertips across her sensitive nipples. "And I cherish every part of you. This nipple." He leaned up to taste each rosy tip. "And this one, too." He laved her until Maddie groaned and dug her hands into his hair.

"Oh, Chase."

"And I love this tender skin." He bent and kissed the underside of her breast. "We will have to make a few changes in this room though."

Maddie pressed her heat against his erection. "Oh, really?"

"Yeah. Those orange nude paintings on the wall have to go." His fingers traced a fiery path down her breasts to her navel as he gestured toward the deflated plastic figure on the floor. "And let's definitely get rid of that pitiful blow-up woman." He tweaked her nipple, spread a little more chocolate sauce on the peak, then licked the tip again, loving her slow and so deep her body responded with an answering, burning ache. "I'd much rather have the real thing."

Maddie moaned at the erotic sound of his suckling noises. "What about the heart-shaped bed?"

"A little too Vegas for me."

"And the strobe lights?"

"They're making me motion sick." Chase slipped a finger down her stomach to tease her curls. "Besides, I'd rather have natural light—I want to see every bit of you."

Maddie reached down and cupped him in her hand, smiling when his sex surged full and hard against her palm.

Chase glanced at the ceiling, and the walls, enjoying the different views of their naked bodies almost as much as having Maddie on top of him. "But we might have to keep the mirrors."

Maddie straddled him. "Oh, so you like the mirrors?"

Chase fit his shaft at the tip of her sex, then pulled her down on top of him, filling her with his throbbing sex. Her moan of ecstasy nearly brought him to the brink. "Yeah, we might want to add some above the sunken tub." He began to rock within her. "And the kitchen island."

She gripped his shoulders and pulled him deeper inside her.

"And the laundry room, and that walk-in closet . . ."

Maddie clawed at his back, pumping him harder as she leaned over to whisper in his ear, "And when we have babies, we might have to think about building that secret tunnel."

Chase thrust inside her again, filling her to the core. Maddie threw her head back and screamed in ecstasy.

"Secret tunnel?" Chase's own release began to spiral as he plunged into her again. "Heck, sweetheart, we might have to soundproof the walls."

His silver-blond hair blows back from his magnificent face. His black leather breeches hug every inch of his well-muscled thighs. He is every woman's fantasy; he is the virtual reality game hero Vad. And Gwen Marlowe finds him snoring away in her video game shop.

She knows he must be a wacky wargamer out to win the Tolemac warrior look-alike contest. But the passion he ignites in her is all too real. Swept into his world of ice fields and formidable fortresses, Gwen realizes Vad is not playing games. On a quest to clear his name and secure peace in his land, he and Gwen must forge a bond strong enough to straddle two worlds. A union built not on virtual desire, but on true love.

___52393-0 $5.99 US/$6.99 CAN

Dorchester Publishing Co., Inc.
P.O. Box 6640
Wayne, PA 19087-8640

Please add $1.75 for shipping and handling for the first book and $.50 for each book thereafter. NY, NYC, and PA residents, please add appropriate sales tax. No cash, stamps, or C.O.D.s. All orders shipped within 6 weeks via postal service book rate. Canadian orders require $2.00 extra postage and must be paid in U.S. dollars through a U.S. banking facility.

Name________________________________
Address______________________________
City__________________State______Zip________
I have enclosed $__________ in payment for the checked book(s).
Payment <u>must</u> accompany all orders. ☐ Please send a free catalog.
CHECK OUT OUR WEBSITE! www.dorchesterpub.com